FLIRTATION
ON THE HUDSON

A JOURNEY OF
CORNELIA ROSE NOVEL

J.F. COLLEN

FLIRTATION ON THE HUDSON
Journey of Cornelia Rose – Book 1
Copyright © 2019 by J.F. Collen

SECOND EDITION SOFTCOVER
ISBN: 1622536401
ISBN-13: 978-1-62253-640-5

Editor: Kimberly Goebel
Cover Artist: Kabir Shah
Interior Designer: Lane Diamond

EVOLVED PUBLISHING™

www.EvolvedPub.com
Evolved Publishing LLC
Butler, Wisconsin, USA

Printed in Book Antiqua font.

BOOKS BY J.F. COLLEN

JOURNEY OF CORNELIA ROSE
Book 1: *Flirtation on the Hudson*
Book 2: *Pioneer Passage*
Book 3: *The Path of Saints and Sinners*

DEDICATION

To: My family and friends;
without your love and support,
I could never have charted this course.

TABLE OF CONTENTS

BACK-OF-THE-BOOK EXTRAS
Acknowledgements
About the Author
What's Next?
More from Evolved Publishing

PROLOGUE
Love is in the Air

West Point, March 1850

Cornelia Rose bent to retrieve her glove, inadvertently setting off a series of sighs from the bench full of admirers. She turned in surprise, her abrupt movement sending her parasol wobbling precariously on her shoulder. She swiped at her parasol and caused a domino effect: her handbag sloshed, its contents erupting from the unfastened top, and her handkerchief escaped from her one successfully gloved hand. A veritable platoon of men sat, sprawled, and perched on the lone bench on the busy wharf at West Point Academy. *Mercy, I am on display!* she thought. Nellie turned crimson in one quick flush. She bent to scoop her belongings back into her handbag and almost lost her balance. Regaining her footing, she tucked a stray strand of hair into her elaborately feathered new hat, and attempted a look of nonchalance. The fifteen-year-old debutante force a smile, with what she hoped was a flirtatious, but refined, expression on her face.

That smile was enough to send one cadet catapulting off the bench. He swooped low to retrieve the piece of pink silk, and turned the motion into an exaggerated bow.

"Mademoiselle, may I say your appearance is akin to an angelic visitation to lost souls sufferin' in hell," he drawled in a Southern accent. Nellie reached to retrieve the handkerchief and the cadet boldly caught her hand in his own large grasp. An onlooker from the bench gave a loud guffaw.

Her mother, still standing next to her berating the sailor from the steamboat, gave Nellie a warning *tsk, tsk*, but did not stop her lecture on proper baggage handling.

"Thank you, gallant knight, for your alacrity, and most chivalrous retrieval of my personal belonging," said Nellie. She extracted her hand and beamed with pride at her own very poised reply.

Encouraged in spite of losing Nellie's hand, the cadet leaned closer, saying, "Your fine airs have captured, I say *simply captured* my heart. May I escort you on a short promenade to Flirtation Walk?"

Numerous chuckles rippled through the bench.

Nellie stepped back in alarm.

"Come, come," said the cadet, realizing his tactical error. "'Tis merely a path to Battery Cove where the Great Chain was affixed during our Revolutionary War."

Cornelia attempted diplomacy. "But for the fact that your offer has come at a rather inopportune time...." She gestured to the ladies and luggage behind her. "As you can see we have just arrived. I am sure our little group would have been delighted to accompany you."

"Cornelia Rose, why must you always be so difficult to locate?" A peevish voice interrupted her intoxicating repartee with the cadet. Nellie stiffened. She had no doubt as to whom that voice belonged. *'Tis plumb irritating that he should choose just this one, singular time to be punctual.* Without thinking she stamped her foot in anger. *I thought he had guard duty for many hours. How truly grating the sound of that whiny voice! Elmer P. Otis. I am quite certain the "P" stands for 'petulant.'*

Just in time, she remembered her manners, even before she heard her mother's *tsk, tsk* admonition. She forced a smile in Elmer's direction.

"Fellows, this is *my* drag for the soiree and its attendant events," Elmer proclaimed to the cadet. He glared at the bench of potential beaus, every one of his regulation twenty-four brass buttons threatening to pop off his dress uniform jacket as he puffed out his chest.

Not only am I stuck with this ne'er-do-well, but my presence is merely a ploy to elevate his social stature! Nellie groused to herself.

The handkerchief-retrieving cadet bowed and walked away. With grunts and grumbling, some of Elmer's fellow West Point Cadets dispersed in different directions to await arriving river traffic at other spots on the landing. Elmer remained standing at attention in front of Nellie, poor-complexioned chin thrust out proudly beneath his grimly pursed lips. A First Cadet rose from the bench and leaned his lips close to Elmer's ear. "You lucky cur!" Nellie heard. Cadet Otis grinned. The First Year punched Elmer in the arm and Elmer changed his position to 'at ease.'

Nellie's mother ended her harangue of the luggage-handling sailor and turned toward them. Elmer came to attention again.

"Mrs. Entwhistle." Elmer P. Otis bowed. "I am most grateful you granted permission to your illustrious daughter to attend this week's festivities."

Nellie's mother smiled with her well-bred grace and extended her hand. Cornelia, her sisters, and her friend Augusta curtsied.

"Ladies." Elmer had the grace to nod and bow again towards Cornelia as he looked at their group. "Say! That's a fair amount of cases for just an overnight stay! Are you ladies planning to enroll as cadets?"

Mrs. Entwhistle coughed and looked chagrined. Nellie's sister Agnes frowned with disdain and Anastasia and Augusta giggled.

Now do you comprehend my concerns, Mutter? Nellie thought. *Elmer cannot summon sufficient social grace to court a farm hand.*

Her mother caught Nellie's eye, *was that sympathy in her gaze?* but did not issue the bristling retort Nellie thought Elmer's oafish remark mandated.

Mrs. Entwhistle shook her head and said, "Cadet Otis, please assist us with these cases. Where is a conveyance for transportation to the West Point Hotel? We must settle ourselves before this afternoon's parade."

"Conveyance?" Elmer scratched his head.

Nellie did not wait for Elmer to formulate a plan. She and her friend Augusta located a dockhand and scurried over to obtain his, and his handcart's, services. *There are only five cases after all,* she thought. *'Tis not excessive!*

"Perhaps I could shoulder one case," Elmer was offering upon their return. "...And I could round up a group to...."

Suddenly, Augusta shrieked, drowning out Mrs. Entwhistle's reply.

"Nathaniel!" Augusta shouted. "My sweet!"

A tall good-looking cadet jumped the last foot from the path to West Point's campus onto the quay and swept Augusta into his arms.

Nellie's mother was apoplectic with disapproval. She frowned at Cornelia as if to say 'I had better never witness this type of wildly inappropriate behavior from you.'

Why cast disapproving eyes upon me? Nellie wondered. *My comportment has consisted of naught contrary to your counseling.* Nellie tilted her head to the side and amended her thought to, *well, naught worse than taking off my gloves on the sloop!*

With Augusta Van Cortlandt secured safely on his arm, Nathaniel Foster from Sparta, New York remembered his upbringing. "Mistress Cornelia Entwhistle, how fare you?"

Nellie smiled and pointed with her head towards her mother.

"Mrs. Entwhistle, forgive me!" Nathaniel bowed low before Nellie's mother. "In my haste to greet my fiancée, I do believe I have forgotten my manners." Nellie's mother frowned, but extended her hand. Nellie's sisters bobbed another curtsey.

Nathaniel gave short shrift to the formalities and turned to Nellie, steering her away from Otis. With a hint of urgency in his voice, he said, "Cornelia Rose. Have you returned the correspondence of Obadiah Wright? He advised you have been incommunicado for some time and it worries him terribly."

Cornelia stole a glance at Elmer, hesitant in formulating a reply. *I do find Obadiah far more charming than this oaf Elmer. But so,* she reasoned, *is one of those trained monkeys that ride an organ grinder's shoulders in New York City.* It was just hard to remember to write to Mr. Wright when she was so busy with her social life.

"You know how those Yale men can be." Nathaniel laughed. "Lonely for a word from his beautiful lady."

"We must continue this conversation later," interjected Mrs. Entwhistle, observing Nellie with a softened glance, sparing her from further reply. "The ladies have had far too much exposure to the sun. We must repair to our lodging and change our attire for the parade."

In the scramble to supervise the luggage handling and assemble the group for the walk up the hill to the West Point Hotel, Nellie evaded further conversation with Cadet Otis.

As they headed toward the path, Nellie felt a tug on her elbow.

"Miss, did you drop this?" A broad shouldered, bespectacled cadet leaned down close to her face. Intimidated by his large size and his close proximity Nellie said 'no', turning away without even looking at the proffered item.

"Beg pardon, Miss." The cadet tapped her on the shoulder. "I know I am nearsighted, but I was fairly certain this glove dropped from *your* hand."

Tarnation! That dratted glove! Nellie blushed, turned, and snatched the glove. "Why th-thank you for your k-kindness," she stammered.

The large young man grinned and leaned close again. He whispered in her ear, "Save a space on your dance card for me! I wish a dance with the belle of the ball too."

Surprised, Nellie looked up into his smiling face.

He winked!

Goodness, I hope Mutter isn't... Nellie did not even finish the thought. She looked away from the cadet; Mrs. Entwhistle had witnessed the entire exchange.

My only sin is removing my gloves on the sloop, Nellie repeated to herself. She picked up her skirts and scurried up the path past her mother.

PART ONE

NEW YORK

CHAPTER 1
Don't Rain on My Parade

Manhattan, October 1842

Seven-year-old Nellie shivered in anticipation, her eyes refusing to close. They had practiced the *Ode to Croton* night and day, singing through their chores. Earlier today, Father led them in song on the joyous carriage ride to Grandmama's. Nellie softly sang it to herself, her metronome provided by the snores of her sister Agnes, sleeping on the far end of the bed, and the sweet puffs of breath from Anastasia snuggled in between them. She moved her hand, checking for the edge of the bed. Not even an inch to spare before she tumbled off the eider down comforter and onto the elegant polished hardwood floor below her. She had better not turn over! Her muscles tensed even more.

It wasn't the starched scratchiness of Grandmama Pffernuss's fine cotton pillowcase irritating her sensitive skin that kept her awake. It wasn't the terrifying formidable grandness of her grandparent's house. It wasn't even the intimidatingly huge city of New York surrounding the house that made her feel edgy and alert.

It was the excitement and anticipation of the next day.

Her parents were in the room next door. Perhaps if she tiptoed in, her father would give her a hug or tell her a story? No, more likely she would wake her baby brothers and her mother would be furious. She stayed put, in her small section of bed, in the mansion packed with her grandparents, her immediate family, and her aunts, uncles, and cousins. All of the Pffernuss family nestled in for the night—in close proximity to the start of tomorrow's grand celebration.

Crystal clear water will spew from the Croton Aqueduct tomorrow.
Papa promised!

The whole grand city of New York will turn out in magnificent ceremony to honor the completion of the new reservoirs and tunnels of the Croton Aqueduct.

Papa invented the new water system for the entire *city of New York,* she thought, pride swelling in her heart. *Sixteen tunnels. The High Bridge. Two reservoirs. And tomorrow we are to be honored guests at the glorious Croton Water Celebration.* She fidgeted with anticipation.

Excitement got the better of reason. She lifted the comforter, slid a cautious toe onto the icy floor, and crept to the bedroom door. The handle made a surprising click when she turned it. She jumped, then blinked, blinded by the refracting light filling the room as she opened the door. Frightened, she slammed it shut.

No one stirred.

Her feet felt frozen.

With a deep breath, she calmed down, opened the door the width of her finger and cautiously leaned one eye and one ear out into the crack of light.

"...even you, *Mutter*, must agree," Cornelia's mother was saying to her Grandmama.

Nellie drew in her breath and pulled back. She thought of closing the door again, but curiosity froze her in place.

"*Mein Mädchen, nein*," said Grandmama. "No, my daughter, I will agree to nothing. I still rue the day that you met that Entwhistle."

"But, *Mutter, Er ist mein Mann* now! Ach! We must speak English. He is my husband now. That was so long ago! James is a good provider. And tomorrow *mein Mann* will be honored."

"*Ja, Ja, ja, du hast recht.* You are right, he is a good man, I will concede." Grandmama drew herself up to her full five-foot height and practically warbled with self-righteousness. "But you are my only daughter. Is he good enough for the Pffernuss family? *Nein.* No. My only daughter marrying an Irishman? *Ach, du Liebe — meine Herz ist immer leiden.*"

Nellie's mother threw her hands up in the air. "Oh, my love, *your* heart suffers, *Mutter*? What about mine? Will you never be happy with me?" She tugged Grandmama's arm, dropped her voice to a whisper, and walked down the hall. The ladies took the candlelight with them.

Dazed from the light and puzzled by the scene she witnessed, Nellie shut the door. *Grandmama does not like Papa? How could this be?*

Sniffling tears, she stumbled over shoes and toys, feeling her way around the footboard, back to her side of the bed. She lifted the comforter. *Oh no!* Anastasia had worked her way over to the edge of the bed. Nellie gave Anastasia a shove, trying to push her back, but her sister was too heavy. She stood there, toes numb now, shivering in her nightgown, tears on her cheeks, overwhelmed, confused, and suddenly exhausted. At last, she crawled over the sleeping Anastasia and burrowed into the blankets, finding a space perpendicular to her sisters at the foot of the bed.

It seemed that as soon as Nelly finally closed her eyes, Agnes, her older sister, was shouting in her ear. "Cornelia, rouse your lazy bones. We will not be delayed by your sloth! If you are not ready, we will leave you all alone in this huge house while we enjoy the festivities."

Frightened out of her sleep Cornelia jumped out of bed into complete alertness, eyes wide open. It was pitch black. She could not even see Agnes, the annoying. She closed them again in confusion. *If it is time to wake up, why is it so dark?* Sleepy little Anastasia cried, "It is too dark to be morning!" echoing her own thoughts. "It is not yet time to wake."

"Listen brainless." Agnes leaned over from the far side of the bed to shake her youngest sister. "The one-hundred-gun salute begins at sunrise. Do you want to miss the most exciting day of your life?"

Anastasia's chubby baby face crumbled into misery. She screwed her eyes closed. Tears flowed and she let out a big bawl. It was unclear whether it was a reaction to the harsh words and the shaking, or the prospect of missing the best day of her life.

Mrs. Entwhistle bustled into the room, baby Matthias clinging to her neck, brother Jonas trailing behind, wearing only one boot. "What is all this fuss and bother? *Raus mit du,* Get out with you! We must get ready! Cornelia, shame on you for keeping your father waiting on his important day."

Nellie grabbed her stockings and began the struggle to tame them enough to transfer them to her legs.

Removing his thumb from his mouth, Jonas asked, "Why is it such an important day, Mama?"

"Baby," taunted Agnes, pointing at Jonas. "*Baby!* I was far too mature to have sucked my thumb at five years of age."

"But you were still a wee little babe, wee-weeing just like all the other babies then, don't you know?" said older brother Jerome, bouncing into the room. He tousled Agnes' hair while he put her in her place. "The parade of cousins leaves from the front door in twenty minutes," he announced, and bounded back out the bedroom door.

Nellie's mother ignored Agnes' rude teasing and said, "Jonas, your father is to be honored as one of the premier engineers, instrumental in the innovative, *and* early completion of the construction of the Croton Aqueduct. Through his endeavors, the thousands of residents of the city of New York will have a ready supply of fresh drinking water, straight from the Croton Dam. We must all be very proud of Papa."

Nellie smiled with pride, which turned to joy when she viewed the new, pretty pink party dress her mother had sewn just for this special day.

"The *President* of our *whole* Nation will be there, brainless." Agnes, already in her dress, tying her bow, did not even look to see the cruel effect of her words on her younger brother. "I'm all a-tremble to hear the speeches. I do hope Governor William H. Seward himself calls Papa to the podium to present him the medal.... Perhaps we will sit near Mr. President John Tyler! Or maybe even near former-president Mr. John Quincy Adams...."

"I want to see the water shoot out of the fountain at the big reservoir," said Jonas. "I wager it will go this high!" he shouted, jumping off the bed into the air.

"Technically, the water will not 'shoot *out* of the fountain,'" corrected Agnes smugly.

"It certainly must," Nellie interjected. "How else would it be possible to have the water works reach the height of 50 feet into the air?"

"You always exaggerate," said Agnes.

"I most certainly do not! Papa and I read it in the newspaper together last night," Nellie retorted.

Agnes shut her mouth, knowing that she could not argue once the highest authority, Papa, was inserted into the discussion.

"As if it would make a difference to us!" Agnes finally said, hands on her hips. Changing tack, Agnes used her superior knowledge of New York City geography to brandish a sword at Jonas. "We might not see the shooting fountain. The water works display of the celebration is at the Distributing Reservoir at Murray Hill which, from here, is the opposite direction from City Hall."

"But Patrick is marching around the fountain! He promised we would see him. Maaa," wailed Jonas. "Can't I see the shooting water?"

"Do not fret now Jonas," said Mrs. Entwhistle. "Our entire family group will egress to the reservoir for a picnic supper. Our picnic will occur precisely during the interval your brother Patrick and his company of cadets will parade at Murray Hill. I am sure we will have a fine view of the fountain and the marching men. After supper, Patrick will join us for our promenade around the reservoir perimeter. This will transpire long after Papa has received his award."

Nellie smiled, thinking of her wonderful oldest brother Patrick, already adult enough at fourteen to march with The Mount Pleasant Military Academy. Head in the clouds, she gathered the flounces of her dress in bunches in her hand, and poked her head into the skirt.

"Not without your petticoats!" Mrs. Entwhistle rumbled like thunder, yet she did not even raise her eyes from the britches she was buttoning over Matthias' behind.

Nellie's eyes stung with tears. *I did not purposefully forget those dreaded, itchy, petticoats,* she fumed. *Where could they be?* She searched through the bedclothes, tossing blankets and pillows every which way. She crawled on top of the bed, looked over the headboard, and then in desperation hung herself upside down over the edge, thrusting her head into the dark space underneath the bed. Tucked in the gloom, the petticoats lay in a little swirl of dust. *Agnes! That's her handiwork,* she thought.

She righted herself and glared at her eight-year-old sister.

Agnes smirked with satisfaction and looked back at Nell in the mirror, raising one eyebrow and calmly arranging her bows on her dress.

Further vexed by Agnes's eyebrow skill, Nellie made one quick, feeble attempt to lift only one of her eyebrows in reply, and then snorted in disgust. There was no time for revenge. Her mother glared at them. Nellie thought better of trying Mrs. Entwhistle's patience.

Nellie pulled on the hated petticoats as quickly as she could, and turned to help her sleepy little sister into her stockings. Five-year-old Anastasia was crying with frustration at the twisted mess. Nellie pulled them off in one motion, stuck her arm all the way into one of the legs and inside-outed them, and then gathered the leg all the way up to the toes. Anastasia watched with her mouth open, and obediently thrust her toes in on Nellie's command.

"Oh, sank you, Nellie," Anastasia whispered in a lisp. "Agnes told me everyone was going to leave without me because I was too dumb to put on my thtockings."

"I would never go without you. We sisters stick together, right?" Nellie smiled, gathered up the other leg of the stocking and put it over Anastasia's other toes.

"Then where did Agnes come from?" Anastasia wanted to know.

Nellie rolled her eyes. "The Lord only knows!" she whispered.

They both giggled.

Agnes scowled in their direction. "*Mutter*, I am completely clad and Cornelia and Anastasia are simply playing. Furthermore, they have not found their boots, much less than buttoned them."

Mother turned an evil eye on the two youngest girls as she pulled cardigans on both boys. "Young ladies, you should be ashamed of yourselves."

Anastasia hung her head and said, "I am thorry, Mother."

Rebelliousness rose in Nellie's throat and choked her apology. She stooped to find her other boot. *Why should I apologize? I did nothing wrong*, she thought. Surreptitiously she shot a glance at her mother with her head still bent. Mrs. Entwhistle bustled around, her beautiful silk dress rustling with efficiency, assembling a bag with some diapers. Nellie felt an apology would not be necessary, or noticed.

"We must leave at once if we are to see our brave armed forces fresh from t' United States Military Academy at West Point deliver the one-hundred-gun salute!" Mr. Entwhistle's cheerful brogue boomed from the hallway below.

Jonas shot toward the door in a surprisingly smooth move, in spite of tumbling over Anastasia still seated on the floor.

"We can't miss the guns and the cannons, Papa," Jonas shouted. Nellie and her sisters rushed out behind him.

The Entwhistle family, joined by the Pffernuss cousins and grandparents, flowed down the grand stairs, out the gate of the stately home, and into the stream of people already hurrying down Fifth Avenue to City Hall to see the historic celebration. *Look at the rainbow of colorful ladies!* Nellie thought, her heart surging with joy at the kaleidoscope of colors blooming in the hats, dresses, parasols, tassels, and ribbons of the ladies in the crowd.

"It'th like being in a parade," whispered Anastasia as they hurried along.

"Indubitably! But as splendid as this is, we will see a gen-u-ine parade after sunrise," promised Nellie, unable to tear her eyes from the bright spectacle before her. As they tried to keep pace with the long strides of the grown-ups, Nellie watched the colors bob and weave through the moving crowd and panted, "The parade will surely be grand! There will be multitudes of marching bands with big brass horns, and ra-ta-tat drums. And handsome soldiers in impressive uniforms and splendid ladies carrying banners, and...."

Anastasia was having trouble keeping up with Mrs. Entwhistle and the perambulator. Nellie tugged her along as best she could, but Anastasia was running as fast as her short legs would carry her. Nellie looked up at the street sign, *we've only come seven blocks since leaving Grandmama's house on 13th Street!* At the rate Anastasia was going, they would never make it as far as City Hall. The bells of a church chimed as they passed, igniting a string of pealing bells in church after church along the route heading downtown that quickened the pace of the crowd. Just as tears threatened and Nellie feared abandonment for the second time that day, her father turned around to locate them.

In one bound, he was at Nellie's side, scooping Anastasia into his arms. "No colleen o' mine'll be left lagging behind today!" he exclaimed, as if reading her thoughts. "Not my angel with the little legs, nor my good lass who assists her!" He smiled down at Nellie and tousled her hair. All Nellie's worries evaporated. She stuck her hand in his giant one, and skipped along next to him.

Soon they caught up with Jerome, who was at the lead, carrying Jonas.

The day was a grand blur of amazing activities. The excitement in the children generated by the ear splitting, one hundred-gun salute at sunrise was enough to carry them to their spot on the parade route. Just in time for the first carriage of officials, eyes riveted on the dancing girls, they picnicked on Grandmama's feast of pickles, ham, and biscuits for breakfast.

The rousing band music, the smell of roasting chestnuts and the attire of the marchers piqued Cornelia's senses. The predawn parade of ladies in their rainbow of finery paled in comparison to the colorfully costumed clowns. Deftly dancing acrobats were resplendent in stripes and polka dots. Carriages of dignitaries displaying elegantly coiffed heads interrupted herds of elephants and exotic animals. Waves of music approached from afar and then engulfed them, carrying them along on drumbeats and melodies, leaving toes tapping in their wake. Peddlers pushed carts exuding tempting aromas: baking potatoes, roasting spicy peanuts, and the tangy citrus of fresh squeezed lemonade.

"The very gall of some people," Grandmother Pffernuss said behind her fan to Nellie's mother. "Observe the thirty-one-year-old humbug from your village, Doctor Brandreth, parading before us with that floosy in his carriage! She's nothing but a guttersnipe from the packing department of his factory. *Ach du Liebe*! Why he is blaspheming this important occasion?"

"Oh, *Mutter*, say 'oh my goodness' like an American! Moreover, they are married now," said Gertrude Entwhistle. She patted her mother's hand in a reassuring gesture.

Nellie's grandmother sniffed. "First wife barely cold in the grave. Putting a bandage on a disfigurement does not make it disappear."

Nellie's mouth dropped open as she tried to make sense of this snippet of conversation.

"Look, Nellie, a flock of peacocks!" shouted Jonas. Tucking the eavesdropped tidbit away in her memory for further study, Nellie gawked at the birds. Two young boys with sticks and a trainer kept the proudly strutting flock headed in the correct direction. "When I am a debutante I shall have a fan made of peacocks' brilliant blue feathers, arrayed just like their tails," she whispered.

The children teased their parents and grandparents for tastes of sweet and savory alike. Fruits from all over the world! They shared a banana, Cornelia trying to take the smallest bites possible, so the sweetness would linger on her tongue. The rarities she sampled made her eyes round. But her favorite was the little button of butterscotch candy her father allowed her to eat all by herself without having to share with anyone. It was far superior even to the nibble of licorice she shared with Agnes, or the lick of Jerome's lemon-flavored ice.

The marching bands are my favorite entertainment, Nellie decided, responding with her whole body. She and her sisters stood, with rapt attention and dancing legs as the rows of uniformed players marched past. Cornelia could not stop moving when the music filled the air. Familiar songs had the whole family singing. Bagpipes had her siblings joining her in dance, Jerome forgetting his superior position as the eldest attending son. A familiar Irish jig even had her father on his feet, stomping along with her. When the last notes of the disappearing band faded from hearing, they turned their heads forward and strained their ears to listen for the next hint of song.

Mile after mile of bands, clowns, acrobats, animals, firemen, and town officials marched before them. Nellie no sooner caught her breath from viewing an amazing spectacle before another marvel flaunted itself before her, snatching her breath away again. The continuous stream of sights strutted and paraded for hours. "In actuality," her mother informed them after consulting her program and her own mother, "the parade is five miles long and will continue until approximately four o'clock."

Agnes jumped up and down, and shouted, "Truly, the duration is almost an entire day!"

In spite of her best efforts, Cornelia had to take a seat. She snuggled herself next to Grandmama's feet, head leaning on the soft volume of skirt, eyes still glued to the wonders marching before her. She felt her eyes closing and tried to pay attention. The colors swirled and blurred before her.

She jerked herself awake as an Oompah Band's tuba wailed close to her ear. "*Mutter*, I cannot stay awake," she cried. "I cannot keep my eyes open—the light is too bright. They hurt!"

"Hush now, *Schatzy*, my little love," chided her mother. But then, with sympathy, she leaned over and gave Cornelia a hug. "The parade lasts all day. You can still hear the fun and the music if you rest your eyes a bit. That way, you will be wide awake when Papa receives his accolades."

Comforted, Cornelia drowsed in the sun while the bands played on.

She awoke to the confusion of her group mobilizing.

"It is preposterous to even contemplate carrying them *all* to City Hall!" her mother exclaimed.

"Yer parents should allow us to take t' larger perambulator," said her father. Mr. Entwhistle was getting a little hot under the collar. He ran his hand over his hair in consternation. The gestured ended with a tug on his ear.

"James, we must leave it here with the picnic supplies and blankets, so they can transport all the necessities *and* our nieces and nephews, first to the ceremony, and then the Murray Hill Reservoir. We have only ourselves to transport in time for the dignitary seating."

"Let's get shinning around!" Mr. Entwhistle thrust his chin forward and through clenched teeth stated, "I'll not abide being late nor bereft o' me family when I am honored."

Mrs. Entwhistle put a hand on her husband's arm. "If we start now and walk to a side street, perhaps we will be able to hire a carriage."

"Wishful thinking woman!" her husband exclaimed. "The whole city is celebrating today, everyone wants to hire a carriage. Jerome, look lively lad and shoulder yer burden."

"I fear I am not fit for this endeavor. I'll swear this brother of mine is heavier now than this morning." Jerome grumbled and jostled the slumbering Jonas, trying to get a firm grip on the sleeping, limp four-year-old, who kept slipping from his hold.

"Mr. Entwhistle, sir, perhaps I could be of assistance?" A young face distinguished itself from the crowd.

"Halloo Clayton," whistled Jerome, cheered by the sight of his older brother Patrick's friend.

"Young Clayton! Your assistance proved invaluable on t' building of the aqueduct, I'll wager it will be of some benefit here as well," Mr. Entwhistle said. He clapped the boy on the shoulder with a friendly hand.

The thirteen-year-old boy blushed, looking uncertain, but then continued, "My relations have a house about four blocks hence. We have an old baby buggy, in want of some attention to be sure, but it might just come in handy transporting your fine family to City Hall."

"Son, it would be a Godsend." Entwhistle picked up the boy's hand and pumped it rapidly in appreciation. "Gertrude!" He turned to his wife. "Gather t' children and begin to make yer way, as best ye can without strife, toward Canal Street. I'll hustle with young Clayton here to retrieve t' carriage, and find ye in progress." He turned and they were gone before Mrs. Entwhistle or Jerome could summon a reply.

With the help of the aunts and uncles, the Entwhistle crew assembled and mobilized. Much complaining and crying accompanied the children's departure from the parade route.

Grandmama waved and the Pffernuss cousins watched Mrs. Entwhistle and the children straggle away.

"Mind your *Mutter*, Cornelia Rose," Grandmama chided. Nellie remained standing on the curb, watching the circus march past, mesmerized by the bearded lady. With a guilty start, Nellie turned and ran after her family, by now, half way down the side street behind them.

Mrs. Entwhistle, already carrying Matthias the baby, picked up Anastasia as well. A strong, determined woman, she rose to the occasion, encouraging her children along. Jerome grumbled about his brother being a lead weight. Sullen faced, Agnes straggled along at her mother's side, dragging her jacket. Cornelia trailed a few feet behind, tired legs lagging and sore feet making her wince and complain.

Mrs. Entwhistle enticed them forward with the promise of future exciting events. "We will next see New York City's Mayor, Robert H. Morris commend your father, along with Mr. John Jervis and Mr. George Cartwright, the chief Croton Dam engineers. Other dignitaries, including our charismatic Governor William H. Seward, will also be on the dais, to congratulate your father on his fine work, and perhaps shake his hand. I will wager that old humbug, Doctor Benjamin Brandreth will not miss an opportunity for posturing on a bigger stage—a speech from him will be forthcoming, mind you!" Mrs. Entwhistle stopped talking to wag her finger, adjusting her children's positions in agitation. Nellie was not sure which person was the object of her ire. "There will be grand speeches, praising the fine work done by the many men devising this engineering feat and extolling the modern technology that engendered the system. Men will speak of the future and make predictions of the great technological wonders to come!

"At the conclusion of the official dedication and honoring ceremony, we will walk to the Murray Hill Reservoir to watch your brother Patrick parade with his Academy. General Aaron Ward himself, Sing Sing's hero of the War of 1812 and our State Representative, will lead Mount Pleasant Academy in his capacity as trustee and alumnus. On this auspicious occasion, our entire family will enjoy a lovely picnic dinner as we watch water flow through the new pipes, filling the reservoir."

Jonas roused himself from Jerome's shoulder and said, "But I want to see the shooting water! Papa promised me!"

"A special commemorative fountain has been erected just for this event," confirmed Mrs. Entwhistle. "Keep my pace, Agnes and Cornelia. You mustn't lollygag on such a grand day."

But as she spoke these encouraging words, sniffles got louder, and even the babies who were carried began to complain. Mrs. Entwhistle had no tolerance for whining, and in spite of her strength under adverse conditions, she lost her patience.

"*Gott im Himmel!*" exclaimed Mrs. Entwhistle. "That is too darn bad about you, now isn't it?" she whirled on Nellie who was in mid-complaint. Nellie saw the grim line of her mother's lips, her clenched jaw, and her raised eyebrows. Nellie burst into tears. Her mother harrumphed, hiked the two offspring higher on her hips and spun on her heel, marching forward. Nellie did not mean to be uncooperative, but her days' worth of walking, crammed into one early morning, had worn a huge hole in her stocking right at the heel, and now a blister was forming. She closed her mouth and limped along. Every step was painful, gingerly undertaken on already tired legs. She tried stepping only on her toe so her heel would not rub, but it only moderated the pain slightly.

She tried to hop, but it was almost impossible to keep going. She sat down on the curb and simply watched as her family paraded away from her. *No one cares about me!* She sniffed back tears. She was going to miss the ceremony that would honor her father!

Suddenly Jonas shouted, "Papa!"

Nellie raised her head and then jumped up, attempting to see what Jonas, a distance away and viewing from his height in Jerome's arms, saw through the throngs of people. She could not. She tore off after her family in a most un-lady-like fashion, and if not for the fact that her mother was so thankful for relief from the task of carrying the children, Nellie would have received a reprimand.

Jerome dumped his brother Jonas into the cart, and pumped Clayton's hand in appreciation.

Mrs. Entwhistle, divested of the two children, was already finding fault with the conveyance.

"*Ach du Liebe*! This could hardly be called a carriage," she muttered. Her husband looked chagrined. "We will arrive at the culmination of your career, the pinnacle of the Great Water Celebration with our children riding in a dilapidated old donkey cart."

"Sure 'n where is thy gratitude, Mrs. Entwhistle?" asked her husband, running his hand through his hair and scratching behind his ear. "This fine strappin' lad has lent this conveyance to us, for no compensation, out o' the goodness of his heart, when our need was dire."

True lady that she was, the reminder elicited a most gracious gratitude, so eloquently expressed to the boy, he blushed, pulled his hat from his head, and bobbed up and down, averting his eyes. Mr. Entwhistle reached into his pocket for a coin, but young Clayton declined it.

"Aye, a right proper gentleman, you are, me lad," said Mr. Entwhistle, nodding his head. He squeezed Agnes into the small cart already filled with his younger children, and picked up the handle. "Forward... March!" he said and sang, "Da-da... Tah da da dut da da...." The wagon lurched forward behind him.

Nellie, last to arrive, stood looking at the retreating, overfull, cart teaming with arms and legs. "No room for me!" she exclaimed.

"I reckon ye'll have to stay behind then Miss." Nellie looked up into Clayton's laughing face.

She was incensed. "My Papa invented the whole water system! If you think I will stay behind, you are sadly misinformed." She stamped her foot, and then winced. The blister on her foot exploded in pain. She caught her lip with her teeth, and scraped at her face where a stray piece of hair was irritating it.

Clayton bowed before her and scooped her into his arms. In two steps, he was beside the carriage, elbowing Agnes into a corner to make a space. He dumped Nellie in the midst of her squirming brothers and sisters. He faded from view as the baby buggy rolled on.

"Do not put your foot near my dress!" complained Agnes.

Nellie twisted her body as far as she could, peering around Agnes to see what happened to Clayton. Matthias squealed and Jonas grabbed Nellie's hair in an attempt to stop himself from slipping. With tears in her eyes from the sting of the pulled hair, Nellie saw nothing but the pants and skirts of strangers.

CHAPTER 2
Summer Breeze

Sing Sing, June 1847

Nellie wrinkled her nose in disgust. *Take care of the pigs! All summer! Again?*

She kicked the ground and looked up. Her father was staring at her, frowning at her lack of response. She swallowed hard, trying to rid herself of the mounting anger she felt at her return to this occupation. She bit back angry words before they escaped from her mouth.

Nellie looked at her older sister. Arm in a sling, face covered in ugly scratches and gashes, some still oozing, Agnes was a pitiful sight.

I would wager she did it deliberately, Nellie fumed, *simply to avoid pig duty.*

She looked back at her father, on whose brow a storm was gathering. He was about to thunder.

She repressed the wave of nausea that threatened to overcome her stomach at the mere thought of the smell of the pigs at high noon in mid-summer. *Even worse than the pig stench was the smell emanating from the nearby outhouse...* "No, the 'privy,' Nellie," she could hear her mother correct her in her head.... Nellie adjusted her apron and amended her thoughts. *Drat that pigpen located so near the privy as to make a perfect combination of stenches.* Blood rushed to her face, and she opened her mouth to speak.

Another glance at her father caused her to close her mouth again and drop her head.

She tucked the stray hair hanging in her face back into her braid. The motion calmed her and changed her heart.

She looked up, rearranged her face into a small smile, curtsied and said, "Of course, Papa, as you wish. I would be happy to resume the care and feeding of the pigs until Agnes' wounds heal."

The flood of tears that threatened to follow this bald face lie was held in check by the instant change in her father's demeanor.

"That's me colleen!" he shouted, and swept her into his giant bear hug.

Agnes smirked. Anastasia, Jonas, and Jerome looked relieved that the chain of command had not dumped pig duty in their laps.

As the group dispersed, Jonas said, "C'mon Nell, pig duty ain't so bad. Me and 'Stasia will help ya, sometimes."

Cheered by that bit of friendliness, she ran back to her room for her old apron. She flew down the back stairs to the kitchen, picked up the scraps Cook had collected from yesterday's meals, and ran the bucket to the pigpen.

Her mother's admonition, "Cornelia, I hope you are not wearing your Sunday frock to feed the pigs," floated over the beautiful Sunday afternoon sky and hung aloft with the puffy clouds, not reaching Nellie's consciousness.

The day was picture perfect, the trees tossing their green heads in the wind. The task usually only took her about twenty minutes. She would breeze right through and not let it bother her.

The stench smacked her in the nose.

She kicked the dirt in anger at her lack of ability to at least respectfully petition that this task should no longer be hers. Why should it be her burden, just because Agnes, the first replacement she had had in one and one-half years, had fallen off Patrick and Jerome's wagon, breaking her arm and suffering multiple contusions? Agnes never should have been racing it. *Leave that wagon riding to the big boys,* she thought.

Agnes should have played jump rope with me! If she had, we would not have had to use a tree as a rope turner... Augusta and Clara would have stayed longer and we could have jumped 'All Together Now'. No, instead that horrid contrarian chose to race with her brothers. She had to go give herself those ugly discolorations and bruises, and I am paying for her mistakes.

Nellie snorted out of her nose. "Humph, I bet she did it on purpose, just to dodge this chore." With that proclamation, her conscious felt a twinge of remorse. Nellie knew that Agnes adored her older brothers and tried to emulate their every move. Patrick, however much he cared for all of his siblings, would not tolerate any hindrance to his important business. Agnes was probably trying yet again to prove to Patrick she could keep up with him, when she took the nasty spill off the wagon.

Nellie's pity was short lived. *How un-ladylike!* she thought.

Cornelia Rose heard the three short blasts of a steamship's whistle, signaling the afternoon steamer's impending departure from the Sing Sing dock. *Can I finish this pig task before the ship leaves promptly at three o'clock?*

Mercy! Patrick is probably sailing his schooner today. Recently graduated from Mount Pleasant Academy, her oldest brother spent the majority of his time at the harbor, either learning their father's shipping business or sailing his own vessel. *I must not dally! I must see his schooner, flags proudly displaying their colors in the bright sun, cruising out of the harbor.*

Like a magnet, the river pulled Nellie toward its bustle and activity. In that one glorious week that Agnes had fed the pigs, Nell watched ships come and go from the harbor every stray free moment during the week and all Sunday afternoon. She helped Patrick with boat maintenance, even volunteering for chores—one evening joining the sailors swabbing the deck, as his schooner lay moored in its slot.

In the middle of the pigsty Nellie suddenly turned an intense shade of scarlet at the thought of her embarrassment last week. Her hand flew to her mouth, spilling slop on her Sunday shoes. She remembered scampering on board her brother's ship last Sunday in a jovial mood only to have Patrick tease her mercilessly, in front of the crew.

"I did not grant you permission to come aboard," Patrick boomed from the forecastle.

This stopped Nellie in her tracks, tears brimming in her eyes. Luckily her brother Jonas stood on deck, practicing his nautical knots. He directed in a stage whisper, "He wants you to salute, remember?"

Nellie ran back down the gangplank and planted herself on the pier, hand to her forehead in a salute. "Permission to come aboard, sir!" she shouted.

"Permission granted, sailor." Patrick's laugh rang out, distinguishing itself from the caw of the seagulls. Nellie was sure sailors two piers away turned to look at the cause of merriment.

Nellie cringed again in remembrance. The butt of the seamen's jokes again. *Now they will never think of me as a young lady!* She squirmed in renewed mortification. *This will never do,* she thought and forced herself to think of other things.

There were many joys that absorbed Nellie at the harbor; its lure wasn't just the ships. Summer brought many fancy folks traveling from New York City. They streamed off the steamships, sloops, and yachts in droves. Nellie observed them all and ogled the gentry's fancy couture.

Fine ladies, beautifully coiffed and plumed, bustled about and fussed over their luggage, until they climbed into grand carriages and rolled up the hill. Nellie looked down at her new Sunday dress, now sporting a bit of mud at the hem. *Certainly not nearly as grand as a New York City Lady, but at least it is finer than my apparel last Sunday,* she thought.

The less grand folk walked, lugging, carting, or even carrying unwieldy bundles and bags. The passengers formed a continuous parade, climbing the hill that was Main Street to one of the many fine inns.

The elite went to the Union Hotel or the American Hotel, both at the top of the hill, with the best breezes and the best views. Bucolic Sing Sing was a mecca for aficionados of fine academies, beautiful vistas, cool forests, and fresh air.

Nellie thrilled at the air of chaos that wafted off the river. But after her week of active participation in wharf life, she saw order and purpose in the jumble and confusion on the docks. Sloops slipped into moorings, discharged their cargo, and slipped away again. Fishing boats docked amid a cacophony of cawing seagulls. Fishermen quickly unloaded their catch with only an occasional reward for those gulls, and then swabbed the decks clean in preparation for the next day's expedition. Ship after ship berthed, had the contents of their hulls emptied, and then repacked with pickles, oysters, cotton gins, cider, apples, files, iron pipes, pills, porous plasters, shoes, stoves, and people, and cast off again.

Farmers are as interesting to watch as sailors, Nellie decided. Hours slipped by as she observed them hurrying their produce down the hills from their farms and haggling with the ship owners for the best price. Last Monday, Nellie watched the grand entrance of one of her father's ship building competitors, Sing Sing resident Thomas Collyer's steamship *Katrina van Tassel*. With an elegant 'come about' leeward in the incoming tide, it moored at the wharf. Smokestacks standing tall, the ship's contents swiftly spilled out of its hold. Waiting produce stood in line to fill the newly created void. Nell followed bunches of long orange carrots, green tops tied together, passing from farmers' carts to market merchants' scales, to shippers' crates. Wisps of green tops escaping from in between the slates, she watched the stacked crates balance on the deck of the steamship as the *Katrina van Tassel* sailed back down the river to New York City. She imagined a family in Brooklyn, bowing their heads, saying 'grace' over the hot carrots on their supper plates.

After the completion of the Croton Aqueduct, her father switched industries and established a shipping company. In addition to schooners and sloops, Entwhistle Enterprises now owned three fine steamships, its fleet built right here in Sing Sing harbor. As shrewd in business as he was skilled in engineering, James Entwhistle had the right combination of expertise to command a successful fleet of ships, transporting cargo and people up and down the Hudson River. Patrick's recent promotion to captain of one of the schooners gave Nellie one more reason to run to the river and loiter about the wharves to watch her father's ships come in.

Now here it finally was, Sunday. She should be gliding along the pier in her new sprigged gingham dress, pretending she was a lady, heading down river to The City. She should be watching the passengers assemble and embark before the third whistle warned of the ship's imminent departure. She pictured herself on her perch of last Sunday, clad in her old Sunday dress, hem a bit too short, hand over the embarrassing stain on the skirt that her mother could not wash out, squinting at the water in spite of the shade of her faded sunbonnet. Her mind's eye again saw the passengers bound for the city leaning on the railings of the two decks in the stern of the grand steamship *DeWitt Clinton* as the sailors at the bow scrambled to cast off the lines and pull the heavy ropes aboard. *What excitement! A voyage!* The sea breeze whipped her hair and her imagination. She saw the steam belching from the engine in black gusts of smoke and the white water of the ship's wake as, anchors aweigh, it set a course south toward The City.

She squealed in pain, setting off reply squeals from some of the pigs.

A pig trampled her foot, in its haste to gobble the slop that Nell was sloshing into the trough. Nellie squealed again at a big splotch of slop the pig managed to get on her dress, just below her apron. She kicked at the pig, sending it squealing in earnest to the other side of the pen.

She would never make it to the dock in time to see the departure of the *Isaac Newton* if she had to stop at the water pump to get the filth off her new dress!

"Cornelia! Corn-eeell-y-ah! Time to scrape the potatoes."

Nellie drew herself erect. *What in tarnation?* She threw up her hands, and the pail hanging off her arm spewed more slop down the side of her dress. *I still have to scrape the potatoes — in addition to performing Agnes' pig duty? This simply cannot be so.*

She tossed the bucket in disgust and ran to the house, clattering up the steps and slamming the screen door. "*Mutter*! You certainly cannot expect..." she shouted.

"Cornelia Rose Entwhistle," enunciated her mother in reply. Her voice was not loud, just intense. Nellie knew that no-nonsense voice—it was terrifying. It commanded attention. It conveyed furrowed eyebrows, a harsh stare, and a clenched jaw. Nellie knew it without even glancing at her mother's face.

Blinking to adjust her eyes to the gloom of the kitchen, Nell clamped her mouth shut and stopped dead in her tracks. Gertrude Entwhistle towered above her. "Such un-lady like behavior will never be tolerated in this house. Stomping up the steps like a cowhand! Shouting like a sailor! I have a good mind to have your father take you to the shed and give you the licking you deserve." Nellie could not look at her mother. She slid her eyes to the right. They landed on Agnes, seated at the table on a chair filled with cushions, smirking at her.

"*Mutter*, I am sorry I shouted," she said. "But..."

"There are no *buts* about it," Mrs. Gertrude Entwhistle said with no lessening of stern anger in her voice. "A lady never chooses to behave in such an indecorous manner."

"*Mutter*." Nellie hung her head. "Mother," she said again, this time as softly as she could manage, knowing she had no choice but to defer to her mother's iron hand. "*Mutter*, since I now have to resume care of the pigs, could not Agnes assume my inside domestic chores?"

Agnes opened her mouth to object, but it was unnecessary. Mrs. Entwhistle immediately sprang to her defense.

"Of course not," Mrs. Entwhistle said, with a vehemence that left no room for arguing. "Your sister suffers terribly from the wounds and trauma of her accident. She must apply herself to recuperating. You will perform a modest amount of additional domestic tasks until she recovers. *Arbeit macht das Leben süss*. Ach, in English! Work makes life sweet. Further, I will not entertain, nor endure, any complaints. It is a sacrifice you will make to aid her recovery."

Nellie's mouth gaped in disbelief. *Once again, I am burdened with more work, courtesy of the special needs of the sneering Agnes.*

"Now, do not shirk your duty Cornelia. Close your mouth. You are a lady, not a codfish. Scrape the potatoes. Improper deportment will no longer be tolerated." Her mother turned back to the stove, and tasted the stew Cook was stirring. "More pepper," she said to Cook Hilda.

"Anastasia, go to the garden and pull some bay leaf for the stew," she called. Immediately, overhead feet audibly scurried.

"Ohhhh, I feel so poorly," complained Agnes.

Mrs. Entwhistle rushed to her side. Kneeling, her mother felt Agnes's forehead for fever and looked closely at her bruises.

"Cornelia, make a poultice for Agnes' wounds. *Gott im Himmel!* Why has that harebrained doctor not come to set her arm? Most likely he bent his elbow in excess last night at O'Malley's saloon, thus rendering him incapable of rounds after Mass today." Mrs. Entwhistle regained her standing position with a groan, relying heavily on a pull on the back of Agnes' chair, which, for an instant, threatened to topple it.

"Dad blame it, Ma! Watch what you are doing or you'll break my other arm," Agnes said rudely. Nellie drew in her breath at Agnes' vulgar language.

But rather than chastising Agnes, Mrs. Entwhistle merely said, "Now, Agnes, do not trouble yourself," and placed a soothing hand on her sister's head.

Tarnation, Agnes can get away with murder!

Agnes pulled her head out from under the hand and said, "How can I be untroubled when no one attends my injuries?"

"I know how to set her arm," Nellie said.

Every woman in the kitchen paused and turned to look at her.

"Now how in God's Kingdom would you have obtained that knowledge, Cornelia Rose?" Mrs. Entwhistle said, putting her hands on her hips.

"Ye gads, do tell," said Agnes, with her trademark smirk.

"Clara's mother is a midwife. After school every day, Clara and I walk to her house. You gave me permission, *Mutter.*" Nellie raised anxious eyes to her mother.

"Yes, I did, *if* you *completed* your chores," Mrs. Entwhistle said nodding. "I am not certain that is the case, but pray, do continue."

"I always complete my chores," Nellie protested. She quickly resumed her story under her mother's wilting glare. "People come to see Midwife Rafferty at all hours of the day, with all kinds of ailments. I have watched her make medicines, boil poultices, and set bones."

"That does not mean you can actually set bones yourself," Agnes said.

"I have had practice!" Nellie declared.

The hired girl in the kitchen giggled and Cook whispered to her, "She'll surely catch hell now."

Mrs. Entwhistle looked furious, but Nellie swallowed hard and continued her explanation. "Clara asked me to stay for tea after school, one day, as was our custom. You know *Mutter*, I rejected her first invitations, and never would have accepted had you not acquiesced."

"The Lord only knows the cleanliness of her kitchen," Mrs. Entwhistle mumbled.

"Why her kitchen is very clean, and her teas are made from the finest herbs, grown in her own garden. She grows a greater assortment than we do in our kitchen garden, *Mutter*. She uses most of them for medicine. I have assisted in harvesting while acquiring some knowledge of a variety of herbs and their varied uses."

"Cornelia, please do return to the subject at hand. I never did see a girl so carried away with her ruminations."

"At first, I merely helped Clara pick herbs for our tea. But Midwife Rafferty is so interesting, while we pick, she sorts the plants, groups them according to their medicinal properties, and teaches their use." Nellie put up her hand and pulled down her fingers as she recounted, "She has shown me similar and related herbs, herbs which act in concert together, and ones which clash. I have learned remedies for many common diseases. The more I learn, the more I yearn to know. I desire Mrs. Rafferty's full instruction in the science of midwifery."

"Bone setting, you humbug!" Agnes burst out, tugging impatiently at the cloth tied around her neck as a sling. "You are supposed to be telling *Mutter* why you are qualified to set bones."

Everyone in the kitchen looked expectantly at Nellie. All activity had stopped, save the bubbling of the stew in the big Dutch kettle on the potbellied stove. Cornelia Rose Entwhistle, heady from the unaccustomed attention, wrapped her arms around herself in a hug, and said, "I watched Midwife Rafferty set Mary Louise Wheeler's broken arm, Susanna McGlew's broken leg, and the broken foot of John Cody, a sailor from the schooner *Cleopatra*." She beamed at her audience.

"*You helped* a criminal?" the Cook whispered. "Cody, the deck hand who stole Captain Brotherson's forty dollars?" she shivered. "So brave, *Mädchen* Nellie."

"Hush now, Cook Hilda," chided Mrs. Entwhistle. "Miss Nellie exhibited no remarkable bravery. We are Catholics. We believe in forgiveness, and works of charity for all in need, including salty sailors."

"*Salty criminals* mind you," muttered Cook under her breath. "*Gott im Himmel! Ach! English*—God in heaven! *Das ist nicht* proper. *Nein!* No, that is not proper. Do not expect me near...."

She stopped talking under the stern stare of Mrs. Entwhistle.

"You watched? You watched?" scoffed Agnes. "Humbug! That don't qualify you for setting bones yourself!"

"Not 'don't' Agnes, the proper words are 'does not,'" corrected Mother with a gentle hand on Agnes' shoulder.

Agnes calls me a humbug and you correct her grammar? Nellie fumed.

Mrs. Entwhistle turned a hard-set face toward her other daughter. "Now Cornelia, while I am sure it is enlightening to see the Midwife at work, observing her doctoring skills is very different from actually employing them yourself."

Nellie flushed a deeper shade of pink. She opened her mouth, but paused a moment. She was weighing the consequences of telling the truth against the ignominy of saying no more.

She rushed to establish her credentials. "In an emergency, Midwife Rafferty sought my aid. The injury required more than just her own and Clara's hands. She said I had natural aptitude! Midwife Rafferty offered to teach me her science and all I have to do in exchange is help her with her work. I am learning how to be a midwife, *Mutter*, and I have already acquired the skill of setting bones."

Her mother stared at her silently. Nellie said, "I can fix Agnes right now, and her pain will shortly abate."

Mrs. Entwhistle opened her mouth to chastise Cornelia for her deception, but decided against it. She frowned and said, "Your means of obtaining this knowledge have been most devious and degrading to your soul, but have no fear, your father and I will discuss this with you at length on another occasion. The town's doctor seems incapacitated by his own evil ways. I refuse to enlist Midwife Rafferty, and it is nigh impossible to lure a doctor from either Sparta or Tarrytown as far a distance as this neighborhood. Therefore, to spare poor dear Agnes another day of pain, you may demonstrate your surreptitiously obtained education by healing your sister."

In spite of the lack of confidence of the assembled ladies, Nellie smiled and immediately set to work. "I just need Jerome to run to Midwife Rafferty's house to obtain the herbs she prepares for healing broken bones after they are set."

"I thought you said you could fix this without the help of anyone?" Agnes, never gracious, was even more quarrelsome under duress.

"I can mix the potion myself, if you prefer, but it would require me going to the apothecary to obtain the Chinese herbs we do not grow in our garden, an hour of grinding and mixing, and six hours of boiling herbs in oil, to reduce them to a paste I can apply to clean linens. Once the linens are saturated, mayhap sometime around tomorrow afternoon, I can begin to relieve your pain. Is that your preference?" asked Nellie.

Agnes mumbled something under her breath, turned her head away, and stuck out her arm.

Mrs. Entwhistle bustled to the back door and called "Jerome" several times before he appeared.

"*Mutter*, I am working on the dry-docked sloop *Eliza Jane* for Papa. If I do not finish repairing the hull and waterproofing it by this evening, he will be most displeased," Jerome said. He did not take kindly to an interruption of 'man's work' from the women in the kitchen, even if one of them was his mother. He was even less pleased when he heard the cause of the summons.

"I am sent as a common errand boy to retrieve some magic potion invented by a witch doctor?" he asked, incredulity written in the freckles on his face.

"Midwife Rafferty did not invent it. The Chinese have been practicing this medicinal art for centuries. It is a medical recipe passed down through generations, and now common knowledge among western Midwives," Nellie said, raising her voice slightly. Jerome hesitated. His mother glared at him and he rushed out of the room. Nellie smiled to herself: another first, having superior knowledge to the all-knowing, learned Jerome.

Nellie arranged Agnes at the side of the table with her broken arm resting in the correct position, and began giving orders to the ladies in the kitchen. "Heat some water on the stove and fetch me a small salt block," she directed.

The women gathered around to watch Nellie dissolve the salt in a large bowl of warm water, and gently place Agnes' arm in, after testing the water temperature with her elbow.

"Why'd you do that?" asked Anastasia, who had come in with arms full of herbs from the garden, as requested.

"The salt water makes the bones float, so I can ensure the correct placement of the two bones in her arm," Nellie explained. She ground a paste of flour and water, adding some herbs she bade Anastasia to fetch. Agnes still twitched and groaned in her seat, looking glum.

Nellie crushed some lavender seeds, smoothed the oil from the seeds onto Agnes' temples, and held the crushed bits under Agnes' nose. "Take a deep breath and then release it slowly as you count to five," she said. Agnes looked as if she would object, but thought better of it.

"Again," commanded Nellie, but with a smile on her face and another soothing rub of Agnes' temples. Agnes complied, and then relaxed, just a bit, into her chair, closing her eyes.

Jerome burst through the door, breathless from his run to Midwife Rafferty's house, and thrust a jar of some vile looking brown paste into Nellie's hands.

She soaked some strips of linen in the paste, then dredged them in the flour and herbs. Carefully picking up Agnes's arm, she bound the arm with the herb-infused linen. When fully wrapped, Nellie held the arm up and looked at it carefully.

To break the absorbed silence in the kitchen (even Jerome was watching her now) and to distract Agnes, Nellie asked her what her favorite thing was. Agnes opened one eye, raised one eyebrow, looked at her suspiciously, and said, "What care you about what pleases me?" But there was no malice in her voice.

That was all the distraction Nellie needed, for as Agnes spoke, she squeezed her hand around Agnes's arm where the bones were protruding, and snapped them back into place. Agnes said, "Ow!" and pulled her arm away but Nellie caught it back and started guessing that Agnes' favorite thing in the world was the pearl necklace from Grandmama. Agnes took up the discussion then, listing cherished possessions, while Nellie kept a light pressure on the fracture, waiting for the linens with the healing medicine to dry on Agnes's arm. After three minutes, Nellie put a splint on either side of the arm using sticks from a young sapling retrieved by Jonas from the front lawn, and then folded some linen into a sling. She tied it around Agnes's neck and rested the arm in it, as Jerome, Jonas, and the women looked on in amazement.

"Does it feel any better?" Nellie asked.

Reluctantly, Agnes nodded her head yes.

"I certainly do not approve of your methods of obtaining this knowledge," Mrs. Entwhistle said frowning. "But I must concede you have, without doubt, done your sister, and in fact our family, a good turn by alleviating her suffering." Mrs. Entwhistle smiled and reached out her arms to give Nellie a hug.

Why does Mutter always wear such a grim countenance, and scold incessantly, when at heart she is so loving? Nellie wondered. *Mercy, she is, without a doubt, beautiful when she smiles.*

"Cornelia Rose Entwhistle," said Gertrude Entwhistle. "I thank the good Lord that He has blessed me with you as my daughter."

CHAPTER 3
Strangers in the Night

Sing Sing, November 1847

Cornelia felt another wave of jealousy crest above her head and crash down upon her, engulfing her heart.

Agnes will debut at Mrs. Warden's Harvest Ball, but I, Cornelia Rose must remain a wallflower!

In spite of spending the summer feeding the pigs slop, and doing Agnes' other chores, Nellie was once again denied Agnes's privileges. *Tarnation*, she thought, *I've earned the right to debut too. If I am old enough to do her chores, I am old enough to share her privileges.*

Twelve is not too young to enter society. I should not be penalized simply because Mrs. Warden is persnickety about birthdates. This exacting adherence to protocol is intolerable! Imagine, only inviting the young ladies of Sing Sing born before 1836 without regard to my qualifications. I am fully "finished" and presentable. I am just as gracious, and far more lady-like than Agnes. Moreover, I am far better versed in the steps to the minuet than Agnes — I practice more!

Mercy! I am 12 years and 10 months. In just 2 months, I will be 13. Mother is utterly unreasonable in complying with Mrs. Warden's rules.

As the ladies of the Entwhistle family bustled about making their final toilette for the fancy dress ball, Cornelia pestered her mother one last time.

"It remains unjust that I was not permitted to debut with Agnes," she complained.

"My dear child, why think you that life is fair? Is it fair that you are well-to-do, on the basis of your father's hard work, enviable intelligence, and my substantial dowry, whilst some of your former classmates are working girls in Brandreth's Pill Factory? *Natürlich nicht!* Of course not." Mrs. Entwhistle applied a bit of powder to Nellie's face, and scrutinized her hair and her dress, for anything in need of correction. "To task then, please turn around. *Mach schnell*, quickly now!" As Nellie turned a complete rotation, Mrs. Entwhistle tugged at the dress's bodice and pulled a thread from its embroidered trimming, finely appliquéd by Cornelia herself.

"Next!" she said to Anastasia, with a wave of her hand to dismiss Nellie.

Nell knew any further mention of the subject would be fruitless. Agnes took her turn pirouetting in twirls of colorful taffeta and creamy lace before Mrs. Entwhistle. Nellie consoled herself with admiring her own eye-catching magenta silk dress. Its tight bodice, embellished with beautiful embroidery, *if I may compliment myself*, fit her waist snuggly, and accentuated her newly curved figure. She picked up two handfuls of the soft material from the beautifully swirling full skirt, and poured them back down. *Liquid silk*, she thought, as it shimmered into place. *I am a blessed child to have such a grand gown!*

No, she corrected herself. *I am a blessed young lady.*

Nellie's excitement escalated when she heard the Entwhistles' best carriage pull around to the front of the house. The horses' whinny and pawing of the ground echoed her own impatience to leave. She hopped from the bottom step of their grand porch stairs directly to the mounting stone carved with their family name. A smiling Patrick bowed over her hand. He placed her into the carriage. *I am a grand lady!* She smiled. The rest of her family settled themselves around her, nestling into the plush velvet seats.

The horses made their way up the Main Street hill, and took a right on State Street. The Warden's house was in nearby Sparta. "Papa, why do we use the carriage when our journey is less than a mile?" shouted Jonas from his perch next to the carriage driver.

"For yer *Mutter*'s fancy ball, we travel only in t' finest style," Mr. Entwhistle replied with a wink of his eye.

Nellie closed her eyes, inhaling and savoring the excitement of the moment.

With all eyes on the lovely debutantes, more or less gracefully performing the minuet, Nellie had a moment to watch the young men attending them. Some looked younger than she was! *How unfair*, Nellie grumped. The dancers wove back and forth, performing the beautiful French dance in time to the rhythm, some of the young men attentive and graceful, some awkward and inept. Pride swelled in her eyes as she watched Patrick, resplendent in tails, and Jerome, wearing his Military Academy uniform, looking exceptionally handsome, dancing with agile steps. They gallantly twirled their partners and deftly guided them through the complicated turns.

Nellie put her fan over her mouth to hide her smile when a gangly youth stepped on Agnes's toe. Nellie watched her sister fight the urge to slap him. The youth was gawky from the top of his angular head, to the thrust of his jaw, to the elbows jutting awkwardly from his body. *Something about his total gracelessness is rather endearing though,* Nellie thought.

In the same quartet, moving beside the angular youth was his total opposite—a tall graceful young man, impeccably groomed and polished, whose slick mannerisms made him positively slither as he danced. She caught her breath in repulsion. *Ugh!* Nellie shuddered to herself as she watched him fawn over his partner and pull the poor girl much too close to himself. He exuded charm; but the sly, knowing manner with which he appraised each of his partners bordered on the unsavory, obliterating any appeal that charm might have had over Nellie.

Cornelia Rose jumped.

"Mademoiselle," a scheming, oily voice said behind her. Nellie turned and immediately flushed. The Romeo was suddenly at her elbow, bowing over her hand, the copious ruffles of his sleeve almost slapping her bosom as he moved in on her, confident of his right to judge her assets.

Nellie's father, standing smiling beside her, turned his head in her direction at the sound of the 'gentleman's' voice. But her father gave her no comfort, nor could he protect her against this socially acceptable attack.

"You unfortunate wallflower, I have watched you waiting in the wings, your lovely feet tapping to the music," the Romeo announced with a disturbing, confident ring to his voice. He stepped in even closer. She could smell his over-scented body, and see a fine mist of perspiration on his thin mustache as his full sensuous lips moved. "I will rescue you from spinsterhood by selecting you for this dance."

Further taken aback by his presumptive and familiar attitude...*did she not even rate the formal 'May I have this dance'?* Nellie blurted "No!" She turned on her heel and fled to the other side of the room.

In the panic of her flight, Nellie very nearly collided with a waiter balancing flutes filled with champagne. Nimbly, the waiter stabilized the tray and simultaneously stepped aside. Grateful to avoid a further gaffe, she tried to rush past, but he addressed her. "M' lady, a bit o' refreshment?" he asked kindly, removing one glass from his tray and touching her hand lightly with it.

Out of habit more than gratitude, Nellie stopped and took the glass. The waiter smiled reassuringly at her. *Something about him is familiar,* Nellie thought, grateful to have a distraction from her social gaffe.

"A bit o' the bubbly makes the world sparkle, me Pap was known to say." The young man winked at her. Nellie flushed, and wondered where she had seen this young man before. "A course when imbibed regular, as was his habit, the sparkle fades into a fuzzy blur...." Comforted by his humorous distraction, Nellie smiled her thanks into the beam of his twinkling eyes. *Those blue eyes! I believe they have twinkled at me before!*

But she had no further time to puzzle as she took a cautious sip, and tried to compose herself. A young gentleman in the uniform of Saint John's Military Academy on Eastern Avenue appeared before her. He, too, took a glass from the waiter, saying, "There's a good chap."

"Clayton!" the head steward summoned in a low voice, and the helpful server moved on.

Nellie took another tentative sip of champagne. The bubbles tickled her nose. *Mayhap Mutter is correct. I am not ready to debut. At least not in a society filled with slick Casanovas like the ladies' man that asked me to dance.*

"I beg pardon?" she asked demurely. The young gentlemen with the sword said something to her, and while she did not hear the words, the sound broke her reverie. *He has a fine handsome face,* she decided, rousing herself from her miserable social disgrace.

"I said: I see the harvest this year is most abundant," the young man repeated. He pointed to a group of matrons clustered by the buffet all wearing hats festooned with dried fruit. Clusters of grapes and piles of pears dangled and shook precariously as the women gossiped.

Nellie burst out laughing. *A sense of humor!* She liked him instantly.

The young man smiled and gripped his sword hilt. "Allow me to introduce myself," he said with a bow. "I am Obadiah Weber Wright, upperclassman at The Churchill School. I believe you town folk know it as 'Saint John's Military'? I hail from this fine state."

"Are you any relation to Senator Silas Wright?" Nellie asked, with another touching of her lips to the champagne glass. She did not drink, since she realized she did not find the slightly bitter beverage at all appealing.

"I see you are astute in the affairs of our government," said the young man with a grin. "In fact, he is my father."

Nellie smiled and tried to look knowing. *He thinks I am politically astute. Hardly! Thank the Lord I overheard Papa discussing the morass Mr. Wright, now our state's governor, created during his time in the Senate....* Nellie pulled at the perpetually loose strand of golden hair tickling her eyes. *I had better not say that!* Scrambling to think of something worldly and witty, Nellie managed to say, "It hardly takes much education to know of the illustrious political career of our venerable Governor of New York." *Mercy, mayhap Governor Wright is no longer the governor? Who won the last election?* In confusion again, Nellie took a gulp of champagne and then made a face, as she tasted it on its way down.

Obadiah grinned at her.

Nellie squirmed.

He cleared his throat. "May I compliment you on your obvious good sense! Your superior powers of discernment are evident in your ability to avoid that Casanova," he said and grinned again.

All of Nellie's mortification and chagrin came rushing back. "Goodness me, was my *faux pas* obvious to everyone?" she blurted in embarrassment.

"Only to me," Obadiah reassured her hastily. Nellie tried to raise one eyebrow, the way Agnes always did, in that taunting, teasing manner, but no luck! They both went up and instead of looking flirtatious, she looked surprised. Nervously she tucked back her unruly strand of hair. *Why should it have been obvious to him?*

He read her look accurately and answered her unspoken question. "I invariably notice when the sensibilities of the prettiest young lady in the room are affronted."

Another compliment! Delighted, Nellie's mind went blank. There was another pause as she searched for something to say.

Once again Obadiah's sense of humor rescued her from her embarrassment. "Every dry-goods store in town is surely devoid of an inch of fabric! Sing Sing's fair maidens are resplendently dressed to the nines. There are more flounces here than on a chorus line of Can-Can Girls," he observed.

Nellie gasped at the racy simile, while he nodded toward a group of girls clustered in the corner fanning themselves, talking to potential suitors. The skirts' circumferences ensured that the young men couldn't get closer than arm's length away from their conquests.

Mercy, I must devise a reply! "Parsimony in attire is not a foible of the evening," Nellie said, with a grave air about her, nervously tucking the strand of hair behind her ear again.

Unfazed by Nellie's serious reaction to his joking banter, Obadiah continued, "Tsk, tsk, the fire engine red blush of certain flounced young debutantes makes their cheeks visible across the room. They are in stark contrast to the lads materializing as rumpled and down-at-heel, as if they never darkened the doorway of a haberdashery."

Nellie giggled gratefully. They passed the next few moments engaged in lively conversation. Nellie, composure regained, enjoyed her opportunity to exercise her wit and conversational skills.

The debutantes regrouped and performed another dance. Obadiah stayed at Nellie's side, smiling, and making bright witticisms. Nellie laughed and smiled, her replies flowing easily. Her sense of good feeling flooded back with the flattering attention of the young cadet. Even the pauses in their conversation began to feel convivial. *This fine gentleman is splendid company,* she thought.

Nellie tapped her feet to the music. Every muscle in her body wanted to dance, but her companion for the evening was oblivious to her desire.

All too soon the candles burned low and the punch evaporated. Only two exotic orange slices were left, floating forlornly on some soggy spices. Their host signaled the orchestra for the last dance.

Obadiah turned to Nellie and took her hand. For a second she thought he would at last ask her to dance and her stomach did a nervous flip-flop in anticipation. He smiled, looked her in the eye, and bowed low over her hand.

Nellie felt her face flush and her heart stand still.

"I thank you for spending lo these few moments with me," he said, his eyes searching hers. Nellie dropped her eyes to prevent him from seeing the surge of disappointment that rushed over her.

He paused. She squirmed, searching for a reply.

Obadiah continued, "The usual tedium of these events was dissipated entirely by your charm and splendid conversation, peppered with your bon mots. It is not often that the comeliest lady at the ball is also the one possessed of the superior wit!" Obadiah's courtly and sweet words mollified her acute disappointment at his failure to ask her to dance. She again attempted a reply but there were no words on her tongue. He grinned and bowed again. Gripping the hilt of his sword, he walked back to a unit of his classmates.

Nellie, wordless for the third time in the night, smiled at his retreating figure.

"Nellie, do you have a beau?" Anastasia whispered excitedly in her ear, bringing her thoughts back into the room.

Do I? she wondered as she twisted her strand of recalcitrant hair and smiled at her pretty little sister.

CHAPTER 4
What a Day for a Daydream

Sing Sing, March 1848

"Sakes alive lazy bones, which knight in shining armor captured your heart today?" Agnes's grating voice burst through Nellie's reverie. Cornelia was at her favorite perch, leaning out their bedroom window, gazing over the Hudson River. She kept her eyes on the blue gray green water flowing north from New York City harbor with the incoming tide, while she searched for an answer.

"Ivanhoe... I was merely...." she stammered.

Anastasia appeared at her elbow, turned her toward the room and gave her a hug around her waist. "Do not favor Agnes's rude words with a reply," she said with a laugh. "Agnes is cross because *Mutter* finally made her do a chore!"

Agnes drew herself up to her full five-foot height, angry look on her face, and shouted, "I perform a plethora of chores and never am I favored with a word of gratitude or appreciation." She flounced out of the room.

Anastasia and Cornelia looked at each other and giggled. Anastasia picked up her skirts and flounced away from Nellie. "Sakes alive! Never am I favored with a word of gratitude!" she mimicked.

Nellie shook her head. "Agnes never completes even her fair share of chores. Moreover, what simpleton expects gratitude for merely performing the tasks necessary to keep us clean and fed?" she asked.

Anastasia moved to Nellie's side and they both gazed out the window. The water rolled swiftly north, bringing salt water from the Atlantic. *Shattemuc*, Nellie thought, recalling the Mohican Tribe's name for the Hudson meaning 'the river that flows both ways.' Sailboats, punctuating the gray green landscape with their brave white sails, struggled to make headway. The 9 a.m. steamboat blew its whistle as it left the dock, coming within inches of a clipper battling the wind and the tide. Nellie could watch all day, dreaming, projecting her emotions onto the weather conditions of the river, if she were allowed such leisure.

"For what pines thy heart *dearest* sister?" Anastasia asked, with an affectionate tweak of Nellie's curls.

"The Methodist Campwoods Meeting," said Nellie. "I *so* look forward to it. 'Tis my favorite part of the year."

Anastasia shook her head in disbelief. "You could not find the Campwoods Meeting superior to our favorite outing—ice skating on the Hudson. It proffers no convivial, toasty hot chocolate party after invigorating exercise."

"*Au contraire!* Last year's romantic outing permeates my dreams."

Anastasia looked skeptical. "But last year you said your favorite time of year was winter. Cornelia Rose, winter is now! Verily, the Hudson's ice has broken, the ice cutter dry docked for the year, but we still have a sleigh party this Sunday. I'll wear my new fur cap with the matching muff, and you can wear your beautiful black shawl with the scarlet flowers. I can see us now. Rosy cheeks, wind whipping our faces, hair flowing behind, all the young men unable to avert their eyes! Who would you like to sit next to, and cuddle, under the big blanket?"

Nellie blushed. They both giggled.

"In truth, you are correct," said Nellie. "Yea, truly we will have one more grand winter frolic, complete with bonfire, hot chocolate, and roasted chestnuts." She gazed at the white clouds scuttling across the sky racing, and then surpassing, the sailboats on the river. Her thoughts raced along with them. "Then I will skip right over the spring mud that follows on the heels of the snow's disappearance, and catapult into summer. Last year's meeting at Campwoods was as thrilling as the white-capped river on a stormy day! It upended my presuppositions of romance. Now the length and breadth of all my ruminations turn to the exhilaration of attending another assembly there."

Beginning in 1831, the Methodists gathered each August to revive their religious vigor in Locust Grove, just east of Sing Sing's village. The faithful encamped with a roster of preachers exhorting the flock to accept salvation. The meeting's fame spread quickly; people came from The City and all over the United States to spend a week in the aptly christened Campwoods. What started as an uplifting and reaffirming religious experience for a few grew to a gathering of thousands, attracting both the faithful and those merely curious. This meeting provided yet another reason for the rich and the elite to flock to Sing Sing to enjoy to the bucolic countryside. The Campwoods Meetings became a social phenomenon.

"It was thrice more scintillating than a three-ring circus." Nellie said, wistful visions of scenes from last year playing before her half-closed eyes.

Not that her Roman Catholic parents approved of her heretical visit to the infidel's camp. Of course, Nellie's family never attended the camp.

"How clever of you to persuade *Mutter* to allow you to go," said Anastasia and frowned. "I am not permitted."

"I merely observed that both our older brothers have been allowed many unfettered visits to the camp, without any scrutiny regarding their plans. It is patently unfair to deny me permission to stay overnight," Cornelia said.

"That observation would hardly have convinced Papa, let alone *Mutter*! I do believe her favorite saying is 'Thinkest Thou Life is Fair?' Moreover, I can hear Papa now, saying, 'Yer brothers are boys, different rules apply'."

Nellie laughed at her sister's imitation, mimicking her father's brogue exactly. Anastasia chewed her bottom lip and twisted her face into a scowl. Nellie knew her sister would not let the subject rest until she deduced Nellie's method of persuasion.

"'Tis true, it took far more calculated cajoling than that simple statement. But I have been pestering them for an overnight stay since last summer — when my visit transpired exactly as I had promised. I established my credibility. Lacking evidence of any tragic incident, or more importantly lacking my conversion to the Methodist faith, I have finally wrested agreement for my overnight stay at the camp... as long as it is properly supervised by trusted aristocratic friends of the family."

"Harrumph," said Anastasia, "You should immediately request the permission be extended to allow me to accompany you!"

Nellie smiled but did not rise to the bait.

"Harrumph!" Anastasia said again, and put her hands on her hips. A petulant tone crept into her voice. "My favorite time of year is still winter. I far prefer watching the ice cutter cut a path through the Hudson to watching a camp of singing heretics."

Nellie laughed. "I still do too," she said loyally and gave Anastasia a hug.

But when she pictured the dashing young Louisianan gentleman, Hannibal Rufus Calhoun, whom she met at the Eve'n song, she shivered with anticipation. Over the course of the year, he had sent two letters, further sparking her eagerness for this year's meeting. Rereading Hannibal's courting words quite literally made her heart throb.

Nellie leaned a little further out her window, watching the motion of the Hudson. She observed a sudden flurry of March snow make the tidal water choppy, and looked through the snowflakes at her memories of last year's camp. She imagined she could feel the August heat that drove thousands from the hot City. She pictured the tents and cottages, filled to capacity with pilgrims, enjoying the blissful cool of the Sing-Sing woods and listening to hourly scripture readings. A continuous stream of charismatic preachers would delight the faithful with their sermons and anecdotes once again when this summer's 'dog days' rolled around.

Nellie sighed, remembering. The Entwhistle family lived an easy forty-five-minute walk from camp, but she rode in style in the Van Cortlandts' lavish carriage to the daylong prayer meeting.

The event was a spectacle: impassioned preachers shouting of Fire and Brimstone, promising grim punishment in Hell for the wicked, which moved the faithful to shout *Amen* and sing *Alleluia*. Interspersed with the preaching and spirit-moved testimony, the congregation joined in heartfelt singing, and loud praising of the Lord.

It was mesmerizing.

Still, she felt that she missed half the fun by going home right after Even'song. She blushed as she confessed to herself the real reason she had not wanted the day to end. The Louisianan. *Were all Southern Gentlemen that dashing, that handsome?* She had spied him out of the corner of her eye at the morning welcome session. After exchanging many looks throughout the day, the young gentleman finally approached her for a conversation before Even'song. So smitten by his attention, she barely knew what she said to him. Nellie shook her head, remembering her disappointment at the brevity of the encounter. The important outcome: he had obtained her address, and her permission to correspond.

Her taste of the camp's carnival atmosphere last year had only whetted Nellie's appetite for more. She envied the devout Church members who spent weeks there.

If truth be told, Anastasia is right. Mutter only granted permission after I produced the trustworthy Mrs. Van Cortlandt, who vowed to chaperone and keep me safe. Her credentials are impeccable: a most esteemed member of the venerable Methodist family who donated their land for the camp. Even Mutter could not argue when Augusta Van Cortland's mother promised her supervision. After all, the Campwoods grounds are located at the edge of the Van Cortlandt estate — it's almost as if I were staying at their house....

This year, I shall stay in one of those darling tents, erected each year for the traveling faithful, Nell dreamed, staring harder through the snow turned to raindrops, trying to remember the stark white canvas of the tents, gleaming in the summer sun, flaps tied invitingly open.

Intuition informed Nellie that Hannibal Rufus would be there this year, even before his letter on Monday confirmed his arrival in August.

The first signs of spring were evident in the warm weather and mud the following Sunday.

The entire Entwhistle family hustled to the warehouse currently housing Saint Augustine's Catholic Parish. They marched, in bunches, down Water Street to Sunday Mass. Mrs. Entwhistle, leading the group, paused to chat with an acquaintance as she waited for the stragglers to catch up. Nellie, already at her mother's elbow, heard the woman say their town anticipated an influx of 60,000 people at this summer's encampment. She could not even imagine that many people in one place at one time. *Of course,* she reasoned, *they would not be gathered exactly at the same time — they would come throughout the course of the summer.*

Their walk to worship ended in Doctor Benjamin Brandreth's storehouse, near the dock of the Brandreth Pill and Porous Plaster Factory. Ever since he was President of Sing Sing, Doctor Brandreth allowed their parish to celebrate Mass in his gas-lit warehouse each Sunday, rent free, while the parishioners raised the funds to build their own Church. *Certainly, it was not as fine as attending Mass at the home of John and Bridget O'Brien, but it was a far sight better than having to take a long carriage ride to Verplank to attend Saint Patrick's,* Nellie thought.

After Mass, a woman in an elegant hat chatted with Gertrude Entwhistle, expressing her joy at the expected number of revival attendees. Nellie watched the ships cutting back and forth in the water, and mooring at the dock as she unashamedly eavesdropped.

"The Campwoods is quite the topic of conversation today! What care you of the infidel strangers inhabiting our wood?" demanded Mrs. Entwhistle.

"Not a whit," assured the woman. "My interest is purely economic. The fashionable ladies last year made quite the fuss at my husband's millinery shop. The annual pilgrimage to Campwoods engenders a bountiful boost in sales."

It has engendered a 'bountiful boost' for me as well. Nellie giggled at the thought.

That afternoon, curled in a cozy spot on her bed, Nellie finished reading *Ivanhoe.* She stretched, yawned, and resumed her reverie from her garret window. She cast rhapsodic eyes on the gray swells of the river, rising, and now more gently curling, and breaking on the sandy riverbank in front of her.

Today the misty spring weather softened the majesty of the Hudson. As she watched, the clouds ceased their race across the sky and gathered into one mighty cumulus, obliterating the sun. In a dramatic move, the huge cloud burst, rain immediately pummeling the entire scene. The shower vacillated from rain to snow, and back again. Nellie's mood fluctuated along with the change of precipitation, alternating from cool anticipation to warm desire and yearning. The black of the naked trees on the shoreline blended into the grey green river, but then revivified in the burnished black of the mountains that hugged its far side. The dreamlike colors corroborated Nellie's suspicion that the river was holding secrets, just like the characters in Sir Walter Scott's novel and those in the depths of her own heart.

'Tis the perfect weather for reading, Nellie concluded, transferring her romantic thoughts back to the Middle Ages. *But Ivanhoe should have married Rebecca! Her acumen and attributes were far superior to Rowena's.*

Howsoever, in spite of the less-than-satisfying ending, Sir Walter Scott must also author the next book I read. He is an adroit weaver of tales. What a complex romance!

With a burst of energy, she ran down the back stairs, almost two at a time.

"Where is your sense of decorum?" Mrs. Entwhistle admonished Nellie's specter streaking through the kitchen.

Nellie closed the door of the library behind her and inhaled. *Yummm, the smell of leather bookbindings is almost as intoxicating, and maybe even as enticing, as the smell of the sea!*

Nellie looked around the Entwhistle library, filled with their precious books. *Although every square inch of these walls are lined with books, from floor to ceiling, I fear I have read most of our offerings. I wonder how many unread books remain?*

In a trance of concentration, Nellie climbed the ladder of the track that encircled the bookcases, trying to remember where the rest of Sir Walter Scott's novels lived. In the process, her hand lingered over *The Spy* from James Fennimore Cooper, a fiction about the Revolutionary War. Rumor had it, the novel was based on the father of Sing Sing's Union Hotel's innkeeper, Enoch Cosby Jr.

I did so enjoy this intrigue too. Perhaps it is more compelling to read a story of contemporary romance, set right here in New York, in our current epoch.

Idly, she put her foot on a shelf and gave herself a little push along the track to allow the wheels to ferry her to the next section of the bookcase.

Suddenly she hurtled forward.

A scream escaped from her startled lips.

The ladder shot down the length of the wall and swung wildly around the corner. Nellie would have fallen off, but for her excellent reflexes. She stuck her foot out to catch a shelf and the ladder screeched to a halt.

Panting, Nellie caught her breath as a laugh peeled from the gloomy recesses of the room.

"Matthias, you little urchin! That was most unfair and most unwelcome," Nellie said, in a loud authoritative, no nonsense voice.

"Aw, shucks Nell!" the crushed little voice said. "Ya didn't like it? Warn't it a grand wild ride?"

Surprised that her brother was not out to cause mischief, but rather to play, Nellie said, "Mercy! I did not even consider whether it was fun.It was too unexpected, too terrifying."

"I could push you again when you are ready," offered Matthias.

That vexing little devil! Could he truly only want to engage me?

Nellie smiled. "Perhaps I should let you have a ride first?" she asked.

"Huzzah!" shouted Matthias. "How did you know?"

"You dickens!" exclaimed Nellie. "Did you push me merely to ensure I would push you in return?"

"Well, it did occur to me that I could never garner enough steam to really whip the turns and then come back to center all on one of my own pushes," said Matthias. "Simple mechanics. Some of the force necessary is lost because I can only push with one foot whilst I balance on the ladder with the other."

Nellie watched him attach himself to the ladder, arms around a rung, hands clasped.

"Ready, steady, go!" she shouted and pushed with all her might.

She launched her brother down the short end of the wall, past the fireplace, around the first curve, down the entire length of the next wall, around the next curve, and across the back wall. When the ladder reached the end of the track at the back wall, instead of grinding to a halt, it rebounded and rushed back from whence it came, all the way around the first curve, stopping in the middle of the long wall.

"Eureka!" shouted Matthias. "I knew it only needed more force."

"That should suffice your curiosity. Now let's stop this foolishness."

"But you did not have a proper turn."

Nellie hesitated. She really did want to see if she could ride the ladder all the way around and back on one push. She walked over to the ladder and put her foot up. But Matthias still clung on.

"An even better experiment would be for you to ride with me, to see if we go as far if we both push!" he exclaimed.

After a few tries they figured, if they both pushed off, and then jumped on, Matthias on the inside next to the book lined wall (he was still small enough to squeeze through the corner) and Nellie on the outside, they were able to ride there and back *twice.*

This is truly exhilarating! Nellie thought, much like sledding down the steep Broad Avenue hill. They tried it one more time.

It was one time too many. Matthias jumped on a bit late and as a result forgot to tuck his tail sufficiently to clear the corner. *Crash!* His rear end cleared a whole shelf of its contents.

"*Gott im Himmel, was ist los mit du*? Ach, what is the matter with you?" growled Mrs. Entwhistle from the back doorway.

The children hung there and looked at the books, and then at the wall, anywhere, to avoid meeting their mother's eyes.

"You will shake the walls from their joists. Pick up those books. What monkey business is this?"

Nellie and Matthias still clung to the ladder, stacked on either side, as if smelted to the rungs.

Mr. Entwhistle came running into the library. When he saw Matthias and Cornelia, he burst out laughing. "For the love o' Saint Paddy! I've nary seen a ride like that. Ye know, I've always wanted to give that fancy ladder a go. *Mutter*, what do ye think?"

"James, you are incorrigible. What kind of an example is that?" Gertrude demanded, hands on her hips.

"A good, scientific one, for our future engineers," said her husband, eyes twinkling.

"Papa, how did you know? I was trying to discover the correct amount of force required to clear the *two* turns and also return to the straightaway without derailing from the track." Matthias jumped down and ran over to his father, while Nellie unhitched herself and began picking up the books.

"Let's see how much force it takes for me!" said Mr. Entwhistle, stepping up the lowest rung of the ladder. He caught the look his wife threw him. "Now, now, colleen o' me heart, 'tis no harm done with a wee bit o' fun and experimentation." He gripped the ladder but then stepped down toward Mrs. Entwhistle.

"Yer right, *Mutter*. What was I thinking?" He ran his hand over his hair in his familiar habitual gesture of contemplation.

Nellie and Matthias hung their heads. "The jig is up." Nellie whispered to Matthias.

Mrs. Entwhistle looked relieved.

But her husband continued, "Where's me manners? 'Tis ladies first!"

Her mother's face was a battle of emotions. Nellie was not sure whether anger, decorum, or fun would win.

"Come on, Trudy, have a go," encouraged Mr. Entwhistle.

"*Ach, es machts nichts!* It doesn't matter," she said, smiling at last. "The thought *has* always intrigued me, ever since I was a little girl."

Nellie and Matthias looked at each other in disbelief.

Matthias whispered to Nellie, "Horsefeathers! Now I want to try Grandmama's ladder too! Their library is twice as big as ours. Their ladder runs around the whole room, not just three sides like ours.

Nellie whispered back, "If I had my druthers, I would ride their ladder *and* read all their books!"

The children watched their father hand their mother on to the lowest rung of the ladder and steer her with gentle pushes around the circuit of the track. Mrs. Entwhistle laughed genteelly the whole way around.

Agnes came bursting through the door and stopped still, hands on her hips, her mouth twisted in an unbecoming pucker of disapproval. "Well I never!"

Suddenly she burst out laughing. "Sakes alive!" said Agnes. "I shall inform *both* my older brothers. Now I needn't feel guilty for keeping lookout while they surreptitiously rode the ladder." Their mother gave a startled, disapproving sound but their father pushed her hard. Mrs. Entwhistle giggled as she sped back to the center of the room.

"Jumping Jehoshaphat!" Jonas burst in the room. "We are permitted to ride the ladder? Why was I not invited?"

CHAPTER 5
Anticipation

Sing Sing, August 1848

Nellie found it impossible to stay still. She squirmed her way through Latin and piano lessons, checking her watch every couple of minutes, not even bothering to replace it in the breast pocket of her middy shirt. That most prized of all her possessions, her Swiss pocket watch, a special gift from her father, dangled on its gold chain down her bodice. As she raced through her chores, the gold watch bobbed and swung with every move.

"I declare, you will wear that thing out!" said Anastasia, shaking the feather duster at her sister. "Fear not, suppertime approaches, and the carriage will arrive shortly."

But it would not be soon enough for Cornelia. After the midday supper, she would journey the short distance to The Campwoods Meeting Grounds for her overnight stay at the Methodist Revival.

In a few short hours, she would be listening to that most eloquent of preachers—Reverend Stowe. Impatiently, she wrestled with her embroidery. She squirmed in her seat to see the Grandfather clock in the hallway, twisting her linen out of its frame in the process, her pocket watch swinging wildly. The needles slid off the material and the threads snarled in a vicious tangle, ensnaring her watch.

"Tarnation!" she muttered, angered not by the hopeless tangle of her crewelwork, trapping her watch, and thus her, but because in the gloom of the hallway she could not make out the second hand of the clock.

Bong! Bong! The half hour struck on the hall clock, followed by chimes from some of the surrounding churches. Nellie sighed, wrenched the watch free, and leaned back in her chair in the sunlit sewing room. She lifted her chin, closed her eyes, and stretched her neck back, trying to relieve her tension of excitement. She opened her eyes, her nose still pointed to the ceiling. The dappled light, reflected off the crystal chandelier of the side-room on the second floor, dazzled her eyes and arrested her fanciful mental wanderings.

She loved this room. The windows on its three sides kept the room awash in sunlight for most of the day. *'Tis a virtual peninsula perched on top of the carriage porch*, Nellie thought. One view faced down the hill to the river, the second across the street past the neighbor's barn to the town, and the third, up the hill in the Campwoods direction. Normally, Nellie looked around the room counting her blessings. It was such a cozy spot to enjoy the company of her mother and sisters. Ordinarily this time was a highlight of a delightfully long summer day. With all its many windows open, its vantage point on the side of the hill, and elevation a story above the street, the room caught all the summer breezes. The tick tock of the grandfather clock was usually calmly reassuring to Nellie. Today, however, its monotone connoted stagnation to Nellie, as if its sound documented time standing still.

Light danced and reflected off the wall sconces and the unlit chandelier with the same electric energy Nellie felt dancing inside her. She tapped her foot and then twisted to look at the clock. She still could not see it.

Tonight! I encamp tonight! I wonder if I will be able to meet him *again.*

She looked at the tangled mess in front of her and threw down her work.

"I must verify I have included clean handkerchiefs in my valise," she said, rising from her seat so fast the chair wobbled and threatened to topple over.

"Cornelia Rose, you are as jittery as a Mexican jumping bean. Now sit up straight and settle back to your handiwork," said Mother.

Nellie obediently sat down again, but only because she had seen the clock in the hallway. *The time* remains *half past noon! Proof positive that time indeed stands still.*

Nellie sighed. Her mother's gaze softened. "I understand how arduous it seems to await the advent of an exciting expedition," her mother began. Nellie sighed again. *Will Mutter make the wait even more interminable by dispensing another lecture?* she thought, her rebellious streak rearing its ugly head.

Her mother's next words surprised and chastened her.

"I recall well my own impatient anticipation of many momentous occasions in my life." Her mother smiled, almost dreamily. Amazement made Nellie stop fidgeting in her chair. "Furthermore, I concede it is thrice as difficult for you, since you lack even a modicum of patience." Nellie hung her head. Mrs. Entwhistle laughed. "I speak not to chastise you, but only to acknowledge the fact that patience has never been your forte." Nellie's jaw dropped and now even her sisters looked surprised. Nellie opened her mouth further to object, but her mother held up her hand. "We all have our gifts, and simply put, patience is not one of yours. But to the point: I was fortunate enough to have many wonderful opportunities in my life, opportunities for fun and glamour for which I awaited in eager anticipation." The sisters looked at each other uncertainly.

"I am merely suggesting that we try to maintain an equilibrium. We must smile through adversity and not unduly elevate the wonder and importance of a single outing in our lives, lest we be cruelly disappointed.

"I will allow it is exciting to attend social events such as these. I would simply counsel that building your hopes and dreams upon the import of one outing might lead to disappointment."

Nellie kicked at the floor below her chair. "Even if I so desired, how could I possibly not dream of this event?"

"Perhaps you can find some diversion and joy in your crewel work," her mother said with a wide but understanding smile.

"Ugh," mumbled Nellie. *Was the entirety of this sympathetic speech merely a tactic to employ me more gainfully?* "This trivial, trying task is merely a waste of time," she declared.

"Cornelia Rose," her mother said. Nellie heard the old familiar voice of steel that had been strangely absent from her mother's prior speech. "This task is your employment. Thanks to your father's hard work and industry we most assuredly could purchase the finest stockings money can buy. But knitting and sewing are labors of love. You young ladies must learn these skills and must always endeavor to keep yourselves employed in the running of your households. Your father understands that 'time is money' and runs his business accordingly. If I may quote Mrs. Child's counsel in her seminal work on frugality and husbandry, '...every member of the household should be employed, either in earning or saving money.' We ladies leave the earning to the men, and we endeavor to perfect the art of saving money."

"I repeat, of what use is crewel work?" Nellie asked, daring to be impertinent.

Mrs. Entwhistle said with a sigh, "It is an indispensable skill. The ability to make beautiful things is one of life's joys! Consider your finely stitched handkerchiefs." Nellie rose and Mrs. Entwhistle waved her back to her chair. "We have shown great economy in rending those very necessary items from larger sheets and linens that have worn in places. Now, with a little creative handiwork, we have made the old into something beautiful and new. An excellent example is your new handkerchief...."

Nellie jumped up again. "I must make certain I have packed my handkerchiefs!"

"Cornelia, have you not been listening?" Mrs. Entwhistle said.

But Nellie had already disappeared down the hall. She flew to her room and pulled everything from her valise. There on the bottom were two lace hankies. Nellie glanced at one, flawlessly embroidered by her mother. *Beautiful! Lace in all my favorite colors,* she thought. Nellie picked up the other, examining the mistakes in the hand crocheted border. She smiled, remembering six-year-old Anastasia laboring at the task. Nellie had taken pity on her little sister's struggles. Together, she and her sister had added colorful flowers, but Anastasia still tussled with crocheting the lace border. One evening Nellie gave up 'play time' to finish it for her sister, adding a whole row of lace. Her reward – Anastasia gave it to her for Christmas later that year. It was Nellie's favorite handkerchief—a talisman of good feeling and fortune. She would take no journey without it.

She snapped the valise shut and sat on it. She looked at her pocket watch.

Now what shall distract me?

At last the carriage arrived.

Augusta Van Cortlandt bounded out of the carriage the second Nellie's butler touched its door. Her friend sprang into Nellie's arms, excitement frothing and spewing into a giant hug. Huge puffy sleeves enveloped Cornelia; unruly crinoline petticoats bunched and wrapped heavily around two pairs of ankles. Jumbled together, the butler handed both young ladies into the carriage as one package, and they were off.

The chatter flew between the two girls as fast as the carriage wheels turned. Augusta's brothers wiggled and squirmed and Mr. and Mrs. Van Cortlandt looked at both camps in benevolent amusement.

"Twenty conversions just yesterday!" exclaimed Augusta.

"Surely that is merely exaggerated scuttlebutt," Nellie replied.

"No, with mine own eyes I have read it in today's *New York Daily Tribune*. But staggering numbers of conversions are hardly newsworthy, these days. They are a daily occurrence. Far more dramatic—fifteen hundred encamped this week. A veritable city has sprung up in our midst in scarcely a fortnight. I thrill to think of the multitudes of attendees!"

The girls giggled in anticipation. The thrill for Nellie was not in viewing the multitudes, but rather something a little harder to articulate. She rummaged in her brain to pinpoint the object of her anticipation. *Was it anticipation of excitement? Not precisely.* Based on her experience of one night at the revival last year, it seemed more an anticipation of participation, even if vicariously, in the emotional highs of the revival. The wonder she felt when she watched people, filled with the Spirit, gyrate, and testify to the Lord overwhelmed her with an emotion like no other.

Her friend had yet another thrill in mind. "I delight to think of the fashionable high society coming in from The City to observe the event, rather at arms-length, evaluating the other participants. We will be mingling with the high muck-a-mucks!"

Nellie did have to concede she rather liked this aspect as well.

"Thus, your luxurious sleeves contrived with yards of fabric," Nellie said, touching the soft folds of Augusta's ruffles.

Augusta giggled. "Yes, my first attempt to dress to the nines. Yet, I am not quite sure I have achieved a desirable fashion effect."

"Indubitably you have!" Nellie cried, hugging her friend. "None of the high society ladies will have a superior claim for better dressed sleeves. Moreover, the blue of the cambric matches the hue of your eyes and highlights the blush of your high cheek bones."

On that wonderful note, Augusta's blush deepened with appreciation and they rolled into the Campwoods' entrance.

In stark contrast to the slow crawl of time throughout the endless day, the carriage ride felt like the blink of an eye. The coachman handed the group out of the carriage. Nellie stood for a moment taking in the scene before their entourage joined the throng of evening arrivals, streaming through the gates down the wide path.

Nellie giggled when she caught herself staring, mouth agape, at the spectacle before her. There was so much to see; merchants hawked all manner of commodities. *Yummmm!* The aroma from roasted chestnuts and hot sweet potatoes immediately set her mouth to watering. General stores had bloomed overnight, their porches spilling enticing goods onto the pathway. Bulging stacks of camping supplies, barrels of pickles, and bolts of fabrics stood on display, begging to be eaten or fingered. Peddlers brandished carts stuffed with bric-a-brac, fans, blankets, pans, and firewood. Nellie had never seen so many goods or so much food assembled in the same place. *Everything from soup to nuts!* she thought. *This is not just a religious meeting – it is a festival.*

The crowd swelled around her as she and Augusta paused, magnetically drawn to the opulent array of wares. A hand on her elbow brought her abruptly to her senses. It was Augusta's mother.

"You girls swarm like bees to honey!" Mrs. Van Cortlandt exclaimed. Then she laughed. 'I cannot fault you for your youth, nor your enthusiasm. No matter! Enjoy the event at your own leisure." Nellie was pleasantly shocked at this unexpected freedom. Both girls thanked Mrs. Van Cortlandt profusely.

She held up her hand. "Keep your heads and your wits about you in this boodle. And, remember at all times your ladylike demeanor. Of course, verily, it is unnecessary for me to utter those words. My one direction is that our tent is near the main dining hall—and may be difficult to spot in the dark. Therefore, I encourage you to locate it, and ascertain your bearings before you lose yourselves in the drama of the events." She gave the girls each a hug, and hurried off after her husband.

Nellie and Augusta could not believe their good fortune. *Unrestricted? Unencumbered? Permitted to wander on our own? We have been given both independence and autonomy? What a novelty – freedom!* Nellie thought.

They succumbed to the attraction of the brightly displayed wares and wandered into the closest store.

CHAPTER 6
Out of the Frying Pan

Campwoods, August 1848

The events of the evening unfolded with a compelling energy that Cornelia Rose Entwhistle did not resist. She flowed from one store to the next, pausing in between at the many peddler's carts. Even'song would begin promptly at eight o'clock, after all sittings of dinner ended. Already at six, bursts of song erupted from the crowd and funneled its way down the long path, through the trees that surrounded the open platform and benches of the main preaching area.

The girls wandered from shop to cart, pooling their meager funds to sample some of the delectable culinary offerings. They bypassed the items they ate daily in the summer—fresh corn on the cob and ripe red tomatoes. They sniffed in derision at the city folks gobbling the plebian farm fare. They honed in on the rarities in their own diet, and finally settled for—honey glazed nuts roasted over an open fire, and a shared glass of fresh squeezed lemonade, a treat reserved for special occasions only, like a grand Independence Day celebration.

The crowd waxed and waned around them as they imbibed not only their delicacies, but the sights and smells as well.

With a jolt of one awakening from sleep, Nellie pulled out her pocket watch and fumbled for the time. "Hurry, Augusta! We have not even journeyed to the main preaching area, much less located our camping site, and it is only five minutes till Even'song."

She placed one hand on her skirts to elevate them to running height, and the other on Augusta's arm. Together, they dashed towards the main area, startling groups of fellow spiritual travelers, leaving some laughing at their unbridled enthusiasm as they passed.

"Plenty o' Spirit to go 'round, young ladies, no need to run," called someone from behind them.

"Save a bit o' grace for me," shouted a bawdy looking woman shambling along.

Nellie looked at Augusta and they slowed to a more decorous trot. "I guess my furious canter is not exactly ladylike behavior," Nellie said ruefully, and they both burst out laughing.

They could hear the first strains of music from the organ long before the path gave way before them and opened up to the main preaching area. They arrived, breathless, just as the choir burst into the first song of the program.

Not an empty square inch of bench visible!

Nellie and Augusta walked away from the platform, along the perimeter, peering through the crowd looking for a space large enough to accommodate two young ladies and their voluminous petticoats.

Finally, in the middle of a bench between two families with many squirming children, they located a space in the farthest recesses of the large natural amphitheater. Stepping over bags, children, and toes, they inched their way along the row, and settled in just as the final chords of the song drifted into the night air.

Dusk was falling softly all around them.

The first preacher made his way up the stairs and the crowd hushed in anticipation of his words.

Firefly time is the most magic part of the day! Here I am in the middle of a magical dream. While the rest of the assembly kept their eyes on the preacher, Nellie's drifted toward the meadow in the shadow of the woods beside her to watch the tiny bugs flash their secret messages. *I wonder if he is at Even'song? Mercy, that fine young gentleman from Louisiana, with that dreamy drawl....* She tried to scan the crowd, but save a few seats to her left, across the center aisle, and a few seats to her right, the blinders of her bonnet prevented her from seeing anything but the back of men's heads, and the elaborate bonnets and hats of the women in front of her.

Augusta caught her wriggling. Behind her fan she whispered, "Is he here?"

"Alas, I see naught but families with well-scrubbed ears," Nellie said.

"Merely because it is the first day of the camp—wait until later in the week, there will be nary a well-scrubbed anything! I have packed some fine Parisian perfume to wear on my wrist. It will form a barrier preventing the barnyard smells, emanating from the gentlemen, from reaching my nose." They giggled.

Of course, Augusta, her only confidante besides Anastasia, would remember, and know full well what really fueled Nellie's anticipation. *Hannibal Rufus Calhoun.* Nellie sighed every time she thought about the romantic young gentleman she encountered last year. *His last missive advised he intended to find me at Camp this week. How fortuitous for a rendezvous,* she thought again – *Rufus, traveling from Louisiana, is attending The Methodist Revival Camp the very week I am permitted to stay overnight with my dearest friend's family.*

She could not prevent her eyes from searching the back of the heads of the crowd again.

The preaching reached a crescendo. One audience member after another rose, shouting and gyrating. Some rushed the platform, some stood up in their place. The crowd gasped and cheered as people shouted in tongues, some temporarily drowning out Preacher Stowe. Undeterred, he simply paused, facilitating the rising frenzy. To further orchestrate the response, he rushed down from the platform among the crowd, embracing those moved to testify, shouting *Alleluia* with them. A man stood, proclaimed God's glory, and ran half way down the aisle toward the preacher. Everyone in Nellie's section stood to watch the drama. The man writhed and yelled and the preacher pronounced:

"Wrestle with that Devil! *Amen* to your struggle." Laying his hands on the now prone man wriggling in the aisle, he cried, "Away evil. Satan be Gone! Release this man. Holy Spirit, *Save Him*! Turn us all from the many paths of evil. Keep our eyes trained on you Lord."

Everyone in the crowd joined the preacher in a loud series of *Amens*. The choir broke into song. Nellie too raised her voice and sang *Marching to Jerusalem* as the choir egressed from the stage. The arena emptied, row after row, as people, and their baggage, poured down the center aisle singing every verse of the hymn. Next came a round of *Alleluias* from Handle's Messiah.

Suddenly Nellie felt a tremendous energy surge through her. It was electrifying! *It must be the Holy Spirit!* she thought. A vibration, almost a shock, starting in her feet, tingled all the way up her legs.

"Alleluia!" She shouted raising her hands and trembling. Augusta looked at her in surprise. Consumed by the thrill of the electric tingle coursing through her body, Nellie did not even notice her companion's reaction. The energy moved her across the emptying row of seats and out into the aisle, right under the waving arms of Preacher Stowe.

"Do you *feel* the Almighty?" he shouted at her. "Do you feel His healing power? You, Sinner, you have been saved."

The shock of being the center of the preacher's attention, and thus the focus of the charged crowd permeated her energized state and froze Nellie in her place. The Reverend Stowe took this as a cue for more preaching.

"Look on this woman! Young though she be, she *knows* her sin, she *knows* her depravity. *She...knows*...she must escape the clutches of the DEVIL and mend her evil ways. *It is the only conduit*, the only true path to circumvent the Fire and Brimstone that surely would be her destiny if she continues her wicked ways!"

Mortified, her embarrassment freed her feet. Nellie turned and ran down the aisle away from the preacher, around the marchers, into a sea of gaping mouths, knocking a small child over and jostling many an elbow.

"YES, run from the Devil, do not permit him to wrassle with your soul. YES! Run to the Lord, embrace your new path. *Go forth, young woman, your faith has saved you!*" Reverend Stowe shouted at her retreating back, and the crowd swelled with *Amens* and *Alleluias*.

Nellie now knew what it felt like to wish the ground would open and consume her, right then and there, even if it be into the fires of hell.

CHAPTER 7
Into the Fire

Campwoods, August 1848

Her rush out of the limelight brought her to the fringe of the woods that gave the site of the revival its name. The pines seemed to move aside to accept her, as she charged further and deeper into their embrace. At last, free from the demon preaching that chased her, she collapsed in a tumble at the foot of a tree, the pine-strewn ground cushioning her fall.

She covered her face in misery. *What a spectacle I have made of myself! Gyrating on display for the multitudes to view! Mercy, the prime example of a sinner! Oh, the images they must conjure of my sordid and horrible life.* True, her conscience told her she *was* forward. *Did I not intentionally flirt with the Louisianan boy at last year's revival, and even allow him to touch my hand?* She felt the full weight of the horror of her transgressions fall upon her again, adding to the ignominy of her public display.

Cracking twigs brought her hands from her face and she looked up from her wretchedness.

Hannibal Rufus Calhoun! She was sure it was his face she had glimpsed through the trees.

She spun her head around to the right as the pine branches of the tree at her elbow moved. Hannibal stepped out of the darkening woods and appeared before her!

Her surprise was not so complete as to prevent her from registering how much he had matured since last summer. *His plantation must be thriving,* was the bizarre thought that flitted through her mind as she scrambled to her feet.

"Bless my soul, I have located the sinner! Repenting further I presume?" the Louisianan drawled with a laugh in his voice.

"I am mortified, simply crimson with embarrassment!" she cried, looking down at her feet.

"But for the fact that you were the *center* of attention, I would not have been allowed the pleasure of feasting my eyes upon you this year!" he exclaimed.

Nellie looked up into his handsome face quizzically.

"Yea, my dear girl, your embarrassment has a silver lining. My delegation has already made its final preparations for departure. The judgment was made to change our week of camping to the *prior* week. Therefore, we embark on our return journey for Louisiana early tomorrow." He paused at the hurt expression on her face. "There was no time to post a letter to advise you — the decision was taken less than a day before we departed."

Nellie stood, mouth agape, clothes in disarray, her wits scattered. Hannibal raised one eyebrow.

"Resuming my narrative then, members of our assemblage requested a departure of this morning to expedite our return to our lands, a few matters urgently needing their attention. However, I petitioned to remain this one final evening and leave post haste before dawn, logic-ing the lion's share of daylight would speed our progress." He twirled his recently acquired handlebar mustache. "Secretly, of course, it surely was merely a ruse to have one more night to find you. I was certain you would be here. I spared no effort perusing the crowd at dinner. Alas, but to no avail. I strolled the entire length of the tent area — no sight of y'all. I neared despair in finding you among the huge crowd for Even'song and preaching. I scanned the rows as the crowds emptied the benches, my en-tire hope ebbing away. Determining I could tarry no longer, as my assistance at the preparation of the wagons for our morning's journey was required, I turned away. Lo and behold! It was at that *exact* moment, the Reverend Stowe stopped his egress from the amphitheater to expel one more demon — you!" He grinned at her with one raised eyebrow and a triumphal smile.

Nellie still looked uncertain. *What a disconcerting smile! Almost a trifle demonic,* she thought.

Sensing her hesitation, he took her gloved hand, bowed low and raised it to his lips.

A tingle of delight, *rather like being filled with the Spirit,* she thought, tickled up her arm, and bloomed in a blush on her cheeks.

"A most fortuitous spiritual cleansing indeed!" Hannibal Rufus' manly, drawling voice, deepened in the year that had separated them, boomed off the pines. Nellie thrilled at the virile sound.

She raised her eyes and smiled. In an instant, Hannibal gathered her in his arms and kissed her soundly!

Nellie drew back in complete confusion.

"I have waited an *en*-tire year to take such an action. Y'all peeked in and out of my dreams with those luscious lips. I have longed to taste them, and now have not left the north disappointed." Before Nellie could gather her wits, he dove in for another kiss. It was overwhelming, and wet and a bit...heavenly...! She frowned as his tongue began to lick her lips...in a wicked way.

She drew back and wiped her mouth with the back of her glove.

He pulled her back in again and this time, with more force, pressed his tongue in her mouth.

Strange! she thought, *but not entirely unpleasant.* Shivers ran up and down her spine. *Should I recoil? Reclaim my lips and tongue?*

As she enjoyed, yet felt a bit repulsed by, his kissing, his hand strayed from around her waist up her back.

She pulled away. Slightly panting, she said, "My goodness, but you men from the South are certainly passionate about your kissing."

He laughed and tried to clasp her again in his arms, but she took a quick step back and began to chatter.

"My thoughts have oft turned to you as well, all this long cold winter. I had hoped we would have a chance for a stroll through the woods, or a picnic supper. Even though I am only permitted one night at the camp, I dreamt that with you in close proximity we might have a chance to become better acquainted. But now you leave before dawn! I am sorry to have but this short encounter."

She looked at him, finally, after her burst of chatter gave her the composure to meet his eyes. He stared directly, boldly, laughingly, into hers. She was frightened by his look of naked desire.

Hannibal took a step forward, his bodily presence somehow a bit menacing to her now. "Our written correspondence acquainted us sufficiently. Now is not the time for dialogue. We have the better part of a night, my darling. I want no more words from those lips, they are now intended for something else." He leaned in and again pressed his lips against hers. At first, she kissed back, but then realized his hand had strayed to her bosom and he was caressing the top of her breasts. She felt an electric shock that thrilled yet repelled her simultaneously. Pressing harder against her, his hand sought and found the lace of her bodice. He tugged the lace to untie the knot!

She wrenched herself free. "I thought you were a Southern Gentleman? That is not gentlemanly behavior." She glared at him.

He took a step forward, and she, a step back.

He laughed, and began to unbutton his coat. "To the contrary, this is precisely the behavior of a Southern Gentleman. It is just not common knowledge to you Northerners." He started to slide his coat off his shoulders.

"Then I'll have naught of it, you cad!" determined Nellie. She turned on her heel and charged out of the woods, leaving the surprised Southern Gentleman tangled in his overcoat, mercifully unable to pursue her.

CHAPTER 8
Lord, Deliver Us

Campwoods, August 1848

Nellie ran with all her might. She burst back into the clearing of the amphitheater just when she thought her lungs would explode from the arduousness of her physical exertion. She looked desperately around for a familiar face in the sparse crowd of worshippers still lingering near the podium. *Nary a one!* she thought, with a flash of alarm.

"There's one of the saved," a man nudged his companion and pointed at her. Nellie hurried through the open space in the direction of the camping tents, ears and heart burning with shame. She forced herself to calm down and focus on finding her group. *Now where did Mrs. Van Cortlandt say they were to settle?* In her distraught state, she could not remember the directions to the tent site. She wandered through a packed area of singing worshippers, praising The Lord as they settled their possessions and people in for the night. She peered into tents and searched for path signs, growing more agitated with each lapsed minute.

She stared down the alley between yet more rows of tents. *Tarnation*, she thought, realizing that she had already walked its length. *I know there must be some area I have not checked.* Lost both physically and in her misery, the sound of her name startled her. She felt a light touch at her elbow. Recoiling at the touch as if bitten, she violently pulled her elbow away. She turned toward the voice, ready to shout at Hannibal, in public, if necessary.

She looked up into the smiling face of the cadet, Obadiah Wright. He bowed low over her hand, and she felt a flush of shame at the similarity of his gesture with that of Hannibal Rufus' earlier one. *Did all men lust in their hearts like Hannibal Rufus?* she wondered. *Or am I truly filled with the devil, eliciting men's wanton ways?*

Luckily, Obadiah took Nellie's blush as nothing more than an echoing of his own surprise in their chance meeting in this crowded place.

"My dearest acquaintance of all the finest ladies of Sing Sing! What a true pleasure to see you peering down the alleyway toward my tent," he said and a smile lit his face with a warm, welcoming expression. "What circumstances have conspired to have you arrive here precisely at this moment, and unattended at that?"

She drew a deep breath.

"Alas, you look a bit distraught. Perhaps I can be of some assistance?" he asked. He smiled with that unruffled manner she found put her so at ease.

Nellie took another calming, deep breath and adjusted her shawl. "As a matter of fact, you might just be of assistance. I am here with my confidante and her family, and I am afraid I have not quite gotten my bearings as to the location of our campsite. Are you familiar with the layout of the tents? I don't recall seeing a plan, or any trace of a map, and I fear I am rather at a loss as to the indications I should be seeking."

"Permit me to offer my arm, my dear lady, and we shall reconnoiter." Obadiah bowed in a courtly yet friendly manner, and proffered his arm. Nellie sighed with relief, and gratefully placed her hand on his elbow. In no time at all, Nellie saw the Van Cortlandt coat of arms fluttering over a tent flap, verifying they had found the correct tent.

Once he had ascertained she was safely in the correct place, Obadiah, true Northern Gentleman that he was, smiled at her, and bid his adieu. "I look forward to our next encounter. Perhaps we might try the lackluster convention of pre-arranging a meeting?" With a laugh in his eyes he strode away.

Nellie pulled down her shirtwaist and composed her face.

She opened the flap of the tent and stepped into the small sitting room. Her tension dissipated with the sight of the comfortable arrangement of some small pieces of her friend's familiar furniture. Mr. Van Cortlandt rocked in a rocking chair while Mrs. Van Cortlandt hovered over him. Her friendly greeting met with anxious chatter from the pair. Not only her absence caused the commotion; Augusta was missing as well.

"I am quite certain it is of no consequence, Mrs. Van Cortlandt," Nellie reassured them. "I am sure she stayed after the divine services at half-seven to sing psalms with the group of young adults gathered around a small campfire. I will go find her, either there, or at the nine o'clock prayer meeting. We shall take good care of each other."

She walked back down the steps of the tent and looked across the path. Midwife Rafferty, her friend Clara's mother, and her teacher and mentor, stood at the top of the stairs to the tent across the way looking anxiously up and down the path.

Now Cornelia felt entirely safe.

"My third chance encounter of the night," sang Cornelia Rose in a determined-to-sound-happy voice, and she flitted across the alley to embrace the midwife.

"Child, 'tis fine to see you, but I'm in a bit of a pickle. I'm a-needing Clara, and simply cannot ascertain her whereabouts." The midwife continued her scan of the path in front of them.

"There must be some mischief in the air!" Nellie said playfully. "All my companions are missing!"

"By the Saints, don't say 'missing'! I need her forthwith! I would be happy to think she was enjoying herself with some fine young people, raising joyous voices in praise of the Lord, were it not for the baby I am about to birth. Mercy," said Midwife Rafferty, wringing her hands. "It is not one of your uncomplicated, ordinary births, I could assist with my hands tied behind my back. No! I need the assistance of an apprentice. When a woman has been laboring for hours already and swelling in this particular fashion, something is amiss. My training and my instincts tell me this baby is breech."

"Might I be of assistance?" Nellie asked. "I know to date I have only been entrusted with the preparation of herbs, potions and tinctures... and of course providing an extra set of hands in setting a broken bone or two, but you know I long to become a midwife. I believe I can be of some aid to you tonight."

Midwife Rafferty folded her in her arms. "Most definitely you will be helpful. I have often told you, you show promise at midwifery. I am happy to have such an able assistant. Now help me assemble the herbs while the woman is resting in her sister's care." Without waiting for a reply from Nellie the midwife started listing the supplies she would need and slipped into her tent.

"Yes, yes, we will also need several of my tinctures, a bit of salt...." The midwife bustled about, pulling bottles and pouches from various baskets stacked on a travel case on the side of the tent.

Nellie stepped in behind her. "You have brought all your medicines with you for this one week in camp?"

"A midwife is always prepared — mind ye, every year the camp spawns one medical emergency after another. I am always ready to ply my knowledge for the benefit of my fellowman and kindred worshiper. Moreover, I did send Phillip, post haste with the carriage to bring me more St. John's Wort salve. We've enough for the birthing tonight, but I saw by the assemblage at Even'song they'll be adding a few more to their flock o' chosen people before the week is out!"

Nellie immediately engrossed herself in preparing and packing the medicines. In minutes, under the skillful direction of Mrs. Rafferty, they assembled all the necessary herbs, potions, and linens. They rushed off, balancing heavy baskets, to the tent of the laboring woman.

The stench of unwashed bodies hit Nellie's sensitive nose as she entered the tent behind the Midwife. She tried to contain her reflexive gag, but Mrs. Rafferty heard it, and said to her in a whisper, "They'll be none of that if ye want to be a proper midwife. Next time arm yerself with a posy of lemongrass, lavender, and clove tucked in yer bodice. Decrease your sensitivity to other smells, it will." Nellie rushed to thank her but the fully prepared Midwife, clad in a huge apron, had already begun to set up shop.

Before Nellie's eyes, and with only a bit of Nellie's help, Mrs. Rafferty shooed away the idling men, who stank from several weeks of unwashed worship and free flowing beer. Once they had dispersed, with strict instructions to wash their hands all the way up to their elbows, the midwife turned to the laboring woman and her sister. Nellie noted the calm reassuring voice the midwife adopted, encouraging the pair, and inspiring their confidence in her abilities. In the shake of a lamb's tail, Nellie watched her transform a corner of the tent around the writhing woman into a clean, clutter free area lined with her baskets of remedies.

A brief examination of the progress of the labor during her absence added to Mrs. Rafferty's continual flurry of preparations. "Mrs. Bachelor, 'tis my understanding we are ushering in your fourth little one, is that correct?"

Nellie leaned forward over the pot of fresh herbs she had been mashing and stirring into some alcohol for a tincture, to get a better look at the woman who was the cause of this commotion. A pale face, with closed eyelids and sweat dampened hair clinging to its temples, twisted toward the Midwife and a thin sound emanated from colorless lips. "Aye."

"'Tis your saving grace then, that this is not your first. Ye know what's expected of ye, and fourth children rush right on through, trying to catch up with their older siblings, don't they now?" Mrs. Rafferty squeezed the woman's shoulder, and brushed the stringy damp hair back from her forehead. "'T won't be long now. But when ye are not feeling any contractions, just focus on resting yer person. I'm going to need all yer strength when I want ye to push."

A flutter of the woman's eyelids was the only reply.

"Ye'll be wanting a rest now won't ye?" Mrs. Rafferty said to the woman's sister.

"Yes, I'm grateful for it. Although I won't know rest—I've got my own brood to contend with," said the woman and she scurried out of the tent.

The midwife turned to Nellie. "I am certain now the baby presents in t' breech position. I'll need you to follow my instructions carefully. We'll want to keep the ripping and tearing to the minimum o' course—and with a breech that is nigh impossible. I am wagering on my combination of herbs—St John's Wort to dull the pain, some oils to increase the elasticity of the skin—and yer fine hands to help me, that will see us through the worst of it."

Nellie's trust in Midwife Rafferty, already high based on all she learned in her herb lessons, swelled with the rational, calm, and reassuring words. A wave of adrenaline surged through her, helping her turn her full attention to assisting and learning.

Mrs. Rafferty cautioned, in between bouts of shouting and screaming as the labor pains overtook the poor woman on the floor, that even though the baby's arrival seemed imminent, it could still be many more hours. After Nellie hauled water from the pump at the corner of the tents' path, and then for the sixth time boiled it at the campfire near the dining hall, her attention and energy flagged. For the first time, she realized how tired she was. She turned to a lump of belongings piled on the floor in the tent behind her and sank into it to rest her feet. It seemed like an instant later Mrs. Rafferty was calling her name, and telling her the baby was crowning.

Nellie rubbed the sleep out of her eyes and inspected the water and the ointments to make sure they were at the ready. The water was no longer scalding hot. She wondered if she should go out to put the kettle back on the campfire.

Nellie glanced at the birthing woman as Mrs. Rafferty uttered her name again. "Ugh!" Nellie involuntarily exclaimed. She gazed in horror at the scene in front of her, at first not sure what she was seeing.

The baby was entering the world bottom first. Nellie stepped forward to lend a hand as the midwife instructed her. At last, the careful handling of Mrs. Rafferty facilitated the shoulders, and then the head, entering the world right after the baby's legs and bottom, without undue loss of blood. The midwife called for the scissors Nellie had recently sterilized, and she cut the cord and successfully tied it off. She handed the baby to Nellie who wrapped the slimy newborn in the soft linen furnished by Mrs. Rafferty as instructed, and began to gently rub the baby.

"We need a cry!" Mrs. Rafferty said. "Is she breathing?"

Nellie looked anxiously at the wizened bundle in her arms.

"Strike her on the bottom!" Mrs. Rafferty said, busy still stemming the mother's bleeding. Nellie scrutinized the warm little wrinkled face nestled in her arms.

"Now," commanded the midwife. *I cannot strike her!* Nellie thought. She lifted the baby up to her shoulder and dutifully gave her a firm pat on the back. The baby uttered a small sound — she was breathing!

Nellie gasped in relief. "She is breathing! She is alive!" Nellie practically shouted. The baby wriggled as if confirming her statement. Nellie stepped carefully over to the mother, cradling the precious cargo, and put the baby on the woman's breast.

"Well now that's just the remedy this mother needs, Cornelia dear. The little one on her breast — mother and child introduced to each other at last! You've good instincts me love."

Nellie beamed.

"Our task is not complete. We now count fingers and toes, we check oxygen levels by looking at fingernail color...." Mrs. Rafferty took Nellie step by step through the medical procedures and pronounced mother and child in the best of health.

Another wave of adrenaline, spurred by the excitement of the event and spiked by the praise, bolstered her spirits and confidence, and carried her all the way through clean up. She assisted Mrs. Rafferty in settling the grateful mother to nursing. The pair soon slipped into slumber.

Everything tidy, the miracle of the birth floated her out of the tent, and onto the path to their campsite.

Nellie bounced along next to the midwife; nearly empty baskets lightly resting on their arms, chattering questions so fast, Mrs. Rafferty finally dissolved into laughter at the futility of answering. The midwife gave her a hug, shushed her to not awaken the sleeping members of her party, and bade her get an hour of sleep before the dawn preaching started. Nellie realized she had gone through the whole night without sleep, and with nary a thought of the early evening unpleasant encounter in the woods.

Was that just last night? she wondered.

Cautiously, she lifted the flap to the Van Cortlandt's tent and crept inside. Someone had converted the sitting room into an overflow bedroom. As Nellie's eyes adjusted she saw two canvas curtains, separated by a narrow hallway, rising, and falling in succession with the sound of disparate snoring. More snoring emanated from slumbering figures on the chairs. Nellie saw two sleeping forms on the floor. She recognized Augusta's beautiful hair done in a sleep braid and laid down on the bedding arranged next to her, up against the side of the tent. She tried to close her eyes and relax, even though still fully clothed all the way down to her shoes.

It seemed that seconds later Augusta was hovering over her, touching her shoulder teasing her to wake up.

"I'll wager my evening was just as adventuresome as yours." Augusta laughed into her ear. "Come, arise, and disclose your escapades! I will match your stories with mine."

Nellie's eyes flew open and she sat bolt upright. She looked around in confusion at the tent's metamorphosis. Transformed back into one large room, the tent was unrecognizable. With the canvas room dividers rolled up to the ceiling, exposing three beds cheerfully made with colorful comforters, sunlight streamed in from an opening in the back of the tent.

"There was another birth?" she asked in confusion.

It was Augusta's turn to look confused. "A birth?" she scratched her head. "Oh goodness, I heard a babe was born. Mother was up with the sun, directing the cooking of flapjacks on the open campfire and gathering all the gossip." She turned to Nellie in horror. "Oh goodness, do you think my early evening absence at our campsite was noticed? Oh goodness, that mitigates some of the delight in my exploits. Oh goodness...."

"Oh mercy, Augusta! Will you stop saying 'Oh goodness'?" Nellie burst, clutching her aching head. "Yes, they did notice your absence, but

I arrived just in the nick of time, and said I supposed you were at the young people's campfire singing psalms, and I would join you there. On my journey to find you, I had a chance encounter with Midwife Rafferty. She could not find Clara, so *I* went to assist with the birth."

"You accompanied the midwife? If that don't beat the Dutch! How did you learn such a skill? I am so jealous! All I do is stitch and sing. I can't even learn more grammar, Latin, or the classics the way my brothers do." Augusta put her hands on her hips and looked perturbed.

"That is a whole other subject!" Nellie said. "I have been surreptitiously learning the secrets of medicinal herbs for two years. Birthing was exciting and awful at the same time. The baby was breech. It was very difficult. Midwife Rafferty is an amazing healer. There was so much blood, so much bile, so many bodily fluids...."

"Ugh! Say no more!" Augusta put up her hand and turned away. "If blood and bile were involved in the study of Latin I should cease to desire to study it!"

Nellie opened her mouth to say more, but Augusta again put up her hand and said, "Upon reflection, I realize I quite emphatically do not have any desire to participate in such a repugnant event. Perhaps not even when forced to — to obtain my own children. My word, such distasteful unpleasantness! Is it possible to hire someone to perform that task in my stead?"

Nellie giggled.

"But my goodness," continued Augusta, "you must have had quite the experience. It is little wonder you slept soundly through the conversion of our little tent to its daytime form.

"And I thought you lingered later than me because Hannibal Rufus Calhoun cornered you." Augusta winked knowingly at Nellie.

"He executed just that maneuver," said Nellie. Augusta smiled.

"Fie on Hannibal Rufus!" Nellie exclaimed, her face revealing her distress. "I never want to hear that name again. No, no, don't press me for details right now — it is not important. I see you are bursting with news of an adventure of your own."

"I never could hide my true feelings from you Nellie!" Augusta said with a happy sigh.

"Nor would I ever desire that you do. Come, come, where were you into the wee hours of the night? Surely, your eyes would not dance with such sparkle from campfire singing alone."

Augusta squealed. "Goodness no! The harmonies around the fire launched me into the most romantic evening of my life! I have met the most wonderful gentleman—he hails from the same learning academy as your beau Obadiah."

Nellie blushed at the implication and looked down. Augusta picked up Nellie's chin, forcing her to look in her friend's eyes. "Spill the beans," her friend commanded.

The traumatic events of the evening before merged together and swam before Nellie's eyes. She shook her head and picked a hopeful thought to communicate to her friend. "Obadiah may very well be my beau! I happened upon him last night when I could not locate our campsite. He is not only charming, but has a wonderful sense of direction, and a logical problem-solving mind."

"Cornelia Rose, what bizarre praise from an incurable romantic," said Augusta, giggling.

The girls readied themselves for the day's events in the back of the tent, in a small space made private by curtains. Gasping at the coldness of the water fetched by Augusta's brother, they freshened up and changed into clean blouses. Nellie joined Augusta in happy chatter, determined to keep the unpleasant incident with Hannibal Rufus from her thoughts.

CHAPTER 9
Rescue Me

Campwoods, August 1848

The high of the night's amazing, dramatic birth and the thought of future romance with Mr. Wright propelled Nellie through breakfast with her host family. She chattered gaily, her heart full of happy energy.

But the task of stilling her body to sit erect, displaying proper posture, for the preaching lowered her defenses against fatigue. Sleep crept over her even before the day's preacher warmed up to his theme. Nellie felt her head bobbing and jerked it upright, squirming in her seat. She looked anxiously at Augusta sitting next to her.

"At what time did you retire from your day's labor?" Augusta whispered.

Nellie gave a giggle, and then clamped her hand over her mouth. Exhaustion made every twist of the tongue seem humorous. Augusta looked at her uncomprehendingly.

"It was night labor, not day labor, and it was not my labor, but the birthing mother's." Nellie giggled.

Augusta gave a patronizing squeeze to Nellie's arm. "Always observing the clever turn of words, my friend. Methinks law or literary works might be better suited to you than science."

"Playing with words is merely a trifling fun. Midwifery is my callin," Nellie assured her.

"Mayhap your linguistic skills will serve you well when one of your suitors is called to the bar. You could match wits with the most erudite of men."

"Instead of 'quid pro quo' it would be 'quip pro quo,'" agreed Nellie.

"Precisely! You have proven my postulation," said Augusta, giving a most un-ladylike snort. "Now if you can contain your interruptions, might I suggest that you retire to the campsite for an hour of rest?"

"You may suggest—but Augusta! You are familiar with my peccadilloes! I would sooner forfeit my best pair of gloves than miss an hour of the meeting. Is it not almost time for the first sitting of dinner?" Nellie tugged at a stray strand of hair and pulled herself erect into her best posture. *Shoulders back!* she could hear her mother say. In less than a minute she found herself slumping forward again, eyes closing.

Nellie pulled out her pocket watch and Augusta giggled at the expression of dismay on Nellie's face. "Two more hours! That will never do!"

Augusta giggled again. She took out her fan and waved it in front of her face. "The heat alone could disengage a lady's attention, without the added burden of blue-under-the-eyes fatigue." She put the fan over her mouth and whispered conspiratorially to Nellie, "Come, as quietly as possible, let us make our way toward the shop-tents. I declare my spirit will find salvation more easily in a perambulation around stores crammed with fine wares than in this state of bored stupor, listening to this preacher."

Nellie stifled her own giggle at Augusta's sacrilegious twisting of their purpose here. But truth be told, the exhaustion from her sleepless night was relentless. She knew even if she stayed to listen, she would not hear a word of the news of salvation, but would continue dozing in her seat.

They stood and crept over toes and petticoats toward one edge of the open auditorium. They were only moderately disruptive of those seated in their row, and perhaps the people settled directly behind them, until Augusta lifted her eyes for one last look at the preacher a moment too soon and knocked a squirming toddler off her seat.

The child screamed. But the wideness of Augusta's petticoats prevented her from seeing exactly what had gone wrong. Flustered, she inadvertently worsened the situation by stepping on the prone child's hand.

The screeching escalated. All heads turned and the young ladies flushed crimson at the ruckus they had created. Thinking quickly, Nellie scooped the child up into her arms to comfort her, but that sudden movement, culminating in coming face to face with a stranger, only further distressed the girl. She drew in her breath and unleashed an earsplitting scream. Nellie winced, while the child kicked and beat Nellie's head and shoulders with both fists.

"Unhand my offspring!" commanded a stern voice. Nellie looked down to see a bulky man with a huge bulging neck straining to rise from his seat to grab his daughter. Augusta snatched the kicking child from Nellie's hands and dumped her on the lap of the man. He struggled under the little girl's weight, knees groaning, his efforts to gain his feet thwarted. With a loud grunt, father and child toppled under the edge of the pew in a tangled mess of legs and ribbons. Augusta and Nellie bent down, determined to assist them back to the bench, but the man roared, "Be gone!"

In utter shame and embarrassment, the girls straightened and turned to run away, tripping over each other in their haste to leave.

Rrrrrrriiippp!

Augusta stepped on the back of Nellie's dress.

Nellie looked over her shoulder in dismay, but they did not stop. Not until they entered the safety of the tall pines beyond the amphitheater did they pause for breath. Nellie pulled the back of her dress around and held it up in her hand.

"Oh Goodness!" said Augusta.

"Now don't start that again!" said Nellie and suddenly they both burst into laughter. "You should have seen your face when you could not see the little girl, but you knew you made it worse by stepping on her," said Nellie between giggles.

"Or your face when you looked down at the man with the bulging neck!"

"Or your face when they tumbled off the pew!"

"Or your face when you turned after we heard the loud ripping noise."

"Yes sir, it was most amusing in-deed," the southern drawl behind them immediately returned both girls to sobriety.

"Hannibal Rufus Calhoun!" Nellie exclaimed. "I thought you left this morning to return to Louisiana."

Hannibal Rufus stepped out of the shadow of the conifer pine, and pulled Nellie's hand to his lips. She snatched it away and stepped back. "Not when my prize was yet to be obtained." He laughed and bowed in front of her.

Augusta stepped closer to Nellie, sensing the trepidation in her friend.

"I see before me *two* fair Northern beauties, so clearly at a disadvantage, having just caused quite the spectacle. It would be most foolish to not turn this situation to my advantage," he said slyly and smoothed his mustache with his gloved hand.

Nellie and Augusta exchanged nervous glances, and backed further away. Unfortunately, that was exactly what Hannibal Rufus anticipated. He was inching them deeper into the silent pines. He leaned in closer, blocking the small gap in the underbrush out to the preaching area with his tall frame. Suddenly thrusting his arm forward, Nellie found herself pulled closely to his chest, her cheek pressed into one of his large brass buttons.

She struggled to pull away but Hannibal was surprisingly strong and held her tight. Luckily, he was also trying to detain Augusta with his other arm, so the two wriggling girls pulled together to detach themselves.

Nellie looked around anxiously for an alternative escape route through the thorny bramble around them. She twisted to the right and Obadiah appeared at her elbow. She rubbed her eyes. *Am I imagining him? Is he a mirage?* she wondered.

"Ah, there you are my fine damsel...appearing perpetually in distress," he said.

"Is this fellow, I certainly don't presume he merits the title 'gentleman', disturbing you ladies? Or perhaps one of you are desirous of this questionable attention?" Obadiah asked.

"Yes!" said Nellie.

"No!" said Augusta.

Obadiah looked momentarily taken aback.

"Yes, to your first question and indubitably *no* to your second!" Nellie hastily reassured him. With a surge of confidence and well-being, engendered by Obadiah's appearance, she felt herself smile.

"Be gone you bounder!" Obadiah said, raising his voice, and stepped closer to Hannibal, his face grim and his fists clenched.

"Stand you down, Yankee, you have no business interfering with my woman," Hannibal said and stepped closer.

Obadiah held his ground, and met his glare. "Do not advance further, I am quite certain neither of these fine young ladies are 'your woman'." Obadiah looked back at Nellie to motion her to slip away. Hannibal Rufus took advantage of his opponent's averted gaze to punch him in the face. Obadiah reeled sideways, knocking into Augusta, who tried to catch him but they both tumbled to the ground.

"Just as I thought, who is to stop me?" said Hannibal. Wearing a grim smile, he grabbed Nellie and pulled her toward him again. She dug in her heels and tried to hold on to a low branch.

It gave Obadiah enough time to scramble to his feet and say, "We Yankees do not crumble to a dandy's sucker punch. I am of far stronger mettle." He moved forward, fist cocked to cuff Hannibal.

Nellie gazed in horror at Obadiah's bleeding mouth, then down at Augusta sprawled on the ground at his feet. Hannibal stepped backwards, dodging Obadiah's threatened punch; Nellie felt him drag her with him.

"And Yanks always travel in packs," said a voice behind the trapped Nellie. Hannibal suddenly found himself on his knees, the hand not pulling Nellie twisted behind him in a dead lock. "Or do they not teach you Southerners that?"

Nellie burst free from her captor.

"Nathaniel!" screamed Augusta. "Oh goodness, you are a sight for sore eyes! How fortuitous that you should appear."

Nellie scurried behind Obadiah.

"By the sword you have excellent timing!" Obadiah said, taking off his cravat and tying it around Hannibal's hands. The two 'Yankees' looked down at their captive.

"You have tampered with the wrong woman's affections!" Obadiah said, grabbing Hannibal's shoulder. "On your feet! I am taking you to the Sheriff."

"I refuse to go. I have done naught off form," declared Hannibal.

Nathaniel scoffed. Obadiah pulled the necktie on Hannibal Rufus' hands tighter. Hannibal winced.

Obadiah said, "This is not acceptable behavior to Yankees, you cad. I would not hazard an hypothesis on acceptable conduct of 'gentlemen' in the South, but in the North, we do not tolerate this untoward behavior. I said, on your feet!" He tugged the tie hard enough to pull Hannibal, grunting in pain, to his feet.

"Now forward—March!" commanded Obadiah. "Nathaniel, I trust you can steer these ladies safely back to civilization? It is high time they were reunited with civilized behavior."

"It will be my distinct pleasure," said Nathaniel, offering a hand to Augusta who nimbly jumped to her feet, and his other arm to Nellie, who gratefully put her hand on top. Their small parade out of the pines did not travel far before they met a group of three men who called to them.

"Hannibal Rufus Calhoun the Third," one big man drawled. "Alleluia! We have had a devil of a time searching the Campwoods for y'all."

"Well I'll be a cotton-pickin'.... How is it possible you appear here in this camp?" asked Hannibal, attempting to divert their attention from his captivity. "I saw our caravan leave with my very eyes. By my calculations you should be well south of New Jersey by this time of day."

"Those calculations failed, apparently, to take into account the tenacity of your mother. While she might smell like a magnolia, she is as tough as a pine knot. When she cottoned on to your disappearance, she refused to continue our journey. Like a mule fightin' over a turnip, there's just no reckoning with a Southern belle, once she settles her mind...."

The man interrupted himself as he saw Hannibal wince in pain. Only then did he realize his son's hands were bound. Obadiah pulled on the tie to compel his prisoner forward.

"Young sir, what is the meaning of this? Unhand my son!" said the man.

"Your son's comportment makes me leery of providing you the respect you may be due, sir. Therefore, I will not 'unhand' him until I have reached the proper authorities," Obadiah said, looking the older man directly in the eyes.

Nellie and Augusta grasped each other's hands as Nathaniel moved forward to stand shoulder to shoulder with Obadiah. Nathaniel clamped his hand on Hannibal Rufus's shoulder, and planted his feet.

"Son, I will repeat myself just one time, in case there is something awry with your ability to hear. Unhand this gentleman."

Neither Obadiah nor Nathaniel moved.

The Southern gentleman tried a different tack, and turned to Hannibal Rufus. "What is the meaning of this here discomfiting condition?" The older gentleman smoothed his mustache with the exact motion Hannibal had employed just a moment earlier in the woods. Any doubt as to the relationship of the two men dissolved with this motion.

With a short laugh Hannibal Rufus tried to dismiss the situation. "These Yanks are under the misconception...." But Obadiah's jerk on the cravat holding Hannibal's hands caused Hannibal to interrupt his own narration with another grunt of pain.

"Perchance you can remember the actual facts as they occurred, and save the fictitious version for your triumphal return to your motherland?" prompted Obadiah.

Hannibal Rufus began again. "An innocent encounter...uuuggg!" Obadiah tightened the tie again.

"Perhaps *I* might enlighten you gentlemen, as this fellow does not seem to be in complete control of his faculties," said Obadiah. "I am taking this chap to the sheriff. He has compromised the welfare of these two fine women. We do not tolerate behavior like this in the North."

Hannibal Rufus' father stepped forward. "I assure you, as the Louisiana Gentleman that I am, your trip to the sheriff is not necessary. I will take him into my own custody, *per*sonally ensure the well-being of these fine young ladies, and vouch for the safety of your Northern society, by delivering this here criminal against civility right to the most fearsome judge a man would ever face — his waitin' mother! Would you fine gentlemen be able to honor that request?"

"Sir, your son has tarnished the word of Southern Gentlemen irrevocably in my eyes. However, I do acknowledge the highest authority to which you refer, and I do believe that a solution might be at hand to easily verify your gentleman's oath, while putting my prejudice at ease."

"That being?"

"Summon this fine lady here, and we will release this cad to *her* custody."

"It might be downright impossible to convince Madam Calhoun to disembark her carriage," drawled one of the accompanying men.

Obadiah pulled at the tie holding Hannibal Rufus's hands and propelled him forward.

"However," the gentleman said, stepping into Obadiah's path. "She did advise she would not return home without her son. Perhaps if we head toward the main carriage entrance?" The man pointed in the opposite direction.

Before the situation escalated to fisticuffs again, a self-assured woman, with a parasol twirling over her head, walked sedately toward the group of three men and tapped Hannibal Rufus' father on the arm.

"Daaarling, whatever is the de-lay? I see our son right here, standin' nonchalant, with hands behind his back, a position no true gentleman should ever find his-self in, yet there is no detectable forward motion in the direction of our carriage. I do declare, I find this disconcerting entirely," drawled the woman, in a quiet, icy tone.

The Southern men all stood meekly listening to this scolding. They looked at each other like chastised schoolboys. The woman stood, awaiting a reply, both hands on her parasol, glaring at them.

One of the gentlemen finally said, "Why ma'am, I—I confess, we had a small bit of difficulty locating this here boy. Close on its heels, I say immediately following, we experienced a confrontation with an unexpected situation."

"Pray, do give me the particulars!" she drawled, twirling her parasol. "I *am* sure I could find no pleasure greater than standin' here, listening to an amusing, long tale when at any moment, I am expected in the fair city of Philadelphia for my dear sister's finest roast pheasant dinner. Do not concern yourself, son, with *all* of the people you have inconvenienced with your little charade."

Madam Calhoun looked each man individually in the eyes as she said, "I could not even imagine what further calamity, whatever misfortune, could be more imperative than disruptin' and disregardin' the scheduled hospitality of so many of our kinfolk in the City of Brotherly Love."

The three southern gentlemen looked extremely uncomfortable. They turned, as one unified body to Hannibal Rufus, clearly implying that he was the root of this whole situation, therefore the burden of explanation belonged to him.

He stepped forward, and grimaced, as neither Obadiah nor Nathaniel advanced with him, and his bound hands stayed behind with them. In spite of his predicament, his ears red with embarrassment, he stayed true to form and attempted to smooth talk his way around the situation.

His patience long gone, Obadiah gave Hannibal Rufus's hands another twist, bringing his fanciful explanation to a halt.

Obadiah bowed to the lady with the parasol. "If you please, Madam, may I provide the service to you of an expedited summation of the circumstances?" He paused, waiting for her approval.

She raised an eyebrow at him, but remained silent. Hannibal Rufus's father cleared his throat. "Boy, Madam Calhoun can hardly entertain your proposal without a proper introduction. Please do us the honor of introducing yourself."

"If this don't beat all," Obadiah muttered to Nathaniel. "So refined they can't talk to me without an introduction, yet a son who does not know how to treat a lady."

"Ma'am." Obadiah breathed out audibly. "If you will, I am Obadiah Wright—"

"Son of the Senator?" the lady interrupted.

"Yes, Ma'am as a matter of fact I am. Now about your son...." Obadiah determined to continue.

She held up a dainty gloved hand. "Regard one moment, sir! I have no *interest* in hearing anything from an offspring of that good-for-nothing Yankee politician. Attacking our way of life, as if he had any proper knowledge of the opportunity we provide to those darkies to be useful, to be taken out of the barbaric life they lead in that most primitive of dark continents, Africa."

Obadiah looked at the father of Hannibal Rufus. "Are these so-called gentlemen all impotent?" he muttered to Nathaniel.

Perhaps Hannibal Rufus heard him, or perhaps he grew weary of further extension of his disadvantaged situation.

"Now Mother, surely I have no love for this fellow...."

Hannibal Rufus' father roused himself to take control of the situation. "Madam Calhoun, I declare you are the finest voice the South has ever had in defending our way of life. Howsoever, I do believe these discussions best be confined to the drawing room, for a friendly conversation aided and abetted with some fine southern brandy.

"We are rudely inconveniencing our northern relations who expect us in Philadelphia. Each moment we delay further removes us from fashionably late to catastrophically overdue. May I suggest we hear this fine gentleman's say and then be on our way?"

"At the risk of being uncouth, I have dallied long enough! It is time to bring this scoundrel to the proper authorities!" Obadiah said firmly, and he and Nathaniel propelled Hannibal Rufus forward.

All the Southerners began talking at once. Hannibal swore so thoroughly, as Nathaniel remarked later, there was not a single known curse word omitted. The gentlemen began to argue with each other, and the lady made proclamations to anyone who would listen.

Past his limit for patience, Obadiah hesitated for only thirty seconds more before striding forward again and jerking Hannibal Rufus along.

The lady hurried over to him, and changed her mode of persuasion to angry insistence. She bombarded the men with a flurry of commands while scurrying to keep up with Obadiah's long strides, and Hannibal Rufus' sideways stumbling. Nathaniel strode behind, constantly righting Hannibal and prodding him to keep up with Obadiah.

Abruptly Obadiah interrupted the verbal barrage. "What of the honor of the fine young women he was accosting? I am sorry Madam — behavior such as your son's is not tolerated up North, in genteel society."

"The honor of a lady?" Mrs. Calhoun twisted her parasol in horror and pulled Hannibal Rufus by the collar, turning him around to face her, all the while keeping pace with the angry Obadiah. "I demand an explanation. I will not have my family name dishonored without a thorough elucidation of all the pertinent details of this allegation."

"This Yankee's active imagination has fabricated slanderous conclusions based on his interference with a private encounter I was having with my lady friend," said Hannibal Rufus, with undaunted audacity.

Obadiah stopped and roughly turned Hannibal to face him. "You still posture and pose in denial of your culpability? These ladies have suffered far too much damage to their sanguinity to be subjected to any more of your preposterous lies! Nathaniel, take these ladies out of this scoundrel's company. I will personally deliver this scallywag to justice and stay to see the bounder horse whipped and run out of town."

"Enough!" commanded Mrs. Calhoun. "I have heard enough to run him out of your fine town myself." Obadiah looked at her in surprise.

Nellie and Augusta looked at each other with amazement.

"You had the *au*dacity to meet a young lady without her chaperone? You have trespassed against your upbringing. Who are your people? What kind of ruffian have we raised? You have brought *disgrace* to our name, and tarnished the reputation of our genteel civilization of the South," she said in her icy tone.

Hannibal Rufus' father finally spoke up. "Now Ma'am, no reason to arrive at a hasty conclusion."

But she elbowed him aside and began her tirade again. She pulled Hannibal's ear and began to move him forward as she berated his arrogance and inappropriate behavior.

Obadiah took a few steps along with them, and then quietly released the tie, freeing Hannibal Rufus' hands and allowing the whole Southern entourage to continue to move forward. Hannibal Rufus stumbled along as quickly as the Southern matron's tongue continued its lashing. Obadiah, Nathaniel, Nellie, and Augusta watched the former aggressor scurry alongside his mother; so miserably excoriated and so wretched he failed to realize his hands were free, and Obadiah and Nathaniel no longer accompanied him.

The three Southern gentlemen had quickly fallen into step behind the still chastising woman, mutely supporting her rough justice with their silent escort.

The quartet watched them go in amazement. They all burst out laughing as the ridiculous parade passed through crowd after crowd, leaving gawking people in its wake.

"Ladies," said both gentlemen at the same time, each offering an elbow. Nellie and Augusta took them gratefully.

"Luncheon is now being served," said Obadiah, with an affable smile. "Shall we?"

The ladies nodded their assent and were escorted to the dining hall.

CHAPTER 10
Some Enchanted Evening

Sing Sing, January 1849

The snow on the hill that rolled from the Entwhistle house to the river glistened under the full moon's silvery beams. Icicles hung sparkling from the eves, framing the window, as Cornelia Rose leaned out into the enchanted night, gazing at the spectacular view of her town perched on the water.

"It's simply magical!" whispered Nellie. The rush of hot breath accompanying her words made a visible puff in the cold air. The whole village of Sing Sing was softly twinkling. She drew in a breath through her nose. The smell of the frosty air cast a spell of wonderment over her. *What further enchantment will such an evening weave for me?* she wondered. *Mayhap a magical Winter Wonderland Ball!*

She pulled her head back into the cozy warmth of her room and again, inhaled deeply. The smells inside were as intoxicating as the crisp night air had been. The aroma of cinnamon was wafting up the stairs from the kitchen. Dressed and ready for what felt like hours, Cornelia turned her attention to the sounds of many hands arranging food on tables, and many feet scurrying from kitchen to drawing room to dining room.

Curious to get a glimpse of the activity, Nellie crept down the back stairs. Stepping into the kitchen she was instantly amidst the main floor's commotion. She dodged servants scurrying here and there, bustling about making the final preparations. Candle lighters walked gingerly about, carefully adding new candles to every freshly polished sterling silver holder, all the large chandeliers, and the many-mirrored sconces that outlined the perimeter of the ballroom. The sterling shone, the chandeliers sparkled, and the mirrors reflected and refracted the light, spreading throughout the beautiful formal rooms. At last, the grand house glowed with hundreds of lit candelabras. The effect was spellbinding.

Her reverie at the magical transformation of the house into an enchanted castle broke, as she inadvertently stepped into the path of one of the men hired to serve at the party. He reeled on his heels, tray in his hand swaying precariously. With a quick show of dexterity, the man caught the tray with his other hand, emitting a quiet oath as the glasses slid together. Her face pink with fear as she waited for the glasses to tumble from the tray's edge and shatter, Nellie gasped, "I am sorry!"

The man righted the tray of rattling glasses, and sounded a soft whistle of relief.

Nellie squeaked, "Thank the Lord!"

The young man's blue eyes twinkled as he looked at Nellie. "I think I had a bit o' hand in averting disaster too."

She looked up into his vaguely familiar blue eyes. She turned a bit redder. "Mercy, most indubitably... I did not mean to imply...."

The man threw back his head and laughed, glasses once again taking a little slide along the tray. "No harm done, Miss Nellie," he said.

Surprised that he knew her name, Nellie grinned shyly and ducked away.

She flew up the stairs for her final toilette, mortification increasing her speed.

The glow from the activity downstairs and her embarrassment was only a dim ember compared to the sparks flying in the girl's bedchamber.

"Sakes alive! What is *my* ruffle doing on *your* sash?" demanded Agnes.

"You said I could have it," retorted Anastasia.

"Since it looks far superior on me, I surely would not have uttered those words," argued the oldest sister.

Agnes' gave an indignant snort as Anastasia tied the sash more firmly.

They turned away from each other to style their hair, an unspoken cease-fire temporarily ensuing.

Nellie watched her two sisters preen in front of the mirror, making final adjustments to their hair and sashes.

I am delighted to see my sisters look so lovely, Nellie thought with satisfaction. Anastasia, a dark-haired beauty with an exquisite sense of fashion and a newly acquired flair for dressing, was stunning in her taffeta ball gown. Its shimmering dark blue transformed Anastasia's hair to onyx. Cut daringly low, and accentuating all of her features, Anastasia was sure to turn heads.

Even Nellie had to concede Agnes looked equally attractive in her own right. Favoring their fair-haired father, Agnes's powder blue gown highlighted her beautiful golden locks.

But truth-be-told, neither of them held a candle to Cornelia Rose. Her honey blonde hair, piled high in lustrous waves upon her head, fell becomingly down one shoulder and framed her lovely face. Nell was aglow in anticipation. Her silk taffeta dress was a deep crimson red that set her eyes sparkling and highlighted her rosy cheeks. While not cut as daringly as Anastasia's, Cornelia's gown did justice to her well-proportioned figure. Around her small waist was a beautiful white sash that ended in a bow. The ruffles at the neckline drew the admirer's attention to the soft creamy skin of her small shoulders.

"Take that ruffle off immediately!" Agnes stamped her foot, reigniting the controversy.

"Agnes, you are an insufferable bully," declared Anastasia.

"*Mutter*, come help Agnes and Anastasia resolve their little dispute." Matthias ran into the room, red-faced, his finger stuck in his already uncomfortable formal dress collar, tugging on it. The darling youngest, Matthias was the only one brave enough to call on the highest authority in the house to resolve the difficulty.

To regain a moment of solitude, Nell again retreated to her window, the only place where she could escape her sisters' squabbling. Her reverie did not disappoint. The magic of the bewitched crystal world before her recaptured her wonder and awe.

She leaned out even farther from the window casement, suddenly daunted by the milestone of this event. Anastasia was making her debut in society tonight. Nellie was somehow presented too, but she knew only as an afterthought. Since she had just turned the ripe age of fourteen, Nellie was too old to officially debut. Furthermore, she had attended Mrs. Wheeler's Christmas Ball last year, so it would not be her first appearance in society. *Goodness, fifteen-year-old Augusta had just become engaged! That Nathaniel was a bold gentleman. When he charted a course he immediately sailed it.*

Even though Agnes had no suitors, Nellie attributed that to her sharp tongue, not the fact that she debuted too early. Nellie felt the attention of many eligible men in Sing Sing, and the neighboring towns of Sparta and Tarrytown but she was not yet allowed to receive suitors in the home.

I anticipate a prospect bonanza tonight, she thought.

Mayhap that certain handsome young ensign at Churchill's Academy will be in attendance. How did Obadiah manage to keep catching Cornelia's eye, as she went about her mother's errands on foot through the length of the town, from the gristmill to the milliner? And coincidentally meet her at Hart's Apothecary, just when she emerged from behind the counter?

Nellie shivered, but not from cold. She thrilled at the memory of the first kiss of Hannibal Rufus and their innocent romantic encounter the first time she went to the Methodist Revival at Campwoods. The thrill immediately became a chill as her terror in the woods and the debacle of this past summer washed over her anew. *How could I possibly recall Hannibal Rufus's touch without total revulsion and indignation? Thank goodness Obadiah came to my rescue. How could I have erred so gravely in my judgment of Hannibal Rufus? He seemed quite the courtly gentleman when we first met. Mercy, the embarrassment of my deplorable lack of discernment in assessing the personalities of men!*

But mayhap, the continuous parade of flirtatious schoolboys that pass through the apothecary will help me develop better judgment, she reflected. *I thank the Lord Midwife Rafferty introduced me to Sing Sing's apothecist, Doctor Hart. And I am more fervently grateful that young men like the sarsaparilla Doctor Hart serves!*

After Miss Sarah's Ladies Finishing School, she happily divided her time pursuing her midwifery training. Three afternoons a week she made tinctures and potions or did rounds with Mrs. Rafferty. The other two she spent behind the counter at the pharmacy. There, the curriculum of Nellie's apprenticeship expanded to include many lessons in coquetry.

Nellie was ecstatic at her biweekly opportunity for flirtations — *there was no occasion to learn this skill at Miss Sarah's.* At first, Nellie's position behind the pharmacy glass allowed her to observe, unseen, the many young boys who loitered to read comics, slurp sarsaparilla, or devour a banana split. She gradually overcame the shyness engendered by the sheltered life of the Entwhistle home to be a more active participant in these young men's society. Once she stepped from behind the glass and started talking directly to one of the young cadets, she quickly mastered the art of charming them. She was not, however, sure she was ready to give up innocent flirtations and turn to the serious business of marriage.

Impervious to the freeze of the wintry night, Nellie kept her upper torso thrust out the window like a mermaid figurehead on a Viking ship. *I thirst for greater knowledge — I shan't permit my attention to be distracted so easily by these handsome young men! If only there had been schoolmarms at the public school who were as learned as Midwife Rafferty, I would not feel so lacking in substantive knowledge.*

Nellie remembered her early education in the one room public school house on Brandreth Street. *When I began my schooling, only a few dozen children attended, with an old matron grimly 'learning us' the three R's: readin, ritin, and rithmatic.* Now, there were so many pupils at the Brandreth Street School there was talk of a new building and adding more teachers; maybe even ones as well-educated as the school masters who taught at Obadiah's military academy, or any of the five other private boy's academies in Sing Sing. But it was too late for her, she had not had any say in the matter — she was transplanted to the Lady's School. Nellie cultivated and accumulated most of her knowledge on her own, through constant reading. When her brothers left their books and assignments from The Mount Pleasant Military Academy lying around, Nellie read the books and, covering her brother's answers, completed the assignments too.

Nellie begrudged every minute she spent at the finishing school. She already knew how to be a Lady! In fact, she was sure she was born knowing more, instinctively, than even the headmistress herself would ever learn. *But Mutter will never be dissuaded from her educational philosophy and worldview, despite the futility and lack of utility of the 'ladylike' curriculum.* The only thing Nell wanted to gain from Miss Sarah's was a greater facility in the classics and literature. *I will study prodigious, renowned authors and acquire my father's command of their works, quote for quote. But stitching and deportment? How futile.* Determined to continue her education in science she learned everything possible about healing - on her own.

She longed for the day when her mornings would be free from her hour of practicing perfect posture and pouring out tea. While she waited for her freedom, she increased her knowledge of tinctures and potions, purges, and emulsions at Hart's Apothecary, in spite of the time she spent flirting during her twice-weekly shifts.

Mutter would hardly approve of my self-education in coquetry, she ruminated. *I daresay she would find it shocking!* So far, she had continued to please her parents by practicing her decorum at the dinner table, and often quoting the classics.

"Shut that window!" Agnes rudely disturbed her reverie. "Sakes alive! You'll have us all catch our death of cold. Goodness! Now you'll be the laughing stock of the party—your nose is scarlet red to match your gown."

Nellie's entire face was actually red, not so much from the cold but from her anger at Agnes's perennial, unflagging rudeness. She closed the window and bit her tongue.

"I suppose it is time to go downstairs?" she asked.

"Past time! You are most fortunate I came back to retrieve you." Agnes informed her. "Patrick and his fiancé have been here for hours and are anxious to get the festivities started. Many of the guests have already arrived and our presence is requested downstairs to assemble for the first dance."

With her red nose and ears ringing both from the cold and the scalding words of Agnes, Nellie felt more apprehensive than lucky entering society.

Nellie's head was spinning, not so much from the dancing, as from all the male attention. The minuet left her breathless. The daring French wheel with a particularly handsome young man made her feel blithe and desirable. *This is an evening of wonders, indeed!* Nellie smiled and flirted, imagining herself the belle of the ball.

She paid no heed to her mother's disapproving stare.

The band burst out in the new Steven Foster song, *O Susanna*. The assembled guests cheered in appreciation and the dancing took on a country twang. Nellie could not keep her body still. For the staider music she merely glided and swayed. But now, with every chorus of *".... don't you cry for me, I'll be coming to Alabama with a banjo on my knee...."* her whole body gyrated to the tune.

Her mother frowned at her every time she caught Nellie's eye.

Her father's approach, characteristically, was less subtle than her mother's. After a partner moved in a bit too close and Nellie made no attempt to step back but rather squeezed his hand, her father suddenly appeared at her elbow.

"Yer lookin' a wee bit flushed, me darling. 'Tis time for a rest at the punch bowl and a bit o' cooling refreshment," he said, taking her by the elbow and gently but physically removing her from the arms of her latest partner. "Time to give the other colleens a chance to turn a square." Nellie made a face at her startled partner who quickly rallied his composure and bowed to her father.

"But sir, I have only now summoned the courage to ask the most beautiful young lady at the dance to do me the honor of being my partner."

"'Tis a pretty speech, best saved for another lovely lass awaitin' in the wings yonder." Not persuaded, Mr. James Entwhistle nodded toward the bevy of beauties clustered together near the delicacies and fruit. He turned Nellie away and pointed her toward the wall sconces.

"Me own daughter, dancing with every two-bit, pie-face scallywag with the insolence to put their hands on her. Yea, an' reveling in it!" her father intoned in her ear as he steered her toward a secluded corner of their spacious ballroom. "Yer *Mutter* is fit to be tied, and I'm a wee bit peeved with ye meself." His brow furrowed further as he wheeled her around to face him.

Nellie hung her head, instantly deflated. "But Papa, I meant no indiscretion! I didn't think...."

"Precisely, me lass. Ye didn't ken," he said, but his face softened. "I'll no' tolerate any of me daughters on the end of a grope like a common bar-maid."

"Papa!" said Nellie; shocked her father would even refer to something so tawdry in her presence, much less than say it to her directly.

"I'm sorry for t' rough language, but when ye play with fire, them lads will sizzle every time. A word to t' wise is sufficient, I'll wager. Ye have always been a bright colleen. This art of ladylike comportment I've left in yer *Mutter's* capable hands. She's t' lady of t' family, a right proper lady, and we'll have all our young ladies behave to t' pinnacle of perfection like her. Ye didn't know the ways o' the world, and the low thoughts o' lads. 'Tis our parental duty to make ye savvy. I'll no' be speakin' on this subject again."

I fervently hope not, Nellie thought, flummoxed.

With this speech completed, his face relaxed into its usual grin and he pulled her in for a bear hug.

Nellie breathed a long sigh. *This heady attention downright clouded my thinking.* Her racing emotions and fluttering heart had got the better of her judgment. She hoped no one else had witnessed her permitting one partner to squeeze her waist, or another to touch her hair. She blushed in the relative gloom of the corner, grateful that the sconces of candles shone more brightly off the polished wood floor just beyond them. Now mortified by her own behavior, she tried to content herself with watching the conclusion of the dance.

I thrill at the male touch. A quaver of pleasure tingles inside me! I am a depraved sinner lusting in my heart, she scolded herself.

Her father's squeeze of her hand did not assuage her bitter self-deprecation. She looked at him as a single tear rolled slowly down her cheek.

"Ah, me Nellie, 'tis not so dire as all that. 'Twere it not for ye *Mutter's* eternal vigilance in the comportment of her daughter, 'twould not have been noticed by me, let alone anyone else. 'Twill be yer own little sin, that a trip to the confessional will make right, there's a good colleen." He smiled down at her.

"Ah-hem," said a voice at Mr. Entwhistle's elbow.

Nellie leaned forward to look around the girth of her father's anterior. It was Obadiah, formal dress uniform impeccably pressed, brass buttons shining, even in the diminished candlelight of the corner. Sword hilt gripped by his white-gloved hand, he was a dashingly handsome sight. Nellie snuck a look at his shoes. *Yes, spit polished and glowing darkly.*

"Good evening sir," he said bowing to Mr. Entwhistle. "Good evening Mistress Entwhistle." He smiled and looked her directly in the eye. Nellie cheered up a bit. *My knight in shining armor! It seems his forte is rescuing me from distress.*

"Papa, please permit me to introduce Mr. Obadiah Weber Wright," Nellie said, and gave a little curtsey.

"I know of ye, lad," said Mr. Entwhistle, with a curt nod of his head as Obadiah bowed.

"If I might have a word with you in private, sir?" he said, surprising them both. "If the lady will forgive me?" Rendered speechless, Nellie only nodded. *Whatever could he want?*

Nellie curtseyed to them both, at a nod from her father, and drifted closer to the dancers.

Mr. Entwhistle raised his eyebrows at the young man.

"Ahem," Obadiah cleared his throat. He blurted, "I will head to Yale University for the spring semester shortly."

Mr. Entwhistle did not react, save to raise his eyebrows even higher on his forehead. Obadiah shuffled his feet, smoothed his mustache, removed his gloves, tucked them in his cummerbund and gripped the hilt of his sword.

"I have eyes for your daughter. I wonder if I might look in on her occasionally, especially in the summer months, when term is out," he stammered.

"Never thought I would see the likes of a 'college man' as good enough for me daughter. What will ye be occupying yer time with during the frequent periods when class is not in session?" asked James Entwhistle.

Not allowing Obadiah any time to answer, Entwhistle rolled on. "Will ye be out on capers, pulling pranks, like t' rest of the sophomoric crowd, idly 'studying' when ye could be earning an honest day's wage *and* getting an eddycation?" Mr. Entwhistle ran his hand over the top of his head and scratched his ear in a brusque dismissive gesture. "I didn't have anyone spoon-feed me an eddycation, I read books and figured by meself. At my employment, I trained me own self—I didn't just do t' grunt work as a laborer, no, I put meself forward, looking at t' plans, learnin' t' principles, figurin' out t' engineering and the like." Mr. Entwhistle paused and looked hard at Obadiah, who stood, expressionless, listening, the only sign of tension his white knuckles on the hilt of his sword.

"Ah 'tis a bit o' sour grapes, I'll concede." Entwhistle shook his head and ran his hand over the top of his head again, ending in a quick scratch at the back of his neck. "I didn't have t' opportunity for formal study. But I should no begrudge it o' you. I know yer father worked hard to get his accolades and obtain his highly esteemed positions of Senator, and Governor of our fair state. 'Though I can no' stand his political views...."

Obadiah grimaced. It was another mark against him.

"...'Tis of little consequence now. Sorry to sour yer milk. Ah, ye can't cast t' sins o' t' fadder on the son. I'll allow ye that lad. Yea, I 'll allow ye to write yer name in fer a dance on her dance card tonight," Mr. Entwhistle concluded.

"Thank you, sir. I appreciate your consideration of my qualifications. Perhaps it might also be acceptable to you to allow me to write to her, in fact regularly correspond, while I am at Ya...ahem, in Connecticut, attending to my business?" Obadiah looked straight ahead at the dance floor while he talked, not daring to look the older man in the eye.

Mr. Entwhistle looked at the dance floor too, seeing the twirling, floating, flirting Cornelia Rose. "...If me colleen desires, ye can correspond with her while ye pursue yer eddycation," he conceded, more than confirmed.

Obadiah frowned; frustrated Mr. Entwhistle would not endorse his request wholeheartedly. He gripped his sword hilt tighter and wiggled the blade in and out of the sheath, deciding if he should advocate harder for himself, lacking the proper words.

Obadiah followed Mr. Entwhistle's eyes to the blithe figure of Nellie, laughing and enjoying another minuet. Realizing further words would be futile, he thanked Mr. Entwhistle for his time, shook his hand and stepped aside.

Standing on the sidelines Obadiah stroked his mustache in dismay. All he had obtained through this interview was permission to *dance?* The band began another song while Obadiah grappled with his feelings. His eyes again lit upon the reeling and smiling figure of Nellie, moving through the chain of hands and a smile returned to his face. When the last breathless reel ended, he moved through the crowd and once again appeared at Nellie's elbow.

"Fairest Lady of the soiree, may I have this dance?" Nellie looked up into Obadiah's eyes and blushed. *He is quite charming, in a distinct, sincere, and intelligent manner,* she thought.

"The pleasure would be mine sir," she said, and dropped a pretty little curtsey. Obadiah took her hand and piloted her on to the dance floor. Nellie felt a delightful tingle at his touch. *Oh Lord,* she prayed, *will I have to confess this too?*

CHAPTER 11
Baby, to You, All I am is the Invisible Man

Sing Sing to Manhattan, January 1849

She did not want to leave the warm coziness of her bed.

Last night, with the help of her feather comforter, she transferred her body heat to her bed, making it a warm cocoon that lulled her instantly into a luxurious deep sleep. Yes, she was awake, but an exploratory foot determined it was frosty cold in her garret room. She rolled over and snuggled deeper into the eiderdown. When she shut her eyes after last night's festivities she continued her dancing and revelry in her sleep, dreaming of the evening's enchanting ball. The dream still floated through her head. Now, comfy, snug, and still drowsy, she re-experienced the panoply of her emotions of that magical event: the excitement of the preparation, the anticipation, the heady attention, the energy of the dance, the thrill of the dancing. The thrill of the flirtations! The thrill of the touching!

The thrill.

She shivered, not from cold, but from delight.

She allowed herself one more stretch wrapped in the warmth of the feather comforter.

At last, the electricity of the still palpable thrill moved her out of the bed into the cold morning. Then it fizzled away leaving her standing cold and tired, searching for her robe, sad the ball was over.

The morning-after-the-ball-blues lasted only until she descended the back stairs to the kitchen. Mrs. Entwhistle looked up from her tea and toast and greeted her with the scintillating statement, "New additions to your wardrobe Cornelia, are absolutely required."

Already this morning, a smattering of invitations to balls, luncheons, and dinners had arrived. Helen Brandreth, her contemporary and the eldest daughter of the wealthy pill factory owner even graced Nellie with an invitation to tea. *Perchance, this might provide an occasion to meet Helen's comely older brother, George Brandreth. Would he make an appearance at Helen's tea? If I had my druthers, I would set my cap for him!* A new world unfolded for Nellie, renewing her interest in the art of ladylike behavior and etiquette—which invitations she would accept, the protocol for replying, what type of script to use on her new calling cards...the plethora of details that required attention astounded Nellie.

Nellie's mother had already arranged a trip to New York City today and an appointment with a dressmaker. *Fittings for new gowns*! Nellie felt like royalty. Her ears still catching strains of last night's music, her head swirling with images of her gown billowing and swaying as she danced, she returned up the narrow back staircase, taking the steps two at a time, to dress for The City.

Fastening her buttons and hooks while she looked out her window, Nellie observed the construction of the new railroad tracks along the river. Soon it would be possible to take a locomotive to The City. *Why would anyone eschew an easy sail down the river?* Nellie wondered.

Mrs. Entwhistle had them booked on her husband's eleven o'clock steamboat.

"I will never travel to the city with the plebeians on that dirty noisy conveyance belching dirt and soot they call a locomotive train," her mother declared yet again, evidencing her staunch endorsement of their family business and their investment in shipping and a genteel way of life. "I do not care if they build the tracks right to our front door! My experience at the central depot in The City was most horrifying, and never to be forgotten. Ladies must never stoop to common transportation when they can travel in dignity via ship."

"May we go to an eating-house and eat oysters like real New Yorkers?" asked Anastasia, bouncing into the kitchen, eager to begin her duties as a debutante too.

"Have you taken leave of your senses? No daughter of mine will enter an eating-house. Furthermore, why would you fixate on a food as common as oysters? Oysters! We have a river-full just outside our door, just ripe for the taking. That is what the common folk eat!" Anastasia's face fell and she looked as if she wanted to vanish on the spot. Mother's tone softened. "However, mayhap we will luncheon at a fine restaurant, in the Ladies Sitting Room. Or, if your father's schedule permits, he will escort us to tea at the Astor House," her mother said.

Aha! Nellie thought, *Mutter has not ruled out the possibility of a sumptuous lunch!*

Excitement mounted as Mrs. Entwhistle ordered the carriage brought around. Soon they rolled down the hill to the dock.

The accustomed rush of exhilaration Nellie felt upon her arrival at the wharf whipped her already heightened senses into a small frenzy. She drew in a deep breath, and a nose full of the salty smell of the ocean rewarded her. *The tide, full of saltwater, is coming in! The journey will take twenty minutes longer. Halleluiah!* Cornelia knew as soon as she embarked on the boat she would wish the voyage would never end. She stood in the middle of the dock for a moment, feeling the wind, watching the sails and the gulls, trying to contain her wild enthusiasm. *No cause, no enticement could ever induce me to forsake this river valley!*

Joy filled her heart as she observed the dock activity. Sailors scrambled to ready their ship. Freight hung suspended from ropes on pulleys while cargo men hoisted the ropes higher and then swung the heavy crates on board, lowering them in front of handlers poised to align them in rows in the cargo hold. Cargo placement satisfactory, the sailors released the winches and sent the lifters back to shore.

When the steamboat was in readiness and the five-minute 'all ashore that's going ashore' whistle blew, she assumed her usual position at the tip of the bow. In breathless excitement, she watched the sailors haul in the lines. The steamboat pulled from the dock, edging out to the center of the Hudson. Mrs. Entwhistle frowned her disapproval when she saw Nellie's perch, but wordless, she disappeared through the hatch into the captain's sitting room.

Nellie turned her face toward the spray as the boat gained speed.

"Ten knots," called a sailor.

Nellie's knees bent in rhythm with the chopping motion of the boat chugging through the tide's surf. *The thrill of a ride on one of my father's steamboats, capped by a wardrobe of new dresses from the finest seamstress in The City? The world could not contain any greater joy than this!*

"Mistress Entwhistle," said a voice behind her. She turned to see a tall, handsome, vaguely familiar figure smiling at her.

"Yes?" she asked, abashed at having someone catch her with what she could only imagine was a look of sheer bliss on her face.

"Your father requested I furnish you this," he said, holding out a huge Macintosh. His grin widened, ear to ear.

Embarrassed, Nellie mumbled her thanks, not looking the man in the eye as she took the proffered garment. *He is not wearing a sailor's uniform – who is he?* she wondered, but she was too mortified to look at him, much less engage in further conversation.

It seemed just a heartbeat later, the steamboat docked at Barclay Street, where father had his port. Only the thought of new additions to her wardrobe prevented Nellie from staying onboard. She stood lingering on the wharf, watching the bustling activity; freight swinging from winched ropes on to shore, passengers scurrying, seamen hustling, consoling herself with the thought that she would be back on the ship this evening.

Nellie was so busy watching some sailors tie their knots on a ship's ropes she did not see that same young man steer her mother and sisters to a waiting hackney.

"Nell!" called Anastasia, with a sense of urgency to her voice. Startled, Nellie looked around to see that her entire party was in the carriage save her sister, who, with half her body and one arm in, gesticulated wildly at her with the other arm. Nellie picked up her skirts and ran to the door as it was closing.

The man who had given her the Macintosh suddenly materialized, catching the door, pulling it wide open. He smiled at her again. *What lovely eyes he has,* she grinned back in spite of herself.

"Your raincoat, Mistress E," he said, holding out his arm. She peeled it off; again embarrassed, as she had forgotten she was still wearing it. "Enjoy the day's outing!" He smiled again, handing her into the carriage.

"At what time shall I have the hansom call for you, Ma'am?" the man leaned in and asked Mrs. Entwhistle.

"We must return to the dock in time for our passage on the evening steamship home," said Mrs. Entwhistle. She handed him a card. "Direct them to this address, at half four." The door closed and the young man faded from sight.

The carriage ride was a virtual tour of Manhattan. The sights, sounds, and smells of the streets bombarded them as they made their way to the dressmaker's shop. The girls marveled at the scenes they witnessed: shopkeepers fussing over merchandise displays, newsboys hawking papers, butchers chopping meat. Noise and odors spilled onto the streets and into their carriage. They turned off a busy street onto an avenue.

"Was there ever such a sunny street as this Broadway!" exclaimed Anastasia, leaning out the window to better view the avenue ahead of them.

"Anastasia, do not dangle from your carriage window like a fisherman's pole from a trawler," chastised mother.

"The colors!" sang Nellie. "Rainbows of color on hats and parasols!"

"Not to mention the gowns," said Anastasia. "Look at these fashions! Dazzling. We must procure a gown with these ballooning sleeves and inaugurate this stylish trend at home."

"Omnibuses, hackney cabs, peddler's carts—this bustle of activity caps the climax! One forgets just how sleepy our little Sing Sing village is," Agnes chimed in.

Not exactly on point, thought Nellie, *but at least she is not adopting her usual strident tone.*

"Broadway is the pinnacle of elegance!" exclaimed Anastasia. "'Tis quite the lively whirl of color, fine carriages and enticing smells."

"Not like the Bowery," said Agnes. "Common carts and wagons, streets full of people wearing ready-made clothes and whiffs of cooked meat."

"Ladies, must you gawk like commoners? Agnes, a genteel lady does not comment on sections of The City where less fortunate people abound. Now, let us put an end to this unseemly behavior. We must move with alacrity if we are to arrive at the dressmakers punctually." Mrs. Entwhistle hustled the girls out of the carriage as soon as it stopped.

The appearance of some ready-made gowns, offered for examination and trial, made the session at the dressmaker's even more delightful. Enchanted, the girls each chose a gown to her liking and assessed the latest fashions.

Nellie donned a lavender tea dress, a soft pink chenille morning frock, and a shimmering blue taffeta ball gown, shivering with delight at each view in the mirror.

"If I may say so myself, we cut quite a fine figure," said Anastasia softly. Both girls, sporting fine creations with yards of fabric billowing over six petticoats topped by a crinoline underskirt, twirled, and posed, admiring themselves in the mirror.

"This tucker of Dresden lace is the perfect complement to your figure," said Nellie.

"As is the majesty of your figure aided by this loop of fabric," complimented Anastasia as she fingered the soft cloth draped on the bodice of the gown Nellie wore.

After they identified fashion preferences, bolts of material passed in front of the awe-struck girls, one more beautiful than the next. Mrs. Entwhistle spared no effort in procuring choice after choice of material and pattern.

Agonizing over the alternatives amid her daughters' barrage of verbalized indecision, Mrs. Entwhistle ordered several gowns for each girl.

"To tea!" cried Gertrude Entwhistle. "With not a moment to spare."

"No oysters?" asked Agnes in a small voice. Nellie wondered that even Agnes dared to question her mother's directive. *After the decadent hours filled with an embarrassment of riches and every couture choice imaginable, even Agnes should have no cause to grouse.*

Mrs. Entwhistle's face took on the appearance of a thundercloud. Agnes had the good sense to change tack immediately. "Just a trifling jest, *Mutter*. We are all in such high spirits after viewing that veritable whirlwind of luxurious fabrics and styles. We have been fêted and spoiled like princesses. Lead the way!"

"Your father's messenger advised, Mr. Entwhistle has contrived to meet us at the Astor House for tea," said Mrs. Entwhistle. "That magnificent structure is just a short perambulation along Broadway from here, no need for a carriage."

"*Mutter*, Astor House is across from City Hall," said Agnes. "That is a rather *long* perambulation."

"Now Agnes, after sitting at the dressmakers the entire afternoon, it is a privilege to be able to stretch our limbs and stroll through the cityscape. Furthermore, your father has rearranged his schedule to afford us the opportunity for the rare treat of tea at the Astor House. This opportunity should not be greeted with complaints."

Agnes did not respond.

"The Astor House! How truly scintillating," Anastasia said to Nellie.

"Did you know it was designed by the same architect, Isaiah Rodgers, who designed our country's first truly elegant and luxurious hotel, the Tremont House in Boston?" asked Nellie, linking her arm with Anastasia's and beginning their saunter. "I saw a picture of it in one of Jonas's architectural textbooks." The pair's noses swiveled back and forth like metronomes, observing the scintillating sights and sounds of The City as they chatted.

"How truly blessed we are," piped the quarrelsome voice of Agnes, walking behind them alongside their mother. "Our own family historian treating us to yet another lecture."

"Ha! I am more than an historian. I am a visionary! I dream of a world where women can dine at a fine hotel for tea *without* having to be accompanied by a gentleman," Nellie retorted.

Just as their entourage arrived at the Vesey Street entrance to the Astor House Hotel, Mr. Entwhistle jumped out of a carriage.

"How very fortuitous," said Mrs. Entwhistle. She smiled fondly at her husband.

He rubbed his hands. "I'm anticipatin' a *grrrand* and tasty meal, accompanied by all o'me beauties. Oh, tarry a moment." He suddenly turned back to the cab. He reached into the hansom and pulled out a colorful bunch of flowers. He ran his free hand over his hair. "Almost forgot, these are fer ye." He thrust them at Cornelia.

Speechless, Nellie accepted the bouquet, the colors so vibrant they brought tears to her eyes. "I have nary seen such a panoply of color gathered in one bunch." She gazed in wonder at the magenta and purple fuchsia, the blue delphiniums, sunshine yellow black-eyed Susans and orange Gerbera daisies; exotic flowers that grew in no garden Nellie ever saw. "Are these enchanted?" she whispered.

"Who has endowed you with such splendor?" Anastasia demanded.

Nellie separated the flowers, revealing a card.

"What does it say?" Even Agnes was interested.

Nellie opened the card, and closed her mouth.

"Do not toy with our emotions," entreated Anastasia. "Whose name is signed?"

Agnes said with exasperation, "Cornelia Rose you have such a flair for the dramatic."

Even Mrs. Entwhistle was curious. "Who is the mysterious suitor?" she asked.

"I know not!" Nellie said. "This note is hardly enlightening. All that is written is 'A bouquet of magical color from your admirer!'" She turned to her father. "Papa, who gave these to you?"

Mr. Entwhistle's eyes twinkled. He replied, "Sure 'n begora, I'll not play cupid."

"Do not amplify the mystery, Papa. From whom did you receive these flowers?"

"I was sworn to secrecy. I know me little romantic colleen loves a good mystery, and to that end I'll only reveal that even I am unsure whether I was given t' flowers from a mere messenger or t' true sender."

Nellie stood in bewilderment, staring at the note.

"Now come along, ladies." Mrs. Entwhistle used her no-nonsense voice. Nellie, Anastasia, and Agnes remained immobile; Nellie looking at her flowers, Anastasia admiring the architecture of the grand Astor House and Agnes leaning with a look of wonderment on the great Doric columns at the grand entranceway.

"Agnes, ladies do not *lean*, they stand straight with good posture at all times. Anastasia, we do not gaze upward at the entablature and gawk, no matter how magnificent the design and construction and Cornelia Rose...*ach du Liebe!* Ladies do come along!" Mrs. Entwhistle nodded to the doorman, who sprang forward to open the door.

"Yea, me stomach tells me 'tis long past tea time. I've traveled a long way for me tea, and I intend to imbibe a bit o' t' delicacies post haste," said Mr. Entwhistle with his hearty laugh.

Nellie stood still as her family filed through the door, held open with continual flourishes by the doorman. She took another look at the brilliant array of colors. A dreamy smile played on her lips, lighting her whole face. *I have a secret admirer! One who has dazzled me with the most exotic flowers, blooming in intoxicating colors! No need to fret over who he be, or spend time sleuthing to ascertain his identity – this is heady enchantment. I do not believe there ever was a lady so inundated with blissful bounty. Truly, I am blessed.*

She tightened her grip on the flowers with her left arm and with her right hand she picked up her skirts and petticoats and swept through the doorway with her own grand flourish.

CHAPTER 12
Sugar, You are my Candy Girl

Sing Sing, February 1849

The days after her "unofficial" debut continued to provide a delightful uptick in the number of invitations Cornelia Rose and her sisters received from various fashionable members of Sing Sing's high society. Now a steady stream of eligible suitors crossed the Entwhistle threshold daily. In a reprieve from instruction at Miss Sarah's, the ladies devoted their mornings to receiving callers.

"Here comes a great paper of candy along with Barney Forshay!" exclaimed Agnes, looking down from their garret window as the girls prepared to welcome their guests. "I shall treasure it better than Barney's company, for he has been to see me every day of this past fortnight and candy has not."

In spite of their annoyance at Agnes's usual ill-tempered observation, Anastasia and Nellie laughed.

"I must agree," said Anastasia, all smiles. "It seems we have no dearth of male attention. However, that treat is less sweet than other delights of the confectionary persuasion."

"Let us garner bonbons of our own," declared Nellie. Her sisters looked at her with blank stares. "We must host a taffy pull! 'Tis the perfect weather, and perfect season for a social gathering of sweets." She winked.

Anastasia squealed with delight. "Another of your delightful puns," said Anastasia.

Even Agnes laughed and said, "Capitol plan."

Anastasia squealed again and Matthias came running. "Another mouse?" he asked, looking around the room. "Where is he, I need another pet."

Now all the girls squealed at that repugnant thought.

Agnes took the lead in disabusing him. "Sakes alive, no. Matthias, ever since we got our new cat Smedley our garret has been free of those loathsome, ugsome creatures entirely."

Matthias looked crestfallen.

Nellie gathered him in for a hug. "However, you might be pleased to learn the true reason for Anastasia's squeal." Nellie smiled down at her little brother. Matthias, disappointment temporarily arrested, looked up expectantly. "We propose to host a taffy pull."

Matthias gave his own gleeful squeal. "Nellie, you are right, that is far superior. It is doubly better, because we'll get candy, and I'll make sure the spills don't get cleaned up and then we'll get more mice too."

The girls laughed as Matthias ran away.

The day of the social dawned fair, crisp, and cold.

"A picture-perfect setting, right out of a print of Currier and Ives," said Cornelia, a dreamy look in her eyes. "I will be hard pressed to tolerate the interminable wait for today's festivities to begin."

Anastasia sniffed the air. The sisters discerned the unmistakable aroma of bubbling molasses.

Matthias ran in. "It's starting to boil!" he shouted, running out of their room.

The sisters all clattered down the back stairs behind him.

"A herd of elephants," grumbled their mother, but she turned from the hot flame over which she was presiding and smiled at her daughters. Several quarts of molasses were gaining heat in four big cauldrons on the massive potbellied stove.

"Steam is gathering!" shouted Matthias and scampered away.

The giggling girls ran back up the stairs to get ready while Mrs. Entwhistle and Cook Hilda monitored and stirred the pots simmering over the low flames.

Before long the guests arrived. The hallway was filled with a party hubbub until the enticing aroma of bubbling sugar lured everyone into the kitchen. Guests wandered in and out, assessing the progress of the cooking molasses. One group gasped when the boiling dark mass in one of the pots suddenly rose to the top, threatening to erupt from its container. But Gertrude Entwhistle was right there, festively aproned, stirring spoon ready. She modulated the flame, stirred the pot, and prevented disaster.

Matthias interrupted Nellies' conversation with Augusta to pull her back into the kitchen to witness the next step in the taffy preparation.

Mrs. Entwhistle bent over the side table, carefully measuring bicarbonate of soda. Matthias jumped up and down as their mother scurried back and forth to the stove, four times, stirring the stabilizer into each of the pots.

"That completes the final step!" he shouted. He smacked his lips.

The crowd ebbed and flowed past the prime pot viewing spots, wandering through the parlor and the sitting room, pausing in front of roaring fire in the each of the magnificent hearths.

Nellie jittered from one room to the next, greeting all the guests, chattering with her high energy vivacity, with one eye on their massive front doors and their butler who alternated between opening the door and gathering discarded wraps. Nellie could not wait to see George Brandreth again. *But will he grace me with his presence? Has my teatime conversation been sufficiently witty to entice his attendance at my taffy social?* Nellie fidgeted with a wisp of hair straying from her newly coiffed hair, poised, as if ready for flight, in the archway of their drawing room. *Where was he?* she worried. A figure reflected in the large mirror temporarily arrested her attention. Hannah Agate stood sideways to the mirror, but from Nellie's angle it was obvious that Hannah was watching herself. *What possesses Hannah? Has she never gazed at her own reflection? No, that is impossible, she is from a founding family in Sparta, living in a veritable palace on Revolutionary Road — there must be rooms full of looking glasses. Mayhap she suffers from extreme vanity?* Nellie stifled a nervous giggle. *What an odious character flaw.*

Hannah shifted her gaze and caught Nellie looking at her. She sniffed and stalked to Nellie's side. "I am eager, yet apprehensive, at the thought of the arrival of Mr. George Brandreth. Ostensibly Mr. Brandreth is the only eligible suitor for a woman of *my* breeding in our entire village! My mother has assured me of his affections. I hope to secure his attentions this afternoon." Hannah turned back to the mirror and smoothed her flounces, not even polite enough to listen to any reply from Nellie.

The conceit! Nellie fumed. *I am sure she only favored me with her agenda of machinations because I caught her admiring herself. Ha! Mr. Brandreth is* my *beau. He will pay his attentions to me.*

"Nellie!" Augusta grabbed Cornelia's hand and drew her toward the kitchen. "Come join Nathaniel and me at the taffy pull."

"I am presently occupied," Nellie said, in a flat voice, with a formal bend of her head. She pulled her hand back.

Augusta did not take offense, rather she laughed. "Pining at the door is your employment?" she asked.

Nellie did not answer. She turned her attention back to the ornately carved mahogany front door again, willing it to open.

Then it did.

"Lo and behold," she whispered to herself. "He has arrived!"

George Brandreth stepped into the foyer with that easy grace men his size and stature seem born with. Nellie could not take her eyes off him. He greeted the butler with courtesy, his mouth smiling, his eyes traveling the room. Nellie saw with relief his eyes passed right over Hannah Agate without a pause. When they landed on Nellie, his eyes lit up. Nellie responded with her own glow.

Brandreth was at her side in a heartbeat. *My own, quite audible, heartbeat!* Nellie thought.

"How dashing you look in your casual cut afternoon jacket," she said, her lightheartedness and happiness spilling into her declaration. Hannah turned her head at the sound of Nellie's voice and gave a look that could kill. Nellie did not even notice.

"I do cut a most romantic figure, do I not?" said George, in such teasing, happy-go-lucky tone it did not sound like boasting.

"Indeed," agreed Nellie. She hesitated. *What is our next course of action? Next conversation?* She panicked, hearing Hannah rustling toward them.

She need not have feared. Brandreth bowed over her hand. "May I escort you to the taffy pulling area, so we might choose the best candy for the prettiest hostess?"

A shade lighter than pink colored Nellie's cheeks, and she brushed that stray strand of hair off her forehead. Brandreth tucked her hand under his elbow and steered her toward the kitchen, right past the foiled Hannah.

Conversation flowed easily between them as Nellie floated in happiness through her own front parlor. In the kitchen, they stopped beside the great cauldron on the stove, watching Mrs. Entwhistle continue to preside over the percolating, fragrant mass.

"Time for testing!" announced Mrs. Entwhistle. Some of the guests pressed closer.

"I am unfamiliar with the taffy testing protocol," whispered George in her ear. The whisper sent delightful tickles through Nellie's ear and down her back.

Nellie said in a conversational volume, "Watch the taffy as my mother extracts it—it will make threads when dipped in cold water, which means the treat is one step closer to ready!"

"Yes," said Anastasia at Nellie's other elbow. "Next, the taffy will form a soft ball when immersed in the cold water."

Augusta took up the instruction from across the room, saying, "Finally, when the tested lump turns from a soft ball to a stiff ball of taffy — the candy is ready to pull!"

The group waited expectantly, as the batch boiled for a few more minutes.

At last, Mrs. Entwhistle pulled one pot from the flame and ladled large scoops of the sticky mass directly onto the marble kitchen table.

"Steam rising," squealed Matthias, eyes level to the table top, pointing.

The whole group laughed.

Cook returned the cauldron to the stove as Nellie and Agnes reached for the already-buttered pans. After only a few minutes of cooling, Mrs. Entwhistle scraped the boiled molasses off the table plopping little portions into pan after pan. The girls ferried them to the great dining room table to cool further.

Groups gathered around the pans, and began to spread butter on their hands. Agnes buttered Matthias' hands. He promptly scooted under the massive table, and licked all the butter off. "Delicious," he giggled.

"If you like the butter, wait until you taste the taffy," said Augusta, with a merry, conspiratorial wink.

"It couldn't be better!" said Matthias.

"You will soon see, you are mistaken," said Nellie. "Taffy is a naughty food — blobs of butter, lashings of sugar and syrup and *Mutter* even put some chocolate in one group's batch!"

Matthias's eyes grew round. "I will join the chocolate group," he promised.

Brandreth and Nellie finally took a turn at the big tub of butter Mother had filled to the brim in preparation for the party. *Mercy,* Nellie thought, peering down into its depths. *It is already half depleted!* Nellie took a scant scoop, hoping there was still enough for all the guests, and delicately rubbed it into the palms of her hands. She held them aloft like a surgeon, careful not to put her hands anywhere near her lace bodice.

Brandreth dug into the pot and gave himself a generous scoop, lathering it all over his hands, both the palms and the backs. "I confess I have been a tad too generous with my portion," he said. He winked at Nellie and stepped in closer. "However, I have devised a remedy for my greed." He reached out and grabbed both of Nellie's hands in his large ones, coating hers with gobs of butter. Laughing, and before Nellie could think of a polite way to protest, Brandreth began massaging her hands and then each individual finger, "I assure you this is the only cure. I must smother these delicate dainties in butter!"

The touch turned from flippant to firm. Nellie felt a thrill of intimacy at the change. She looked down at her fingers. Tingles from the contact traveled up her arms to tantalize her thoughts. *A decidedly romantic figure, pulling on my heartstrings via my digits! Simply heavenly.*

Forgetting where she was, Nellie looked up into Brandreth's eyes and flashed a big smile. *He seems smitten too!*

"Ahem!" a voice said loudly in her ear. The sound broke the spell and Brandreth removed his hands. Annoyed, Nellie wheeled around to give a quiet tongue lashing to the fool who had caused this folly. She looked up into the angry eyes of Obadiah Wright.

"Mercy! Mr. Wright. You have materialized out of thin air!" Totally flustered Nellie spoke in a voice two octaves higher than a cat screech. "A distinct pleasure to see you again, sir."

"Verily?" Obadiah's voice was as angry as his eyes. "I intended to surprise you with attentions and a visit, but I see the surprise is my own."

Brandreth inserted himself into the conversation, in an effort to be gallant. "Wright, good to see you old boy. I would shake your hand, but I see you are not in the proper form to participate in this frolicsome taffy social."

Obadiah turned those angry eyes on Brandreth. "If I may have a moment of conversation with this young lady?" he asked. The frost on the windows was less icy than his voice.

Brandreth stepped closer. "I am not quite sure the occasion affords it. You see, the taffy pulling is about to begin and we'll not miss it. We're buttoned and buttered in fact. I am afraid we must postpone indefinitely any tête-à-tête between you and my candy girl."

Undeterred from his pursuit of Nellie by an apparent rival, Brandreth grabbed Nellies' buttered hand with his own slippery one and steered her to the pans of molasses waiting to be pulled.

A terse "Good day" grated from Obadiah's throat. He turned on his heel and marched out the door.

"Good riddance to bad rubbish. What bee was in his bonnet? A most disagreeable chap," proclaimed Brandreth. His hands grabbed hers again, hardly touching the taffy.

Nellie blushed and stammered, "I... he is...."

"It makes no never mind." Brandreth waved his hand in dismissal. "He is gone now and we can resume our merrymaking."

Nellie viewed the groups gathered together around their allotted portions, laughing, and talking while they pulled and stretched the warm sticky masses. She had a sinking feeling in the pit of her stomach. She pulled at that stray hair, the strand again dangling this time over her eye, leaving a streak of butter on the offending clump.

Brandreth leaned down toward her. "Come, come, that fellow can get in line. Is he a farmer? Does he not know the proper protocol, to obtain permission before coming to call? 'Tis of no consequence, I tell you." He reached out and brushed that sticky strand off her brow with the tips of his buttery fingers. Now her hair was so full of butter it stuck to her forehead. In spite of the unpleasantness of the situation and the tackiness of his fingers, Nellie giggled, for the tingles came back with that light, intimate touch.

I will wrestle with the devil and my conscience later, she decided. *This is an entertainment I look forward to with great anticipation each year. Furthermore, this year, I am this social's hostess. I will not let one disgruntled suitor dissuade me from my enjoyment.*

Nellie joined in the merriment with all her guests and admired the various shapes that emerged as the product of the gathering's labor. Some groups lay single sticks of taffy, twisted, or curled with a knot on the end. Others braided their sticks, making sure they had enough for each member of their group to take a piece home. Still other groups consumed the candy as they pulled, having little to show for their efforts except full stomachs and happy affects.

Nellie felt a tug on her sleeve as she admired Nathanial and Augusta's neat rows of pulled taffy sticks. She turned to find Brandreth grinning down at her, now hiding his hands behind his back.

"Pray tell, for what have you summoned my attention?" she asked, smiling with a mock stern expression on her face.

"You heartless flirt!" said Brandreth. "I wish to give you *my heart.*"

Nellie drew her breath in sharply, astounded at the boldness of his proclamation. But when Brandreth pulled his hands around and opened them before her she laughed with delight. In his hand was a small pull of taffy, twisted and shaped into a heart. With a flourish, Brandreth bowed and presented the candy to Nellie.

"Take good care of my heart now," teased George.

CHAPTER 13
Downtown

Sing Sing, May 1849

"I did not know you were a shop girl." George Brandreth's frowning face separated itself from the bunch of young men hanging out in front of Hart's Apothecary as Nellie dug her apron out of her bag and closed her parasol to enter the shop.

"A *shop girl?* Of course not," said Nellie with a small laugh as she continued through the door.

"I beg to differ. You are employed by a shopkeeper," said Brandreth, following her into the drugstore and talking to her as if instructing a person of meager intelligence. "Therefore, you are a shop girl."

Mercy! Mutter warned me that working here would give suitors the wrong impression of my social status. Nellie shrugged. *What of it? A 'shop girl' is not worthy of his time? I'll not enlighten him.*

Nellie decided to turn the tables. She gave a flirty little laugh. "I might ask you, kind sir, why you were loitering outside the premises of this fine and noble establishment like a truant schoolboy?" Nellie gave what she hoped was her most engaging smile.

Brandreth hesitated.

"It does not seem worthy of Doctor...." Nellie paused dramatically, "No! *Senator* Brandreth's son to be seen about town, idling and dallying, not gainfully employed."

"I am inventorying Hart's stock of *Brandreth's Pills*, of course. Just monitoring the marketplace for our locally manufactured wonder cure." Brandreth's face relaxed, but his eyes were still hard.

"From *outside* the establishment?" asked Nellie, laughing aloud.

Perhaps her laugh was a bit too taunting, or perhaps young Mr. Brandreth just did not have a sense of humor about himself. He stiffened and said through clenched teeth, "A *shop girl* is not acceptable company for a Brandreth!"

Nellie refused embarrassment, drawing her shoulders' back and standing ramrod straight. "First of all, I am not a 'shop girl,' I am studying herbology and apprenticing to be an apothecist, and secondly..." she said, tossing her head, stray hair whipping into her eyes. "...Your stepmother would have little forbearance for the hoity-toity vagary you just communicated to me! As a former factory-worker, *her* social status was several echelons *below* 'shop girl.'"

She turned on her heel and walked to the back of the store. She slipped behind the counter and put on her work jacket. Brandreth hesitated for a second, but then turned on *his* heel and stalked out of the store. Nellie shook her head. *What did Brandreth say when Obadiah Wright executed that same maneuver? 'Good riddance to bad rubbish.'*

Straightening her apron, she hurried to Dr. Hart, all smiles, in anticipation of her two hours of mixing tinctures and studying medicines.

The time flew by, as Dr. Hart was not only knowledgeable about medicinal remedies unknown to Midwife Rafferty, but was also a great talker, with a dry, droll sense of humor. Nellie absorbed information as fast as it was offered. *When Doctor Hart's chin-wagging gets dry,* Nellie thought to herself, *I can find just as much amusement from the schoolboys hovering over the penny candy, peppering me with questions about the items for sale in the shop.*

In what seemed like only a few minutes, Nellie's lesson ended. Blinking from the late afternoon sun as she stepped out of the apothecary, Nellie almost bumped into Obadiah Wright.

"Good afternoon, Mistress Entwhistle," Obadiah said, giving a stiff bow. "I thought I might just find you here."

"Mercy, you startled me, and very nearly trampled me!" Nellie hoped her focus on the physical near miss would cover her confusion over the fact that he was seeking her company in the first place. *Did he not march out of my house mere months ago? Has he been hiding under a rock? I never expected him to resurface or pursue my favor again.*

"Perhaps you are surprised to see me? I must confess I am a tad abashed at my behavior during our last meeting. I was unaware of your family's taffy social and had presented myself at your dwelling to advise you of my plans to attend Yale University, beginning that very week. If I could have kept but longer away, I might have waxed this speech more poetically. However, some embrocation did assuage my bruised ego during my absence, and now, as the academic term has ended, I find myself back in Sing Sing. I am still uncertain myself as to why I have waited for you to finish your intellectual pursuit at the apothecary to gain an audience with you."

Nellie looked at Obadiah, a frown creasing her forehead. She was unsure whether she wished to continue their conversation. *After that long, waffling, dissertation the import of his desires still remains obtuse,* she thought.

Obadiah hesitated, as if still making up his mind what he wanted to say. Nellie tapped her foot. *I must practice forbearance,* she thought, and forced herself to give a little smile.

Obadiah seemed to reach a decision. "Perchance, I happened to be strolling past this establishment several hours ago, just at the very moment a certain odious Mr. George Brandreth had the audacity to belittle your very noble pursuit of knowledge of healing skills."

Nellie smiled, pleased at the almost hidden compliment.

"I must also confess the earwigged incident gave me pause to reconsider a perhaps hasty decision on my part to abandon all hope of courting you after witnessing the inappropriate comportment you displayed at the taffy social in your own home," Obadiah said.

That was too much for Nellie. Her smiled disappeared and she twisted her mouth to defend herself.

Obadiah held up his hand. "No need to refute my judgment. I am here not to foist it upon you but rather to formally apologize for my hasty departure. Your handling of Mr. Brandreth today leads me to suppose that perhaps I have misjudged your character, yea, your very principled temperament."

These words acted as an incendiary on Nellie. She began to sputter, "By the horn spoons, what gobbledy gook is this? I have a notion to...."

"I see my words have the very opposite effect to the one I desire to achieve."

Obadiah closed his mouth and stepped away from Nellie. "Mademoiselle," he said, pointing his toe forward and bowing very low in an old fashioned courtly gesture. "I would like to apologize for any behavior heretofore, which I may have exhibited, which may have transgressed your delicate emotions or trespassed on your very fine humor. I beg leave to seek an audience with you. To that end, I beg the honor of accompanying you on a promenade across Sing Sing's finest architectural feat, the grand arch of the Croton water supply system."

Recovering her good humor, intrigued by Obadiah's interest in 'courting her,' Nellie had the grace to smile her consent to a walk. "'Tis a lovely afternoon for a walk. It would be a pity to let such an opportunity pass, unheeded. Have you strolled the aqueduct trail before? Are you familiar with its history?" she asked.

"I have viewed the magnificent arch, spanning the wide Sing Sing Kill from many an angle — the mill on the bank, the haberdashery window, the path beneath it. I confess however, I have never walked across it."

Mercy, so many confessions in one short conversation, Nellie giggled to herself.

Obadiah took her arm. They crossed the street, Obadiah deftly shielding her from a stray dog and an errant hay cart driver, walking towards the entrance of the wide promenade that led across the arch.

"Verily, this promenade is one of my favorite strolls, any time of year. Nonetheless in spring, festooned with luscious blossoms...." Nellie gestured to the wisteria that hung over the entrance and the morning glory wrapped around the post. "...The perambulation is transformed into a journey through heaven."

Obadiah glanced down at her, an amused smile peeking out from under his mustache. That was all the encouragement Nellie needed.

"This juncture in the conversation demands presentation of the element of man-made ingenuity. The span of the arch is eighty-eight feet — and every heady foot affords spectacular views both up the kill and down toward and across the mighty Hudson River. Why, did you know that the centering of the arch was based on the architectural design adopted for the famous Waterloo Bridge at London?" she asked.

Surprise halted Obadiah. "Man alive! Through what course of education have you acquired this depth of knowledge of the properties of the arch?"

Nellie smiled, proud of her expertise. "As you will recall, my father engineered the Aqueduct project."

"Yes." Obadiah rubbed his mustache with a rueful gesture. "I was schooled in great detail in his workplace education, as I recall."

Nellie gave him a funny look. *By whom, I wonder?* she thought. "Yes, well, for a quick dispatch of the matter, let me advise that through an inquisitive mind, a photographic memory and hard work, my father went from a common laborer to an assistant to the chief engineer, Mr. John Jervis."

"Verily, you remember Mr. Jervis discussing the mechanics of the construction of the bridge?" Obadiah smiled down at her as they walked. "You were a mere child at the time of its construction. Surely you were not that precocious, even if as a little pitcher you had big ears."

"I did *rather* enjoy Papa regaling us at the dinner table with the trials and tribulations of the construction project. However, I do confess the chief engineer himself gave a fine lecture right here at Town Hall last month, presenting the intricacies of the considerations of construction in anticipation of the tenth anniversary of the project's completion."

Obadiah had steered them towards the perimeter, and now Nellie paused at the wall protecting sightseers from toppling down the chasm into the kill. "The most spectacular aspect of this engineering wonder of course, is not the engineering at all."

Obadiah's smile turned into a quizzical expression, his interest again piqued. "Is that so?"

"Most decidedly. The most spectacular quality of this arch is the view it affords of God's engineering—the glorious Hudson River and its surrounding mountains."

"Well spoken," Obadiah confirmed. He tucked her hand back into the crook of his elbow. Both smiling, they continued their walk across the span.

CHAPTER 14
School Days

Sing Sing, October 1849

An invitation to a Soiree at The United States Military Academy at West Point! Nellie smiled from ear to ear at the thought.

But, with Elmer P. Otis? She sighed. *Could any alliance be more repugnant? How ever did Mutter manage to place me in this predicament? Mutter says I must entertain this most eligible suitor, but truly Elmer? The mere thought makes me bilious.*

"*Mutter*, can I accompany Cornelia on her trip to West Point Academy? After all, I have also made my debut, and seem to have a dearth of qualified suitors," Anastasia said. Her lips twisted with self-doubt and uncertainty as to the cause of the lull in suitors. She shook her head, and jumped back into selling her plan to their mother. "I would ensure that she had good companionship, whilst assessing the eligible suitors residing there myself."

"*I* would ensure that both Cornelia *and* her suitor were properly chaperoned," said Agnes. The women turned to her in surprise.

Agnes interested in West Point society? Unimaginable! But thank you, Agnes, thought Nellie, for her mother immediately rose to the bait and charged forward.

"It is lovely to see my daughters championing each other's welfare," her mother declared. "You young ladies have banded together in such a pragmatic fashion. Yes! Of course, we should *all* go. We will make a grand foray into West Point society! I will correspond with the Superintendent's wife, and the wives of other officers responsible for arranging the social activities and advise them that you three *lovely* un-betrothed women will be attending *all* of the festivities, appropriately chaperoned, of course, by your mother."

There's the sticky wicket. Mutter will chaperone. Mercy, what am I thinking. The sticky wicket is of course suitor Elmer P. Otis. No! No! I will never *even* consider *Elmer an eligible suitor.*

Within minutes Mrs. Entwhistle had outlined all the details necessitated by this adventure from new dresses to a stay at the West Point Hotel. In spite of her dread of the actual person responsible for the outing, Nellie could not resist anticipating the exciting excursion to the famed Military Academy. *The new dresses alone may well be worth suffering through an intolerable interaction with old Elmer.*

How vilely shallow, she thought. *Surely, I have sufficient social graces to competently handle even this most troublesome companion.*

"Since you have such a fine outing all arranged, *Mutter*, I will be off to practice my midwifery skills with Mrs. Rafferty," said Nellie. "Then I will be joining Augusta and Mrs. Van Cortlandt for tea."

"No, your tea time and afternoon will be spent learning the history of West Point. Along with your sisters, you will familiarize yourselves with the names of some of its professors and leaders, and all its illustrious graduates. We only have six short months." Her mother shook her head to affirm her better-not-argue-with-me tone.

Nellie threw back her head and raised the back of her hand to her forehead. "Mercy, if I must labor under such stress, I propose that we include my dear companion Augusta in our merry group." Her sisters giggled.

Mrs. Entwhistle looked as if she was about to object, but Nellie elaborated on her argument. She said, "After all, Nathaniel Foster entered the Military Academy along with Elmer. Since he and Augusta are betrothed, it stands to reason that by the time of our outing, Augusta will already be an authority on the etiquette and protocol demanded during a West Point visit."

"Very well. But be advised, you must include 'paying attention' in your afternoon agenda of whispering secrets, giggling, and over-all merry making," said her mother. "I will be testing your knowledge before our voyage, to ensure you have retained the proper information and can conduct a well-educated conversation with the Superintendent, his wife, and the other dignitaries." Her mother nodded her head to emphasize her point.

"An examination of all that I have retained? Surely you jest!" exclaimed Nellie.

"I kiddeth not. An ability to converse with intelligence and wit on a subject dear to the listener's heart must be sedulously cultivated.

"You ladies have a very fine example of excellent social skills in our recently replaced First Lady, Julia Tyler. The 'Rose of Long Island' is an exemplar of the behavior I wish you to emulate." Nellie's mother was already in instruction mode.

"Mrs. Tyler is definitely gay, charming, and fashionable," agreed Anastasia, with the clasped hands and dreamy sigh of a lady trying to imitate a princess.

"Sakes alive! *Mutter,* how very shallow. I shall choose to emulate our current First Lady Sarah Polk. It is behind her skirts that President Polk rose to power. She is his personal secretary and confidante. *I* believe Mrs. Polk is the intellect that actually writes the president's speeches. She is the epitome of a modern, accomplished woman," said Agnes, with a single raised eyebrow to emphasize her point.

Land sakes! thought Nellie. *Agnes lavishing praise on a prominent lady? Who knew she valued articulate, educated women so?*

Nellie's rebellious streak reared its ugly head as she decided to correct Agnes and establish her independent thinking in one dramatic proclamation. "Agnes, you are incorrect. Our *current* First Lady is Margaret Smith Taylor, a First Lady *I* will emulate! Since her husband's inauguration this March she visibly remains the pistol carrying, soldier nursing, bold frontier woman she always was, leaving the frivolity of the high falutin' entertaining of the nation to her youngest daughter."

"*Ach du Liebe!* Must you insist on accolades and admiration for a backwoods frontier gal? Cornelia Rose, I expect more educated aspirations and emulations from my daughters, especially my historian turned midwife," reproached her mother.

"If compelled to be the rendezvous of Elmer P. Otis for the length of an *entire* escapade at West Point, eschewing other romantic liaisons, making it possible for my sisters to meet the men of their dreams, while I am at the beck and call of a *dolt* of a boy, then I must be allowed to express my true feelings elsewhere," Nellie replied, trying once again in vain, to raise only one eyebrow.

"You have charted a course to endure all this pain of apprehension although the offense may never occur. Tsk, tsk." Mrs. Entwhistle shook her head. "Now, *raus mit du!* Be industrious in your pursuits until teatime. We will take tea in the library, as it provides a fitting ambiance for our lessons."

Mrs. Entwhistle drew on her own vast intellect and store of knowledge to devise engaging sessions of study. Not only did they explore the history of West Point, but also the current affairs, policy, and politics in and surrounding the Academy. While Nellie most enjoyed the week they studied the various authors and dignitaries who were frequent guests at the campus, even she had to admit learning the illustrious history of West Point with her sisters and her friend Augusta was scintillating.

One evening during dinner preparation, apropos of nothing, Mrs. Entwhistle asked, "Did you read in the morning's paper of the death of Edgar Allen Poe—that macabre poet who attended West Point?"

"Why should I learn about him? He was expelled from the Military Academy in 1838," replied Nellie.

"Well done, Cornelia Rose," approved Mrs. Entwhistle, smiling and turning back to her leg of lamb.

"I would not award her response such swift sanction," said Anastasia. "That answer hardly merits a 'fair reply'." Nellie looked up from fetching the pickled beets, surprised that Anastasia sought to discredit her knowledge.

"*Warum?* Why would you be miserly with your praise?" asked Mrs. Entwhistle, her back turned to them, leaning into the oven, sprinkling pinches of salt and garlic over the lamb.

"Because Nellie did not mention that Poe's dismissal sprang from a nefarious incident," said Anastasia with a smirk.

"Now Anastasia, please remember your manners. Is it absolutely necessary to delve into those tawdry particulars?" Mrs. Entwhistle's disapproval was evident.

"Stasia, are you referring to Poe disobeying orders to wear white gloves at muster for roll call?" asked Nellie.

Agnes interrupted with her too-ready opinion. "That is *hardly* tawdry, *Mutter!*"

"Goodness no," Anastasia agreed, innocuously enough. "In fact, Poe obeyed *that* order."

Agnes and Nellie looked at each other, shrugging.

"He reported to roll call wearing *only* white gloves!" said Anastasia.

Agnes gasped aloud.

So did their mother, which was shocking since none of her daughters had ever heard her emit such an unladylike noise before.

Nellie tried to stifle a giggle, but failed. *Only Stasia possessed the audacity and impertinence to convey that anecdote to Mutter!*

"Anastasia — Penelope — Entwhistle! What a shockingly insolent fact to recount! *Was ist los mit du*?" Mrs. Entwhistle wiped her hands on her apron in agitation, as if she were trying to wipe out the obscene image of the unclothed Poe.

"*Mutter*, I am merely complying, and in accord, with your desires," Anastasia said. Her eyes danced in glee. "I agree that to appear well informed we must be able to discourse on a variety of subjects, *but* to be truly interesting and witty conversationalists we must propose many *different* points of view!"

CHAPTER 15
Sit Down, You're Rocking the Boat

From Sing Sing to West Point, March 1850

Cornelia shivered and pulled her cape tighter around her shoulders.

Goodness this wind earns March its reputation for bluster. Would that it was April. One would never contemplate such gales in April. But Mercy! April could saddle us with rain showers. Far worse. Oh, I should never curse the weather — each season has its beauty.

She scanned the sky from her perch at the bow of the Hudson Day Line steamboat, making its way toward the final loop in the 'S' curve of the river which signaled the imminent appearance of the West Point quay.

Nary a cloud visible, she thought with satisfaction. *I shall wear my orchid organdy to the parade. Thank the Lord I added that to my valise at the last moment before closing my cases.*

Lifting her head as if to match the full force of the stiff breeze with an energy of her own, Nellie squeezed her companion Augusta's hand and whispered, "We have almost arrived at this long-anticipated destination."

"Ladies, ready your parasols, but do not open them until we land," Mrs. Entwhistle commanded. "Lord knows your complexions have already suffered from the overexposure to wind and sun afforded by your insistence in riding *above* deck rather than in the ladies' sitting room below."

"I am sorry to be such the contrarian," Augusta offered. "I suffer horribly from seasickness. I could not stomach the ride in the compartment — I would fret and sweat so below."

"Goodness! Ladies never sweat! Horses sweat. Men perspire. A lady merely glows." Nell's mother was perturbed by Augusta's vulgarity and mercifully thrown off the subject of their exhilarating ride at the bow of the ship. "Cornelia. I *instructed* you to *never* remove your gloves in public!"

"But *Mutter*, they itched so horribly. Determining the source of the irritation necessitated their removal," Nellie defended herself.

"Never in public. You will see, that small *faux pas* will have large repercussions," her mother warned.

The boat nudged the dock and the girls lost their footing, falling against each other and the rail. Their possessions spilled from their hands and tumbled around the wet deck.

Praise the Lord! Naught fell overboard. Nellie and Augusta scrambled to retrieve their dropped items. Mother remained erect, with perfect posture. She raised one eyebrow in reproof, but turned to gather her own hand luggage, and her other daughters.

Diving down to the deck to retrieve her glove, Nellie noticed men loitering about the dock, waiting for the arrival of the ships bearing weekend guests.

"I am all a-titter with eagerness," she exclaimed.

"As am I," Augusta confessed.

The girls rushed to the gangway to disembark.

PART TWO

NEW YORK

CHAPTER 16
Before the Parade Passes By

West Point, March 1850

"I was rather overheated hiking up the hill to our hotel. Perhaps it was the indignity of following the handcart like a common bar maid," Augusta admitted. She puffed another application of powder on her round shoulders, peeking out of the tops of the sleeves of her gown.

"But of course, you did not perspire!" Nellie giggled.

Augusta laughed. "Goodness, never! But my glow would have outshone a field of fireflies on a June night!

"I hope my sweltering state did not lead me to choose too light a silk for our attendance at the parade."

Mrs. Entwhistle charged into their dressing room when she heard that question. "Too light? I think not. Too scant about the shoulders for day wear—I believe so!"

"*Mutter!* Augusta is not your daughter! She can choose whatever lawn gown her heart desires," declared Nellie.

"Cornelia, while Mistress Van Cortlandt is in my charge I am bound and determined to ensure no ill befalls her. In that gown, outside in the bold sunlight, in the midst of literally an army of men, I will not be responsible for her safety." Gertrude Entwhistle threw back her head and glared at her daughter.

Quite melodramatic Mutter! thought Nellie, but did not dare to contradict her.

Augusta did not quibble. "I will choose another gown *post haste*. I do not mean to give you a moment's concern Mrs. Entwhistle! I am so appreciative of the opportunity to visit my dear Nathaniel, especially since my own family was unavailable to chaperone me on this trip. In point of fact, I struggled to choose between this gown and my ruffled taffeta in the first place."

Ribbons, flounces, a buttonhook and even some powder flew as Augusta changed and the girls scurried about making their final toilettes. The girls chattered happily. Agnes, in a rare good mood, generously lent Anastasia her second-best bonnet, since it matched the trim on Anastasia's gown perfectly.

Augusta used the time it took to change into her new gown to lecture the Entwhistle girls on her prior experiences of the scheduled events. "The parade will be thrilling! Oh, my heart stood quite on edge when I saw the rows and rows of cadets, keeping brilliant time to the music, all marching together, as with a single, unified step. Cornelia, *you* most certainly will be roused to poetry upon viewing the grandeur and symmetry of this patriotic exhibition." The girls sat, spellbound at Augusta's words. Pleased with her captivated audience, Augusta continued, "The dinner will be a four-course meal—one of the many reasons it was so wise, Mrs. Entwhistle, that you prepared only a light repast for our picnic basket on the river." She nodded to the fair lady who graciously inclined her head.

"But the most exciting event by far will be the cotillion tonight! West Point soirees are unparalleled in their opulence."

Nellie shivered in anticipation. Anastasia, so captivated by this fascinating information, stood listening, hairbrush in hand, half her hair pinned and the rest, still wildly undone from the windy boat ride, cavorting on her head.

Reveling in the attention, Augusta lowered her voice to increase the drama. "Ladies, the most important piece of information of all concerns a certain promenade dubbed 'Flirtation Walk'."

All the young ladies began to talk at once. Augusta held up her hand, commanding silence.

"That handsome cadet already explained it to me," Nellie said, before Augusta could continue her lecture. "Flirtation Walk is merely a promenade to the historic site where the Great Chain was strung across the Hudson River during the Revolutionary War. Its path begins near the dock where our steamboat anchored."

"No!" Augusta said with such a vehemence the other girls jumped. "*Formerly* it was a path to the Great Chain earthen fortification. *Now* it is the only place on this military base where cadets are permitted to take their female visitors *unchaperoned!*"

The girls gasped. Anastasia dropped her brush. Even Agnes looked duly impressed by this scintillating statement.

"Sakes alive!" Agnes whispered.

Augusta, pleased with this reaction, continued, "Ladies, I have not yet disclosed the most shocking part." She paused for an even greater theatrical effect. Thrilled that she commanded their rapt attention, she leaned closer and dropped her voice to a whisper. "The culmination of the walk..."

The sisters all took two steps closer to the mirrored table where Augusta sat. Even Mrs. Entwhistle paused in her preparations to listen.

"...The figurative apex, a compulsory stopping point, popular with *all* of the cadets is... 'kissing rock'!" Augusta leaned back and smiled broadly, waiting for the melodrama of her statement to cause a response from her listeners.

The Entwhistle sisters all began talking at once.

"It cannot be so!"

"The gentlemen cadets try to *kiss* us?"

"Kissing! How scandalous!"

"Augusta Phillipa Fredericka Van Cortlandt!" Mrs. Entwhistle said. "How on earth did you obtain such information? Have you frequented this place?"

Augusta had the grace to look shocked. "Frequented? Most certainly not!"

Mrs. Entwhistle gave a 'harrumph.'

"Howsoever, my *trusted fiancé*, has escorted me on this promenade, upon occasion, which conduct I do not think inappropriate, in any manner, for an affianced couple." Augusta stood up and looked Mrs. Entwhistle squarely in the eye.

"Now, now, dear Augusta. I certainly did not mean to imply anything to the contrary. Howsoever," Mrs. Entwhistle repeated Augusta's words and raised her eyebrows. "As your guardian for this expedition, and in the interest of steering my own impressionable daughters on a smooth course to matrimony, I must make all the relevant inquiries concerning every obstacle and potential pitfall which might veer us off course," said Mrs. Entwhistle patting Augusta on the shoulder.

Nellie raised her eyebrows but said nothing.

"Come, come, ladies. Make haste! It is time to be underway." Mrs. Entwhistle turned toward the wardrobe for her shawl and parasol, took one final glance in the mirror to make sure her hat pin was still secure and moved to the door of their chamber.

Agnes and Anastasia scrambled around in the wardrobe for their final accessories.

"Am I presentable?" Nellie asked Augusta.

Instead of a reply, Augusta pulled her in close and whispered in her ear, "Do you still correspond with Obadiah?" Nellie pulled back in surprise but Augusta continued, "You managed to avoid answering Nathaniel's direct question at the wharf upon our arrival. Furthermore, your head seemed to be turned many a time by the men straggling about, in the brief duration of our appearance at the dock."

Nellie blushed at the memory of the many romantic approaches she fielded from the bench full of cadets at the quay in the short time after their arrival. "I *do* correspond — quite regularly, in fact with Mr. Wright. Obadiah has beautiful penmanship."

"Beautiful penmanship?" Augusta stepped back and gave a merry laugh, but raised her eyebrows in an arch expression. "Nothing quite turns a girl's head like beautiful penmanship." She winked at Nellie.

Cornelia Rose blushed, but mercifully was spared the necessity of a response as Mrs. Entwhistle opened the door and sailed out into the hallway of the hotel.

We are on our way to the parade! Nellie thought. She marched toward the door, but then turned and ran back to the table for her itchy gloves.

Mrs. Entwhistle escorted the ladies to the one o'clock parade since all of the cadet escorts were already in formation; platoons stacked one behind the other. Their group joined a stream of beautifully attired women, silks sailing in the brisk gusts of wind, coursing into viewing stands on the northern part of the Great Plain. The merry maidens passed the long gray line of men, in a colorful, blithe parade of their own.

The pageantry of the cadets marching across the parade grounds, feet rising and falling in unison, in perfect cadence, thrilled the female spectators. The rousing music of the United States Military Academy band further quickened Nellie's heartbeat.

Behind her fan Augusta whispered to Nellie, "'Tis a marvel how striking each man looks in his uniform, whether he be a pasty-faced city boy, or weathered, sun-kissed youth who heretofore knew only the plow or the rifle in some backwoods country. Truly, the training and the uniform homogenize these disparate men into a squadron."

"I understand that men from all parts of the country seek admission to this prestigious Academy, yet these men all blend together as one unit," responded Nellie.

Augusta giggled. "I was here the first week after Nathaniel reported for duty. The assemblage was not the well-oiled machine it is today. It was a rather ludicrous spectacle of tobacco chewing Westerners stepping on the toes of scowling Southerners, with New Englanders watching, mouths agape, instead of marching along. Backwoods Frontier boys trod the wrong way, on the wrong foot, all prodded and pushed by instructors and drill sergeants. Verily, those Plebes represented every state of our Union, from Maine to Texas."

"In a few short months, marching and drilling transformed them into a blended and harmonized corps of soldiers," marveled Nellie.

"How sweet does this music fall on one's ear," Anastasia leaned over to exclaim.

The parade held the enthralled attention of the ladies. When the cadets cleared the field and the last note died, the ladies heaved sighs of disappointment.

The cadets broke rank and began to filter over to the groups of spectators, milling in front of the Superintendent's review stand.

Nathaniel bowed over Augusta's hand as she said, "We've had such a jolly good time at the parade—we might well be satisfied with martial music at the cotillion tonight!"

"My silly sweet pumpkin," said Nathaniel, tenderness evident in his eyes. "We would not disappoint the bevy of belles gracing us with their presence tonight with anything less than a twenty-piece orchestra, playing all of the dance favorites."

The girls twittered in delight.

The only deleterious note of the day was the agony of watching Elmer P. Otis's maneuvers during their formal dinner.

Elmer only stumbled once on their promenade into the formal dining room. But as they found their assigned table, Otis crumbled to pieces and fumbled with the protocol. Befuddled, he couldn't pick their seats at the long table. First, Elmer held a chair for her and sat down to her right. Then, he immediately stood back up and indicated for her to do the same so he could sit at her left. Finally, blushing, with perspiration already streaming from his pockmarked face, he leapfrogged over her and sat across the table from her. At last he moved back to the seat he first claimed at Nellie's right. His ineptitude and anxiety was excruciating to witness, yet Nellie was powerless to help.

"*Mutter*, my heart palpitates painfully at every awkward misstep," Nellie whispered, her lips practically touching her mother's ear, as her mother sat down next to her.

"Hush, *mit du*," chided her mother.

But when Otis picked up his dessert fork at the top of the plate, rather than the salad fork on the outside of the setting, in the process neglecting to take his cloth napkin and immediately place it on his lap, Mutter leaned closer to Nellie and said, "Mayhap he is a bit green, and unskilled in the social graces."

The group began conversing, first with the dinner partner to the left. Nellie was privy to some observations and instructions from Mrs. Entwhistle.

"I do wonder how it is that I am seated next to *you, Mutter*. Should I not be seated next to that gentleman on the other side?"

"*Natürlich*," said Mutter. "Naturally. I am loath to admit it but, mayhap, your escort did not seat you correctly."

Nellie turned to Elmer, but any thought of conversation flew from her head when she saw that Elmer sat, still perspiring heavily, beads of sweat gathering almost to the dripping point on his forehead and nose. "Are you ill?" she asked, concern for his wellbeing taking precedence over any point of etiquette.

Startled, Elmer looked up, eyes wild and shook his head no.

"Mercy Elmer, then whatever is the matter with your food?"

Elmer kept his gaze on Nellie, misery swimming in his eyes. Then he looked from left to right, and then finally back into her eyes. "We did not say the blessing," he whispered. "Protocol demands that we do not touch a morsel of food until we say the blessing."

Nellie glanced around the large dining hall for evidence of a preacher. None apparent, she noticed the other cadets were already eating. "I am unsure of reason for the lack of benediction," she said. Elmer didn't move. He sat at attention at his plate, his woeful eyes staring straight ahead; sweat now dripping on the tablecloth.

"*Mutter*, I think Elmer needs a priest," Nellie whispered to her mother.

"*Gott im Himmel, was ist los?*" Mrs. Entwhistle broke protocol and leaned around Nellie to look at Elmer. "God in heaven, whatever can the matter be? He looks terrible. Is he ill?"

"No, *no!*" said Nellie. "He cannot eat unless they say a benediction."

"*Ach du Liebe*," said her mother, fanning herself.

"Wait a minute," Nellie said, frowning. She turned to Elmer. "Could you not simply say a blessing to yourself, silently, as I did? Would that not suffice to conform to the protocol? Mayhap that is exercise the other cadets performed?"

Elmer broke into a huge grin. "But of course! That's how we prayed at home! It's just that here, they always order someone to say a blessing out loud and we are forbidden to touch a morsel until the benediction is announced to the platoons."

Mercy! I thought Elmer was a simpleton before he joined the Academy and started following orders. Now the excess of commands has reduced him to dimwitted. Will he never learn how to think for himself?

Nellie shook her head. *Not while he remains in training — independent thinking is not a skill highly regarded here.*

CHAPTER 17
Oh! I Wanna Dance with Somebody

West Point, March 1850

I survived a tedious dinner, filled with multiple faux pas on the part of my escort, and enormous amounts of truly unsavory food, only to be a wallflower *at the cotillion?*

Nellie jealously watched her sisters field lines of bachelor cadets rushing them. Their dance cards were already full. Nellie spied the tall, good-looking cadet who had retrieved her handkerchief exercising his social graces, greeting the hostess and the planning committee. But before she ascertained whether he would approach her, three other cadets approached and each asked for the pleasure of a dance. At each request Nellie hesitated, but then accepted. She was unsure of the protocol as an 'escorted lady.' She quickly scanned the room looking for Augusta. *She would surely provide me sage counsel. If there are only twelve dances at this cotillion, and I am 'escorted' by Elmer for the night, for how many dances am I free to choose another partner?* Since her friend was nowhere in sight, Nellie impulsively allowed each of those three cadets to claim her for a dance, but she did not dare accept any other requests.

Now she stood on the sidelines, listening to the glorious music compelling her to dance. She tapped her feet in tempo with the music, but also with impatience. *Not only am I without a partner for the first dance, but Elmer is curiously absent. What mayhem could he be instigating now, and where?*

Finally, he appeared at her side, midway through the second number, sweat once again beaded on his forehead, his poor complexion unfortunately prominent even in the soft gaslight.

That dance ended and a Virginia reel began; yet Elmer stood, immobile in front of her, but for wiping sweat from his lip. *Must I tell him it is customary to* dance *at a cotillion?* she thought.

A cadet stopped right in front of her and bowed. "May I have this dance?" he asked.

Out of courtesy Nellie turned toward Otis, her eyes seeking his permission.

"Oh, did you want to dance?" he asked, as if the idea only just occurred to him.

The other cadet flushed and requested his name be placed on Nellie's dance card for the next unclaimed dance.

"Lizard," Otis muttered. But Nellie gratefully penciled it in.

Now, in the middle of the first dance with the gawky Elmer, Nellie was quite relieved that her dance card showed a Cadet Zetus S. Searle was soon to be her partner. *How many times must a lady smile through her crushed toes?* she wondered. *And this is a Grand March, such a simple formation, with a Dance Master leading.* She tried to look as if she were enjoying herself and promenade without stumbling over the clumsy Elmer's feet. *Goodness, I thought the cadets all took dancing lessons.*

Elmer smiled down at her. "Is this not wonderful? You are heaven in my arms and my lucky charm. I can never execute these steps during dance instruction. Tonight, I have mastered them! My assigned partner, Cadet La Rhett Livingston must have two left feet and an elbow that is certified as a bayonet. I was beginning to think *I* was deficient, but with you as my partner, I am floating like a dream."

Nellie smiled a genuine smile at the naivety of the statement. *This hardly qualifies as floating! Still, it is somewhat endearing that Elmer P. Otis believes I am 'heaven, and a lucky charm.'* Nellie relaxed just a bit. *After all, he thinks we are floating!* Somehow, she found herself tripping over him less. She took advantage of Elmer's concentration on his steps to look around the huge hall. *Any attempt at conversation seems to further confuse his footwork,* she thought, *I'll just 'float,' preserve my toes that remain unbroken, and observe the other dancers.*

Anastasia swept past her in the arms of a short, stocky cadet who was surprisingly light on his feet. Nellie suppressed a giggle at the look of consternation on Anastasia's face. Anastasia was looking at her feet. *Oh no!* Nellie thought, *'tis a sure path to a misstep.* She caught her sister's eye and gave Stasia a wink. *Smile!* Nellie mouthed. Stasia blushed, but then smiled at her partner who broke out in a broad grin. Stasia swooned in his arms and her next steps flowed more freely. Nellie overheard the cadet say, "Mona Lisa! Your smile is so disarming, an August breeze could knock me flat." Anastasia beamed and the couple danced away.

Nellie glanced around the dance floor again and spotted her sister Agnes with a tall, trim cadet, gliding easily around the perimeter of the dancers. Agnes had an enraptured look on her face. *My goodness, she must be sweet on that cadet,* Nellie thought.

The music stopped and Elmer looked uncertain. The tall cadet that had just been dancing with Agnes appeared at Nellie's side. "Plebe, make foot! I have the next dance," he drawled.

Elmer stiffened to attention; hand still on Nellie's gloved hand.

"Sir, with due respect, sir! This is my drag for the soiree and its attendant events, sir!" Elmer made an attempt to stick up for himself.

"Check the Ladies' dance card, you neophyte," commanded the First Cadet. "For the fifth dance, it lists 'Armistead L. Long.' As you are no doubt painfully aware, this is a superior officer before whom you stand."

Armistead stepped around the still-confused-looking Otis and took Nellie's hand, leading her to the dance floor. Long smiled down at her. "My dear, you cannot be expected to dance this here Virginia reel without a true Virginian."

A Virginia ham by the size of his ego! Poor Agnes, Nellie thought. *Why is this cadet dancing with me when Agnes is so clearly smitten with him?* Nellie looked around for Agnes, and spotted her next to the punch bowl in conversation with yet another cadet.

"You are a splendid dancer, much too good for Otis. Howsoever, I have not come to court you, I have come to ask for your advice." The tall cadet leaned in and swept her around the floor. *Such a graceful dancer and he only wants my advice?*

Surprised, Nellie stepped back, and almost do-si-doing into the couple making an arch next to them. "Don't be alarmed, I simply learned that you are the sister of the lovely Anastasia *and* the enticing Agnes." The smooth dance moves of Long were unbroken by his dubious dialogue.

Enticing Agnes? That's a fine kettle of fish.

Nellie covered her surprise by replying, "Yes, brilliant deduction. However, I am quite befuddled as to why you seek *my* counsel."

"I cannot decide which lady suits me better!" Nellie looked up at him in surprise but the cadet was staring at her two sisters, head moving back and forth as if watching a child's game of shuttlecock.

"For what purpose?" blurted Nellie.

"Why to give my spoony button, of course!" The cadet looked at her as if he suddenly discovered she was half-witted.

Nellie burst out laughing. Long looked offended.

"I beg your pardon for my outburst. I am overcome with shock. Methinks it might require more investment of time than just a few, paltry turns around the dance floor with each of my sisters for you to discern which sister's beauty, temperament, and personality most suit *you*," Nellie said.

"No doubt that is a *fine* flowery speech, but I will be graduating in June and will return to my home state of Virginia. I must have my bride accompany me," said Armistead with a pleading look on his face.

"I am afraid *I* cannot determine the fate of my sisters," declared Nellie. Armistead's face fell; he looked crestfallen and hopeless. Nellie's heart softened. "Ahem, well, has either sister returned your affections?"

"I am afraid I lack the know-how to ascertain that information, I confess. I have no sisters, and no experience with your fair sex. Howsoever, I will rectify this deficiency tonight. I will make one of them my Oh An' Oh," declared Long.

At Nellie's blank stare he explained, "My 'one and only.' Perhaps you could monitor the affections of your sisters as we circle the dance floor and then report back to me."

"You make a preposterous request that I will not honor," declared Nellie.

Armistead stepped back and stopped dancing. The couple behind them stepped on Nellie's foot, and their whole reel derailed. In the ensuing commotion and flurry of apologies Armistead stood looking confused. Nellie felt sorry for the man, in spite of crippling pain in her small toe. *It is undeniably broken*, she diagnosed. The other couple rejoined the formation and danced away. Nellie stood facing Armistead thinking *this dance is an eternity longer than even the ones with Elmer*.

Against her better judgment, and motived by compassion for the dejected, indecisive character standing before her, Nellie said, "Whilst I cannot tell you which of my sisters you should 'spoony button' I am willing to observe their countenances while they dance and inform you if *either* of them appears smitten with you."

"I owe you a lifetime of gratitude," said Armistead. He bowed and turned on his heel, leaving her facing a new partner in the last advance and retire of the reel. *That was rather abrupt!* Nellie thought as she watched him sprint toward Anastasia, breaking in on her dancing partner as the last strains of the fiddle hung in the air.

Elmer immediately appeared at Nellie's side. "No more dancing with other cadets," he decreed.

Nellie looked down at her dance card, tied with a pretty pink ribbon around her wrist. Only the name 'Zetus S. Searle' remained, but Nellie believed he was the stocky cadet who had danced repeatedly with Anastasia. *A rather sad state of affairs,* she thought, *battalions of men and I cannot scare up a dance partner save Elmer and a cadet not only not remotely interested in me, but also simultaneously pursuing both my sisters?*

When Elmer saw only Searle listed on her card he steered her to the punch bowl. Nellie made polite conversation, dredging up interesting facts about West Point drilled into her head by her mother. She offered them to Elmer a tad more willingly when she saw how delighted he was to receive them. The bits of history she communicated sparked Elmer into almost interesting conversation.

"What 'nanty narking'! Who says you even have to dance to have fun at a cotillion?" he asked, his wide smile making his face not displeasing.

Mercy, this is a cruel blow. Tarnation, it is a waltz, Nellie thought. The introduction to *Guntswerber,* the new composition of Johann Strauss II, played softly, the music gathering momentum. Another cadet bowed before her and Nellie's hopes rose.

"Mistress Entwhistle?" he asked. Nellie nodded. "I am Zetus S. Searle. I requested a dance on your dance card...." Nellie handed Otis her punch cup. "...But I am loath to fulfill my obligations." Nellie's face must have registered the shock and chagrin she felt. The cadet rushed on at a pace ill-suited to his southern accent. "My word, my tongue is quite higgledy-piggledy. I humbly apologize for my befuddlement. But I must advise I am too smitten with your fair sister Anastasia to risk trespassing her good nature, even to fulfill an obligation assumed before I made her enchanting acquaintance. Since you are her sister, I am sure you will grant me your understanding."

Nellie sighed. She nodded her head in agreement, not trusting her voice to conceal her disappointment. Cadet Searle bowed again and hurried back to Anastasia.

Nellie resigned herself to tapping her feet from the sidelines. But then she rebelled. *Why must I be deprived of an opportunity to engage in my favorite activity?* She attempted coquetry. "I do *so love* to dance. Perhaps you could find it in your heart to chance another turn around the floor with me?"

Elmer looked unsure.

A passing cadet gave Nellie an appreciative appraisal. He sized Elmer up and growled, "Request the honor of a dance with the lady, you cur."

Nellie tried not to giggle. She decided to help Elmer save face. "I'll strike a bargain with you. I will regale you with all the Academy history I have learned through the careful tutelage of my mother if you promise to soldier on and escort me in a few more turns on the dance floor."

She checked her dance card. "The next dance is a lancer, so it should be rather easy to glide around the floor," she said, trying to sweeten the pot.

"It's a deal!" Elmer said with genuine enthusiasm. Delighted, Nellie bit back a wince as Elmer stepped on her foot yet again when they entered the stream of dancers. True to her word, she continued to chatter while they circled the dance floor, and found it prevented her from counting how many times Elmer kicked her in the shins.

"Halt!" said a voice behind Nellie. Startled, she stopped, making Elmer step on her foot *and* kick her shin, a dance combination he had not mastered before.

"Aw, don't make trouble Magruder," said Elmer, trying to lead Nellie in the opposite direction. Nellie turned and stared at the cadet.

"Plebe! Has one night of festivities caused you to forget how to speak to your superiors?" barked the cadet. Elmer froze, crimson red creeping up from his gray uniform collar.

"Good evening First Cadet William T. Magruder, sir." Elmer spat the words. Nellie thought the cadet looked familiar.

The cadet's face was a thundercloud. But then he glanced at Nellie, who was frowning. "Unhand that young lady," the cadet commanded. "She is far too high for your nut." Elmer reluctantly stopped trying to pull Nellie away and dropped his hands to his sides. *Mercy! It is the cadet from the dock who retrieved my glove. He certainly looks dash-fire without his spectacles.*

"Attention!" the cadet barked.

Elmer snapped to attention stance.

"Were you or were you not 'Absent Without Leave' on Friday last, and spotted at Benny Havens' Tavern?" shouted the cadet. He leaned his massive body so menacingly close, his nose actually touched Otis's.

"But sir, I...."

"A simple yes or no answer is required here."

Elmer hung his head. "Yes, sir." He almost whispered.

"Guilt established. I am plumb certain this will be more painful to me than to you," said William Magruder with a sarcastic grin. "However, as a First Year, it is my *duty* to place you on report and personally supervise your immediate punishment for this disciplinary infraction."

"But sir, you went to Benny Havens' *with* me! In fact, I only accompanied you because of your coercive insistence that I obey a direct order from a superior officer."

"It was most fortuitous that you followed the command. *That* was my direct order last week. *This* week I command you to make reparations for your transgressions against our code of discipline. Ours is not a regiment tailored to the soft at heart."

Elmer stood stock still at attention, embarrassment creating intermittent, disturbing splotches of crimson on his neck and ears.

Magruder raised an eyebrow in amusement and continued, "I assure you my good fellow, at times we all think of 'Dear Mother and Home' and wonder why we voluntarily chose to attend this miserable excuse for an educational establishment."

Elmer opened his mouth to protest further, but Magruder's two cohorts, witnessing the whole exchange, surrounded him. "Time for some extra guard duty," one said. Lifting Elmer under the elbows they propelled him across the dance floor. Stopping only to allow him to retrieve his dress hat from the table of cadet hats, they quickly escorted him out of the ball.

Magruder turned toward Nellie and bowed. "I request the honor of your presence as a dancing partner," he said. Nellie hesitated, disconcerted by the prank and unsure whether she should try to help Otis.

"You needn't look astounded—this is my second request, after all! Did you not honor my entreaty at the dock, to save me a dance?" the cadet smiled with disarming charm somewhat incongruous with his large frame. "Surely you have written me into your card as 'that marvelous mystery man'!"

Somewhat mollified that at least the cadet would not act like a cad to *her*, Nellie reluctantly took his offered hand. The man gracefully led her in the first steps of a polka.

"Now then." Cadet Magruder smiled down at Nellie, not at all winded as they danced the polka around the floor. "I have released you from your sentence of dancing with the inept! You may begin to shower me with your undying gratitude."

Nellie had to confess to herself she *was* a bit relieved to see the back of Elmer's head as he succumbed to the cadets hustling him away.

William followed her gaze. "'Tis a pity, for sure. I have no desire to affect him injuriously. It is an upperclassman's task, nay *responsibility* to have a bit of fun with pulling rank, even if it is at the expense of a bewildered neophyte."

With no other gracious course of action evident other than to acquiesce to the change of escort for the evening, Nellie jumped into the next promenade around the dance floor with buoyant enthusiasm. *A polka would have intimidated poor Elmer so thoroughly he would have retreated in terror.*

When they switched linked arms, William winked. "All is fair in Love and War! I have quite early grasped the maxim — the end most certainly justifies the means. Moreover, this maneuver bolsters my reputation for being a man of my word — I told you on the wharf to save a dance for me."

Mercy! Who would have thought the cadet who retrieved my glove would be this charming and persistent? My goodness, he truly looks handsome without his spectacles.... But I hope his vision is not compromised.

Nellie cast about for a subject to begin the socially required brilliant banter. Mercifully, the next song was another waltz, so there was more breath for conversation. The stays of her corset did not dig in quite so deeply during these steps.

Suddenly, Magruder's huge arms and hands crushed her into his chest and her stays constricted all breathing. Nellie drew back in alarm. William laughed at her. Attempting to recover from her awkwardness in trying to maintain her distance, Nellie said, "I could not help but notice you have more buttons than many of the other cadets."

"Your powers of observation are quite keen," said William. *Because you crushed me painfully and restricted my breathing with your ungentlemanly, inappropriate, button-battering, embrace,* Nellie thought.

"Through my brilliant scholarship, natural intelligence, and exceedingly hard work, I have earned the considerable distinction of an appointment to Acting Assistant Professor," William bragged. Nellie's face expressed the proper amount of admiration for this accomplishment. "This honor not only entitles me to three rows of *fourteen* buttons, rather than the usual eight, it also qualifies me for an

additional pay of ten dollars a month and a light after ten o'clock taps."
After a glance at Nellie's expression of confusion, Magruder added, "I
can continue to study long after plebes like your former escort must
turn off their lights."

"Whenever would the intense rigors of battalion training permit
leisure time to study dancing? Your skills are quite apparent," Nellie
said.

"Our fencing master, Pierre Thomas, will be most delighted to hear
that his diligent efforts at dancing instruction on Tuesday evenings have
reaped compliments." William smiled down at her. *He is not only a very
large man he is also exceedingly tall! It is quite surprising that he is so light on
his feet.* Nellie thought, feeling petite. "However, it was not he that first
inspired my interest in this social grace. A Boston dancing instructor
began our lessons during summer encampment before our first year of
academic instruction...."

Dancing with all her heart, searching the room with both eyes, and
listening with one ear, Nellie was enjoying the evening to the hilt, multi-
tasking included. She spotted Armistead L. Long, and this time...Nellie
craned her neck to see behind her tall partner as he swung her in a wide
arc...Agnes was smiling in Long's arms. *Mercy! I have never seen Agnes
smile so broadly, nor look so content,* she thought.

"If so enamored with my dancing, why cast your eyes around the
room, as if to find a more suitable partner?" asked William.

Nellie gave an embarrassed laugh. "Please forgive my
indiscretion."

"It grieves me to hear you confess to wishing to replace me," said
William, thrusting his lip out and hardening his eyes.

"Please, no! Mercy! That is a false conclusion—not the true reason
for my tactlessness."

William grabbed Nellie's arms in each of his large hands, almost
encircling her arms' circumference completely, and looked her straight
in the eyes, without missing a step of the minuet. "I'm all atremble to
hear," he said; voice barely a scintilla short of a snarl.

Intimidated, Nellie looked over her shoulder and said, "You will
make sport of the true cause." Her eye caught sight of Armistead Long
again, this time with Anastasia in his arms. *In mid-dance Long switched to
Anastasia? Mercy, neither sister looks happy about that!* With her
trademarked gesture of indignation, hands upon her hips, Agnes'
glowering anger was evident from across the room.

"I'd rather the true reason than the torture of speculating as to my deficiencies," said William, again following her gaze.

Nellie drew her eyes back to her dancing partner, shook her head and said, "First Cadet Armistead L. Long...."

"That indecisive fellow?" asked William. "You are sweet on Long?"

"He is sweet on my sisters. But he cannot make up his mind which one he prefers and he enlisted my aide to...."

Magruder threw back his head and laughed. "If that is not the bee's knees.

"That Armistead, he can never pick sides. While I confess, I do have a bit of a reputation for being indecisive...well more accurately, I have a remarkable ability to see both sides of a situation...I certainly know what I like when it comes to the ladies!"

Nellie pulled her hand away from his at this bold proclamation.

Magruder hastened to make amends. "Please do not take offense. I meant only that I was smitten by your charms immediately upon my first vision of you." *Maybe you should not have taken off your glasses?* Nellie giggled to herself. "I could see forthwith that you were a person of refinement and character, as well as a beauty." William had the audacity to wink at her. "I *knew* I wanted to get better acquainted.

"Hang that Armistead Long. He'll have to decide on his own. I would like your undivided attention for the next dance, for alas, it is the last one of the evening." Magruder led her to the punch bowl for a quick sip from a lovely crystal glass in the short interval before the orchestra announced the last dance.

Nellie took a long grateful sip and smiled at Magruder over the crystal. *This foray into West Point society has surely been full of surprises,* she thought, *mostly happy ones.*

Suddenly she caught the gaze of her mother, across the room with the other chaperones. *Tarnation! 'T will be quite the task to elucidate this state of affairs,* she thought.

But when William Magruder, smiling at her with dancing eyes, took the cup from her hand, placed it on the tray of a willing server, and led her to the dance floor, Nellie forgot everything else but the pleasure of twirling with a handsome, brilliant dancer.

CHAPTER 18
Tea for Two

West Point, March 1850

Augusta clasped her hands in delight. The women, taking off their wraps and hats, looked up expectantly. Augusta turned away from the messenger, closed the front door and announced to the ladies, "Nathaniel has sent word that he, and a veritable posse of willing cadets will be awaiting us at the receiving area of our hotel at nine o'clock tomorrow morning to escort us to services at the Cadet Chapel."

The girls' exclamations of delight resembled the twitter of birds at the first blush of dawn.

"I am aglow in anticipation. Slumber will be quite impossible," declared Anastasia.

"*Nein*," stated Mrs. Entwhistle. "No, I have arranged for our concierge to hire us a conveyance. We will egress to the Catholic Church in Buttermilk Falls at half Eight. Anyone found tardy, or deficient in dress can make their own way to join our party, at the Catholic Church."

Augusta dropped her hands to her sides and hung her head.

Nellie rushed to her defense. "*Mutter*, Augusta at least, must be free to worship in the Church of her desire. If she and her fiancé are accustomed to attending services at the Cadet Chapel...."

"Conveniently located on the Great Plain across from our hotel rather than in a different town via a bumpy journey through rutted roads...." Anastasia whispered in Nellie's ear as she paused for a breath.

Nellie stifled a giggle, continuing her defense of her friend, "...then it is not our duty to change that arrangement."

Mrs. Entwhistle looked as if she thought differently on that point, but merely shrugged her shoulders. "Very well. Augusta Van Cortlandt, I presume we can part company in the lobby of the hotel where you will await your escort. We will then recommence companionship at our luncheon in the dining room.

"Daughters, we *will* leave promptly."

The carriage ride to the Catholic Church was not as long, nor as bumpy as Cornelia Rose had dreaded. The tediousness of the trip was somewhat relieved by catching glimpses of cadets, in full dress uniform, in groups of two and three marching through the woods. The ladies giggled as they saw big black dress caps bobbing up and down with the hurried pace of the cadets. Speculations as to the purpose of the early Sunday morning march, in what appeared to be random spurts, flew around the carriage. *How comic they look, wearing those puerile parade hats with the excessive plumage!* Nellie thought. When the ladies neared their destination, they delighted to see more cadets trudging out of the woods in those staggered groups, fancy dress hats now in hand, picking twigs and leaves off the plumes, mounting the church steps to attend Mass.

Walking back from the altar to her pew after Communion, Nellie took a quick inventory of the rest of the congregation, tallying how many cadets attended Mass. She noted the last ten rows were crammed full of cadets. She and her sisters, kneeling with hands folded over their reverently lowered eyes, watched the gleaming line of handsome uniformed men march up to receive the Sacrament.

Tarnation, Nellie thought, when she caught a glimpse of Elmer P. Otis, lurching with an awkward gait down the aisle after partaking, hands jutting at a strange angle from his wrists and folded in front of him. Anastasia saw him too, and giggled.

"Maybe he will not detect us." She tried to reassure Nellie.

"And maybe a camel will pass through the eye of a needle," replied Nellie in whisper, and then blushed at her wicked blasphemy of today's Gospel.

There are only two groups of ladies here—even Elmer would not be so oblivious and unobservant as to overlook them.

When they exited the Church after the recessional hymn, sure enough, there was Elmer, standing with two of his company, blinking goofily in the sun. Nellie looked quickly left and then right. There were no other paths to their carriage. There was no way to avoid him.

No way 'round it. Better to simply face the demon! She walked right up to him and said, "Good morning Cadet Otis." She smiled her most charming smile.

This dazed Elmer so completely he simply stood there, opening, and closing his mouth. Nellie giggled to herself, *Mercy, what was he expecting me to do?*

One of the cadets nudged Elmer. "Speak boy," drawled the other, in a quiet voice.

Elmer said, "Um..." and closed his mouth.

Mrs. Entwhistle, the exchange of pleasantries with the pastor completed, swept with grand grace towards the group. "Cadet Otis, how very pleasing to see that you, quite literally, will go the extra mile to attend Mass, rather than compromise with an obliquely named 'Christian Service.' Your mother will be exceptionally proud of you when I report that I not only found you in excellent health, in tip top form, but also operating on the highest of moral grounds."

For some reason, rather than flummoxing Elmer further, this excessive praise helped him find his tongue. "Madam Entwhistle, good morning." He took off his tall dress uniform hat and bent forward in a bow. "I am delighted to see you and the ladies in such fine form this morning and relieved that you were able to find a conveyance to Church."

"Might I offer you a return ride to the Military Academy?" asked Mrs. Entwhistle. "I believe my daughters will be willing to squeeze on one side of the hackney, if you will be so kind as to sit with me." She looked at the two other cadets, who both looked hopeful. "Your fine companions can ride with the driver."

Anastasia gave a surprised squeal of delight. Nellie had been too engrossed handling Elmer to realize that Otis's companions were none other than Zetus Searle and Armistead Long. *This certainly cannot be a coincidence!* Nellie thought. *They are both Southern men, not likely to be Catholic. How in tarnation did those two glean we would be attending Mass here today?*

Elmer took Mrs. Entwhistle's arm and escorted her to the carriage. Cornelia moved behind her sisters toward the carriage but Cadet Long stepped in front of her, blocking her path.

"Never mind," Long said, leaning close to her ear as the others continued to walk. "I have chosen."

Startled, Nellie looked at him. "But of course. You have chosen Agnes," she stated.

Now Long looked startled. "Why no, I have chosen the dark haired one. You are mistaken, she is called Anastasia."

Nellie repressed a giggle. "Cadet Long, I hesitate to overstep my bounds, especially now that you have relieved me of my duty. But surely you can see, Anastasia seems to have made the choice for you." Nellie turned the cadet around so he could see that Zetus Searle held on to Anastasia's elbow as if it were an anchor. Both Anastasia and Zetus blushed and giggled as they conducted an intimate conversation. Long opened and closed his mouth, indecisive as to his next move.

Agnes, spying them from the seat she had already claimed in the carriage, ran back over.

"Armistead, here you are! I was so pleased to see you attend Mass this morning. You dance like a dream, and I dreamed of our dancing all night. I do believe you have swept me off my feet...." Agnes slipped her hand through Long's elbow and steered him to the carriage. He grinned down at her, relieved that his choice was clear.

Nellie threw up her hands and followed the party alone. *'Tis for the better*, she tried to tell herself when suddenly, she felt her own elbow gripped.

She looked up in surprise.

"I simply could not *abide* an outrageous beauty such as yourself walking unescorted to her carriage," a cadet drawled with a smile. "Whilst I have not had the pleasure of a formal introduction, I take the liberty to provide this here gentlemanly service of properly seeing you into your surrey. Indeed, I await the further opportunity to become so acquainted."

Nellie had to remind herself to close her mouth, while she listened to this courtly speech in amazement. Before she had a chance to reply, or remember where she had seen this man before, the cadet handed her into the carriage, tipped his plumage-waving hat to her mother and her sisters, closed the door and the carriage rolled away.

"Cadet Otis," Mrs. Entwhistle interrupted him in mid-sentence. "Who was that most courteous cadet?"

Elmer looked irritated at the interruption and muttered, "Second class Cadet Lawrence S. Baker."

He swatted at the cuff of his uniform as if to shake off crumbs of ill effect from Baker and turned to Nellie as if no interruption of conversation or time had lapsed since they last spoke on the dance floor. "I will arrive after luncheon to escort you to the glee club concert, which will be held in the Academic Building." He turned back to her mother. "If I may then have your permission Madam, to accompany Cornelia

Rose on a walking tour of the old embattlements and some of the more scenic vistas of the campus?"

"We would *all* appreciate the opportunity to survey the highlights of the Academy grounds, both historic and scenic," said Mrs. Entwhistle. *Was she being intentionally oblivious to the import of Otis's request,* Nellie wondered, *or is she protecting me?*

Otis's plea received aide from an unexpected source. "No, we would not, *Mutter,*" disagreed Agnes. "Armistead Lindsey Long invited me to promenade down 'Professor's Row' after the Superintendent's Tea."

Mrs. Entwhistle tried a different tack. "Mercy, we have quite a full schedule. I am not sure time will permit these last-minute additions."

Elmer blushed and opened and closed his mouth several times again. "If you please Madam, there are a few spots on the campus that the cadets are permitted to walk their ladies and I wonder if you would allow me to...."

Good Lord! Nellie thought, for once in complete accord with the maneuver her mother was executing. *Does he think he can corner me into accompanying him on Flirtation Walk? Is it not sacrifice enough for me to be in his company? Must he deprive me the small grace of having my chaperone attend me?*

She had plenty of time to devise strategies for maintaining her distance from Elmer while she listened to the rapturous music of the cadet glee club concert. Unexpected guard duty prevented Elmer from escorting her. *I am mercifully unaccompanied and can enjoy this fine performance unencumbered by the inept Elmer,* she thought, her heart and spirits soaring with the music.

Nellie stopped her tapping feet at a scowl from her mother. Composing her dignity, she murmured to her mother, and Anastasia, who sat beside her, "The discipline of practice is quite evident in the excellence of these skilled musicians and vocalists."

Zetus leaned over Anastasia in his enthusiasm to inform Nellie, "We have the best band, and the most melodious voices in the United States."

"It certainly does keep a fellow's spirits up," agreed Nathaniel from his seat on the other side of their row.

"Not only are they talented," whispered Augusta to Nellie from behind her fan, "they cut quite fine figures in their white band uniforms."

Nellie, giddy feelings whooshing back with that lighthearted remark, whispered her agreement, "My breath was clean taken away at the sight of the grand Drum Major when they marched through the auditorium on to the stage."

The day flowed sweetly, the events sugar-spun together into one honeyed confectionary treat. The concert ended in a triumphant march as the band processed back to Center Barracks. The audience dispersed, some to stroll along the Hudson paths, others to the mess hall or the hotel for dinner or tea. Nellie and her group, by special invitation, made a beeline to the late afternoon tea at the Superintendent's Quarters.

At first Nellie was rather at a loss as to how to join a conversation. She and Anastasia stood awkwardly next to the cucumber sandwiches, trying to figure out the proper way to snag and eat a delicacy. As they eyed the serving platters, their mother swooped over and selected a sandwich. In one graceful and dainty motion, she secured the tasty tidbit on a plate and tucked a napkin underneath. Cornelia made an attempt, but was not as successful. She chased a butter and egg sandwich all over the serving tray and then settled on a cucumber one that broke as she lifted it. Luckily no one but Anastasia was watching when it plopped back on the tray.

It is far too difficult to eat under such circumstances, she thought, and stopped trying. Anastasia giggled and looked uncertain. In the end she, too, turned from the table without sampling anything.

"Superintendent Thayer was avant-garde in his promotion of the Military Academy. Thayer established the Academy as the quintessence of a superior education and a benchmark for our nation," said their mother in a sotto voice. "Once he tightened this operation into a smooth sailing ship, he showcased the Corps of Cadets to the world by dispatching envoys of marching men, choral singers, and bands of musicians around the country to allow our citizens to observe firsthand the fine quality of soldiers in training here." Anastasia and Cornelia listened as they observed the guests in the room.

"Allowing our compatriots to visit the Academy and experience the fashioning of our future leaders is another tradition set by Thayer and continued by our current Superintendent and host, Brevet General Brewerton. Cornelia Rose, you must take advantage of this opportunity, use your wit and best conversation to hobnob with these esteemed visitors and forge some social connections."

Instructions completed, Mrs. Entwhistle went off to join a conversation with a distinguished looking gentleman, an officer with many medals and a lady with one of the most elaborate tulle and feather hats Nellie had ever seen. In spite of a second of self-doubt while she adjusted her own comparatively plain millinery concoction, she dutifully perused the crowd in the large drawing room. She spied Superintendent Brewerton's wife, and realized a sincere 'thank you' for the opportunity to attend the tea would do as an opening for conversation. Anastasia joined her, bolstering her confidence.

By the time Cadet Searle appeared at Anastasia's side, and drew her into their own tête-à-tête, Nellie had hit her stride. She was chatting with Mrs. Brewerton, and former Superintendent Richard Delafield. "I believe the Gothic architecture with its slate-gray granite, turrets, serrated rooflines, and sally ports is not only pleasing to the eye, but well suited to the scenery. It is one 'great stone castle' becomingly nestled in the famed Hudson River Highlands, so romanticized by the Knickerbocker movement."

"I take that compliment to heart, young lady," Delafield replied. "In fact, it warms me to my toes to hear those words, as that was the very effect desired when I instructed their design."

"Did I hear mention of that *famed* and *world-renowned* group of brilliant writers?" A white-haired gentleman joined their conversation. "If not for the Knickerbockers, few would know of the sublime, yet picturesque nature of these Highlands."

"I most heartily agree," said Nellie warmly. "Although I do dispute some of their methods, they have served our country well. I recall when the famous British actress Fanny Kemble viewed the ruins of old Fort Putnam in 1832 she lamented that we Americans had named our glorious mountains and vistas such uninspired names as 'Butter Hill' and 'Anthony's Nose.' We needed writers and poets such as these great men to take up their pens and their paint brushes to showcase this transcendent, bucolic scenery to the world."

The gentleman threw her an appreciative, appraising look. "I know exactly the passage of her memoirs to which you refer. I believe she wrote, 'Even the heathen Dutch, among us the very antipodes of all poetry, have found names such as Donder Berg—thunder mountain— for the hills.... How very grateful I am to the Knickerbocker's Nathaniel Parker Willis for getting 'Butter Hill' changed to 'Storm King'.'

"Yet you dispute some of their methods?" The gentleman waggled a questioning bushy eyebrow at her.

"You must concede, in their haste to cast a spell of legend and history over the mountains and valleys of the Hudson, some of the authors did more than 'borrow' ideas from old European literary forms," stated Nellie.

The gentleman bellowed a loud guffaw. Mrs. Brewerton looked around the gathering with nervous, furtive darts of her eyes, as if checking to see whom the man had offended. As none of the other guests interrupted their own conversations, or even glanced their way, the hostess took a nibble on her petite four.

Nellie blushed. "I believe in my desire to be an interesting conversationalist and share my passion for this beautiful scenery I am privileged to call 'home,' I have overstated my views to someone to whom I have not yet been properly introduced." Nellie paused for a breath, and then dropped a curtsey with the words, "I am Cornelia Rose Entwhistle, of Sing Sing, New York."

The gentleman laughed again. "I wish you had been present for tea last week, when my friend *Washington Irving* and I passed many pleasurable hours, hobnobbing with the Superintendent and other fellow Knickerbockers, followed by an evening of overindulging large quantities of food and drink across the river at Gouverneur Kemble's summer cottage in Cold Spring."

Nellie's heart sank to the bottom of her toes. "Mercy, I am dreadfully sorry! I meant no offense!"

"Nonsense, young lady, no offense was taken. It's all capital fun. My sole regret is that the other boys are not here — we would be unanimous in our desire to have you converse with us all evening," the man replied, bushy white eyebrows raising and lowering as if to emphasize his words.

"Good sir, I fear I am still at a disadvantage." Nellie was blushing now from frustration. "I still do not know to whom I have the pleasure...."

The woman accompanying the white-haired gentleman interrupted, "Mercy child, forgive his rudeness. Allow me to introduce my husband, Mr. William Cullen Bryant. A learned poet, writer, and editor, to be sure, but his social skills apparently still leave much to be desired."

Nellie heard none of the pleasantries offered by the woman after she said the name 'Bryant.' *How positively mortifying!* Her eyes darted around the room, looking for an escape. Nellie spied Elmer P. Otis loping toward her from the dining room, precariously balancing two cups of tea.

William Cullen Bryant, still smiling broadly, said, "I must speak to your chaperone to arrange for you to join me and my group for an evening of conversation. Gouvenor Kemble's house, our usual haunt, is just a short row across our mutually admired river."

"I have tea for two persons," Elmer interrupted the all too interesting conversation to announce. Oblivious to his rudeness and the fact that the three dignitaries were vexed at having their conversation disturbed, Elmer looked only at Nellie and said, "I have reconnoitered a cozy nook by the fireplace in the library."

Suddenly realizing his faux pas, Elmer's ears turned bright red. Instead of apologizing, he blurted, "There is only room for two." He jerked his head in that direction as if summoning Nellie to follow him, turned on his heel and practically cantered away. Nellie could see the tea sloshing out of the cups he held at bizarre angles away from his body.

Nellie thought fast. "Mercy, I do apologize for my acquaintance's rude behavior. I confess I do not know him well and am at a loss to explain his peculiarities."

"It is obvious his judgment is clouded by your beauty. You must forgive a man so smitten," said Mrs. Bryant with a sympathetic smile.

Mr. Bryant laughed again.

Nellie searched for an appropriate way to end the conversation. But she remained silent, at a loss for words. Embarrassed and further distracted by the sight of the woebegone Otis peering at her from around the arch of the library, elbows still protruding awkwardly, she blushed. Still tongue-tied, she curtseyed her leave with as much grace as she could muster and made a beeline to Otis.

He was perched on the end of a seat, balancing the teacups on his knees. His face brightened so upon her arrival her heart melted, grateful that with Otis at least, she had not fallen from grace.

"I certainly appreciate your thoughtfulness—obtaining a cup of tea for me," said Nellie.

"After you drink it, can we go for a walk?" Otis asked.

He is nothing if not persistent, Nellie thought.

Nellie shook her head in the negative. "I am sorry, *Mutter* has given me strict instructions in tea protocol. I am afraid I am a quite committed, obedient daughter and must pay my respects to other guests of the Superintendent."

Elmer's face fell.

Cornelia, do not add 'heartless' to your list of sins, she thought. Aloud she said, "Cadet Otis, after I perform my obligations as a proper guest at this fine tea, we may go for a *short* perambulation."

A half hour later the exceptionally educated and learned dignitaries began to drift away. The number of guests at the splendid tea dwindled as the afternoon shadows lengthened. Nellie, still engaged in animated conversation, watched groups of invitees take their leave, cross the Academy's Great Plain and head either to their hotel rooms or back to the steamboat to continue their tour of the Highlands.

CHAPTER 19
There's a Kind of Hush

West Point, March 1850

Mrs. Entwhistle was busy collecting her charges. Agnes and Armistead Long lingered in the library, deep in conversation. Anastasia and Zetus Searle continued their tête-à-tête over yet another cup of tea and plate of sandwiches in the drawing room. Their mother circled each couple, edging them closer toward the door in an effort to corral them into leaving. Elmer P. Otis, taking advantage of Nellie's change of heart, appeared at Mrs. Entwhistle's side and followed her around as she maneuvered.

At last they were all out of the parlor and walking down the front walk. Otis stopped still, blocked Mrs. Entwhistle's path, snapped to attention and said, "Permission to escort your daughter Cornelia Rose on a sunset walk along the paths of our scenic Highlands, Madam."

Even Mutter has to stifle a grin, observed Nellie.

"Not so fast, plebe," Armistead Long spoke. Everyone looked at him in surprise. *Here's aid from an unexpected source,* Nellie thought.

"Don't you have a date with Anna Lytical?"

A sense of relief flooded Nellie.

Elmer blushed a brilliant shade of red. *My he is a colorful fellow.* Nellie giggled to herself at her own pun. Otis' ears alone were a frightening color of sickly scarlet. Nellie secretly felt joyful. *He is pursuing another? Alleluia!* she thought.

"Speak boy," commanded Long. "Don't let old Albert Church down now."

The group closed in together, looking at each other, confused. Augusta and Nathaniel spotted them and sauntered from the garden path to join them.

Agnes spoke from her position on Long's arm. "Is Mr. Church the mathematics instructor you just spoke of, the one cadets call 'an old mathematical cinder, bereft of all natural feeling'?" she asked. It seemed to Nellie Agnes' mouth twisted into a question mark. "What has Church to do with Otis' courtships?"

"Otis. Speak," repeated Long, in a low voice, an inch from Otis' nose.

Otis opened his mouth took a deep breath, and recited without stopping:

> *"Of all the girls I ever knew*
> *The one I've most neglected*
> *Is called Miss Anna Lytical*
> *For her I've least respected.*
> *O! Anna, Anna Lytical*
> *I'll never love you more*
> *For you, I fear will cause my fall*
> *And make me leave the Corps."*

Otis saluted Long while everyone except Nellie laughed — even Mrs. Entwhistle could not hide her smile.

"*Tarnation,*" whispered Nellie.

"There but for the grace of God go I," Nathaniel said quietly to Augusta. She gave him a sympathetic squeeze of his arm.

"May I escort your daughter on a promenade?" asked Elmer, ears still flaming red.

Mrs. Entwhistle's resolve broke. Perhaps it was Elmer dogged repeating of his request, but more likely she felt a twinge of sympathy for the poor embarrassed cadet. "While it does go against my better judgment, I do suppose you can steal Cornelia Rose away for a brief expedition. I believe I really must supervise the repacking of the luggage and ensure it is ferried to the dock in readiness for our steamboat departure."

Dadblame it! Nellie's ire rose. There was no escaping it now. *Mutter, how could you think I desire to undertake this unchaperoned excursion?*

Mrs. Entwhistle shooed Cornelia down the path.

In an instant Otis was at her side, steering her along the Superintendent's front walk. He walked her briskly across the Great Plain, skirting Execution Hollow, the rift in the lawn so-called after its alleged function during the Revolutionary War. He averted the path toward the Central Barracks and the heart of the campus, practically galloping towards the ruins at Fort Putnam.

The pace was so rapid they were past the old fort in less than five minutes. Nellie had a stich in her side and her corset pinched her back as they entered a path both lovely and remote.

"Are you quite certain it is permissible to be this far from your barracks un-chaperoned?" asked Nellie. Apprehension at the distance between them and the rest of her companions compelled her to make one last attempt to rejoin the others.

"This is an area off limits to everyone *but* the cadets. We are actively *encouraged* to enjoy the view and the beauties of each season here," replied Elmer.

Each season's debutantes? Nellie thought. *Could Otis be capable of a double entendre? The thought certainly amuses me.*

They stepped through the trellised archway. Otis' voice soared and sang, "I've oft had occasion to imagine the ecstasy of my feelings would the woman of my dreams accompany me on this walk. You will observe—the path is just broad enough for the passage of two. The pleasing peal of laughter will alert us to the close proximity of another couple."

Nellie reined in her runaway imaginative fears. *It is rather foolish to fret!* she thought. *After all, Elmer Petulant Otis attends me—hardly a situation fraught with danger. 'Tis but a lark; and my good humor will ensure it thus.*

"Listen to the birds sing. Songs so melodious are not oft heard on more plebian paths," Otis continued, oblivious to Nellie's qualms.

"Early spring, I am told, is the prime season to make this journey. The tiny buds on the otherwise bare trees only just hint their future glory, keeping the vistas unimpeded by flora, yet intimating the lush green color to come."

Elmer is certainly waxing poetic! Nellie thought.

They continued down the path fragrant with early spring blossoms of crocuses and daffodils. Nellie admired both nature's beauty and the man-made marvels highlighted by Elmer. They passed Gee's Point and had their first glimpse of Constitution Island; winter browns retreating as green buds commandeered the landscape. The path wound around to the west and Otis pointed out the ruins of the earthen fortification where The Great Chain originated during the Revolutionary War.

"The capstan still stands, stalwart, awaiting further use," said Nellie, pointing to a large round metal fixture.

"On April 30, 1778," intoned Elmer in an officious voice. "Rafts made of wood, covered in pitch to prevent waterlog, floated enormous link segments of the chain forged in nearby Sterling Iron Works."

I underestimated Elmer's vigor to be tour guide. Nellie smiled to herself. *Perhaps there is hope that I will not have to parry any unwanted romantic advances.*

"Until the war's end, troops hauled the chain in, link by link, every winter before ice choked the water's navigability. Every spring they repositioned it. Its mere presence was so effective—this fort so secure—that those damn Brits never even approached our country's first fortress.

"Verily, they did not risk navigation this far up the river," said Otis, with so much pride Nellie got the impression he had personally forged and strung the chain himself.

They paused in front of a boulder on the mountainside of the trail. Before Nellie knew why they had stopped, Otis whisked her into his arms and placed her gently on top of the perch. In one quick scramble, he was by her side. "Cornelia, here we are, just the two of us. There's no one else in sight. We are present in this romantic location, with an unobstructed view of the sunset behind us, its colors already playing on the water before us." Otis made grand, almost graceful, sweeping motions with his hand, behind them toward the mountains and then in front of them at the view of the color-dappled water. He now looked side-to-side, anywhere to avoid her eyes, his pimply chin wobbling. "I am truly smitten by your charm. Will you do me the honor of wearing my spoony button?"

Tarnation! This is a most compromising turn of events, thought Nellie. In the dead silence, she chose her words carefully. "Elmer, I am truly flattered. Howsoever, I fear you perhaps might be laboring under some preconceived notions that bear little correlation to a harsher reality. You have only just made my acquaintance."

"No—not true, I knew you when we attended the one room schoolhouse on Brandreth Street."

"Elmer, I was a mere child. As truly were you. Now surely, this is quite the scintillating excursion, packed with many exceptional events. Furthermore, this pathway, with its lovely spring blooms festively decorating our wanderings, fills our senses with heady fragrances, perhaps overwhelming our emotions. I am quite certain that many a young man has spouted protestations of undying love on this path. *Never-the-less,* I would like to forestall any such confessions until such time as we have become better acquainted."

Elmer protested, "But you have not given me pause to indicate my true intentions. I need no further information to make up my mind—my heart has already made clear its desire to me. I will not be delayed nor silenced. I must tell you, I wish to seek your hand in marriage."

Nellie grimaced. *Precisely the exact words I hoped to circumvent.*

"Elmer, dearest. I cherish your sentiment, and am truly touched. Be that as it may, I am forced to admit I cannot reciprocate those affections at this time," said Nellie, trying to extricate herself from this awkward situation without humiliating her escort.

"You're not sweet on that stupid Buckskin?" demanded Elmer, grabbing her hand.

"Buckskin?" asked Nellie, withdrawing her hand from his grasp.

"You know—the Virginian," said Elmer.

"My goodness, I never did get to convey to you my deep distress at the impudence of that First Cadet, hustling you out the door, trespassing on your good nature under the guise of rank and military discipline, in order to monopolize my attention. Such boorish behavior! I do hope such tricks and chicanery play little role in your daily life here?" Nellie asked.

Distracted by her question, Elmer unburdened himself. "Daily? More like hourly! Furthermore, the humiliation of the tasks they set us to—sweeping rubbish, scrubbing kitchen pans, is enough to shame even a saint. Pshaw! Manual labor. Making us scullery maids and ditch diggers."

"I garner from my reading 'tis merely a hazing period, a training exercise to ensure that no matter how odious, a soldier will perform the task commanded. Does this initiation period not terminate when the new class is enlisted in June?"

"Rumor has it. However, the degradation does try me to the quick and I begin to doubt if I will ever put it behind me." Elmer sighed and Nellie knew his thoughts were heading back toward her. "I had thought, 'if I but had Nellie as my betrothed, wearing my spoony button, this ignominy would be easier to endure.'"

Tarnation! Must he tug on my heartstrings, using my pity to ensnare me?

"Elmer Pet..." Nellie caught herself before saying 'petulant' as his middle name. "...Otis, I will not stoop to the feminine frailty of giving you false hope by promising myself to you."

She tried not to notice how crushed the cadet looked.

He said, "Then all is lost. All is for naught."

Nellie took his hand with sympathy, but with no less resolve. *This unwanted attention must end now,* she thought, and said, "I am sure that time will reveal to us both the way forward from here."

"Do you mean to say we will progress no further on this path?" asked Elmer.

Thinking he meant the figurative path towards marriage, Nellie nodded her agreement.

Elmer made a face. "I can't even take you to kissing rock?"

Nellie smiled with relief at his simplicity—she most definitely wanted to dodge that bullet. "No, we will have to save that for a later date." *And a different companion,* she finished in her head.

Elmer jumped down, and pulled Nellie off the perch. Then he turned her around and marched her back up Flirtation Walk. In his haste to hustle her off the path, he brushed rudely by several wandering intertwined couples, practically dragging Nellie as she apologized in his wake.

CHAPTER 20
Benny Havens, O!

West Point, April 1850

"Come along, Cornelia. I never took you for an overly cautious wench," urged William T. Magruder. His long strides across the damp and uneven terrain immediately left Nellie winded and his words left her speechless.

Wench? How very uncouth! Nellie thought, scurrying, taking three steps to his one. Her tongue wiggled free of her labored breathing. "Consumption of liquor is pernicious to your health! Playing cards, nay any game of chance is forbidden, I read it in Thayer's Rules myself. Why, even having cards in your possession is grounds for dismissal."

Cornelia's intrepid spirit wavered. For over a month William Magruder had been courting her through the mail, wooing her to his side, seducing her with words that whispered of adventures and thrills. Intrigued by the idea of a new trip to West Point with an escort she actually desired, intoxicated by the thought of high society *and* romance, she schemed with Magruder to devise a visit with a less diligent chaperone than her mother. *I would never have had any latitude for intrigue under Mutter's watchful eye. But a clandestine trip to the cadet watering hole? This madness was not included in our agreed agenda. Furthermore, this trudge through the woods is entirely devoid of romance....*

"Cadet Magruder," Nellie said, pulling at his jacket to slow him down. "I have no desire to imbibe an alcoholic beverage."

Magruder was unperturbed. "Beer is not alcohol. At least that's what Jefferson Davis said—his pranks are legendary! Yet his escapades at Benny Havens' certainly did not retard his career. Officers in the know say the President is considering Davis for Secretary of War," said Magruder, easily clearing the log blocking the path into the woods behind the Central Barracks.

Nellie's hem caught rough bark and she heard a rip as she struggled over that same obstacle in their path. "Did you not reprimand poor Elmer P. Otis for this very infraction?" she panted.

Magruder laughed and said, "'Tis but part of the hazing of the plebes.... I see you still require some education as to the real workings of this institution. In any case, the occasions for 'extra training' have all passed now. In just four short weeks the plebes will graduate to second year cadets whilst I receive my diploma. The time is ripe for just a bit more amusement before I begin my commission and head out West to fight those savage Indians." William pulled Nellie's hand and she reluctantly followed him further into the dense woods.

Savage Indians? What an uninformed prejudice. He is the height of conceit and rudeness, she thought.

"You have already received your commission?" asked Nellie. Focusing on this new piece of information, rather than more confrontation, Nellie followed William across a short meadow toward another path. "I thought commissions were only granted after passing the June examinations."

William's look of pride shone even in the meager moonlight. "Thayer's merit roll for ranking a cadet's performance still dictates the commission I receive at graduation. Since I have an exceptional, in fact outstanding, record of academic merit...."

There is barely even a footpath, Nellie thought, as she stumbled over an enormous root protruding from the sticks and leaves that formed the path. The trail was rough going in the dark, with only the scant light of a waxing crescent moon to periodically illuminate the way.

"...extraordinary performance on the drill field, superior riding skills and conduct...."

Nellie interrupted, "Eureka! Conduct. I am quite certain a trip to Benny Havens' is an infraction of the disciplinary codes. I assure you, from what little I read of former Superintendent Brevet Lieutenant Colonel Sylvanus Thayer, and his copious rules, I am sure he has prescribed against just this sojourn. Thayer would be outraged that a first classman, one who is ranked high enough to have already received his commission, would even contemplate sneaking off to the tavern."

Magruder emitted an expansive laugh that reverberated through the forest. "I will soon be free of Thayer's legacy and that infernal book of rules. Any infractions I may receive between now and graduation will be as naught, once I surpass my entire class with my performance before the Board of Visitors and Professors. I intend to 'bone it' with all my might to ensure I excel at the upcoming examinations. I am determined to rise to the top and earn the rank of general. All to make my state of Virginia proud."

"Strange that I did not realize you were from the South," Nellie said.

"I *was* from western Virginia, but now I am from West Point. This fine education in engineering and maneuvering, coupled with my innate, naturally superior abilities...."

As they hustled through the dark woods and Magruder droned on and on singing his own praises, Nellie ceased to listen. *Thank goodness, I heeded Mutter's advice and wore my sturdy but stoutly unattractive walking boots. This would be quite the journey in my fancy dress boots. But thank goodness, I did not listen to Mutter and stay in Mrs. Van Cortlandt's suite at the hotel. Even Mrs. Van Cortlandt, with her more lenient chaperoning style, would never permit my absence at night for this this length of time.*

I should not fret – my absence allows Agnes some unchaperoned time with her beau Armistead in the comfort of Professor French's drawing room. Some well-deserved 'spooning' time. Aware that she was merely rationalizing her behavior, Nellie tried to revive her adventuristic spirit. She pushed some hair, loosened by her stumbling steps, away from her eyes. *Magruder's Professor's house permits the freedom to make this daring expedition. Did I not desire adventure and intrigue?* Finding little comfort in these thoughts, Nellie tried to think of other things. *Might I have a husband who is a professor here someday, dwelling in such a darling house?* Nellie stole a glance at Magruder, who continued to list his strengths and accomplishments, oblivious to the fact that Nellie was no longer paying attention. *How unfortunate that upon closer study, William is a blowhard braggadocio, and little else. I suppose it is necessary to suffer many encounters with potential suitors in order to ascertain their true colors....*

Before Magruder ran out of laudatory compliments for himself they had completed the mile trudge to their destination: Benny Havens' Tavern, on the bluff in Buttermilk Falls.

In the darkness, the building did not look very impressive. *Seems hardly worth the trek,* Nellie thought. She was even less impressed when they ran the last few feet from the woods and dashed inside. In the dingy light, she saw a glowing pot belly stove, a few cadet's faces ringing the fire, several more men lining the stools on the bar, and groups of two and three men clustered around some small tables.

Magruder brought them directly to the bar.

"Son, 'tis good to see ye again. What'll ye be imbibing tonight?"

"No need to ask—A Hot Flip!" said Magruder, pumping the bartender's outstretched hand with enthusiasm and plopping on a barstool.

"And you, little lady?" asked the bartender.

"Oh, I am not prepared to.... I would like to have.... goodness no, I could not...A mint julep?" she finally asked, in such a timid voice no one save the bartender heard her, and he laughed so loudly that Nellie, in spite of being totally flustered, knew that she would not see the bartender make this drink.

Is mint not in season? Nellie wondered. "What in heaven's name is 'A Hot Flip'?"

"Just about the finest concoction ever conceived. You must try one. Just watch Benny whip one up," said Magruder, leaning forward to watch Benny more closely.

Nellie timidly perched on a stool and watched the process. After thirty seconds she blurted out, "I most certainly would not drink that. It is not made of beer—it is made with rum! I saw the bartender put *rum* into the flagon."

"That's no bartender, that is our host and the proprietor, Mr. Benny Havens himself," said Magruder.

At the mention of his name, Benny touched his head, miming a doffing of his cap, and approached Nellie. "An' who might this fair colleen be?"

"Mr. Benny Havens, may I present a member of the fairer sex, who hails from just a short float down the Hudson, Miss Cornelia Rose Entwhistle." Cornelia jumped down from the stool and curtseyed.

"'Tis a pleasure," said Benny, laughing. Feeling a bit foolish she blushed and climbed back up.

"A Hot Flip w' a touch o' cider then, will it be?" Benny smiled with such an engaging, friendly smile Nellie felt a bit more at ease.

A cheerful, robust man, Benny took delight in tending to his cadet customers. As he beat three eggs for Nellie, he inquired after Magruder's state of being. The two carried on a conversation as if they were the dearest of friends.

"Mercy," said Nellie to Magruder when Mr. Havens turned to wait on another customer. "One might speculate that you and Mr. Havens are quite intimate companions, by the length and subject of your conversation."

"Benny's a best friend to every cadet who strolls in here. His genuine and hospitable manner is the reason that poor old misfit Edgar Allen Poe wrote of West Point, 'Benny Havens was the only congenial soul in the entire God-forsaken place.'"

Nellie watched Benny throw a dram of cider and a generous dash of sugar into the pewter mug containing the eggs. He followed that with a shake from each of four jars. *Those must be spices,* she thought. *Maybe nutmeg? Cinnamon? The enticement of this beverage increases....* She was surprised to see him reach into the fire and grab one of the hot pokers. Benny thrust it into the mug and held it there for about thirty seconds.

It gave a scintillating, sustained sizzle.

"Why have you put a hot poker in the mug?" Nellie called, her curiosity overcoming her reticence to speak.

"Trade secret, m' dear." At Nellie's confused face, Benny laughed. "I could tell ye, but then I'd have to hang ye!"

Nellie blushed a crimson so deep it was visible even in the dim light of the tavern.

"Jest 'aving a bit o' sport w' ye, is all." Benny winked and leaned in closer. Nellie noted with surprise that he did not reek of beer, but rather had a pleasant fresh-scrubbed scent, with a hint of pot roast. Benny tapped his head. "The real secret is in knowing jist when to remove the poker for that special caramelized flavor.

"Ye be the judge o' it fer yerself." He thumped it down on the bar in front of her.

She took a cautious sip. *It was pleasing to the palate,* she thought. She took another, larger sip, appreciating the bouquet of flavors in her beverage.

Magruder regaled her with the history of the tavern. "At first Benny sold only ale, cider, and buckwheat cakes. But now that the military has seen fit to remove him from the convenient location he occupied for so long near the hospital on campus, forcing him to set up shop over a mile and a half distance from us, Benny rewards our extra travel with a repast a bit more substantial."

I told you Thayer would not approve of this venture, Nellie thought. *I wonder if it were he that removed this establishment from the campus grounds?*

Magruder winked at Nellie, seeing that she was enjoying the concoction.

Benny took up the tale, "Aye, colleen, the chaps what come here are homesick and hungry, and me and the missus take care o' them like they was our own. Many of the regulation-breaking cadets we have befriended have gone on to achieve high ranks and fame."

"But don't the instructors and sergeants come looking for the cadets?" Nellie was getting less nervous by the sip, but still, she felt compelled to ask.

"More likely they come looking for a piece of that fine fowl Benny has roasting there," Magruder answered. He pointed to the spit Mrs. Havens was turning over the fire. "And a bit o' Hot Flip for themselves!" he added. Magruder laughed into his drink and ordered another, with a side of buckwheat flapjacks.

"Letitia, bring a slice o' your tasty critter for our new guest," Benny called, busy wiping out mugs for the next customer. "Let her try a sample of our finest."

In spite of herself, Nellie's mouth began to water at the tantalizing smell permeating the tavern. She hadn't eaten much at tea. *Had there even been tea?* She could not recall. She gratefully took the sampling from Mrs. Havens and was trying her first juicy bite when suddenly two tables of cadets in the back stood up and sang:

> *"Come, fill your glasses, fellows, and stand up in a row,*
> *To singing sentimentally we're going for to go;*
> *In the army there's sobriety, promoting's very slow,*
> *So we'll sing our reminiscences of Benny Havens', OH!"*

In one motion, every cadet seated in the tavern stood and they all joined in the chorus:

> *O! Benny Havens, oh! O! Benny Havens, oh!*
> *We'll sing our reminiscences of Benny Havens, oh!"*

They all sat back down again and resumed their drinking as if no interruption had occurred.

Benny winked at Nellie again. "I 'av a system, yes, I do. I employ a scout nightly and we hustle the underclassmen out when the big brass come in," he said.

No sooner had he made that statement when a boy came running in. "Ye've got less than ten minutes before General Ambrose Burnside arrives!" the lad panted.

"That scalawag!" said Benny. "'T'will be good to see 'im again."

Nellie jumped up, ready to run. But Magruder took another sip of his second Hot Flip, and banged his fork on the bar. "Burnside was in here so much when he was a cadet, he had his own stool! Eventually he carved his name on it. Dawdle awhile. You haven't even taken more than three sips of your cider Hot Flip."

"How can you be so cavalier when the fruits of your four years of hard labor are in jeopardy?" Nellie demanded.

"The lookout is stationed at the top of the cliff stairs. We still have plenty of time to leave, if we deem it desirable. The carriage road winds way around before it meanders here. Therefore, I propose you drink your beverage while we discuss the pros and cons of this important decision," said Magruder, unperturbed.

Nellie took another sip. *It is actually quite delicious.* "I am forced to confess I do enjoy the caramelized flavor."

The fire crackled nearby. Many uniformed cadets still lounged about, eating their comfort food, chatting companionably with each other and with Benny and his wife.

"I confess I remain unenlightened as to why they call it a 'Hot Flip,'" said Nellie.

"Well now, what ye might call a 'red-hot poker' apparently some fine folk call a 'flip dog.' We couldn'a rightly call a food a 'hot dog' so that left 'Hot Flip,'" answered Benny, again bestowing his ready smile on her.

Nellie looked skeptical at that explanation, but she had no time to retort.

Emerging from the murky shadows of the back of the bar, Zetus, Anastasia's solid-framed cadet suddenly loomed in front of her like an impenetrable wall. A gasp of surprise escaped Nellie.

"Zetus S. Searle," she exclaimed as simultaneously he said, "Cornelia Rose Entwhistle!"

"I am shocked to see you here!" They both said at the same time.

"You must leave at once." They both said together again.

Anastasia's beau is correct! Nellie thought. *I care not a whit for the opinion of William T. Magruder, whose motives are questionable, even in the mildest of circumstances.*

A second urchin burst through the door. "Burnside just got joined by bigger brass than him. Ulysses S. Grant...."

"To the windows and back door men! Make haste!" said Mrs. Haven in a loud whisper.

Nellie turned to follow the command, panic rising in her heart.

Magruder pulled her elbow back. "Why do you scamper like a scared squirrel? You are a civilian. You have every right to be here, accompanying me."

"You're *not* leaving?" asked Nellie.

"For Burnside and Grant? They have logged too many hours by this fireside for me to leave this cozy perch for the likes of them."

"Nellie, come on!" Zetus tugged her other elbow. Maybe it was the fact that he used her nickname. Or maybe it was because he was 'buttoned' to Anastasia, and Nellie knew that under her youthful silliness Anastasia had good judgment of character. But in any case, she pulled her elbow out of William's clutches and allowed Zetus to pull her along.

"Cornelia Rose, if you retreat like a coward at the first sign of conflict, you are not the lady for me," William said in a booming voice, partially rising from his barstool.

"Mayhap you are correct." Nellie threw the words over her shoulder without even looking back.

In an instant, the crowd pushing to get out the back door consumed Nellie and Zetus. "I'll take the window after I push you through the front of this ungentlemanly group," Zetus shouted.

He steered Nellie toward the door. The crowd pushed and shoved around them. Zetus could get not any closer to the doorway than behind the door. Planting himself behind it, he reached a large arm around the door and shoved Nellie out, just as the pack of cadets pulled him back and squeezed ahead of him.

Nellie ran around to the side windows, stumbling in the shadows where the light from the tavern did not reach the ground.

Cadet after cadet spilled out of the two windows, tumbling against each other as they hit the ground in their haste to evacuate the premises. Nellie looked for Zetus but in all the uniformed arms, legs and backs she could not distinguish even *his* most recognizable build.

A loud clatter from the window's shutter caused her to look up in time to see two cadets burst through the window at the same time. One landed on his feet and the other on his side. In the light from the suddenly vacant window, Nellie could see that the one on his side was at last Zetus. She ran to him, wondering why he did not immediately spring up. She reached down to pull his hand only to find it was thoroughly wet and clammy.

"What has soaked you so?" she asked, repulsed by the ooze still on her own hand. "Mercy, what has transpired during your attempt to escape?"

Zetus stumbled to his feet, hand clutching his thigh, whispering, "As soon as we clear the area we can see." He turned but remained crouched as he tried to scramble for the wooded footpath.

"Why ever do you not stand erect? Moreover, what is the source that drenched your hand and cuff so?"

Nellie looked down at her current escort. He was breathing rapidly, shambling in an awkward manner at her side, when suddenly he collapsed.

"Cadet Searle, what ails you?" Nellie cried. She tried to pull the cadet upright, but he lay there gasping for breath. Cadets ran around them, desperate to get away. Nellie tried frantically to ascertain the cause of Zetus' inability to walk.

In between labored breaths, Zetus gasped, "Not... wet.... Bloody...."

Nellie grasped his hand and tried to examine it to determine the cause of bleeding. The blood was drying up and there was no cut that she could feel. Her panic was beginning to ebb as she asked, with what she hoped was a calm medical manner, "How did you hurt your hand?" *Furthermore, how would that injury prevent you from walking?*

"No... no," was all Searle could reply.

"There is no wound evident. Furthermore, even a severe hand wound should not prevent ambulation," said Nellie. *In point of fact, it could have been someone else's blood, since you do not appear to be bleeding.*

But Zetus remained on the ground, his hand now clutching his muscular thigh. Nellie decided she had better investigate, although she was reluctant to examine the cadet's body further.

Just then light from a kerosene lantern suddenly beamed upon them. Nellie saw in a flash that Zetus' hand was again covered in blood. "Halt, please, who-so-ever conducts the lantern. Your assistance is required," she said.

The lantern obediently came closer. Nellie did not even look to see who carried it. She focused on the alarming dark red patch, growing bigger by the second on Zetus' upper thigh.

"No...." Zetus whispered. "Don't let the patrol cadet catch me. Do not call attention to me."

Those words you have breath for? Nellie thought, almost amused. "I am reluctant to alarm you but you have a wound on your leg, and I must have the light to determine its magnitude."

CHAPTER 21
Homeward Bound

Highland Cliffs, April 1850

The light bearer shone the beam full on the pair, and illuminated the wounded cadet's face. "Searle, a fine pickle you're in!" someone said.

Searle rolled his eyes back in his head in response. Nellie clamped her hand over the ripped material jaggedly covering the skin below, trying to stem the flow of blood.

"Searle, buck up. It is I, Gouverneur Kemble Warren, friend, not foe. Did the fact that I accompanied you to Benny Havens' somehow slip your mind?" the steady, practical voice continued.

"Gouverneur Kemble, the senator and industrialist?" Nellie almost released her hand from applying pressure to the wound at her surprise.

"No, no," said Warren, a trace of annoyance in his voice. "A common mistake, to be sure. I am his namesake."

"I beg your pardon. It was my understanding that the Senator was a confirmed bachelor, but obviously he is your father," said Nellie, while trying to figure out her next step in providing medical aid.

"He is actually no blood relation. He and my father are fast friends, so I am named to carry on his legacy. No, no, I am no industrialist. I am a classmate of old Searle here."

"My apologies, 'tis such an unusual name." Nellie kept her hand on the wound while she tried to gauge its depth. She shuddered at the thought. *I can't possibly have him remove his trousers. I must continue to apply pressure through the cloth.* Nellie summoned the lantern closer, lifted her hand off the wound and took a long, probing look.

Wordless, both men stared at her.

"I am afraid, good sir, that Cadet Searle is in no condition to answer. It seems he has quite a wide, but mercifully fairly superficial, gash on his leg. I must bind it immediately to stanch the bleeding, or he will not have the capacity to ever make it back to the barracks."

As she spoke, Nellie lifted the bottom of her dress. Warren sucked in his breath at the lamplight sight of her ankles, but Nellie paid him no heed. She tore an arm's length strip off the bottom ruffle of her best petticoat. *No matter, can't be helped. In any case, that rip I suffered earlier in the evening, when I stumbled over that log caused irreparable damage. I would have had to sew on a new ruffle to salvage this petticoat anyway. It is the least I can do for my sister's beau,* she thought. She clamped her hand back on Searle's wound. Quickly but methodically she applied the ruffle to the wound, and then wrapped it as tightly as she could around his thick, muscular thigh. *I will need a whole petticoat for this large limb,* she thought. The slight pressure at least held the bleeding in check while she ripped the entire length of her bottom ruffle off her petticoat and into equal length strips. Warren made himself useful by holding the lamp and summoning another comrade to hurry back to the tavern and ask Mrs. Havens for some beer.

Nellie wound the last strip tightly around the other makeshift bandages, and tied it into a firm knot. *Midwife Rafferty would be proud,* she thought. Mrs. Havens came running out with the beer.

"How in t' world did this occur? Was there an altercation? I noticed a bowie knife lying under t' window as I came out," Mrs. Havens panted, breathless.

Warren said, "Old Searle here would not hurt a flea. By the sword, he is our pacifist. He could not have been fighting."

With one swig of the beer, Searle revived enough to confirm, "'Twas not pugnacity but merely stupidity—in the scramble and press to climb through the window my fool knife decided to burst its sheath."

"I told you to re-sew that old leather sheath, Zetus," Warren said with a fond rub of Searle's shoulder. "Did I not tell you it would poke free some day and slice you?"

"It was certainly fortuitous that you had a lantern Cadet Warren," said Nellie, standing up and gathering herself. "How did you contrive to have one when all the other cadets seem to sneak about in the darkness?"

"I am a first-class cadet. I always arm myself for battle. I stash this securely in the woods for just such occasions—walks to and from our home-away-from-home."

Does mayhem like this occur often? Nellie wondered.

Mrs. Havens gave Warren an affectionate pat on the arm. "'Tis a blessing you did, son." She turned to Searle and asked, "Well enough to walk, now cadet? I'm afraid t' big brass is cozy in front o' my fire, no room now for an A.W.O.L. the likes of you."

"I can probably assist him on the walk back," said Nellie, wishing they were underway already.

Mrs. Havens and Warren turned to her in surprise, as if they had forgotten she was there. "'Tis a blessing *you* kept such a cool head. You are a most fortunate soldier, Zetus, to have received instant aid under these exceptional conditions," said Mrs. Havens.

"My goodness, Florence Nightingale, in all this commotion we have not been introduced," said Cadet Warren. "Searle, rouse yourself from your self-inflicted misery and introduce us to your fine lady."

"She's no fine lady—she is the sister of my spoony button girl," said Searle. *Was it pain that made him state her relationship in such an unflattering way?* she wondered.

"Ye always were quite the flatterer now," said Warren with a hint of vexation in his voice. Nellie and Mrs. Havens burst out laughing.

Then Nellie remembered they were not that far from the tavern, so not only were they still at risk of discovery, but also a long distance from the barracks.

"I am Cornelia Rose Entwhistle," said Nellie. She extended her hand.

Warren bowed with the grace of a knight over a duchess's hand. Nellie smiled. For a second her world righted itself.

"Mercy!" she said with a sharp intake of breath. "I fear we have been distracted from our sense of urgency. Perhaps I am being overly cautious, and the threatening visit was a false alarm?" She looked from the still pale face of the prone Zetus into the flushed face of G. K. Warren and then to Mrs. Letitia Havens.

"Alas, my dear, 'tis a real danger for these lads. There are not often raids such as these, but when they come, t' consequences can be dire. Two generals and a posse of cadet guards and patrols, tossing back Hot Flips and wolfing me roast pork! I do recall one patrol such as this capturing a certain Jefferson Davis. Goodness that lad got in more scrapes! Although I must say, he does not seem to be worse for the wear. Governor of Mississippi, with an eye toward Secretary of War, for the right President."

Mrs. Havens commands an impressive knowledge of the whereabouts of one of her 'sons,' thought Nellie.

Warren emitted a low chuckle. "Every cadet in the long grey line knows the tale of Jeff Davis damn near falling to his death on these very cliffs, trying to escape a raid."

"T' lady is right," said Mrs. Havens. 'Ye must 'make foot' now."

"Come," Warren said. "Zetus stand and lean on my shoulder. Mistress Entwhistle, if you will be so kind as to support his other shoulder, I shall attempt the journey back to camp."

Nellie dutifully shouldered Searle's right arm and his weight almost sent her pitching forward. The team started off down the rocky path well enough, but when they came to the crude wood steps leading to the top of the cliff, and the treacherous woods above, Nellie's heart sank in trepidation.

She drew in her breath and placed her right foot on the first step with determination. "Up we go then," she said.

They climbed three steps.

Nellie was already out of breath. *Where were the rest of the fleeing cadets? Have they all gone ahead?*

Just then, a light shone below them.

"Busted!" moaned Searle.

"The cavalry!" rejoiced Warren.

"Most definitely not t' cavalry young man," said a stern voice in a thick Irish brogue. "As for ye Cornelia Rose Entwhistle...."

Nellie turned in disbelief and looked straight into the glare of the lantern, which blinded her. Her companions blinked in its brightness too.

Rough hands grabbed Nellie and two bodies brushed by her to assume the weight of half of Searle.

Nellie tried to pull away from the grasp, but the perpetrator held the lantern up to his own face. Nellie was gob smacked to see it was her own father.

"Papa? How did you get here? What business do you have here?" Nellie sputtered.

"I might well be ask'n' ye t' same sort o' questions," her father replied, tightening his grip on her arm and pulling her away from her two companions. "Tho' I suspect the answer is 'monkey business'!"

The men with her father steered the two cadets around the other way to face them.

"Sir, be you friend or foe to this lady?" asked Warren, as Searle gasped, "Unhand this angel of mercy!"

Mr. Entwhistle and his companions burst out laughing. "Well, I see ye be in the company of gentlemen at least. Unchaperoned, aye, jist as yer *Mutter* worried, but a wee bit o' redemption in t' fact that t' men appear to be gentlemen. Come this way lads, ye appear to be in a bit o' lather. Let's get ye to me sloop and we can determine where to set course from there."

"Your sloop? But where is...? How did...? ...Come here? When...?" Nellie's tongue, still in a stupor of surprise, stuttered more bits of questions.

"Yer *Mutter* sent me, yer brother Patrick, and young Clayton here on a fact-finding mission, finding, in fact that only *one* Entwhistle colleen was present and accounted for, resting with her chaperone at t' instructor's fine home...." he said. Nellie winced because her father tightened his grip on her arm.

"Papa I can explain...." Nellie interrupted.

"An' ye surely will. But for now, suffice it to say that Agnes was worried about you and her sister's beau here...." Her father gestured at Searle. "...and relived to see me appear with t' same concerns. She was only too willing to tell o' yer whereabouts."

Mr. Entwhistle turned to Patrick and Clayton, "Do not err, like I have meself. Do no' ever underestimate t' powers of our better half's sixth sense." To Nellie he said, "Yer *Mutter* was beside herself with worry, sure that a grave ill befell ye. I could no' placate her. I had to come to find ye."

"'Tis well that you did," said Nellie as her father said, "'Tis well I did."

In the process of moving the wounded cadet, Patrick gave Nellie a reassuring clap on the back. *Thank the Lord for small favors, 'tis my brother Patrick come to rescue me and not Jerome or Jonas. Neither of them would ever let me forget this humiliation,* she thought.

In minutes, they were at the sloop, anchored at a flimsy dock less than a quarter of a mile down the cliff from Benny Havens'. On the other side of the dock, several rowboats were in various stages of launching, with cadets perched on every available spot. Other small craft were still berthed, ostensibly awaiting other members of the cadet corps.

"Do you mean to say that instead of that trek through the dark and dangerous wood, I could have journeyed to that tavern via the river, with a short stroll up a well-trod path?" Nellie asked, fists raised as if to punch someone. "That Magruder is a ne'er do well!" She stamped her foot.

A big belly laugh rang out over the water. Nellie could only surmise it came from one of the crew or her father's cohort, Clayton.

"You'll be less than pleased to learn then," said the still laughing voice from the shadows, "the float up the river to the cadet barracks is a scant five minutes."

If that doesn't make me a goat! Nellie thought.

Her two cadet companions, however, resuscitated her self-esteem. They talked over each other in their haste to exculpate her, explaining in detail, with laudatory words, how Nellie rescued Searle from certain death by her medical skill and cool head.

Somewhat mollified by learning the details, Mr. Entwhistle brought his craft to a small dock in close proximity to the barracks. Patrick and Warren almost lifted Searle ashore.

Nellie moved behind them, ready to disembark.

But Mr. Entwhistle laid a restraining hand on her arm.

"I'm afraid yer stay at T' Point has ended m' dear," he said in a soft voice, no anger or rancor apparent.

Nellie drew back in surprise. "But Papa, I am to attend services in the Chapel in the morning and the band concert tomorrow afternoon."

"Not any more, ye ar'n't. Yer sister will send word to that cad who was to escort ye, and that will be the end o' it."

Nellie was actually grateful. *I expected punishment and humiliation. But Papa is sparing me the ignominy of having to tell Magruder I never want to see him again.*

She threw her arms around her father and gave him a giant hug. He immediately hugged her back. She said, "Oh Papa, thank you and *Mutter* for saving me from my own imprudence and folly."

The world was right again as, in the ship's light Nellie saw her father grin back.

CHAPTER 22
Wedding March

Sing Sing, June 1850

Tarnation!

The memories that sprang to Nellie's mind each morning, as soon as she awoke, washed her in a fresh wave of embarrassment and mortification. Scenes from her exploits, which she privately dubbed 'The West Point Debacle,' repeated in her head for what seemed like an eternity. *When will I learn some restraint?* she asked herself over and over, head bent in shame. *When will I learn how to accurately assess the merits of a young man's character? I will never return to that Academy – that location of my humiliation.*

However, the invitations, received continually since the Entwhistle ladies' debut last year, continued to come. The indignity of her father retrieving her from West Point, like some wayward, disobedient dog, remained within the family. But it needled her, prickling like a thorn within Nellie's heart. She busied herself with the social life in Sing Sing, happy that the picnic social scene was budding with the June flowers. She eschewed invitations to West Point and declined Anastasia's request that Nellie accompany her to see her beau Searle.

One Sunday evening, Nellie sat on her bed in their garret room and watched enviously as Anastasia and Agnes unpacked their cases from their weekend at West Point.

"Pshaw, Nellie, you should have come!" Anastasia looked at her with big, sympathetic eyes. "Elmer still pines for you. You also received inquires as to your whereabouts from that scallywag Magruder, and some cadet named Baker who did not look familiar. Can you enlighten me as to his identity?"

"I am afraid I cannot." Nellie dismissed the message from the mystery man with a wave of her hand. "Magruder is a scallywag indeed..." she muttered.

She shook her head, as if trying to shake off his memory. "How fares Zetus? Any repercussions from his tragic injury?" Nellie stifled a grin, determined to focus on the lighter side of the whole sophomoric incident.

"Only his undying appreciation for you and your midwifery skills. He claims you saved his life! Instead of skulking about here like a culprit, you should be regaling all of society with anecdotes of the episode." Anastasia threw her hand wide in a dramatic gesture. "Every man, woman and child should know of your heroism."

"Pshaw," said Nellie, face again burning with humiliation.

"Most truly, Cornelia," said Anastasia with an earnest expression on her face. "There is no shame in the incident. 'Twas just a bit of a lark of a caper, turned sour—followed by an act of selfless bravery."

"Bravery? I merely applied my training." Nellie scoffed at herself.

"Even Papa and *Mutter* speak of the incident with pride."

"I almost believed you, until you proffered that proclamation. Our parents will *never* be proud of having to find and rescue me from that scrape." Nellie buried her head in her hands.

"You would be surprised," whispered Anastasia, her hand on Nellie's shoulder in a comforting gesture. "They are human. And they were young once too."

Nellie looked up in disbelief, but Agnes, standing with her hands on her hips, captured her gaze.

"I am waiting for your undivided attention, sisters," Agnes said, tapping her foot. Both girls dutifully, or perhaps from force of habit, deferred to Agnes's orders, and turned expectant faces toward their domineering sister.

"I am engaged to be married," she announced, and folded her arms across her chest, smug expression on her face.

Her two sisters crowded around her, hugging her, and squealing in delight. Agnes's facial expression turned to satisfaction.

"So exciting! How wonderful!" the sisters chorused.

"How ever did you persuade that indecisive Armistead to make up his mind?" Nellie demanded. "I do believe that man truly could talk out of both sides of his mouth."

"He is a man of action, once a firm woman takes him in hand," replied Agnes, and then she grinned a smile so big Nellie was sure her sister had never before smiled that broadly.

Agnes held out her hand and her sisters saw a large, heavy ring. Nellie grabbed her hand and Anastasia bent to view it.

"Goodness that is massive!" exclaimed Anastasia.

"Why the black onyx contains an image of West Point," said Nellie.

"Yes, it is Armistead's class ring from the Academy. It is merely a placeholder for an engagement ring of my own," replied Agnes.

Nellie examined the raised design of the almost triangular onyx stone set at an angle in intricately wrought gold. "A most remarkable placeholder indeed," she confirmed.

"We must plan your wedding!" shrieked Anastasia. "Which do you prefer: a ceremony of splendor and spectacle in New York City like the viscountess at Trinity Church or a quiet one in our small village setting?"

"Viscountess? Sakes alive! Now that she has married a common American, for his wealth, that Hungarian 'viscountess' has been stripped of her honorary title," said the bossy Agnes. Nellie would have challenged her statement, but somehow, she vaguely recalled that Agnes' point of societal etiquette was correct.

"Therefore," Agnes continued, "henceforth she will only be referred to as 'the Honorable Mrs. Dunlap'."

"Mercy, do you remember the pomp and circumstance of that wedding?" asked Nellie. The ladies nodded. "It was grander than even *I* could have imagined."

Agnes raised a solitary eyebrow in a smirk of recognition at the vast capacity of Nellie's imagination and the true grandeur of the nuptials they had the privilege of attending.

Anastasia took up the narrative. "The reception for the viscountess was both ostentatious and magnificent. The feast sumptuous and overabundant! After dancing the evening away, the guests were invited to say their farewells to the couple." She traipsed through the sitting room as she recounted the tale. "The whole party filed across the grand lawn in a colorful parade of fancy couture. We sashayed down the steps in the exquisitely manicured landscape to the river estuary abutting their imposing estate."

Anastasia stopped in front of them and whispered, "A hush fell over the assembled guests as we waited for the happy couple to board their boat and ship off to some exotic location in their own private sloop. As one, the crowd leaned over the bridge to bid the blissful newlyweds adieu...."

"And *Mutter*, of all people, dropped her glove!" Nellie started laughing as she uttered the words. Her sisters joined her.

"I truly thought it was you Nellie, for I will swear to this day, as the glove hit the railing and then plopped off, I heard your favorite excited utterance, 'Tarnation'! Could *Mutter* truly have employed such boorish language?" asked Anastasia.

Agnes tossed her head, and defended their mother. "I only heard her whisper what any *lady* would say — 'my best kid glove!' with a small groan."

Nellie was literally holding her sides now, tugging at her corset, she was laughing so hard at the recollection. "The entire crowd watched the lone glove float like a lily pad on the still waters of the river, as if it were taunting *Mutter*."

Anastasia started laughing again, and even Agnes smiled.

Anastasia resumed her tale. "The glove floated downstream and then came back, as if it were saying goodbye."

"Yes," sniffed Agnes, now with a small giggle. "At last, with a small wave of its fingers it took it off on an adventure all its own." Agnes waved 'bye bye.'

"Mercy! The prospect of wedded life most truly agrees with you," said Nellie and caught Agnes' hands affectionately.

Agnes sniffed again. "Yes, it is all well and good. But *'es macht nichts'* as *Mutter* would say. It doesn't matter what style wedding *I* would prefer. Indeed, *I would prefer* a grand and glorious wedding at the biggest Catholic Church on Manhattan Island. *Mutter* has decreed a simple church wedding at Saint Patrick's in Verplank, like our brother Patrick's nuptial Mass two years ago. Sakes alive! No! *Verplank*? Pile on the agony!"

Agnes sighed, feeling sorry for herself, and picked at the loose threads on Nellie's eiderdown. In a subdued voice, she said, "The site of our wedding has already been determined. Since Mr. Armistead Lindsey Long is from way down south in Virginia, and I refuse to entertain the idea of ever even visiting there, let alone travel there for our nuptials, *Mutter* has arranged we will be wed in the boondocks of Verplank."

Anastasia and Cornelia exchanged glances. *Yes, this is the Agnes we both know.*

"Mayhap *Mutter* will allow some concession to Armistead's exceptional education and excellent pedigree," said Anastasia.

"Surely, you can use your extraordinary persuasive powers," Nellie chimed in, "and convince *Mutter* to allow you some nod to Long's heritage, in the form of fancy dress uniforms on the groom and his men?"

Agnes paused in her grousing, interested. Anastasia looked amused at Nellie's choice of words.

That was all the encouragement Cornelia needed. She continued, "The pièce de résistance—the happy couple exiting the church through the crossed swords of the honor guard as the parade band plays Wagner's new *Bridal Chorus*. It will be unreservedly romantic, just like the weddings reported in the Society Pages of the newspaper."

"A true fairytale," said Anastasia, batting her eyelashes.

"Every ounce as romantic as plain old Nancy Osgood marrying 'Baron' Charles Steadman Abercrombie," declared Nellie. "It is only by tracing his lineage back to his Scottish great-great-great grandfather that can he even *pretend* a claim to that moniker. A claim made all the more tenuous, by-the-by, through virtue of the fact that he, himself, has never even stepped foot in Scotland. But I digress! Indubitably, a West Point infused wedding is far more glamorous, and stylish, than either couples' ostentatious exchange of vows in New York City's Trinity Church."

The sisters smiled at each other in happy anticipation of a most satisfactory, glamorous, storybook wedding.

CHAPTER 23
Don't Know Much about History

Sparta Cemetery, July 1850

"A cannonball blasted through a tombstone?" asked Obadiah. "Was that precise shooting or mere happenstance?"

Nellie smiled at him, happy to be heading out for a picnic on this lovely July afternoon.

"Is there some military advantage to firing on the dead, untaught during my education at Saint John's Military Academy?" Obadiah demanded, with a mock look of consternation.

Nellie laughed, swinging her light bag containing a tablecloth, their napkins, and other necessities for a dignified picnic. Obadiah switched the heavy basket containing the food and drink from hand to hand. *I have the proper equipment, the proper nourishment and the most splendid of companions,* she thought.

Obadiah took his history seriously. "Do not abdicate your responsibility to supply me with all of the requisite details—namely, whose eternal rest is marked at this site?"

Nellie said, with appropriate solemnity, "A poor little boy, Abraham Ladew, who died in 1774 after only a brief seven years on this earth. The poor Ladew family! The tomb next to Abraham is a sister he never would have met. Tragically, she died as a mere five-year-old, before he was born.

"Life was more arduous then. Happily, today we are far better armed to weather life's diseases and hazards, with a greatly increased store of medical knowledge," Nellie said.

They arrived at Sparta cemetery at the top of a grassy knoll, overlooking the new Post Road to the east and Revolutionary Road to the west.

Nellie led the way to the Ladew family plot, almost centrally located in the cemetery at the top of the hill. A fancy black chain link fence encircled the family's section.

"Here is Sarah," said Obadiah. He read, "'...died Aug. 15, 1764. Aged 5 years, 7 months, and 11 days'. My that is precise." He traced his finger across the chiseled words.

Obadiah's fingers next probed the cannonball hole, not with the idle curiosity of a thrill seeker, but with reverence and respect for the dead and their history.

He looked around the pleasant, tree shaded spot. "This area is the picture of tranquility and repose. It seems strange that a stray cannon ball damaged this tombstone, yet nothing else in this area was harmed."

"Verily, *today* only this solitary, isolated, bit of damage is visible. But I must inform you—the old Presbyterian Church of Mount Pleasant used to be right there." Nellie pointed past a group of young pines toward the far corner of the cemetery. "A farmer named Arnold Hunt donated part of his land to build the original church. It was so damaged during the Revolutionary War, why, it was shaken to its very foundations, triggering alarming stress fractures. For many years the visibly damaged, old rickety building worried its parishioners as they sat worshiping. Finally, the congregation garnered sufficient funds to build their current church."

"Yes. I have seen the church in its new, prime location," said Obadiah. "Right downtown in Sing Sing on Pleasant Square."

Nellie nodded. "So today, we have an open, tranquil, spot, on the top of a hill to catch breezes, and an occasional glimpse of the Hudson through those shady trees, to enjoy our picnic—just the landscaping design for final resting places that is currently in vogue."

Obadiah shook his head and laughed.

"William Cullen Bryant's poem *Thanatopsis* springs to mind in a setting such as this. His concept that the beauty of nature is here to support us and console us, especially in the face of death, is ratified by the pastoral beauty of this spot," she said.

Ever ready to provide a theatrical performance, Nellie recited:

> "To him who in the love of Nature holds
> Communion with her visible forms, she speaks
> A various language; for his gayer hours
> She has a voice of gladness, and a smile
> And eloquence of beauty, and she glides
> Into his darker musings, with a mild
> And healing sympathy, that steals away
> Their sharpness, ere he is aware...."

Obadiah clapped with appreciation. Nellie stood up and curtseyed, with a laugh.

"Your tongue warbles the sweetest music," he said.

Smiling at the compliment, Nellie shook the picnic blanket. It fanned out in the breeze and landed under a shady tree. She sat down, removed her gloves, and opened the picnic basket. They settled in the comfy spot for some cold fried chicken, cucumbers, popped corn, and pickles.

"And the *pièce de résistance!*" Nellie exclaimed as she pulled out a large flask.

"With an introduction like that, that flagon cannot contain water," said Obadiah. "But what tempting liquid refreshment could it be?"

"Lemonade!" Nellie announced. "Fresh-squeezed this morning by my very own hands."

"How thoughtful." Obadiah smiled. "And very clever of you to package it in such a way to survive our little hike to this nesting place."

Their conversation flowed as liberally as the lemonade.

But when they bit into the chicken all that could be heard was the sound of the breeze in the trees.

Satiated, Nellie looked at the great puffy clouds racing over the tops of the trees and then gazed out to the beauty of the mighty Hudson. Good feeling lapped at her like the small waves of the river lapped the rocky shore below. She smiled at Obadiah and he caught her ungloved hand and raised it to his lips. The touch on her bare skin sent tingles racing up her arm to her heart.

After a cozy moment of munching pickles and bantering bon mots, the conversation turned again to local history.

"The British Navy was *here*," said Obadiah. "It seems a trifle peculiar, upon reflection, when teaching local military history to circumvent the significance of naval battles."

At Cornelia's puzzled look, Obadiah said, "I recall my military academy devoted excessive amounts of time studying land skirmishes, when teaching the strategies of the battles of the Revolution. It seems they quite ignored the fact the British Navy sailed this far north on the Hudson."

"They went much further north than Sing Sing!" Nellie rose to the bait. "Surely your lessons included study of the original fort at West Point and the chain across the river to Constitution Island? Surely, they recounted the dramatic rendezvous of the battleship *Vulture* with

Benedict Arnold? Or the tale of the farmers, organizing in a Bedford Tavern to reclaim their livestock 'appropriated' by the British for food, instead thwarting the escape of the British Spy Captain Andre?"

Obadiah laughed again. "There may have been some mention, but the details are fuzzy. You, however, have put some heart into the tale."

"That ship was the very same *Vulture* that fired the cannon shot into poor Abraham Ladew's tombstone," she said.

"That was to be my very first question. From whence did that historic cannonball originate? But then I caught an aroma of the delicious repast you prepared and I am afraid all other interests quite fled from my thoughts!"

Mollified by the culinary compliment, Nellie drew a deep breath and smiled. "No matter, there is no dearth of information concerning local Revolutionary War intrigue. Why, I recently enjoyed reading a tale involving one of Sing Sing's own local spies, recounted by James Fennimore Cooper in *The Spy*."

"I do adore your passion for local history, and I pray you continue with your narrative." Obadiah leaned back against the nearest elm tree, put his hands behind his head and smiled.

Nellie's smiling eyes met his. Her heart did a little flip-flop at the beguiling attentiveness she saw there. She cast down her eyes, searching for an appropriately charming rejoinder. Thinking of none, she reverted to communicating her subject.

"Revisiting my earlier tale of that same ship, *The Vulture* wreaked havoc on the no-man's land of Westchester County. The British Naval Fleet controlled New York City harbor, but the territory north was in continuous flux. The British occupied some of the land, but the Revolutionaries had strongholds in other parts, triggering constant battles for the unclaimed areas. The poor residents! Daily, ships patrolling the Hudson River skirmished, firing canons willy-nilly. Causalities were constant, including decapitation by cannonball!"

"Decapitation? Surely there is no proof that a cannonball ever decapitated a soldier," protested Obadiah, still smiling.

"Decapitation was the cannon's very purpose. Moreover, my extensive study of local history led me to the journals of a certain American General, William Heath. He documents that in the Battle of White Plains he witnessed an American cannonball decapitating a Hessian artillery man," said Nellie, triumphant that she was able to offer the direct proof Obadiah desired.

"So eloquent are you, I have no choice but to believe you," said Obadiah. He jumped up and gave her a bow and a hand flourish, formally deferring to her opinion. She smiled in response. He winked and settled back down into his comfortable listening position.

Nellie nodded an acknowledgement of the compliment and continued. "In addition to the eye witness account, there is the less scientific folklore, claiming that a decapitated Hessian soldier still haunts the Northern part of Tarrytown, riding out every night from the Old Dutch Church on the Post Road, in search of his head."

"Is that story not the product of the imagination of the writer, Washington Irving?" asked Obadiah. "Does he not reside somewhere near here, along the Hudson River?"

"The product of *Irving's* imagination? Ha! That literary thief! In nearby Slapershaven, the original Dutch name for the sleepy harbor inlet in the hamlet of Tarrytown, there circulates some witchery—a traditional story of Brom Bones' race with the headless horseman for a bowl of punch. Washington Irving is merely a scribe—his *Sketchbook* only records legends and fables that have been part of the local folklore for generations. Irving learned them from a Dutch family named Van Wart with whom he summered as a child during a 'fever' scourge in New York City, similar to the yellow fever plague to which poor Sarah Ladew succumbed, decades earlier!"

"Man alive! I have touched yet another nerve. I can certainly concede that Irving might have based his well-written short story on a circulating local legend, but one 'embellishment' does not make him a literary thief. Let us not forget that he is singlehandedly responsible for starting the 'Knickerbocker' movement," said Obadiah.

"Mr. William Cullen Bryant, in fact my personal acquaintance, would certainly disagree with the moniker 'single-handed'!" Nellie said.

"Perhaps," conceded Obadiah, "however, Irving put this American landscape in artistic vogue. His claim that the world's finest scenery abounds in the Hudson Highlands inspired many poets, pundits and the Hudson River School of artists." Obadiah paused and looked a tad sheepish. "I might not have been drawn to Sing Sing to attend the Academy had my father not been a devotee of the Knickerbocker movement. At the time, he was Governor of our fair state, and, smitten himself with the quixotic pull of this region, he enthused me with the romantic appeal of the Hudson. Truly, I have not been disappointed in that amorous regard." He winked at Nellie.

"Furthermore," Obadiah continued, "Irving also garners fame for his other Knickerbocker stories. *Rip Van Winkle* is one that jumps to mind."

"Pshaw! That story is *stolen* from an Old Russian folktale! Mr. Bryant can continue to wax poetic in defense his friend — it will never persuade me. Irving, the alleged literary giant, is merely an embroiderer of folklore. He has never had an original idea. Even his settings are merely poetically written descriptions of this, our own historic Hudson River Valley.

"Truly, he has set the tales in flowery verse, painted a picture of this area with his words, but the stories themselves, *Rip Van Winkle* and our Sleepy Hollow legend are not of his own making. He has stolen them and touted the literary creations as his own." Nellie folded her arms and shook her head.

Obadiah smiled at her with tenderness in his eyes. Nellie saw those tender eyes flicker to her lips and she tingled at her speculation, *how would those smiling lips feel against mine?*

"Today you have tapped several facets of history that are foreign to me, therefore I dare not refute them. It is evident you are quite the ardent defender of causes you champion. An admirable trait in a woman," Obadiah said. He cleared his throat. "If truth be told, I admire *you*. I envision... I hope we share many future picnics together, discussing any passion of yours — in fact, whiling away the hours undertaking anything your heart desires."

Nellie looked at him in wide-eyed delight.

Obadiah leaned over and caught her hand again, gently pulling her toward him.

Nellie's heart galloped.

He kissed her hand and looked up at her. At the touch of his lips a tingle of pleasure traveled up her arm. She caught her lip in her teeth.

Seeing her favorable response, he gathered her in his arms and kissed her lips in earnest.

Mercy, the day grew suddenly warm! Nellie thought.

If this isn't butter upon bacon! History and... some mystery.

CHAPTER 24
Déjà vu

Sing Sing, August 1850

"But Papa, this time I will be the escort of just one cadet," Nellie pleaded.

"As ye were with that young lad Otis?" asked her father, still shaking his head in the negative.

Nellie had finally relented and decided to accept another invitation from a cadet at West Point. The mysterious Lawrence Simmons Baker, the cadet who had escorted her from the Catholic Church to their carriage such a long time ago on her first visit to West Point, had been corresponding since then. When Agnes announced her engagement to Baker's friend Armistead Long, Baker's letters took on a tone of desperation, petitioning Nellie to grace him with her presence.

Nellie made up her mind to accept his latest invitation, and now pleaded her case. "But there were no incidents when I accompanied *Otis*. Of course, I *did* entertain advances from some of the other cadets, but solely because I was Elmer's companion under protest. This time, I would be appreciative of the opportunity to become better acquainted with a potential suitor, most especially as he is a suitor of my own choosing. Surely the difference is readily evident?"

Mr. Entwhistle still stood, rigid, looking from the invitation to Nellie and back again.

Nellie turned her persuasive talents on her mother. "*Mutter*, West Point has become quite the destination during the summer months. Dignitaries from all walks of life—artists, writers, politicians, merchants, and industrialists converge there for the sublime scenery and the scintillating musical performances. The Academy in the summer provides just ambiance and distinguished society, just the right *milieu* in which a young debutante should circulate."

Her mother remained unmoved, the hem of her sister's dress turning rapidly through her hands as she shortened it with quick basting stiches.

Nellie tried a different tack with her father. "*Mutter* can accompany me."

Mrs. Entwhistle looked up from her mending with raised eyebrows. "Thank you for permission. *Natürlich,* I will accompany you," said she, with the expression on her face that most people use when they are lighthearted and teasing.

"Then it is quite settled," said Nellie and scampered out of the room before either of her parents could contradict her.

They caught a luxurious day boat to Albany, packed with tourists, flush with newfound leisure time. Nellie eschewed the steamboat's fancy dining room and the lavish staterooms and assumed her usual post at the bow of the ship, feeling the adventure and the joy of the salty spray.

When the river channel narrowed and they turned the first curve of the serpentine "S" course the river followed, the sure indication that their destination was imminent, Nellie thought her heart would burst with happiness and anticipation.

Life at The Point was very different during summer tourist season. A fine carriage met the steamboat, and ferried the visitors up the hill in style.

Anastasia giggled and whispered from behind her fan, "A far cry from our first visit, don't you agree Nellie? No toiling up the hill watching our luggage lurch and tip precariously at every hairpin turn of the path."

Nellie giggled back. "No fear of *glowing* today."

From the luxury of a nicely upholstered seat in the carriage, Nellie's first view of the heart of the campus was quite different from the sweeping barren scene she witnessed last April. A sea of tents, white canvas sailing in the breeze, flooded the wide-open Great Plain. The rift in the lawn known as Execution Hollow, usually the only interruption of the grass, was not even visible. The glare of the sun reflected by the tent tops transformed the Plain from forest green to nautical white.

The encampment on the Great Plain was the home of the cadets through the summer months. When the carriage skirted the perimeter of the camp toward its West Point Hotel destination, she could see cadets lounging about in a rare moment of free time. A bugle blew and abruptly leisure time terminated. Nellie blinked, and the cadets were already in platoons, scurrying to obey its command.

Leaning back on the plush velvet cushions next to her, Anastasia lamented her inability to locate Zetus S. Searle among the throngs of people and cadets.

"I am quite certain you will find him with all due haste. I am equally certain he is anxious to find you!" said Nellie.

"Do you think he will be at the reception desk at the hotel waiting for me, since he could not meet us at the landing?" Anastasia asked. She twisted her fan in her hands.

"Verily, it seems likely. He is now a graduate of this fine Academy, an elevated status from cadet. Therefore, I would assume he has greater flexibility, and command of his schedule." Nellie reassured her.

"I would make the very same assumption," said Anastasia, "but for the fact I have heretofore seen little evidence of schedule flexibility. I was more than ecstatic to learn of Zetus' decision to resign his commission immediately upon graduation. It is not as if our country is at war. Moreover, Zetus is a pacifist at heart, and has no interest in 'taming the West.' So, it seemed the best course of business for him is the business of academia. Where better to start than here? His position understudying a professor and tutoring remedial students during the cadet summer encampment has been a Godsend."

They mounted the grand stairs of the hotel and crossed into the cooler recesses of the capacious lobby. There, near the reception desk stood Zetus, in front of the grandfather clock, looking even more massive in his civilian clothes.

"My humble apologies, my sweet pumpkin, for failing to greet you at the dock. I was forced to oversee some last-minute details of the program for tonight's Hop."

"*You* are the new dance instructor?" The words popped out before Nellie considered their appropriateness.

Zetus blushed.

Anastasia surreptitiously kicked Nellie in the shins for her excited utterance. "Cornelia Rose! What impertinence! Zetus is an exceptional dancer," Anastasia said and grabbed Searle's elbow, giving it a reassuring squeeze.

"The head dance instructor from Boston suffers terribly from gout this summer. His continuous employment here at the Academy since Superintendent Thayer hired him, causes general reluctance to relieve him of his duties. As a junior instructor, I am assigned to oversee dance lessons in his stead," said Zetus regaining his poise, even though his large ears remained bright red.

"I have also had a hand in fashioning the program, to ensure the cadets showcase the steps they have worked diligently to master. Mademoiselle, may I present your dance card for this evening?"

Anastasia squealed with delight. "Nellie, observe the clever design. The dance card is a fan!"

She artfully snapped the fan. Its folds sprang open, revealing pretty pink flowers emblazoned around printed words on heavy gold pressed paper, laced together with pink ribbon.

Nellie stepped closer and admired the program. She read, "Summer Hop Friday August 29th, FINAL COTILLION 1850 Summer Encampment," as she ran her finger over the engraved words on the fan's outside closure.

"How delightfully intricate! How finely executed!" Anastasia gushed.

Zetus's grin lit his whole face.

He looks pleased as punch, Nellie thought.

"Each dance is listed," said Zetus, taking Anastasia's gloved hand and running her finger over each fold. Anastasia read, "1-Pigeon wing, 2-Double shuffle, 3-Hoe-down, 4-Waltz, 5-Reel, 6-Quadrille."

"Only six dances?" Nellie cried, her dismay at missing any opportunity to dance making her tactless.

"Cornelia! What ails you? Must you blurt every gauche thought as it enters your head?" cried Anastasia. She practically clucked like a mother hen as she patted Zetus's hand to reassure him.

Mercy, Anastasia must be truly smitten to react so.

Zetus patted Anastasia's hand in return. "It's of no consequence, my beloved. Cornelia, as you must have already perceived, our Hops are strictly regulated. However, if you spread the fan out so...." Zetus pulled the fan out further, revealing four more spokes and continued. "...You will see we have the usual number of dances, including a polka. The paper was stuck."

They all laughed.

"Our Hop will conform to the regularly apportioned time, of course, from 8 o'clock to 10 post meridiem precisely. We have ample time for ten dances, and I promise you, my men have excelled at their lessons. I must say, I enjoyed a bit of sport and levity myself in the process. You will not be disappointed in the cadets' execution of my instructions."

After they supped on a delicious light tea.... *Dash it, even the food is finer!* Nellie thought... they had just sufficient time for donning their evening dresses before the hour of the Final Cotillion arrived.

When Nellie, her sister, and mother came down the hotel stairs into the soft evening, it was not the last vestiges of the evening sun that took her breath away, but the candlelight flickering in the dusk along the path around the perimeter of the tents on the Great Plain.

"How dreamy... the candlelit path enhances the already romantic scenery to the point of leaving me starry-eyed!" Nellie said, drinking in the scene.

"The sight engenders my delighted swoon," confirmed Anastasia.

"Where does it lead?" asked Mrs. Entwhistle.

"To the Cotillion!" both girls replied.

The ladies had barely entered the main floor equestrian-practice-area of the academic building turned dance hall when someone grabbed Nellie's elbow. She swung around.

"At last we meet again. I have often despaired that this most desired reunion would only ever occur in my fantasy," boomed a drawling voice.

A tall courtly cadet bowed low over Nellie's hand, the act obliterating his face, leaving Nellie unsure of his identity. He straightened and she deduced he must be the mysterious Lawrence Simmons Baker. *He remained shrouded in mystery until the last possible moment,* she giggled to herself.

Cornelia curtseyed and said, "Cadet Lawrence Simmons Baker, I presume? It is truly a pleasure to at last be properly introduced."

"Here you are in the flesh!" exclaimed Baker, and Nellie gave an inward gasp at his rough language. "I do thank you for your gracious and faithful correspondence as I endeavored to turn our long-ago chance meetn' at the quay and then later in the Churchyard, into a courtship." Baker practically sang the words in the cadence of his deep Southern accent.

A courtship? Nellie thought. *If that don't beat the Dutch!* But when he quite literally swept her off her feet for the first dance, she relaxed in his arms and savored the blissful movement. She smiled and floated through the 'pigeon wing' as if her feet had wings of their own.

"I have long dreamed of dancing with one so skilled in this fine art," Nellie said, as she swirled and swayed. "Moreover, I am not merely speaking in platitudes, nor am I simply flattering — my speech is quite sincere."

"I so very much appreciate your honesty. And of course, your highly desired compliment," said Baker.

Nellie raised her eyebrows with a touch of irritation at his immodesty.

But when she sighed with disappointment at the dance's end, Baker sighed too. *'Tis a bit surprising for such a self-assured, bold man to sigh,* she thought. *Mayhap we have sentiment in common after all.*

He held on to both her hands, pulled back and took a long look at her. Nellie smiled in return.

Suddenly Baker dropped her hands and ran off.

What in Tarnation? Nellie thought. She watched him dart through the crowd and make a beeline towards the table at the entrance. She leaned slightly backwards, and saw him talking with animated facial expressions to the hostess.

Mercy! He procured a writing instrument?

In an instant, he was at her side again and grabbed her fan program, signing his name on all the spots on her dance card, with a flourish.

The two hours of dancing flew by as swiftly as Baker and Nellie's feet flew over the riding hall floor. The music swelled louder with the final Strauss waltz. The grandeur of the musical arrangement and the excellence of the musicians culminated in producing the stirring music that filled her head and heart. Flushed with excitement, the music coursing through her veins, Nellie abandoned herself to the joy of dancing.

With the last strains of music still playing in her head, Nellie floated on Baker's arm out of the building into the star-lit night. They paused at Fort Putnam, the citadel perched on the highest point of the campus, observing the spectacular view of the Hudson, easily visible in the moonlight.

Before she floated back down to earth, they were upon Flirtation Walk.

Meandering down the path, still dancing in her head, Nellie let the softness of the moonlight feed her heady mood. They paused at a nook on the path that served as yet another scenic overlook.

"'Scenes of wild grandeur, peculiar to our country,'" Nellie whispered.

"'Tis the middle watch of a summer's night,'" recounted Lawrence.

"'The earth is dark, but the heavens are bright'...." Nellie recited in reply. In an instant Cadet Baker was standing behind her, pulling her back into his... *buttons! Oh no, button-crushed from behind...* tight against his chest. He encircled his arms around her small waist and drew his lips close to her ear.

"'The moon looks down on ol' Cro'nest,'

"'She mellows the shades on his shaggy breast....'" The cadet turned her toward the bump dubbed 'crow's nest' protruding from Storm King Mountain, one of the two 'frowning hills' just within sight from their nook on Flirtie. Nellie felt enchanted by the charm and romance of the evening. The moon was high and bright and the stars, indelible bursts of light in all sizes from pinpricks to fists, seemed close enough to touch.

She smiled at the stars and said softly, "'...and seems his huge grey form to throw,'"

"'In a silver cone on the wave below.'" They both said together.

Nellie said, "The Knickerbockers have done a capital job of filling the Highlands with new legends. Why that very mountain upon which the crow's nest rests, would still be called 'Butter Hill' instead of 'Storm King'" were it not for the fine persuasive essays of Nathaniel Parker Willis."

"Yes, if y'all examine that water closely, I am sure you will join me in seeing Drake's 'Culprit Fay,'" teased Lawrence. "As enamored as I am with this romantic scenery, though, it does not hold a candle to the river-wrapped woods of the mighty Mississippi Delta."

Nellie turned around in his arms to face him. Hot words of protest rose to her lips.

Baker placed a long, slender, tapered finger on those lips and drawled, "Now, now, Ma'am. I do humbly apologize for striking a sour note during our lovely perambulation. I can see that I should not exhibit the audacity to compare the *fine* scenery of your native *land* on a magical night such as this to any place as plebian as the muddy shores of my native scenery known as Ol' Miss."

Placated, Nellie visibly relaxed. Lawrence moved right in and planted a long, lingering, passionate kiss on Nellie's lips. Nellie's heart shot over the moon, catapulting her whole body along with it.

Before she could protest, or even catch her breath, Lawrence turned her around again, pulling her back into his buttons, twisting her petticoats around her legs. He leaned his head close again, this time lining his ear with hers. "See here," his arm brushed the side of her breast as he pointed to a spot across the river, a tad up from the shore.

"The lights of the grand industrialist Gouverneur Kemble's estate in Cold Spring...." His arm moved along her breast as he lifted it towards the sky. *Intentionally?* she wondered. "...Mimic the little stars of light around that constellation."

"Truly the moon creates a perfect night for viewing the scenery," Nellie agreed, but she stepped away from his embrace. Baker caught her hand to pull her back. Before she allowed herself to be tugged back into his arms she tried to subtly thwart his intentions, at least verbally. "However, 'tis a pity we missed the moonlight serenade boat ride, proposed by the others."

"We have not missed it. Quite the contrary! I have chosen this exact spot to position you for maximum enjoyment and optimum experience of that very boat ride. I do believe you will find far greater excitement and *exhilaration* here. You shall participate fully in the event without the compulsory ride in that rocking, unstable, boat." Once again, those strong arms encircled her. He pulled her back into his buttons. He turned Nellie, this time toward the south.

"The boats will pass around Gee's Point in a matter of minutes. I believe there is only a mild wind, so we shall be able to hear the serenade selection just as perfectly as if we were in the boat next to the band's."

As he finished speaking, the first boat came around the point into full view. In the bright light of the moon, Nellie could make out the white gloves of the cadets flashing in unison as they pulled on the oars. A murmur of delight rose from the boatload as they viewed the moon's beams playing on the waves in front of them.

"With the serpentine twist of the river at this bend, I suppose the boats would have been in the shadow of the Point on the other side of the mountain," said Nellie.

"Hush now!" commanded Lawrence. "Listen!"

He was right, the first strains of music wafted up to their perch as the boat carrying the band rounded the point. *'A Little Night Music'! This selection is perfect,* Nellie thought. When the boat completed the turn, the music rose to their ears clearly and sweetly in the still summer air.

Baker's breathing was getting louder in her ear. She pulled her head a bit to the side to hear Mozart's *Allegro* better but Lawrence's head followed. Suddenly wet lips began to nibble at her ear. Nellie's initial irritation at not being able to hear the music soon shifted to tingles of delight. *How decadent... how scintillating... how titillating....*

Nellie could feel herself melt at the warmth and passion of the kisses on her ear and then her neck.

Once again, literally to the tune of *Romanze, Andante*, the cadet turned her around, sliding his lips from her neck to her ear to her cheek... to her lips. *Mercy...* she thought. *Skillfully done.* He kissed her again and ran his hands down her arms, sending shivers of delight along the same path. Once again, he encircled her in his arms and swung her around.

He whispered in her ear. "Next we will hear Weber's *Hunter's Chorus* as the oarsmen steer the Moonlight Serenade boats right under the Crow's Nest of Storm King."

"'Where the eagle builds her eyrie,'" Nellie whispered back.

"Watch," Baker ordered, turning her head toward the boats now squarely in front of Storm King.

"Why have they stopped rowing?" Nellie asked.

"From this point on the oarsmen will rest on their oars, thus allowing the tide to drift the flotilla back down the river. When this musical piece concludes, they will dock at the North Dock, and *we* will proceed to 'Kissing Rock'."

Nellie's stomach did a flip-flop at that declaration, quivering in anticipation. She watched and listened, pulsing with the music and the heat of the kisses the cadet bestowed lavishly and in rapid succession on her ear and neck. *This spot must be re-named kissing lookout!* The thought ran across her brain, dodging in between the mind-numbing passion ignited by Baker's kisses. As the music swelled to its crescendo, Baker swung her around again for another long, passionate kiss and an encasing embrace, in a smooth and seemingly well-practiced move.

Well practiced? Why does it seem that this well-orchestrated interlude is well practiced? She thought with only part of her brain as the other part soared with her emotions.

When the cadet moved his lips down the front of her neck in a long slide down her décolletage to the top button of her bodice, Nellie's brain snapped to attention. *Dash it! I am a fool.*

She put her hand under the cadet's chin and pulled his eyes up to her own eye level. "While quite enamored of this surfeit of affection, I do hate the niggling feeling tugging on my intellect that perhaps this is not quite the spontaneous outpouring of affection I supposed."

Baker laughed and said, "If you mean has this escapade been premeditated, then *yes!* I stand guilty as charged. I told you when I first met you at the dock and retrieved your handkerchief that I wanted to take you to Flirtation Walk. I have dreamed of it ever since."

Nellie stood still in his arms, remembering her first foray to West Point and the long-forgotten flirtatious exchange she had with this cadet. *Mayhap he has merely rehearsed this scenario in his mind?* she thought.

Lawrence, perhaps thinking her silence meant she had no further objections, slid his hand into the top of her sleeve and rubbed her bare shoulder with his palm, his thumb straying toward her breast. Nellie stepped back.

"You have stood in this exact spot and performed this exact maneuver before."

The cadet's hand froze. He flashed startled eyes at Nellie.

Nellie knew her answer.

"Well, butter my biscuit! I have *not,* I mean, would *not....*" Breathing heavy, Baker fumbled for words.

"Ahem," Nellie said to silence him, and pulled further away. "I do feel a tremendous softness for you Cadet Baker. Howsoever, I do believe carrying on in this manner any further is detrimental to the fostering of this gently budding relationship. I would like to be escorted back to camp now."

The cadet looked at her in disbelief. "I assure you...."

Nellie's jaws tightened with that look of determination her family, at least, knew all too well.

"This response is hardly necessary," said Baker, reaching for her hand.

But Nellie used that hand to tuck a stray hair into her elegant, coiffed curls, pat it, and pull up her shawl. She turned to go.

"I am departing back to camp now, *with* or *without* you," she said.

She walked away, not really even caring that she heard no footsteps behind her.

Twice to the most romantic spot on the West Point campus and twice nothing to show for it! Why must I have this unerring knack for entangling myself in compromising positions with Southern Gentlemen? My penchant for Southerners must cease entirely, straightaway.

CHAPTER 25
Color My World

West Point, August 1850

Nellie did not want to open her eyes. If she did, she would have to face the aftereffects of yet another humiliation on Flirtation Walk. *Or any type of walk at West Point!* She screwed her eyes tighter shut, turning her face into her pillow.

"Nellie," called Anastasia from the front foyer of their West Point Hotel suite. "Nellie, look!"

Nellie put the pillow over her ears and kept her eyes shut.

Suddenly the pillow was lifted from her head and the formidable figure of her mother loomed over her. "Cornelia, rise this instant! Late evening hours must never keep a debutante from appearing fresh and chipper in the morning. Any lack of healthful sleep can be reclaimed during an afternoon nap."

Mrs. Entwhistle leaned closer. "A little surprise just arrived for you which I am sure will rejuvenate your spirits and animate your morning. Come, gather yourself and take a look."

Curiosity overcame her discomfiture and she followed her mother to the foyer, donning her silk dressing gown as she stumbled out of her room.

On the entry table was the largest bouquet of carnations Nellie had ever seen. Only a few of the flowers were the plant's natural color of purplish pink. Other blossoms were white, red, and curiously, the majority were blue.

"Cadet Baker sent you flowers!" exclaimed Anastasia. "How blissfully romantic!"

Nellie ran to the flowers and gazed in wonder. There were so many blue carnations she began to count them, and then counted the others. "Thirty-six!" she announced. "But why? I cannot even hazard a guess."

"What magic makes some of the carnations are blue?" asked Anastasia. "Wherever would one obtain blue carnations?"

"Horticulturists and expensive hot houses in The City cultivate carnations all year round in this day and age of progressive technology," said Mrs. Entwhistle, her love of flowers evident in her knowledge. "They now have patents for growing carnations in red and white...but blue! That color is novel, even to me."

Her mother pulled the card out of the bouquet and handed it to Nellie. "In any case, perchance a reading of the card might shed some light on the mystery?"

Nellie opened the envelope addressed:

> To: *Cornelia Rose Entwhistle,*
> From: *Lawrence Simmons Baker, First Class.*

The card read:

> *"Carnations for my little flower's January month of birth.*
> *Thirty-six for the year she first appeared, bringing the world mirth.*
> *Rainbows of color, with a predominance of startling blue,*
> *Color my world with the hope of courting lovely you.*

In between her reverent praying, through her lowered lashes, she scanned the pews full of cadets for a glimpse of Baker.

Truth be told, she admitted to herself, *instead of reverent praying, my thoughts dwell solely on that enigma, Cadet Lawrence Simmons Baker, and my emotions flit from tingles of delight to outrage at his behavior.* She again perused the pews in front of her, but still could not detect the back of his head. She could not possibly look behind her without turning her back to the altar—a serious breach of etiquette. She sighed with frustration one too many times and received a glare from her mother. Unable to concentrate, her feelings for Baker leapfrogged from one extreme to the other.

At last she located him when she returned to her pew after Communion. She inhaled sharply, in an involuntary tribute to his tall good looks and lean muscular physique. He was kneeling near the back of the Church. Nellie knelt down, lowered her head, folded her hands under her chin, and leaned her elbows on the back of the pew in front of her, to allow her eyes to follow Baker as he walked down the aisle to receive the Sacrament. As she watched, the cadet stepped with an easy grace to the altar, back erect, hands angelically folded in front. *There were no awkward, Elmer P. Otis-esque angles to this cadet!* Nellie thought.

Baker looked directly at her on his way back to his pew and had the audacity to wink.

In Church!

Though truly, it is his wild, passionate behavior that so attracts me. She shook her head. *Of all the thoughts for a lady to think, these are especially inappropriate in church. Oh! If I had my druthers I would allow him to sweep me off my feet in a mad passionate romance! Mercy, this is truly a 'near occasion of sin.' I had best avoid him on my way to the carriage. I must not allow my head to be turned even further.*

But her mother, of all people, prevented her from carrying out that resolve.

Cornelia made a beeline for the waiting carriage only to see her mother interrupt her exchange of pleasantries with the pastor on the church steps and motion Baker to join her. After a few minutes conversation, her mother looked around and summoned Nellie to her side.

"Cornelia, I am sure you are anxious to thank this fine gentleman for the beautiful arrangement of flowers that arrived this morning, so I will step aside." Mrs. Entwhistle turned to Baker. "But first I must ascertain *how* you were able to procure *blue* carnations in the dead of night?"

"My dear Mrs. Entwhistle, while I am loath to dispel the myth that I might have magical powers to conjure a rarity like blue carnations on a whim in the middle of the night...." Baker's drawling voice oozed with charm and good upbringing. "...I do confess the appearance of these flowers was actually a well-planned and well-executed feat."

"Do give us the particulars," said Mrs. Entwhistle, flashing her rare smile. "I am sure the details will be just as bewitching as the thought that you charmed the little beauties from thin air."

"I am afraid the details are rather dull—in fact, plebian. As you know I have corresponded with your daughter for some time now, and through our written exchange I have learned the intriguing fact that carnations are the flower of her birth month. Furthermore, I have deduced she has a penchant for bold, vivacious color. Therefore, last week, in anticipation of Miss Cornelia Rose's arrival, I procured some carnations...."

"Quite the feat in and of itself, here in the north," interjected Mrs. Entwhistle.

Baker smiled his acknowledgement of the compliment and continued, "I then employed my rudimentary knowledge of botany, obtained at this *fine* institution. I immersed the flowers in indigo dye for a week. The flowers drank the blue water and voila! Rare, blue carnations for a rare and precious flower of a lady."

Mutter, at least, is positively smitten by this explanation, Nellie thought with a wry smile. *Truly, I would be enchanted, but for that ungentlemanly exhibition last night on Flirtation Walk. It is no small matter.... 'Tis a breach of conduct not easily overlooked.*

Baker bowed to the ladies. Mrs. Entwhistle cast her eyes around the churchyard in search of her other daughter. Anastasia was giggling near the carriage with Zetus, and Mrs. Entwhistle turned to join them. "Won't you join us to break fast?" she asked on her way past Baker, so assured of his affirmative reply she did not wait for it.

"That depends," Baker said in a low voice to Mrs. Entwhistle's retreating back. He picked up Nellie's hand and looked into her eyes. "If you will forgive me for my transgressions last evening?" Baker held up his hand as Nellie opened her mouth to reply. "Bide a bit, and hear my plea. I am truly repentant for causing you *any* distress last night. Usually, I am quite deft at ascertaining the desires of my female companions...." Baker smiled at her.

"You have hit the nail on its head!" Nellie exclaimed. "I do *not* appreciate the thought that you have practiced these bold overtures on many unsuspecting ladies and that I am somehow an interchangeable commodity in your quest for intimate relations." Nellie put her hands on her hips.

"Come, come, surely neither of us is a babe in the woods. A belle such as you surely has had a string of admirers?" Baker squeezed her hands.

Nellie could see that she was not making herself clear. "You have confirmed my unfortunate experience, and proven my conclusion that Southern *Gentlemen* do not live up to our northern standards of gentlemanly behavior," she said and pulled her hands away.

Baker's voice dropped a whole octave. "You cannot fault me, my sweet primrose, for I am a *man* with *manly* urges and de*sires.*" Baker leaned closer and almost panted in her ear.

"Mayhap I can," Nellie said, through compressed lips. She tightened her shoulders on her already ramrod straight back and continued, "In private we can reflect upon these feelings. However, they are best held in check until we have clarified the intentions of both parties."

"Surely, I say surely, you understand it is a compliment to *you.* Your beauty is simply so compelling...." Baker paused. His quick scrutiny of Nellies face enlightened him that his line of reasoning was only repelling her further.

He tried a different tack. "I am truly smitten with you Cornelia Rose, and I aspire to prove my intentions are both honorable and desirable. Shall you not find it in the goodness of your heart to offer me another chance?"

Nellie considered for a second. *All of today's activities will be chaperoned by Mutter. I suppose I should allow Lawrence the opportunity to redeem himself. If only for the hope of dancing with him again!*

She nodded her consent and took his elbow. They walked to the carriage, Nellie smiling in anticipation of the afternoon concert, dancing in the arms of the charming, lissome Southerner.

CHAPTER 26
It's Christmas Time in the City

Sing Sing, December 1850

It is magical! thought Nellie.

The soft, late-arriving dawn projected sunlight slants of buttery yellow, warming the accumulated snow's brilliant white to a cozy ecru. The beauty of the snow and the twinkling of the frost sent Nellie's mind into a romantic fairyland. *Could there be a finer view from any girl's garret window?* she wondered. Saint Paul's church bells chimed a quarter past the hour. She imagined she could *see* the musical chimes floating through the cold and frosty morning, perching on rooftops, wafting up the hill to her window, and then undulating down the hill to the river. A plethora of boats, from canoes and rowboats to the grand steamship *Rip van Winkle* crowded the port. Her dreamy eyes wandered over the docks' intense activity. Holiday wreaths, bows, and garlands strung on countless sloops, barges and schooners tied ships to shore as the decorations ran up the hills from the docks via lampposts and cheered doorways. *Heralds of the Christmas season adorn the cityscape!* The festive scene induced daydreams of future romantic encounters.

The harsh cry of the locomotive and its belch of dirty smoke awoke her from her reverie and obliterated her view to the north, dirtying all the fresh snow around the depot and interrupting her surveillance of a gardener hanging boughs of holly on Brandreth's gazebo.

What a loathsome reminder of the grimmer and uglier aspects of life. The Hudson is no longer William Cullen Bryant's 'water streams never deprived by culture', Nellie thought.

"Cornelia Rose, you'll catch your death of cold one day. Why must you constantly hang from your window like a tenement dweller supervising her children?" Scolding, her mother materialized once again without Nellie detecting her silent, stealthy, step. Already burdened with a basket of freshly laundered unmentionables, Mrs. Entwhistle surveyed the clutter of the garret room and Nellie's unmade bed. She needed no words; Nellie understood perfectly and hopped to work.

"Good morning *Mutter*," she said, with what she hoped was a businesslike briskness, trying to shake her enchanting thoughts.

Unexpectedly, a smile crinkled Mrs. Entwhistle's eyes. She said, "I well understand how beguiling you find the solemnity of the Octave of the Nativity. I well know 'tis Christmas Eve and our feasting and celebrating will begin with caroling tonight. Our late night festal supper, so ebullient in its own right, is a mere preamble to the grand finale, Midnight Mass. I too, cherish the wonder and awe of the Christmas liturgy." Mrs. Entwhistle adjusted the basket on her hip and reached a tender hand to stroke Nellie's recalcitrant hair back off her forehead. "'Tis a luxury to walk through life with your head in the clouds Cornelia, one enabled by your father's hard work and industry. You must balance always this dreamy nature with hard work and industry of your own."

Nellie opened her mouth to protest. "I most certainly do." She defended herself.

Her mother smiled again. "*Ja, ja*. But in all matters, one must be a bit practical... extending to matters of the heart, such as how to select a husband."

"Were *you* merely 'practical' when choosing a suitor, *Mutter*?" asked Nellie, recalling the long-ago snippets of heated exchanges she had overheard between her mother and her grandmother.

"Touché!" admitted her mother. "I fell for your father's blunt charm and charismatic jovial personality.

"Be that as it may." The softness left Mrs. Entwhistle's face as she regained her point. "I have well-honed practical instincts. Let us take a moment to review your current cache of suitable men."

"This very moment?" asked Nellie, pointing to the laundry basket and her unmade bed. Her mother sat down on the bed in reply. *Mercy, how very uncharacteristic! This precise moment!*

"Cornelia, your father and I are here to guide you. We have kept a vigilant eye on your stream of romantic pursuits and we feel the suitor best *suited to you*, the one who most agrees with our values, the most Catholic, is Elmer P. Otis, your cadet who still pines for you. He will be caroling with us tonight, and I believe you should entertain his petitions."

"That sickly boy? Honestly, I fear the United States Military Academy has failed that lad. Their instruction and discipline serve merely to increase the number of his ailments!

"*Mutter,*" said Nellie, her hands begging. "I cannot summon the slightest interest in him. Not even a remote curiosity! Please, can you let his cause rest?" Prioritizing her extensive list of objections, Nellie readied herself to launch her best arguments.

But her mother stood up, picked up the laundry basket and said, "If you continue to reject Elmer Otis we must begin all over again to find you someone suitable."

"I confess to having a fondness for Mr. Wright. I hope I do not transgress your desires by entertaining his overtures?" Nellie asked.

Mrs. Entwhistle hesitated. She opened her mouth and then closed it. Nellie pursued. "Perhaps I am smitten by his charms, the way you were with Papa. Might we not entertain this possibility?"

"*Ach du Liebe, Kind.* Child, we do not like what we know of his political views. Moreover, he is not a member in good standing of our parish, like the Otis family. *Ach* why is the path of conformity such an anathema to you?"

Nellie's anger rose to the bait. *Tarnation! My sisters did not choose beaus from our Church either. Why persecute me?* But before she could say a word, she sensed the subject was closed. Her mother's face assumed a hard expression. From her look, Nellie could see that having said her piece, her mother's thoughts turned back to her chores for the day, and arrangements for tonight.

Nellie closed her mouth at the sight of her mother scurrying out the door. *There is certainly no practice of democracy in the Entwhistle household. This totalitarian regime affords not even opportunity for discussion.*

"But what if I simply cannot abide the thought of squandering my life on a spineless jellyfish like Otis?" Nellie asked the stir of air left in the room by her mother's rapid departure.

Her mother's excellent hearing caused Mrs. Entwhistle to poke her head back into the room and sigh. "Very well, some accommodation might be made for such vehement feelings. I thank the Lord you at least had the God-given sense to send that devil Magruder packing.

"*Aber... Ach!* Mrs. Otis will be so disappointed."

At Nellie's pained expression, Mrs. Entwhistle acknowledged Nellie's unspoken objection. "*Ja, ja,* it is not our objective to make Mrs. Otis happy. *Ja.*

"*Aber — was ist los mit du?* Obadiah Weber Wright? *Gott im Himmel!* That marriage would not be prudent. It is always something unexpected with you Cornelia Rose.

"*Ach!* Your father and I could also reconsider the viability of Lawrence Simmons Baker. He should suit you well enough — tall and handsome with good prospects. And a romantic streak too, as I recall the large bouquet of carnations he conjured out of the blue." *More accurately 'in blue',* Nellie smiled at her own pun.

"However, I dare say it is unlikely that we can convince *two* Southern Gentlemen suitors to forsake the South and allow our daughters to remain in their native land...." Mother whisked back out of the room tsk, tsking, and an *'ach du Liebe'* floated up the back stairs as she descended them.

This discussion is hardly concluded, thought Nellie. *I will not be an idle bystander while my fate is decided for me! Lawrence Simmons Baker? Pshaw! They would not be quite so enamored of him if they knew of his antics on Flirtation Walk.* She stomped down the stairs in rebellion. *Yes Mutter, like a cowhand!*

At the bottom of the stairs, Anastasia grabbed her by her waist and pointed into the drawing room. "Isn't yuletide the most magical time of year? Every doorway, every mantel festooned with boughs of holly and every window cheered by candles."

Nellie smiled, trying to shake her disgruntlement. *I must not forgo the enchantment of this season. 'Tis Christmas Eve!* she thought. She returned her sister's hug, her good feeling rushing back. "My thoughts exactly, my dear, sweet sister." Anastasia tied the red ribbon she was preparing for the drawing room doorknob into Nellie's hair. Nellie draped a single strand of precious tinsel on Anastasia's head.

"*Ach, Kinder,* save the tinsel for the *Tannenbaum.*" Mother 'tsk, tsked' scurrying past them, now carrying a basket of fresh bread. The girls laughed and began to decorate the rest of the room in earnest.

The day of preparation for the Christmas pageantry passed quickly as the Entwhistle family and their help scurried about, baking, decorating, cleaning, and polishing.

With the only pause from work a hasty lunch of bread and broth, Nellie and her sisters donned their cloaks over their warmest pretty dresses, complaining of fatigue.

But at the sight of Nathaniel, Augusta, and Zetus singing at their front door to earn entrance, all thoughts of fatigue left them.

Mrs. Entwhistle pulled the mulled wine from the stove and carefully poured it into the company-sized sterling silver punch bowl. The group broke out in a rousing chorus of *Here We Go Wassailing*. The young people clustered around the punchbowl, singing and filling their glasses. Nellie's mother added her beautiful alto voice to the song and poured herself a glass too. Obadiah came into the drawing room, still brushing snow from the shoulders of his great coat. "'Tis a perfect night for caroling!" he announced. Nellie smiled in delight.

They gathered around the beautiful Christmas tree she and her siblings lit only minutes ago. The strategically placed tinsel magnified the light of the small candles, bathing all of her mother's precious ornaments from Germany in their soft magical glow.

"*O Holy Night...*" sang Nellie, "*...the stars are brightly shining....*" Everyone joined in, Obadiah's tenor resounding, loud and clear. Nellie grinned at him in surprise. "What a pleasing singing voice you have," she whispered in-between stanzas. He bent close and whispered back, "We will make a great duet." Delighted, Nellie grabbed his hand and gave it a squeeze. Obadiah raised his eyebrows and stepped in even closer, sliding his arm around her waist as they stood watching the Christmas tree shimmer.

Mrs. Entwhistle leaned forward, so her frown was visible to Nellie, in spite of her lack of physical proximity. Nellie heeded the small wiggle of her mother's finger, which she understood all too well. She took a half sidestep away from Obadiah, in compliance with her mother's wishes. Nellie smiled at Obadiah to soften the blow of the new distance between them and surreptitiously squeezed his hand again.

In high spirits, the group raised their glasses in toast after toast to everyone's health and prosperity.

In the middle of a long toast proposed by Zetus, winding its way through the history of the past year toward the promise of the next, the door again opened. Elmer P. Otis appeared from behind the heavy velvet curtain hanging over the entry alcove, shielding the ballroom from the chill weather.

Obadiah made an angry noise in his throat and pulled his arm away from Nellie's waist in an abrupt gesture of displeasure. But as Otis made the rounds greeting everyone, *showing off his newly acquired manners?* Nellie wondered, the door again opened causing a mighty flap in the curtain. Clara Rafferty, Nellie's school chum, blew in.

"I do so hope I have not missed *all* the fun!" she exclaimed. "Mother had a woman ready to deliver when complications set in. As usual, she needed an extra set of hands. What she will do when Otis and I wed and are off to the wild, Wild West, I do not know!" she tucked her hand under Elmer's elbow and faced the assembled guests, smiling.

In seconds, the import of those announcements sank into Nellie's brain. Obadiah's too, apparently, for his arm encircled her waist again. *Certainly, if anyone can mold that sickly boy into a healthy man it would be Clara!* she thought.

Nellie broke away and dashed to Clara's side. "Mercy! You are a sly one! Sneaking a wedding announcement in the middle of apologies for tardiness. Whatever shall we do with you?" She gave her a big hug.

"Celebrate!" proclaimed Anastasia and Zetus, almost at the same time. They looked each other in the eye and they giggled.

"This momentous turn of events in my life has only just occurred," Clara said, with a vivacity and exuberance that spread to everyone in the room. "Suddenly, just a few moments ago, Cadet Otis appeared at our door and requested to speak to my parents!"

Obadiah approached Elmer and said, "May I be the first to congratulate you sir, and wish you all the best." He pumped Elmer's hand up and down, grabbing Elmer's elbow with his other hand in his enthusiasm. Otis withstood the hand pumping with flame red ears and a chagrined expression on his face. But when Clara turned toward him, his face lit up like a Christmas candle surrounded in tinsel.

Mercy! Mutter did not waste any time advising Mrs. Otis, Nellie thought. *Tarnation! Otis did not waste any time changing course. Mercy, he wears quite a happy affect.*

Nellie smiled. *My sanguineness increases tenfold at this news. The happy couple's joy makes me even merrier.* "I propose a celebratory song. It may be a trifle ambitious, but what say you to singing *Gloria in Excelsis Deo* in rounds?" she asked.

Anastasia squealed in delight. "'Tis my favorite Christmas Carol, made even grander by singing in rounds. I will organize us into groups. Baritones, you stand over there.... Tenors...." Anastasia was pointing as everyone shuffled around.

In the ensuing confusion, when Clara was lining up with the sopranos, Otis sidled up to Nellie and whispered, "'Twas a cruel blow to find you had dismissed me as a suitor." At Nellie's thunderstruck face Otis asked, "Was I misinformed? Do you still carry a torch for me?"

Nellie pulled him over to the front door alcove on the pretext of pointing toward something outside the window. "No, no, of course not."

Otis looked crushed.

"Elmer Pet... Otis, there is not sufficient time for me to either mince words or merely intimate what I must communicate to you. I did not, was not, nor never have I, been smitten with you, carried a torch for you, nor felt anything close to love. Pity, sure, but love—never.

"The only critical inquiry now is whether you truly love Clara or are merely toying with her affections." Nellie's breath came in short bursts from the exertion of carefully choosing unambiguous words. She was beside herself at the thought that this silly man would hurt her true friend.

Otis blinked. "No, no of course not. I have always loved Clara. She is a dear friend and a worthy helpmate. But I have been besotted with you ever since I sat next to you in the Broad Street School...."

"Otis, a school boy, puppy love cannot compare to mutually exchanged affection," said Nellie. "I cannot...."

Otis smiled and gave a rueful shake of his head. "I have come to that realization. Howsoever, I was compelled to declare my undying love one last time. I must certify your full cognizance—you forsake your chance for my affection forever by refusing me now."

Nellie shook her head. *Of all the egocentric, absurd declarations this one takes the cake....* She could think of nothing to say in reply.

An icy breeze again ruffled the heavy velvet curtain at the front door. Nellie pulled it aside. The front door swung open fully and a blast of cold air whooshed in Lawrence Simmons Baker.

"Just the very female I de*sire*," he drawled. He pulled her through the curtain and swept her into his arms. *My word,* thought Nellie, *it's a conspiracy!*

"Please, Cadet Baker, we are in the middle of forming our caroling groups," Nellie protested, pulling back.

"Then I submit, my impeccable timing perseveres. I need but a moment of your time. I must inform you, I depart on a specially negotiated furlough to Mississippi. Some important family business urgently needs my attention. While I am loath to miss my usual Christmas Day feast at the Academy, consisting of Professor Kendrick's spiked peaches, waffles, and maple syrup, do not pine for me. I cherish the opportunity to assiduously perform my filial duty. My sweet, I will see you immediately upon my return." Baker swept her back into his arms, kissed her hard on the lips and opened the door, dashing back into the cold.

Nellie was flabbergasted. She turned to see Otis, face beet red, peeking in at the edge of the curtain, his mouth hanging open.

"Cornelia, Elmer, please. You have delayed our festivities long enough," called Anastasia. Nellie gratefully ran past Otis, back toward the group flanking the great hearth on both sides. She stood next to Anastasia in the alto section.

Suddenly Obadiah's angry gesture, beckoning her to stand next to him, caught her eye. *But he could not have heard Otis...he could not have seen Baker! The heavy velvet curtain hung over the alcove....* She started singing, ears burning red, thoughts jumbled.

In the middle of the first 'Glo-or-or-or-or-or-or-or-or-i-a' refrain, Obadiah appeared at her side. She looked up with apprehension on her face. He whispered, "I don't care if I am a tenor and you are an alto, my position is beside you!"

Nellie laughed, right in the middle of the "in excelsis Deo."

The evening had an impish Christmas magic all its own.

The magic still crackled in the air when Nellie awoke the next morning, nose tip cold, but feet still cozy. She did not have the luxury of turning over for one more snooze, however. She felt a presence.

Her eyes flew open. Matthias's face was almost touching her cold nose. "Nellie, how many times do I gots to tell ye? It's Christmas Day and we get to open our stockings!" he shouted, jumping up and down.

Half asleep but wrapped warmly in her robe, shawl, and the magic of the season, Nellie let Matthias lead her downstairs to join the others.

"*Warum bist du* the last to awaken?" asked her father, his eyes projecting their magical twinkle. He winked at her.

Who knew Papa could speak German? Nellie giggled.

Even Mother was in a teasing mood. She paused from pouring the morning coffee just long enough to pronounce, "*Ach,* I remember the many years you did Matthias's job, awakening us before sunrise on this most holy and festive of all holy days."

"Still wrapped in your enchanting dreams?" asked Anastasia, with a conspiratorial wink. "Merry Christmas."

Nellie woke up fully to the joy of an exotic orange, imported by her father all the way from Spain, peeking out of the top of her stocking. She held it appreciatively to her nose, sniffing the intoxicating citrus smell. "Papa, thank you," she whispered to him. "You spoil us with such luxuries."

"'Tis a grand thing, 'tis it no'?" asked James Entwhistle his face festooned with his broad smile. "'Tis a taste, a tang such as I couldn't even dream when I was a wee lad in t' old country."

Matthias squealed in delight at the same time that Jonas jumped straight into the air. "A banana!"

"Hopping Horsefeathers! I received one too," said Jerome.

"An ol' orange wouldn't do for three monkeys t' likes o'ye," said her father with a laugh.

Anastasia and Cornelia shared an orange, counting out the sections fairly so that they could save a whole unpeeled one for later.

Patrick, his wife Katrina, and their little girl Theodora, blew into the ballroom. There was a wild scramble of greetings and hugs. The three-year-old girl sprinted to the Christmas tree and crawled underneath, setting it rocking. Nellie's sister-in-law ran over to pull her child out as the tree wobbled, the candles flickered and the precious ornaments trembled.

"Dora, love, be careful," admonished Katrina.

Mrs. Entwhistle ignored the near miss, *if one ignores Mutter's hand clutching her heart*, Nellie thought.

Her mother sang, "*O Tannenbaum, O Tannenbaum, wie tru sind deine Blättern.*" Everyone joined in, the melody wafting around them, wrapping them in the warm cozy feeling of family.

During the third verse and final chorus of *O Tannenbaum*, Nellie smoothed her stocking flat along her lap and found, to her surprise, a lump at the toe. She worked her hand through the stocking, careful to not further loosen any of the pulled threads on the inside, the only evidence of its years of hard labor.

Her squeal of joy interrupted the first stanza of *Good King Wenceslas*.

A tiny brooch lay wrapped in golden tissue paper. "*Mutter*, how precious!" she cried, jumping up to give her mother a hug.

Her mother smiled and returned her hug. "I agree," she said. "*Aber*, but the brooch is not from your Papa and I. Our gifts for you are under the *Tannenbaum*."

Nellie looked at the beautiful brooch with its pink enamel overlay of flowers on twisted knots of sterling silver. "Who has graced me with this perfectly precious gift? What magic conjured it here?"

"What does the paper say?" asked Jerome, tapping his head to show Nellie she should be thinking logically.

Right on the golden tissue-thin paper, written in Obadiah's smallest handwriting, were the words:

> *I love thee so, that, maugre all thy pride,*
> *Nor wit nor reason can my passion hide.*
> *Do not extort thy reasons from this clause,*
> *For that I woo, thou therefore hast no cause*
> *But rather reason thus with reason fetter,*
> *Love sought is good, but given unsought better*
>
> *For where thou art, there is the world itself, and where thou*
> *art not, desolation*
> *Your Obadiah*

"It's from Shakespeare!" she said. Everyone laughed.

Jonas said, "Surely you would not have us believe Shakespeare sent you the brooch!" just as Matthias asked, "Isn't Shakespeare dead?"

Everyone laughed again, with Mr. Entwhistle's chuckle the loudest and longest. "Papa, your laugh is the merriest sound in the world," said Anastasia.

Nellie could not help but agree. Her father's laugh always made her feel happy, loved, and cozy. She clasped Obadiah's words on the fragile gold paper to her heart. *This kind of giddy romance is exactly to my liking!*

CHAPTER 27

Caught Between the Moon and New York City

Sing Sing, January 1851

The yuletide festivities always concluded on January 6th, with the Entwhistle's annual Twelfth Day of Christmas ball. "'Tis the Epiphany and the feast of the Holy Family," intoned Mr. Entwhistle. "We'd best not lose sight o' the solemnity o' the occasion in the high spirits o' the fancy soiree."

Even though his admonition fell on deaf ears as Nellie and her sisters only talked about dancing, Mr. Entwhistle circled back to his theme at their morning breakfast after Mass on Holy Family Sunday.

"Ye heard Father O'Flaherty! 'Wives be subordinate unto your husbands, as is proper in the Lord,'" he said. He looked at Mrs. Entwhistle with twinkling eyes as she bustled around the table, pouring tea. She just smiled at him in return, knowing he was warming up to his lecture. "'Children honor thy parents, be obedient and attentive....'" he continued.

"'Fathers, do not provoke your children, lest they become downhearted,'" quoted Nellie right back.

Everyone laughed. Mr. Entwhistle made a chagrinned face. Nellie rose from her place at the table and ran over to give her father a big hug.

The soiree was in full swing, quite literally as the dancers twirled and turned to the ten-piece orchestra. Nellie gazed at the beauty of the gas-lit scene swirling in front of her as she swayed around the ballroom in her brother Jerome's arms. *Mutter has outdone herself,* she thought in admiration. Even as her eyes wandered over the beautiful Christmas arrangements of pinecones, holly, and red satin ribbons interlaced with rare poinsettia pots, her feet stayed focused on dancing. In the year since she made her unofficial debut, she had not missed a single opportunity to employ every step leaned in dance lessons. Tonight was no exception.

Dancing a waltz, a polka, and a Virginia reel in rapid succession left Nellie overheated and Jerome breathless. *An uninspiring concerto is a good time for refreshment,* she thought to herself. She led Jerome to the sidelines, curtsied, and set him free to pursue his own romantic interests. *I will only dally long enough to quench this thirst,* she thought, trying to stem the perspiration spawned from her enthusiastic dancing.

Obadiah appeared at her side. "My fair lady." He bowed. "Unsurprisingly, the belle of the ball."

Nellie lifted her eyes from her crystal cup to him, appreciating anew his dashing appearance and ready smile. He bowed again, low over her hand, their eyes meeting over her fingertips as he kissed them. She dropped a cute little curtsey and he chuckled.

"You have charmed me completely," he said, keeping her hand in his.

"And you, I," she said. "Especially with this enchanting brooch you cleverly hid in my stocking!" She touched it lovingly with the fingers of her free hand as she spoke. "You must imagine my delight upon discovering it, Christmas morning, along with your bewitching words."

"I have lost my heart to you." He leaned in and frowned in mock consternation. "Treat it well, and tenderly, for it is a fragile thing."

Nellie smiled. "One more I shall add to my collection!" she replied with a blithe and saucy toss of her head.

Obadiah's grip tightened on her hand and a frown hopped over his eyebrows. "No!" he whispered, with such intensity Nellie frowned back. "I thought I made myself clear at the caroling. I will not allow my heart to join an ever-elongating string of hearts."

"Why of course not! I merely jest." Nellie realized with a pang that it was of paramount importance to ensure she had not inadvertently hurt his feelings. "I did not intend to make light of your feelings or trespass upon your emotions. I did not realize my quip was at your expense. Please forgive me," she added, bobbing another curtsey.

Obadiah nodded, but the smile did not return to his face.

Nellie tried some pleasant chatter to help him regain his jovial mood. It fell on deaf ears. The band struck up a Strauss waltz, one of

Nellie's favorite, and she looked at Obadiah and inclined her head toward the dance floor. He merely frowned again. Nellie began to tap her feet, scanning for another partner.

"See here, then," Obadiah suddenly said. "I am giving my heart to you, but only if you duly cherish it, above all others."

Somewhat taken aback, Nellie thought for a moment. She offered, "My dalliances with other suitors were a progression, a necessity of searching for 'Mr. Right,' Mr. Wright! I do concede, my pace was rather leisurely. Howsoever, I found discerning my heart's desire quite the arduous task. But I must confess to you—I have found its promise in you. I pray my foolishness has not placed this sentiment in jeopardy...." she looked him in the eye with such tenderness and compassion that Obadiah was placated.

He stepped closer and took her hand. Nellie gazed at him with eager anticipation... when her father interrupted their conversation. She took a step back.

"Good evening beautiful colleen 'o mine," he said in his usual effusive way. "'Tis a joy to a fadder's heart to see ye shimmering along with t' candlelight!"

"Good fellow," Mr. Entwhistle nodded as he turned to Obadiah.

"If I might have a word with you, sir?" Obadiah said, dropping Nellie's hand, and turning toward her father.

Mercy me! Nellie thought. *What occupies his thoughts now?* She smiled at her father and then at Obadiah, curious to hear what he had to say.

"Cornelia, perhaps you would be so kind as to fetch us some punch?" Obadiah asked.

Mercy me! Nellie again said to herself. *Why am I again excluded from their conversation?* But obediently she nodded and waltzed, in time to the music, to the punch bowl. She poured some punch, calming her fluttering heart by inhaling the pine fragrance of the festive bowers decorating the bowl.

"Sir," Obadiah continued, as soon as Nellie was out of earshot. "I know it is improbable that this is an optimum time, nor is this a likely or favorable place, but I would like to make an appointment to speak to you at a later date."

"'Tis a bit irregular to be sure, to don a serious visage and refer to a mysterious conversation to be scheduled for t' future, right in t' middle o' our Twelfth Night of Christmas celebration. Might I inquire as to t' purpose of this conversation, before I grant you an appointment? In anticipation o' yer inquiry, I must warn you, Yale man or not, I am no longer recruiting men for me shipyard, nor for t' maintenance of the Aqueduct. My engineers have t' daily operations of t' water supply well under control with no need for further personnel, and t' plans for expansion of t' operation have currently been curtailed...But yer right, this is hardly t' time or place...." Mr. Entwhistle frowned.

"I beg pardon for my interruption, sir, but I fear I have given the wrong impression entirely. I am well employed. I studied law as well as military maneuvers at both Saint John's Academy and Yale, and I am apprenticed to one of our village's finest judges, Mr. Justice Urmy, Esquire, whilst I complete the final semester at Ya... er, my study of the law."

"No doubt your late fadder's antics in t' Senate, his time as Governor of our illustrious state, and the nod for t' office of Vice-President has kept the powerful sway o' his name over local judges and politicians," Mr. Entwhistle said, a trifle dismissively. He passed his hand over his hair, ending in scratching his head, and adopted a different tone. "Politics aside, I was saddened to hear o' your fadder's passing. He was a fine man. And anyone'll tell ye I do not dispense this moniker lightly. Taking a stand against t' abomination of slavery — earning respect as Secretary of State. I doff me cap to him."

"Thank you kindly, sir. I was fortunate to have him as my father and blessed to have his guidance for as long as I did," said Obadiah, his face elongated with sadness, his right eye twitching. Momentarily, he forgot his mission.

Mr. Entwhistle cleared his throat.

At Obadiah's continued silence, James Entwhistle resumed his own train of thought. "A fine and honorable gentleman such as Silas Wright will continue to command a powerful legacy. I'm sure his reputation at t' bar of Attorneys is still sterling, not to mention his Senate connections in Washington or his gubernatorial pull in Albany." Mr. Entwhistle chuckled. "Though he musta had a whole mess o' clout to get a Whig-loving judge to even entertain t' idea of the son of a Jacksonian present in his own office, much less than to be strong-armed into having that scallywag work for him."

Obadiah's lips twisted into a polite smile. He said, "Whilst I wager that is usually the situation, sir, without blowing my own horn, I do believe my apprenticeship was given to me based on my own merits and scholarship. Judge Urmy indicated to my former headmaster he was looking to take on a young man, appropriately schooled and meeting his strict criteria. Headmaster Churchill remembered me from my days at his Military Academy and sent word to Yale of the opportunity."

Obadiah's smile broadened as he continued his story. "The old coot judge has a bit of a sense of humor about himself. Judge Urmy allegedly told Churchill, 'I'm a prejudice son of a gun, and I want to prove a theory. Give me the last semester's proofs of your three best graduates now studying law, without any names or indicia of origin, and I'll pick my man blind. I'll be a three-legged toad if the best qualified be not a Whig.'

"The old judge guaranteed that he would pick a Whig or forever punish himself with a Jacksonian apprentice. When he selected me, we all had a good laugh; the judge laughing hardest of all. And that, sir, is how the son of a Jacksonian is working for a Whig."

Mr. Entwhistle threw back his head and laughed. Obadiah joined him. The portly Irishman scratched his head. Nellie looked over from the punch bowl at the sound of her father's laughter, but she could not hear their conversation. *Dare I edge closer?*

At that moment, Cadet Lawrence Simmons Baker materialized from nowhere, swept a low bow before her and asked her for the honor of this dance.

Nellie hesitated. *What to my wondering eyes hath appeared? 'Tis too strange a twist of events to not have had my mother's hand in it! I must see what is afoot. I have my demeanor firmly in hand. I will mind my comportment.* She blushed. *Surely it is acceptable, nay merely compliant with Mutter's wishes, to attempt another dance?*

She so loved dancing. She had unconsciously been tapping her foot to the music, even after the rebuff from Obadiah. The young man eagerly held out his hand.

It was too tempting. With a backward glance at her father and Obadiah, Nellie allowed herself to be lead to the dance floor. Baker jumped into conversation as easily as he executed the dance steps. He swung her to the music as he drawled softly in her ear, "Cornelia Rose, can you find it within your heart to forgive my overseppin'? For that's all it was, plain and simple, merely gettin' ahead of myself."

Nellie laughed, "That is water under the bridge. I am pleased to continue a cordial friendship with you."

Baker frowned. "I had a more intimate relationship in mind than mere friendship," he drawled.

Nellie hesitated a moment. Baker and the music suddenly turned her, permitting an unobstructed view of Obadiah and her father conversing. Obadiah's eyes found hers across the room, and she suddenly knew her answer. "I am afraid that, based on our history, we must discard that possibility."

Baker frowned again, but said nothing. Thrusting his chin forward over her shoulder so she could not see his expression, he turned on his magical dancing. Nellie frowned in turn, but allowed herself to succumb to Baker's dancing charm. Lawrence twirled her with ease and grace, and she floated to her favorite waltz, *Sträusschen*. The magic of the movement, her passion for dancing, induced her to soften her words. "At least for the time being, this is the optimum arrangement," she said. With a furtive glance in Obadiah's direction she added a whispered, "But I suppose one never knows what the future will hold."

Baker pulled his chin back. His entire face was lit with a grin. "I am smitten with you Miss Cornelia Rose. I will prove my undying love for you. You will soon understand how deep a man's passion runs and the many benefits for its recipient." Baker pulled her closer and spun her quickly and adroitly.

A girl could quite lose her head with such piquant treatment. Is this mad passionate feeling Baker elicits from me true love? Or is love the sweet but heady attention of Obadiah?

As Cornelia and Baker waltzed past her father and Obadiah, both pairs of eyes followed her. Nellie caught Obadiah's gaze. She was a bit taken aback to see jealousy written all over his face. But before she could react, Obadiah crossed the dance floor and cut in on Baker.

Surprised, but gallant, Baker bowed out, managing to whisper in Cornelia's ear, "Never fear, I will not be dissuaded."

Obadiah steered her around the floor, his dancing competent but methodical. "I could not abide that cotton-picking Southerner monopolizing all your time. Certainly not at the precise moment *you* are the very subject of our discussion," he said. Obadiah did not look at her as he spoke, and it was difficult for Nellie to tell his mood.

"Pray tell, do enlighten me as to the specifics of this discussion," she said. Cornelia decided to maintain her light and airy good humor, engendered by the thrill of the dance with Baker, and carry on the conversation in a joking, flirting tone.

"Well... um... the specifics...." Obadiah hemmed and hawed a bit, and then stopped making sounds completely as he concentrated on turning Nellie around the dance floor. The music stopped.

"In point of fact, I haven't actually spoken to your father about any subject, I am still trying to work the conversation around to that point." With those puzzling words Obadiah left her standing in front of the orchestra, in the middle of the floor and went back to stand next to her father.

Nellie played with a strand of hair straying on to her cheek. Before she could speculate as to Obadiah's mission and motives, Lawrence Baker appeared at her side again. In seconds, the orchestra launched into a minuet. As they floated among the dancers, Baker began to sing a parody of Stephen Foster's popular song in her ear, strangely in tune with the music the orchestra played. "Nelly is a lady, what a lucky man am I, toll the bell for lovely Nell, I'll win her as my bride."

Nellie looked into Baker's attractive face and laughed.

Surely a charming man, this Southerner, Nellie thought. *One who will not be deterred from his purpose. I once told him if I had but the opportunity to know him better, I would not be so averse to his advances.... Mayhap I should give him a second chance.... So blatant in his forward overtures... yet he elicits in me a strange passion.*

Nellie closed her eyes and yielded to the music and the romance of the evening.

Baker, sensing his advantage, backed Nellie near where Obadiah stood waiting to speak to her father again, then whisked her to the other side of the room. Nellie, floating on a cloud, did not notice Baker twirl them past his rival.

Obadiah patiently waited for Mr. Entwhistle to finish his exchange of pleasantries with two of the guests. Entwhistle granted him an audience after the couple danced away. Obadiah frowned and cleared his throat. "To return to the subject at hand, sir, seeking employment is not the focus of my request for an interview."

"A bit o' enlightenment then, son. What *will* be t' topic o' our discourse?" Mr. Entwhistle's face resumed its usual jovial demeanor. Cheered by that affability, Obadiah cleared his throat, tore his gaze from Cornelia's whirling figure and looked Mr. Entwhistle in the eye.

"I did not want to broach it in this manner," Obadiah said uncertainly. "It seems a bit unseemly."

"Now son, I don't know what they learned ye in that fine Military establishment, nor that college, but I never go into battle unarmed. I won't allow my adversary knowing the scope o' the battle, and me in t' dark." Mr. Entwhistle softened his words with his broad Irish grin.

"Oh no, sir. I hope never to be your adversary," said Obadiah. He nervously wiped his brow and his blue eyes flickered in dismay at the turn in the conversation.

"Then spit 'er out son, what is t' topic at hand?" asked Mr. Entwhistle as his voice rose just a half octave.

"Ahem. Yes, hand—unwittingly appropriate." Obadiah's words only further obfuscated his meaning. Mr. Entwhistle raised his eyebrows impatiently.

"Ahem, the subject at hand will be the hand of your fine daughter Cornelia Rose, sir," said Obadiah, eyes searching the room for the sight of Nellie, seeking visual reassurance.

As if by magic, Nellie danced past him, turned her head, and smiled into Obadiah's gaze, catching his eye.

Startled, Mr. Entwhistle took a step back and asked, "Have ye discussed this with me daughter now?"

Obadiah looked startled in return. "Oh no, sir. That would be most forward of me, sir. I had consulted with my own father before he passed away of course, but as to Cornelia...."

Mr. Entwhistle drew his eyebrows together. Obadiah detected subtle disapproval. "Of course, sir, I have ventured to converse about weighty matters with your daughter upon occasion, and I do enjoy her intelligent conversation and sparkling wit. If I may say sir, she appears to inherit these charms from you," he said.

Mr. Entwhistle clapped the boy on the back and gave a hearty laugh. "Aye, flattery and a bit o' blarney never hurt a conversation none, did it? Ye'r all right lad. I right admire ye'r gumption to make advances to me and me daughter. And I know, we'll have a proper airing o' the situation, we will. Come by Thursday next, a mite after t' supper hour and me and me wife will be happy to receive ye.

"Not a word to me daughter about this now, eh?"

"But sir, then how will I persuade her to be my bride?" Obadiah asked. His agitation so great, he rubbed the hilt of his sword with one hand and twirled his mustache with the other.

"My approval is all that's needed, ye must know," said Mr. Entwhistle. "I'll not abide t' opinion o' a woman trumpin' a man, even me if it be me own daughter. No woman need make big decisions — Nell don't know better than one as wise as me. Have ye not t' manly sense God gave to ye lad?" Mr. Entwhistle shook his head and went off muttering. "T' lad may be good at learn' 'n soldiering, but me faith in his judgment might a been misguided."

"I will employ the utmost caution of utterance," Obadiah called to his retreating figure. Mr. Entwhistle did not turn around.

Obadiah hung his head, chagrined — worried that he may have ruined his chances of obtaining the older man's permission. Fretfully he grasped and released the hilt of his sword, staring over the heads of the dancers, reviewing each word of their conversation. At last he got a hold of himself, and muttered, "Whatsoever enterprise must be undertaken to achieve this goal, that girl is truly for me! I *will* make it transpire." He returned his gaze to the dancers, boisterously prancing past him, and frowned at the sight of Nellie, still swooning in the arms of Lawrence S. Baker.

CHAPTER 28
Stuck in Colder Weather

Sing Sing, February 1851

"We *will* have a grrrrrand Church for our parish, *if* we *all* participate. My announcement today serves as a parish-wide call to arms. We must join in a concerted effort to raise funds," said Father O'Flaherty. He looked around the Brandreth warehouse and his stocky body almost ran over to a stack of boxes. He climbed on top of two, balancing precariously, in spite of the audible gasps of the ladies seated in the front. His large frame teetering, the ladies vocalized their opinions on the boxes' stability.

"We grow weary of saying Mass in this warehouse and in stray buildings which have outlived their purpose," he announced from his box pulpit. "And in our parishioner's homes.... Thank you, Bridget O'Brien." The priest interrupted himself to give Mrs. O'Brien a nod. She stood up and made a theatrical curtsy. "Yes, well, we must redouble our efforts to garner money for the building fund. As generous as my parishioners are...." He paused, beaming affectionately at the assembly. "...We must augment our weekly collections if we are to build a church in this century! I believe it is time to widen our purview beyond our own pockets, and seek funds from the village at large."

The minute the last strains of *Hail, Redeemer, King Divine,* the recessional hymn faded, the parishioners gathered in excited clusters, whispering fund-raising ideas. The excitement grew so strong, voices escalated from whisper, to conversation level, to shouting. Father O'Flaherty was incensed. "This is our house of worship!" he admonished. "Need I remind ye t' keep quiet and respectful?"

"'T isn't that just t' point of yer sermon Fadder?" asked Mr. Entwhistle. "This is *not* a proper house of worship at all, it is a warehouse."

There was a moment of dead silence.

Papa, correcting our pastor, in front of our whole parish, right after Mass? Nellie was incredulous. Her father ran his hand over his hair and scratched his ear, but did not retract his statement.

Father O'Flaherty looked abashed. The whole congregation seemed to hold its breath.

"What am I saying, son?" Father O'Flaherty asked.

Son? Nellie giggled to herself. *Father O'Flaherty is half the age of Papa.*

The priest rushed over to Mr. Entwhistle and clapped him on the back. "Yer correct: that *is* just t' point. Once t' Blessed Sacrament is put away, this place reverts to its original state—a warehouse!" Father O'Flaherty laughed and Papa's hearty laugh echoed off the rafters. With more than a touch of relief, soon all the parishioners joined in the laughter.

Ideas tumbled out, fast and furious: craft fairs, picnics, potluck dinners. Mrs. Entwhistle wrote them on the warehouse slate board. Right then and there they unanimously decided to organize a series of fundraisers. Any feasible suggestion was seized and added to the list.

In no time at all, the parishioners scheduled a dozen events, everyone volunteering their expertise. Nellie wanted no part of any of them. *What could I possibly contribute to a craft fair?* she wondered. *My crewelwork is unexceptional. The stockings I knit are all spoken for. I barely finished my needlepoint in time for Mutter's Christmas pillow....*

Her parents urged all their children to participate in their parish's worthy cause. But Nellie couldn't think of any particular talent she possessed that would lend itself to fundraising.

Then a stray comment of Agnes set the wheels in motion.

Nellie had been entertaining her sisters with an anecdote involving a boy, some pilfered penny candy, a chase, and an overturned barrel of crackers at Hart's apothecary.

After laughing with Anastasia and Jonas at the conclusion of Nellie's dramatic retelling of the incident, Agnes stood up and put her hands on her hips. "Sakes alive Cornelia Rose! You are excessively theatrical. Surely your melodramatic storytelling cannot possibly be the *only* benefit derived from all your years of reading, attending theater, and acting in school productions?"

"That's it!" Nellie shouted. "Our parish can stage a play. I can help. In fact, I can produce it."

Mr. Entwhistle embraced her idea. Together they met with Father O'Flaherty to pitch it. Nellie was ecstatic when Father O'Flaherty announced from the 'pulpit,' the aforementioned pile of boxes at the warehouse, that the parish counsel and the pastor of Saint Patrick's in Verplank agreed a play would be an excellent fundraiser. "Miss Cornelia Rose Entwhistle, we would be honored if you spearhead the entire project," the pastor beamed down at her and Nellie nodded yes.

Nellie ran home from Mass. She had to find a play. Nellie knew the idea was to include as many of the parishioners in the cast as possible — so they would sell tickets to all their relatives.

The next several weeks were spent in the library trying to find the right play to perform. At last she decided on a musical revue, writing to several publishers for the rights to perform snippets of a few different plays. With her father's help, she also chose several songs and purchased sheet music. She and her father scripted an hour show and proposed it to the planning committee. Save one dour old lady who thought *any kind* of singing other than of church music was scandalous, the parishioners rousingly approved the show.

Nellie was busy recruiting stagehands, musicians, and artists, and scheduling try-outs, when an invitation arrived for a winter hop, in celebration of Saint Valentine's Day at West Point.

She approached her mother. "Lawrence Simmons Baker has invited me to...."

Mrs. Entwhistle interrupted her. "You may attend. What dates shall I mark in my diary?"

Nellie stood with her mouth opened. *Mutter's preferences and allegiances are certainly crystal clear,* she thought.

Every morning after Nellie accepted the invitation she threw open her shutters and anxiously checked the temperature. "Freezing again!" she moaned. She looked at the icicles hanging from the eves around her. "Further lengthened, overnight." She looked out at the dock; ice held ships frozen into place. She expanded her gaze across the river. "Merciful Heavens, no! Ice and more ice all the way across the Hudson."

Anastasia lifted her sleepy head from her bed on the far side of the room. "I am confused," she yawned. "I thought we *liked* winter, and relished snow and ice."

Nellie turned around. "Ice accumulation on the Hudson means less navigable channels for the ships. According to my calculations, the river is just a few frosty nights away from solid ice, shore to shore! I must then abandon all hope, for the ice cutter ships will abandon the river to the ice harvesting industry."

Anastasia shook her head with a grin at Nellie's dramatic hand wringing. "Cornelia, this is hardly news. Why, every winter we long for just this day, when the ice skating parties can begin. Why in the heavens does this well documented, yearly phenomenon perturb you today?"

Cornelia closed the window and sat on Anastasia's bed. She sighed. "I yearn for another voyage to West Point! I have been invited to the Valentine Cotillion, and I could not bear it if I were unable to attend."

Anastasia looked puzzled. Nellie explained, "The River hasn't frozen over entirely since 1848. Why, proponents of the shipping industry have argued—we do not need railroads, the river almost never freezes completely. Yet today this 'rare occurrence' is happening again! I anticipate the Valentine's Day Hop with great longing. I have set my hopes and desires on an evening in the arms of the dancing dream, Lawrence Baker."

Anastasia still wore a blank look.

"Stasia, if the ships are frozen into their moorings, I will not be able to attend. I can hardly take an ice boat all the way to West Point," Nellie cried.

Anastasia looked thoughtful. "Hmmmm, I never had occasion to travel such a distance in winter, so I never contemplated that impasse before."

Despite her impending tragic calamity, Nellie smiled at her sister's inadvertent pun.

Anastasia drew her legs, still encased in her eiderdown comforter, up toward her face and leaned her chin on her knees. "Could you not take the dreaded locomotive?"

Cornelia shook her head a firm 'no.' "In addition to my well-principled loathing of the beast, the train would be such a long journey. And *so* costly. I must purchase tickets in two directions."

"Of course," said Anastasia. "Going there and returning home."

"No! The journey necessitates southerly travel, to cross the Hudson near The City where the river is not frozen." Nellie held down one finger. "Then, I must travel that entire length again on the *opposite* side of the river, and then even farther north to get to West Point!" She waggled her second finger. "*Mutter* and Papa will never permit it. Expensive travel is for emergencies only." Cornelia shook her head again, feeling sorry for herself.

"There is still a fortnight before the cotillion, perhaps you will be able to find an alternative method of travel, like sled? Or perhaps you will be able to persuade our parents to let you take the train." Anastasia tried to cheer Nellie.

"Harrumph," Nellie sniffed. "Even *I* do not possess the requisite persuasion skills to convince Papa, let alone *Mutter*."

Anastasia made one more attempt at an optimistic outlook. "Mayhap something will change. Perhaps the river will thaw just before that day."

Nellie just shook her head saying, "That is far too much wishful thinking, even for me." She went back to her side of the room and began to get dressed, gloom and doom written all over her face.

The weather continued cold, even frigid, which did not lighten Nellie's mood. Nellie lingered at the breakfast table, slowly stirring milk into her tea, melancholy expression a now permanent feature of her face. The newspapers forecast a cold snap of daytime temperatures in the single digits; Nellie despaired that she would ever see Lawrence again.

"Nellie, cheer up." Anastasia urged her. "At least this morning's mail contained Obadiah's weekly correspondence *and* a nice fat letter from Cadet Baker."

Cornelia lifted her head from its doleful position in her hand. "I have not seen either," she said.

"Matthias is playing postman up in his room. I do believe he has absconded with the morning's mail," Anastasia replied.

"Stasia! Why did you not snag it for me?" asked Cornelia.

Anastasia laughed. "You have been moping around for days. I thought searching for it would give you some constructive employment."

Cornelia indulged in one more frown, paying homage to her righteous contrariness. Then she laughed.

"Goodness," Anastasia said. "My strategy worked wonders, even before you found the missive."

Cornelia ran upstairs to Matthias's room. She caught herself before she tripped over his collection of locally gathered arrowheads scattered across the floor. On the other side of the room, her brother had a green shade visor on his head, garters on his sleeves and was busy stuffing the family's mail into the cubicles of his brother's roll top desk.

"Tampering with the United States mail is a felony, Matthias," Cornelia said in an authoritative voice. "You could be fined or imprisoned, or both! Give me my letters."

"Which ones, Nellie?" Unfazed by Cornelia's threat, Matthias did not look up when he spoke; he kept his eyes on his sorting.

"How many have you taken, you artful dodger?" asked Nellie, no longer just feigning anger.

"Which day's mail do you want?" asked her brother. He started looking through piles on the floor.

"I want every single letter addressed to me!" said Cornelia, resisting the temptation to stamp her foot.

"But then I will have less letters to deliver," Matthias complained.

Nellie gave him a look that could kill and Matthias coughed up three letters. As Nellie turned on her heel to exit the room, he caught her skirt. "Oops, one more," he said with a sheepish grin.

"For goodness sakes Matthias! You deliver *all* this mail directly to the person to whom it is addressed *immediately* or I shall report your theft to *Mutter.*"

Matthias looked like he was about to protest, but his eyes widened at the thought of their mother's disapproval. He stood up and started pulling all the letters out of the cubicles, stuffing them in his mailman's pouch.

Nellie ran to her room. She scanned the return addresses: one from Lawrence, three from Obadiah and one from Clara, postmarked Fort Laramie, Dakota Territory. *Mercy, where in the wilderness is Fort Laramie? Certainly, nowhere I would ever want to go....*

She carefully opened the seal on Lawrence Baker's enticing, fat packet. In beautiful script using every inch of space, she read:

> *My dearest Cornelia Rose,*
> *It is with heavy heart that I contemplate the icicles ever elongating in front of my window. All the talk among the cadets is of the frozen river and the unending ice. I fear, my dear, your Valentine travels will be curtailed by the un-navigable river. Therefore, I enclose a tintype of myself I have purchased from a local photographer. If I cannot see you my little flower, I will at least find comfort in the thought that you can see me.*

Cornelia extricated the picture of Lawrence carefully from the half dozen or so pieces of stationery that swaddled it, icy gloom again freezing her heart.

Perhaps it is for the best.

In an attempt to enjoy this horrible cold that you Northerners seem to tolerate so readily, I endeavored to try ice-skating on the river with a great many other men from my barracks. I am exceedingly coordinated and graceful at all times, as you well know. Imagine my surprise then, when I got on the ice to find myself most perfectly awkward. I have never experienced the sensation of struggling to keep my feet underneath myself! I fear I was quite the comic sight, slipping and sliding, spending more time on the seat of my pants than on my skates. Oh! I had visions of glory before donning these apparatai of disaster! I had pictured myself gliding with my usual grace; twirling, on the ice as I often do in dance. I do believe my natural athleticism might have helped me make a go of it, had it not been for one of my classmates, taking advantage of my temporary ineptitude, sneaking up behind me, whirling around me, startling me, and then actually tripping me! Instead of merely resuming my place on my seat on the ice, up and away I went, arms flailing, limbs splaying in separate directions. Of course, I struck head first as is the case with all unfortunate skaters. I did not know I was hurt until the blood came streaming down my face from a wound above the eye...I will not try your patience with any more of the details.

I now regret the incident even more on account of the invitation to the Valentine Cotillion and the party at Col. Bowman's. I fear I am now unable to participate in the festivities as my head still hammers with pain and they will not yet release me from sickbay.

So, my dearest flower, the frozen river has doubly thwarted our plans. I fear I must alone wait until healing and a thaw enable us to....

Cornelia could read no further. She bit her lip, catching a sob before it escaped. *It is all to no avail!* Overcome with emotion, she threw the remaining unread pages on her bed. Less than a second later, she threw herself down in the midst of them, sobbing.

Agnes stuck her head around the corner. "Cornelia, don't carry on so. Sakes alive! The ink will run. I have not received a letter from my husband in days...but you do not seem me dramatically wringing my hands, nor carrying on so. Furthermore, you still have two other letters to read...."

Cornelia paid no attention to her and continued crying.

Agnes edged closer, staring at the envelopes. "One at least is from Obadiah, I see. I'll wager it contains several more of those quotations from great literature you find so charming...."

Nellie looked up at her, surprised by her uncharacteristic kindness. In spite of her frustration and disappointment, her heart melted enough for her to extend kindness in reply.

"If you have not received any mail from your faithfully corresponding husband, I do believe you should investigate the room of our newly self-appointed mailman, Matthias," Cornelia said through her tears, punctuated by a loud hiccup.

"That bilious little wake-snake!" Agnes shouted and turned on her heel.

Nellie felt a cold gust blow through her glass window and resumed her crying, the scuffling in the other room not fully penetrating her misery.

Matthias ran into the room and threw a large packet at her. It was heavy and banged her on the elbow. "You can stop crying. I *think* this is the last of your mail now," he said and ran out before Nellie could reprimand him again.

Nellie looked down at the package, and the return address arrested her in mid sob.

It was from a publishing company. She sniffed. *Could it be...?*

"It must be the rights to preform our chosen excerpts, and the corresponding scripts!" she cried. "We can finally begin to rehearse the dramatic pieces."

Blues forgotten, she tore open the envelope. A dozen scripts fell out. Nellie picked them up one by one, tearing through the listed titles, summaries, and the cast of characters. The heat of her passion for her new project jump-started her from her frozen inertia.

Nellie embraced her dual role as producer and director of her parish follies with all the energy and talent she possessed. Her first tasks were completed the same week the parish board entrusted her with the event. She recruited volunteers, put Anastasia in charge of costumes, and Augusta, the budding artist, in charge of the sets. She begged Jonas to play the piano as the musical accompaniment, knowing she could round out the band with other musically proficient parishioners. She persuaded her father to take charge of recruiting singers from their parish's choir.

She even approached George Brandreth, via his sister Helen, requesting permission to turn the Brandreth warehouse into a theatre for the performance.

Now that the scripts had arrived, she would be prepared for the scheduled try-outs and could cast all the parts. Nellie's eye lingered over the pile of skits and sketches she had chosen, a budding smile warming her face.

Nellie's selections for the performance included two dramatic pieces, one farcical routine and two slapstick bits. Now she made a list of additional 'acts' she thought would lend themselves nicely to her theme *No Song, No Supper*, after the comic opera first performed in 1790 as a benefit.

She moved to her desk, opened her inkwell and drafted a flyer publicizing try-outs. *I must announce the would-be actors should prepare selections from their favorite plays, poems, or literary work for their audition. I will consider their audition pieces suggestions for inclusion in the show. At those same tryouts, I will cast the skits and scenes I have chosen.*

I shall become a famous director, Nellie schemed. *I will abandon my desire to be a midwife without a backward glance. I was born to be in theater!*

CHAPTER 29
True Colors

Sing Sing, March 1851

"Cornelia Rose Entwhistle, I called you!" The authority in the voice did not diminish despite the long distance it traveled from the kitchen.

Nellie again re-read Obadiah's latest quote from Shakespeare, delivered last night by messenger after they parted, written in his beautiful hand:

> *"Did my heart love till now? Forswear it, sight! For I ne'er saw true beauty till this night."*

She smiled, raised her hands over her head in delight, jumped up out of bed and threw open the shutter. She gave a sharp intake of breath, as she did every morning, in fresh appreciation of her majestic view. Her expansive good feelings wobbled a bit, however, looking at the mood of the Hudson. A one hundred and eighty-degree scan of the panorama subdued her fiery feelings. This morning was grey, with a low cloud cover. The river was flat, the color dull. It was still breathtakingly beautiful to Nellie, albeit chilling to the spirit. The ships were quietly berthed, barely moving in the almost still water—caught and suspended in the frosty cold of the morning. She moored the passionate feelings of her dreams and her exuberance from Obadiah's quotes of courtship along with them. *On to the business of the day*, she thought, closing the sash. Risking pneumonia, she stripped off her nightgown in search of her pantaloons.

Her name again floated up the stairs on the impatient voice of her mother.

Saint Paul's began to chime the quarter hour, joined by the Calvary Baptist, Trinity Episcopal, and the United Methodist Churches. *I'll never tire of this grand symphony,* Nellie thought. *Triumphant music with a lofty purpose — how would one know the hour without the Church bells?*

When the horn of the 7:20 steamboat leaving for The City blasted, she knew she had dallied too long.

She threw on petticoat after petticoat in quick succession. One last look out her window revealed the 7:25 train headed toward Tarrytown, on the way to Grand Central Station, belching steam and tooting its whistle so loudly, it was impossible to hear anything over its noise. Nellie slammed the inside shutters closed and wished, along with the town Aldermen, the newfangled contraption's tracks never extended north to Croton, through their fair city. *Speed is not the bees' knees,* she thought. *Was there truly such a dire need to arrive everywhere faster? Keeping one's eardrums intact had its merits.*

Merits to which Mr. Washington Irving convinced a court of law to ascribe a dollar value. Nellie smiled. At a younger age, she simply adopted wholesale the beliefs of her father, the engineer turned shipping magnate, who touted the benefits of water travel over rail. Now she followed politics and policy through her own extensive reading. The Knickerbocker movement championed the steamship's cause, providing a megaphone for the townsfolk's complaints that the railroad, running right along the river, forever compromised their bucolic life.

She chuckled to herself. *Most likely the impetus for the Knickerbocker School taking pen in hand to decry the evils of the railroad sprang from that folklore thief, Washington Irving.*

The lynchpin of the Knickerbockers did more than complain about the railroad's noise, dirt, and tremors. He filed a lawsuit against the railroad company for tortious interference with his right to peacefully enjoy his property. Irving sought damages for loss of his acres on the waterfront. The tracks cut off Irving's access to the river and caused his land value to plummet.

"How could the railroad put the tracks on Irving's land in the first place without his permission?" Nellie had asked Obadiah.

Proud to display his legal knowledge, Obadiah had replied, "The government's right of Eminent Domain." Nellie tried to look all-knowing at this answer, but Obadiah rightly guessed she did not fully understand this principle. He explained, "The Right of Eminent Domain gives a state or the federal government the power to take private property for public use. So Mr. Irving was powerless to stop the track laying. Nevertheless, the doctrine also mandates 'just compensation' be given the original owner. I believe Mr. Irving prevailed in his lawsuit by arguing the money he received only covered the railroad's attendant nuisances of noise and dirt. The loss of water access devalued the property completely; therefore, the original payment from the railroad company was not 'just compensation' for the total value lost. The crafty, avenging man made a brilliant argument! The Railroad was found culpable for destroying the value of his property and Mr. Irving received an astronomical compensation of $5,000."

Nellie wondered, *why does Doctor Brandreth not follow Irving's suit and file his own complaint? His Glyndon Estate mansion is now perpetually shrouded in grimy soot, shaken to its foundation from the iron monster's tremors.*

Nellie was still a frequent guest at the successful pill factory owner's thirty-five-room mansion on Spring Hill. In spite of her estrangement from George Brandreth, his sister Helen continued to invite Nellie to her parties. Last week, the railroad ruined Helen's splendid tea. The noise and steam of a belching engine's arrival at the Sing Sing train station halted all conversation. *Mercy! The malodorous soot from the locomotive caused me to quite lose my appetite. Did not the soot turn the white frosting on the teacakes quite grey? How can the Brandreths ever again enjoy their food, whist those horrible engines arrive hourly?* Glyndon Estate had been beautiful inside and out with intricate grillwork of fine iron wrought over the façade. Nellie still admired the mansion's style, borrowed from the New Orleans custom, but the train ruined its beauty and value. *It grieves me to think this 'improvement' not only devastated the outside irreparably, it also shattered the home's inside serenity.*

While she was angry on behalf of the Brandreths, now she was selfishly glad that the Entwhistle house was just a bit higher up on a different hill, farther from the station. The severity of the noise of the train diminished before it reached their abode. But even still, it was loud.

I was taught the utmost reverence for Mr. John Jervis's genius in engineering the Croton Aqueduct. But using that genius to lay tracks for his confounded new locomotive engine right along our precious river ruined its natural flow and the surrounding environment. Mercy, that fool conveyance contraption is hardly an improvement! Yet they call this progress?

Nellie sighed and shook her head at the loss of the pristine world of her childhood.

Then she shook a leg. *I must put some hustle in my bustle! It will never do to anger Mutter today. I do not want to jeopardize my outing to Nelson Park to see the 'Native Warriors, Braves, and Beauties of the Seymour Company Traveling Troupe.'*

Her high spirits returning in spite of her outrage at the despoiling of her beautiful countryside, she bounded down the stairs from her garret and received a chastising from her mother as a greeting.

"Staying in bed until after nine like a princess and then bounding down the stairs like a common deck hand? Shame on you Cornelia Rose!" she said.

But her mother's face softened as she caught Nellie in her arms and bestowed one of her precious embraces. Nellie's confusion mired her happy smile. Upon brief reflection, she did not dare risk asking why she deserved a hug; she just squeezed her mother's arm in gratitude.

The day passed in the usual whirl of chores and studies, and before she knew, it was time to dress for her outing.

Nellie carefully completed her toilette and just as carefully chose her wardrobe: four petticoats, her re-worked satiny-pink silk gown sporting new ruffles down the bodice, new magenta piping and trim at the bottom of its full skirt, her crimson hat, and her new boots. Anastasia bounced on the bed in front of her, peppering her with questions as she took off her apron and blouse and began donning petticoats.

"Who is your beau today Nellie, Cadet Baker or Mr. Wright?" Anastasia asked.

"Mr. Wright," Nellie declared.

"So, Obadiah is 'Mr. Right'?" asked Anastasia, her face wearing a coquettish smile.

"For today! Forsooth, he is quite charming and handsome," said Nellie, pulling her corset tighter, as if to brace herself for an onslaught of questions about her two beaus. But to Nell's surprise, Anastasia seemed satisfied with that answer and changed the subject.

"Have you seen the advertisement for the performance today?" Anastasia asked. Nellie nodded, thinking of the sensational handbill disseminated at Hart's Apothecary and elsewhere through town yesterday.

"Aren't you just a bit afraid to see the Indians, Nellie? Don't you think they are frightening? Are they truly bona fide Natives? Do you think they are unfeigned, existent Chippewa, Nell, like the advertisement proclaims? If Red Jacket and Chief Okatahuse were truly from Oregon, why would they want to come here? Do you sincerely desire to witness a staged scalping?" Anastasia paused for just an instant, consulting the pamphlet again. "Or be privy to a theatrical burning of Miss McCrea at the stake?"

Anastasia shivered, her pale white face blanching.

Nellie gave her sister a reassuring pat on the hand and said, "You understand these dramatic entertainments, Anastasia. The topic must always be incendiary and the 'reenactment' most terrifying in order to garner a large audience. I would not think one could generalize about a whole nation based on a traveling show."

Nellie twirled before the mirror.

"Incendiary!" said Anastasia, laughing. "You have such a way with puns, Cornelia."

"I 'spose I would want to attend Red Jacket's narration, if he truly is 'the most eloquent Indian orator living!' Furthermore, it most certainly would be remarkable to see the largest collection of Indian curiosities."

Anastasia shook her head again before continuing, "No, I think I will content myself with watching the Troupe make their grand entrance into town mounted on their ponies, painted, and fully equipped for war. That will be quite enough adventure for me! They certainly could not be intimidating when marching peacefully behind Tom Cathaggle's Bugle Band."

Anastasia speech concluded with her emphatic final jump on the bed. Not waiting for an answer, she bounded down the stairs, shouting, "Jonas, walk with me up Main Street so we can see the Indian Parade."

Nellie giggled and shook her head. She probably would take a peek at the parade through their drawing room windows only. She would wait to see the show in its entirety when Obadiah escorted her, after he concluded his day's work with Judge Urmy.

Mrs. Entwhistle and Nellie both ran to the drawing room's ten-foot high windows at the first sound of a bugle. The parade truly was a spectacle. The young Chief looked fierce, sitting on his pony, dressed in a full buckskin jacket and pants, chest decorated in beads and strings of shells, head crowned with a headdress of many feathers. An older, wizened man wearing a red jacket sat astride a pony cantering after the Chief's. Nellie explained to her mother, who had not seen the advertisement in the newspapers, nor any of the bills of particulars posted at the nearby Union Hotel, that the older Indian was probably Red Jacket, the great orator.

"Lord save me from the terror of war with those people!" her mother said. "*Gott im Himmel*, I thank God we live on the civilized east coast. When I hear tell of the horrors of the West, I pray my kith and kin be spared from enduring that trial."

Almost before the parade ended, Obadiah's carriage pulled up to the entrance on the north side of the Entwhistle house. Just the sight of him, jumping from the driver's seat, throwing the reins over the dappled mare's head, sent those now deliciously familiar tingles down her spine.

He jangled the entrance bell with a happy energetic touch and almost preceded the butler's escort into the drawing room.

Nellie rushed over to him and extended her hand. He kissed it, and she looked up to see her mother frowning at her. *Was that not lady-like?* she wondered, with a bemused smile on her face, as Obadiah bowed toward Mrs. Entwhistle.

Obadiah saw her wry smile and said, "What troubles you, my fair lady? Do you quake with trepidation at the thought of seeing the dramatic presentation of the Chippewa and their acting troupe?"

"No, kind sir," said Nellie. Then, since she felt at a loss to otherwise explain her expression she said, "Although it does give a lady pause when she considers whether or not it is suitable entertainment to witness a re-enactment of a vicious burning at the stake."

"My intelligent Cornelia, how very well articulated!" exclaimed Obadiah. "I myself am rather reluctant to support such a spectacle as this with my twenty-five-cent admission. I have done rather an expansive study of the Plains Indians and their civilization at the Academy, and I find that those paraded about as 'curiosities' are hardly reflective of the civilizations and people who inhabited this land before us.

"If you concur, and if your mother deems it prudent...." Obadiah turned and bowed again to Mrs. Entwhistle. "Perhaps we should switch of our scheduled activity tonight, and instead view the circus?"

"'Tis such a strange happenstance. Two extraordinary entertainments competing simultaneously for our twenty-five cents on the very same night," said Nellie.

"I saw the colorfully ornamented circus wagons pulled along North Highland Turnpike not more than a quarter of an hour ago," said Obadiah. "At this very moment, they are unloading their menagerie and setting up their canvas tent right alongside the Indian show in

Nelson Park. I do believe they intend to begin their parade through town to garner attendees at their big top tent shortly."

"Prudence would rather counsel against attending either event," Mrs. Entwhistle said with a frown. "Why just last month our *Hudson River Chronicle* reported George McNutt had his pocket picked at the last circus. I would wager he is hardly the only man who has ever been robbed at the circus. Moreover, his pocket book contained seventy-five dollars! Rest-assured it was his own folly, to carry such a treasury upon him to the circus of all places! Howsoever, I do believe we would be well advised to heed this confirmation of the circus as an unsavory place."

Mrs. Entwhistle paused for a breath, and Obadiah and Nellie looked at each other uncertainly. Nellie's happy anticipation of the evening dissipated with her mother's negativity.

"Nevertheless," Mrs. Entwhistle continued, looking at the disappointed faces in front of her. "While I hardly approve of the circus and the life of its showmen, I suppose it *is* the lesser of two evils. Further, I will warrant traveling circuses have rather become acceptable forms of amusement over the last quarter century." Mrs. Entwhistle nodded for emphasis. "Fairly respectable people have been known to enjoy an evening at the circus ring."

"Verily!" cried Nellie. "Why I read in *The Daily Herald* just the other day its editor, and my personal acquaintance, William Cullen Bryant thought the circus was unparalleled as a modern form of entertainment."

"Then to the circus it is," said Obadiah, and bowed to Nellie.

"Still," said Mrs. Entwhistle with a cautionary wave of her hand. "It was not too long ago that many churches condemned the circus as immoral, and the traveling menagerie little better, due to the inhumane treatment of those curious animals. Why even the equestrians, whose great acrobatic feats thrill us with their daring, have been known to live rather ungodly lives."

Obadiah said, "I could not agree with your wisdom more, Mrs. Entwhistle, especially when considered from the legal perspective, as many states still ban circuses from performing, making it a misdemeanor to conduct a show of that nature within their borders." Mrs. Entwhistle nodded approvingly, even though she continued to scrutinize his demeanor with a critical expression on her face.

"Howsoever, tonight's traveling show should be beyond reproach as Somers' own Benjamin Lent, the former partner of the very respectable Hachaliah Bailey is its host," concluded Obadiah.

"Ah, yes, Mr. H. P. Bailey," said Mrs. Entwhistle, giggling like a schoolgirl. Nellie smiled in amusement and relief. "In truth, the era of the traveling menagerie began with him. Yes, sir, he caused quite a stir in my day when he landed his sloop containing an elephant at the old Sing Sing dock, and then surreptitiously, and only by night, walked the poor beast from Sing Sing to Somers, so that no one got a free preview. *Ach du Liebe,* how our town gossiped about it for days, when the incident came to light! Why some of the schoolboys even swore they had seen it, while others pumped all the deckhands on the sloop for descriptions of the captured creature.

"Ever since, folk have come from all around to pay their twenty-five cents to see the elephant. And I have seen the elephant!"

"*Mutter!* You have never made me privy to that confidence!" Nellie exclaimed with her hands on her hips.

Her mother smiled kindly. "We were all young and foolish once my dear."

Nellie was not sure, but she somehow inferred a criticism of her from her mother's remark. Her unease quickly diminished however when her mother proffered yet another hug. *Goodness, what can be happening? Two embraces from Mutter in one day. This must portend of world changing events.*

"Old Bet. Such a strange name for an elephant," said Obadiah.

"But, good sir, Mr. Bailey dubbed him 'Old Bet' for he called his oldest daughter Elizabeth 'new Bet,'" said her mother, in an airy, charming tone that Nellie could not remember ever hearing.

They all laughed.

Obadiah revealed he possessed a bit of knowledge of this elephant's history. "Old Hachaliah was sure proud of that elephant. Even after she met with such an unfortunate and untimely death, H. P. Bailey, inveterate showman that he was, devised a method for continuing to make a dollar on her."

Nellie looked confused.

"Mr. Bailey had Old Bet stuffed and continued to take her on the road, charging admission to see her taxidermied remains," her mother explained.

"As smart a businessman and showman as there ever was!" Obadiah concluded with a flourish of his hand.

"Howsoever, not such a wise father," said Mrs. Entwhistle. Cornelia and Obadiah duly looked puzzled. "My friend, Calista Bailey was forever reminded that her father named the elephant after her older sister, not her."

"Was there not some *other* exotic animal named after your friend?" asked Nellie, anxious that the oldest in the family not have all the fame and good fortune.

"No," replied Mrs. Entwhistle. "But she had the last laugh. She is now Calista Crosby—Cornelia, you know her, Enoch Crosby junior's wife. Widow Crosby still runs her husband's Union Hotel. She competes with her father's Elephant Hotel in Somers for the tourist trade and last year she was named 'innkeeper of the year' for our county."

Everyone laughed.

Obadiah, still grinning from the convivial conversation said, "By your leave, Mrs. Entwhistle, I will now escort your fine daughter to an evening of entertainment and education. I promise I will return her with full knowledge of all the animals in the menagerie, and their natural habits and habitats."

"As for the pick pockets, I will certainly be wary and guard my pocket book." He chuckled with a rueful smile. "I am rather loath to confess, but my pocket book is far lighter than the unfortunate Mr. McNutt. It would, in fact, behoove the pick pockets to ply their talents on some other victim." Obadiah bowed formally, but with a merry flourish, and the pair hurried outside to his waiting carriage.

Nellie flushed with excitement as they drove off. "I thrill just to think of the daring feats of the horseback riders!" she exclaimed.

"Know ye from whence the circus derived its name?" asked Obadiah as he turned his gaze from the road to her.

At the shake of Nellie's head, Obadiah continued his scholarly explanation. "A famous equestrian from Brittan's Seven Years War, a certain Englishman named Astley, performed his daring horseback riding in a circle, or a circus, so that the audience could fully see the length and breadth of the entire performance."

"You may be assured, Mr. Wright, I well recall from my studies of Latin that 'circus' means 'circle,'" said Nellie, feeling like a schoolgirl trying to please a favorite teacher.

"Very good my dear," responded Obadiah, much like a teacher pleased with his pet pupil. "And do you further appreciate why Astley chose to perform in a ring?"

Nellie shook her head uncertainly.

"Centrifugal force!" announced Obadiah, with triumph in his voice. Nellie looked back at him with an uncomprehending expression on her face.

"The circular nature of the ring actually helps keep the rider on the horse during the daring tricks."

"I have never seen a rider standing on the back of a galloping horse. I am all a-tingle!" Nellie clapped her hands together as if to prove her enthusiasm.

Obadiah smiled at her and flicked the reins lightly on the back of his mare to urge her to pick up the pace. "I assure you my dear, that will not be the only event of the evening that will set you a-tingle."

With that tantalizing suggestion of romantic events to come, Nellie impulsively took his arm. She nestled next to him, allowing the wind to whistle in her ears and cool her flaming cheeks as they trotted briskly toward the circus tent.

CHAPTER 30
Send in the Clowns

Sing Sing, May 1851

Nellie held her breath, watching her brother balance on a large ball, and juggle three smaller ones. *Who knew Jerome was so talented?* Jerome's dog, in a clown hat, suddenly deviated from the script and lunged at his master's unstable platform, sending Jerome headlong into the bale of hay waiting to be used as a prop in the next skit. *Not such a talented finale!* she thought.

Everyone near the makeshift stage laughed.

"That haystack is surely fortuitously placed," said Nellie. She frowned. "But the show is just one month away. Not much more time to rehearse." She pulled Jerome out of the hay. He looked so funny with straw sticking out of his hair that she giggled.

Jerome held up his arm, wincing in pain. "I fear I have snapped a bone." His face twisted in a grimace as he moved his hand gingerly.

Nellie bent in concern and took his arm.

"Ouch," said Jerome through clenched teeth. "It is painful in the extreme. It must be broken."

"Extreme pain is not necessarily the indicia of broken bones," said Nellie, gently probing the length of his arm, starting at his elbow. Jerome sat with teeth clenched through the travel of her fingers, until she got to his wrist.

Nellie's touch elicited an involuntary jerk of his arm, and Jerome winced again.

Ah, thought Nellie, probing each bone in Jerome's hand, and the joints in his wrist.

"Broken, right?" asked Jerome, eyes closed, turning white.

"No, to the contrary, your bones are sound," said Nellie.

"Then why does this part...." Jerome pointed to the outside of his wrist. "...Hurt so dearly?"

"Sprained muscles are just as painful as broken bones," said Nellie. "The good news is we will avoid the uncomfortable step of snapping your bones back into place. Furthermore, there is no requirement your wrist idle immobile for weeks in a plaster."

"What is the bad news?" asked Jerome, just a bit of color returning to his face.

"Sprained muscles do take fully as long to heal as broken bones." Nellie ran for her midwifery supply bag, always ready and waiting, this time under her cloak backstage. She hurried back, already digging in her bag. "Observe! I have right here an unguent of wheat bran stirred in cold vinegar and then boiled to make the concoction salve. Just the very quick cure for sprains. I will wrap it for today, to give the strained muscles some support. Mayhap you would even like a sling?"

"No sling," said Jerome. He remained seated, center stage, enjoying all the sympathy from his fellow thespians.

"I will have Jerome up and running in two shakes of a lamb's tail," she announced. "Will the next act please take your positions?" She wrapped the wrist in a clean strip of linen.

"I must do my act again, now...." Nellie looked up with sharp disapproval on her face. "...Without the dramatic finish," Jerome concluded. The crowd laughed and gave a 'huzzah.'

"Not today," said Nellie, tying off the linen. "In fact, you may wish to explore another talent and save this daring feat for the next charity extravaganza."

"Never!" exclaimed Jerome. "My public clamors for my act." He swept his good arm around the stage in a grand gesture. Everyone laughed. Enjoying the attention, Jerome continued, "Why, all of my acquaintances have inquired about purchasing tickets. I cannot deprive my public of this long-anticipated performance. Mayhap I can even make my dramatic fall from grace part of my act." Jerome jumped up and everyone laughed and clapped.

Nellie giggled as she reassembled the emergency supplies in her basket.

Tap. Tap! Cornelia whirled around, mid-giggle. Obadiah, smiling and reaching for her hand, stood before her.

"So, this is where you have been hiding? Brandreth's warehouse." He smiled in mock-reproof. "This is my competition? An area surrounded by boxes and filled with minstrel acts?"

"Obadiah! So wonderful to see you, in person." Nellie squeezed his hand. "So marvelous that you have returned to our community."

Obadiah raised her hand to his lips and kissed her fingertips, sending a lovely tingle up her arm, like a spark traveling a jute rope fuse, igniting a blush from ear to ear. "At your service, M'lady."

Nellie beamed at him. "I wonder if I can enlist your aide in publicizing this fundraiser?"

"I am a mere serf at your disposal, M'lady." He grinned. "Although I had hoped your delight at my presence would stem from more than the joy of having an additional plebian to do your bidding."

Nellie laughed. "You know my current responsibilities demand I assess talent and enlist it as I see fit. Unfortunately, at this juncture, you are a mere pawn in the game of fundraising."

Obadiah bowed with a great flourish, and repeated, "At your service, M'lady." He kissed her hand.

She blushed, playing with a stray strand of hair. She stood erect, laid a hand on his shoulder, and said in her most regal voice, "Obadiah Weber Wright, I command you to lead the charge of publicity for this charitable event. I further command that you battle to sell as many tickets as possible, *waging* the entire monetary campaign of our war."

She paused, feeling a little silly, but decided to fully play her role. "To that end, I dub thee Sir Wright!" she said, giggled again. She grabbed a broom lying on the floor and tapped him on each shoulder, lightly. "Arise and assume your duties."

"What say you to that?" Nellie smiled again.

"Twenty-five cents a seat," Obadiah said with a decisive shake of his head. Nellie raised her eyebrows in a question. "My first decision in executing my duties — twenty-five cents a seat, and not a penny less! This is a fundraiser, we must not set our sights too low."

"Sir Wright, extraordinarily well put!

"Oh Obadiah, do you truly believe people will pay *twenty-five* cents to see this show?" Nellie tucked that stray strand of hair behind her ear with a hesitant, doubtful gesture.

"If people will pay twenty-five cents to see Old Bet, the elephant, you can bet they can part with that coin for a premiere theatrical performance," Obadiah said and winked at her.

"But we are amateurs," Nellie protested. "Performing in a warehouse."

"That act of your brother's we just witnessed is bang up to the elephant!"

They both laughed.

Obadiah continued, "Cornelia, fret not! If your dramatic nature can transfer to the other actors, I am sure the audience will be privy to a superb show." He pulled her closer. "Most assuredly, my sweet Lady Cornelia Rose," he whispered into her hair. "Your talents ensure you will give them their money's worth."

From that point on, Obadiah assumed responsibility for more than just the publicity. He handled the duties of business manager and stagehand too. Faithfully becoming her right-hand man, Obadiah never missed a rehearsal, set design, or strategy session.

Tarnation! Rehearsals bi-weekly for months and we have some 'actors' barely remembering their lines, Nellie thought, as she watched Hannah Agate stand like a statue and butcher Juliet's lines. *Romero is little better. Mercy! There have been many fits and starts to this endeavor, beginning with the difficulty in casting only* talented *members of our parish in the show....* What a chore it is to remain in everyone's good graces. Nellie used her diplomacy to persuade certain hopeful actor/parishioners to accept alternative jobs. *I spared them the embarrassment of revealing to Sing Sing at large their own lack of talent,* she told herself again. *Forsooth, perhaps I should have spared a few more!* She shook her head at Agnes' former beau Barney Forshay bumbling across the stage.

Some modicum of talent graces most of the chosen actors and actresses, she reassured herself. *Moreover, the great enthusiasm of the entire ensemble compensates for many an amateur mistake.*

Most parishioners auditioned with pantomime, burletta, and light opera arias they had honed themselves. Nellie took these as suggestions for incorporation into the show. She and her father spent many enjoyable hours together, picking musical numbers and deciding which acts, actors, and singers should play the parts. There were piano players, singing quartets, and brass bands. Nellie's favorite had to be the Hi Henry Minstrels who wore silk top hats and gaudy uniforms. *Their costumes are quite theatrical and buff,* Nellie thought. *Furthermore, Hi has three diamonds in the valves of his coronet – surely a good talisman, thrice over!*

No Song, No Supper, will unquestionably evolve into a masterful production, she vowed.

One evening, while Nellie endeavored to re-stage George Brandreth's particularly dicey performance of *My Old Kentucky Home,*

Obadiah snuck up behind her. He whispered into her ear, "Lady Cornelia, I have quite the surprise for you!" It sent delightful tingles down her spine, for more reasons than mere curiosity.

"Let Anastasia and Hannah take over the direction of *this*...." Obadiah pointed to the small area, sandwiched in between stacks of boxes they called a stage, unable to contain his laughter at the off-key singing of George. "You must come with me."

Cornelia opened her mouth to protest, but Obadiah pulled her by the arm. "I most solemnly swear, while our mission may seem tangential, it is not only a worthy occupation of your time, but you will, in fact, be delighted."

"I will follow thee wither thou goest!" Nellie struck a dramatic pose and laughed. Obadiah smiled and gave a flourish of his hand to indicate the direction. "But soft. First, I must see that the enigmatic Doctor Long Some Faker is again told he may *not* sell his ineffective tonics after his vaudeville act," she said.

Obadiah raised his eyebrows and laughed. "Surely Doctor Faker is not his chosen moniker!"

"Quite truly it is," replied Cornelia, with a merry toss of her head. "The Indian Medicine Man quite proudly wears this mantle, of his own accord."

"Advertising his quackery? Boldly warning of his chicanery?" asked Obadiah, shaking his head again, so amused by the stage name he waited patiently while Nellie cornered the man.

Finally, Nellie left her post, smiling, albeit a bit chagrined at the interruption. *Every minute of rehearsal is precious. Mercy, the day of the performance looms, mere weeks away,* she thought.

She balked again when Obadiah dragged her outside to his carriage.

"Jump in!" he commanded, with a familiarity she found annoying yet exhilarating. "Do not assume a dour countenance," he warned, picking up the reins. Nellie was about to dig in her heels and refuse to go.

Obadiah sensed her mood and said, "Cornelia, my dearest, I will keep you in suspense no longer. I sense I must let the cat out of the bag in order to coerce your cooperation. I have persuaded my old headmaster to allow us to use the stage at Saint John's for our performance!"

"But I already made inquiries there and was told a most emphatic, 'no.' The stage is for the Academy's use only," Nellie replied. She looked at him with a quizzical expression.

"Apparently, you did not send the right knight on that quest," rejoined Obadiah.

Nellie smiled, delight stealing over her face. But then she frowned. "We have not the means, the finances, to support any rental fees...How much will it cost?"

"The lack of expenditure is the icing on the cake!" proclaimed Obadiah. "Not a single, red cent. In honor of the credit I bring to the Academy, Mr. Marlborough Churchill himself is letting it to me! As a personal favor, he said, to one of his prize pupils."

Obadiah turned to her, his eyes sparkling.

"My, this is a magnanimous gesture," she said. She smiled, squeezing his arm. "I am quite overwhelmed by your kindness."

Obadiah looked disappointed.

"Have I not adequately expressed my undying gratitude?" Nellie asked, with mock concern.

"No, no. 'T was a gesture meant to win your heart, to secure your affection for me, above all others," he said with a meaningful look, which somehow the gaslight shining from the lamps lining Main Street magnified, as their horse trotted along.

"You have my heart, you can be assured of that," said Nellie with a light voice, but she looked away.

"But do others?"

The question hung in the air as Nellie used the relative darkness in between the streetlights to hide her face. *I am at a loss for words. I certainly am enamored of this man beside me, but Lawrence still commandeers some of my affection.*

At that moment, they arrived at Saint John's. Obadiah turned to her, still waiting for a reply. But the headmaster himself popped out from a shadow on the front path and jumped into their carriage.

"May I steer you to the stage entrance?" Mr. Churchill asked, without preamble. "I do believe you will be enchanted with the venue I am able to offer you!"

Nellie smiled and voiced her gratitude as their horse trotted along the path. Churchill guided them on a tour of the facilities.

The headmaster was so effusive in his eagerness to do Obadiah a good turn he would not let the evening end. Churchill directed their attention to every nook and cranny of the stage, praised the dressing rooms, and extoled the virtues of the orchestra pit. When they happened upon some old sets backstage, Churchill claimed the sets were just begging to be reused.

After well over an hour of his guided tour, he turned to Nellie and said, "What say you to a quick carriage ride home to allow your knight in shining armor the pleasure of a shot of whiskey with his old schoolmaster?"

Beholden to the headmaster and owner of the Academy as she was, Nellie could do nothing but acquiesce to his wishes.

In minutes, she found herself standing in her own carriage doorway, waving her handkerchief at Obadiah's retreating carriage.

She sighed at the empty, bright moonlit street.

Nellie shook her head. *No matter, I will see Obadiah again tomorrow at rehearsal.... Mercy! We can rehearse on a real stage! Mercy! This new stage adds quite the mystique of Broadway, quite the aura of real theatre to my production.*

She rushed into her front door and pulled off her stole, shouting, "You will never guess."

Nellie was arrested in midsentence at the sight of none other than Lawrence Simmons Baker standing in the middle of her drawing room.

"You have the most disconcerting habit of popping up in my front parlor!" said Nellie, her surprise making her almost discourteous. *Thank you most gracious Lord on High that Mr. Churchill prevented me from asking Obadiah into the parlor for a visit tonight!*

Lawrence, taking that statement as a compliment, rushed forward smiling, and bowed low over her hand.

"My heart has been overwrought with sorrow at your lack of faithful correspondence. I decided I must visit, to personally assess the situation. My calling here is a bit of first hand recognizance, if you will, to determine the reason for your lack of diligence."

Nellie bristled, but Baker drawled on.

"My ardor for you and my desire for your constant company has not abated in the least. While I am fully cognizant of the fact that logistical difficulties have thwarted our ability to properly court in person, I suffer from the disconcerting feeling that distance alone cannot explain the aloofness of your pen. In fact, I rather suspect a waning affection on your part." Lawrence took her elbow and looked deep into her eyes.

Nellie remained motionless and silent.

"This is where I had quite expected an immediate and heartfelt denial of any diminishment of passion." Lawrence shook his head. "While your silence leaves me bereft, I do hope it does not portend dire occurrences. I hope to persuade your attendance at my graduation from the Academy in two weeks' time. Heretofore my many invitations to partake in the festivities have remained unanswered."

Nellie still hesitated. *I do still adore Baker, but do I not also know there is a time when I must choose* one *suitor....*

"I can see that I have surprised you into uncharacteristic silence," Baker said. But he stood there, holding her elbow, waiting for a reply.

Two suitors in one night petitioning for exclusivity in my attention and affection!

"I confess I find myself in quite the quagmire," Nellie said. She snapped her mouth shut, unsure what to say next.

Shrugging her shoulders, Nell took the easy way out. "Your graduation celebration takes place on the very same days as our grand theatrical fundraiser. I immediately advised this in my letter responding to your invitation, thus tendering my answer. As the show is performed on both Saturday night and Sunday afternoon, I am afraid it would be impossible for me to attend your graduation festivities."

Baker stepped back, dropping her elbow. "I see." He thought a moment.

"Perhaps I have a compromise. The actual graduation ceremony is on Monday at noon, followed by a celebratory tea. While I would prefer my sweetheart attend *all* the festivities, I will content myself with your presence on Monday.

"Therefore," said Baker, and he paused for dramatic effect as he went over to one of their horsehair chairs and retrieved his hat. "I will retire for my much-deserved furlough and return to my native South. But I do intend to receive a reply from you before my graduation.

"Good evening my little flower." Lawrence bent over one of her hands and kissed it. "My little primrose," he said, kissing the other hand. He put on his hat and with a dancer's grace, waltzed out the door.

Slowly, in deep thought, Nellie climbed the front stairs to her room.

Anastasia raised her head from her pillow on the other side of the room. "Which beau was in the drawing room?"

"Lawrence," said Nellie with a heavy sigh.

Anastasia sprang from her bed and ran over to Nellie's. She lifted the eiderdown and jumped underneath it. She said in a dreamy voice, "What a splendid twist of events. A midnight tête-a-tête with your true love! How truly romantic."

"Romantic, yes, but my true love? Mercy, I am so uncertain!" Cornelia sat down on her bed, patting the duvet at a lump she assumed was Anastasia's toes. "How will I ever ascertain for which gentleman my heart truly pines?"

"Perhaps we can make a tally," suggested Anastasia.

"Oh, Stasia, what a foolish idea. Love cannot be quantified," Nellie said, shaking her head.

"Not love, exactly, but we can score the attributes of the suitors. So far, I have heard you describe Obadiah as charming, and Lawrence as enchanting," Anastasia said. She jumped back out of the bed and rummaged for some paper in the writing table.

"Mercy, you are no help," said Nellie with a sigh.

"Come, come you are not applying yourself," said Anastasia. Leaping back into the bed, it only took seconds before she poised her pen over her scrap of paper on her writing tablet. She looked up at Nell expectantly, pen leaking a blob of ink, making a splat on the page.

"Lawrence is a charismatic dancer and Obadiah is bewitching with his pen," said Nellie.

Anastasia started laughing, and then could not stop.

"Whatever possesses you?" asked Nellie, in vexation.

"I had nearly forgotten, 'Lawrence is a Casanova,'" she said, almost unintelligibly though a fit of giggling. "'Obadiah has beautiful penmanship'! And I quote you directly."

Nellie twisted her face and shrugged her shoulders at the ridiculousness of those statements. Then she dissolved into fits of laughter too.

"Is it truly a difficult decision?" asked Anastasia, laughing so hard she came dangerously close to upturning the inkbottle.

Nellie and her sister sat on the bed, clinging to each other, laughing until tears ran down their faces.

CHAPTER 31
The Show Must Go On

Sing Sing, June 1851

Cornelia had chosen a small, *but imperative,* she thought to herself, role in the production. She was to perform Ophelia's first soliloquy from *Hamlet.*

Finally, it was the night before the show, and dress rehearsal was in full swing.

Midway through their musical revue, Nellie stepped out of her role as director and onto center stage.

Looking up to the heavens, arms flung wide, Cornelia took a deep breath and began:

> *"Oh, what a noble mind is here o'erthrown!*
> *The courtier's, soldier's...."*

Bang!

Cornelia's eyes jumped to the temporary cat crawl; the place for the spotlight was empty. The stagehands were busy one deck below, repairing a problem with the limelight burner, in order to reinstate the spotlight. Another loud noise distracted her and caused her to pull her hand from its dramatic pose and dash it over her eyebrows, shading her eyes from the stage lights so she could scrutinize the activity of the stagehands.

Bam!

One of the men knocked over a can of paint and it came crashing down right next to her. She jumped back in alarm. It narrowly missed her, splashing green on the hem of her dress. She looked back up into the gloomy recesses of the ceiling. "What else can befall me?" she joked. The stagehands laughed.

"Apologies!" someone called down. *Mercy and Tarnation! Is that Lawrence Simmons Baker up there in the shadows?*

It simply cannot be.

"Nellie," the man shouted and waved. *Lawrence! There is no mistaking that voice,* she thought. She waved back out of mere politeness, her heart skipping a beat. *There is nothing I can do without causing a scene other than to let the show go on.*

Cornelia returned her arm to its dramatic position:

"*The courtier's, soldier's, scholar's, eye, tongue, sword....*"

She glanced nervously around, looking for Obadiah. *I must contain my hysterics! Obadiah has gone to fetch more material for the ballad farce's backdrop.*

She continued:

"*Th' expectancy and rose of the fair state,*"

Out of the corner of her eye, Nellie saw movement, *Mercy, no! It cannot be. Obadiah has returned from his errand. If I can but keep Lawrence on his perch, perhaps the two men's paths will not cross. I must exit the stage and entice the departure of one without the other knowing the first was here.*

Cornelia rushed through the next lines:

"*The glass of fashion and the mold of form,*
Th' observed of all observers – quite, quite down!
And I – of ladies most deject and wretched"

Cornelia gulped for breath. She only paused from necessity – she ran out of air. *Oh, why do I have to breathe?* She tracked Obadiah's movements around the back stage with bile of fear rising in her throat.

She tried again:

"*That sucked the honey of his music vows – *"

Obadiah walked to the ladder of the cat crawl and began climbing. *Help me Lord, I must stop him!* she thought. But she had a few more lines to deliver:

*"Now see that noble and most sovereign reason
Like sweet bells jangled out of tune and harsh...."*

Augusta walked over to the ladder and said something to Obadiah. *Thank you, Augusta! And Praise to You, most merciful Lord,* she thought. Obadiah scrambled back down the ladder and walked over to the large backdrop, inspecting the spot where Augusta pointed. He disappeared behind it. It rose up, Obadiah's feet visible underneath, and moved toward her.

"That unmatched form and feature of blown youth"

Obadiah emerged from behind the set directly at her side. Nellie glanced at him, mouth open to form her next lines. He winked at her. He sauntered off with the backdrop, moving away from Augusta who gestured more instructions for moving some boxes of costumes.

"Blasted with ecstasy."

Her eyes darted furiously from the cat crawl to the side stage, now watching Obadiah lift boxes for Augusta and Lawrence tinker with the ceiling lanterns. She drew a shaky breath, and with more heartfelt wretchedness than she had ever been able to deliver the line before, said:

*"Oh, woe is me
T' have seen what I have seen, see what I see!"*

One of the other actors in the audience gave a slow clap. A whistle came from the cat crawl. *Lawrence!* Nellie thought, and refused to look up. She turned to exit. Before she could reach Obadiah, Augusta swung her to a different part of the stage and said, "Such a lovely dramatic rendition. Now, concerning this backdrop for the love scene from *Romeo and Juliet,* do you think we have drawn enough ivy on the tower?"

"Augusta, you have to help me!" Nellie whispered, grabbing her arm.

Augusta turned around, raised her voice, and called, "Obadiah, be a dear and fetch me some wood from the tinder pile outside." Obadiah put down the box and looked at her with annoyance.

"Sorry to be a pest, but I need it immediately," Augusta shouted. Obadiah threw up his hands and stalked off.

Augusta leaned in close. "Did I spy *Lawrence Simmons Baker* atop the cat crawl? Is the cadet joining our merry cast of characters? Do you have two competing suitors gallantly assisting you in your herculean charitable thespian endeavor?"

Nellie opened and closed her mouth and then finally nodded her head 'yes.'

But before Nellie could conspire with Augusta, a stagehand pulled her over to inspect a ripped curtain. One question lead to another, leading Nellie deeper and deeper back stage, all the time her thoughts spun, trying to devise a plan for keeping her two beaus from bumping into each other.

Suddenly, in her ear, someone whispered, "Get thee to a nunnery!"

Startled, Nellie whipped around. Lawrence put his arms around her, grinning from ear to ear.

"Why, Lawrence, what a horrible thing to say to a lady," Nellie said, making a big show of upset at his words, rather than revealing how upsetting she found his presence.

Lawrence looked startled. "Do you not twig my reasoning for my greeting, Nellie? It's from *Hamlet,* just like your pretty little speech."

Nellie only shook her head. *Merciful heavens!* "Lawrence, do you know what that phrase means?"

"I was forced to memorize parts of *Hamlet* at West Point, but I was not forced to understand them. Never did I contemplate that memorization would actually be a *useful* endeavor. I am so pleased I was able to retrieve that little tidbit of poetry from my noggin."

Nellie continued to shake her head. "But why are you here, Lawrence?"

"Your letters, all winter, spoke of nothing other than your excitement and hard work to produce this theatrical burlesque extravaganza," drawled Lawrence. He scratched his head. "I said to myself, 'Lawrence, if you want that girl, you're going to have to win her over!' I figured I would place my humble talents at your service to assist you in this noble venture."

"Well, thank you, that is most considerate," said Nellie, remembering her manners. "But when we last met, you were off to South Carolina."

"My furlough is almost spent. I have returned from my treasured *Mississippi* homeland in order to see you! I wish to use these precious few days to persuade you," Lawrence said, picking up her hand and bringing it to his lips. "I will coax you into a serious courtship and make you my wife."

Nellie drew in her breath and gazed into his eyes. She sighed.

Remembering her predicament, she looked over her shoulder to determine Obadiah's whereabouts. He had disappeared.

Nellie jumped at a loud whinny coming from the stage. Behind them, on stage Dr. Hart, Cornelia's employer, was literally performing a dog and pony show. The horse relieved himself on the stage.

"If I had had to perform, I might have had similarly expressed stage fright," Lawrence stated, and vanished into the backstage to distance himself from the odious smell. Nellie chuckled, in spite of herself.

Augusta called for Nathaniel. "Be a love, my dear husband and clean up the stage."

Nathaniel laughed and shook his head in the negative, starting to head in the opposite direction saying, "'Tis unexpected."

Augusta charged toward him, pointer finger raised.

Nathaniel laughed again and picked up a shovel propped against a drying backdrop. "'Tis unexpected to ever recall any of Elmer Otis's words as words of wisdom." Augusta looked at him with a quizzical expression on her face. "Otis warned me, 'once we engage in this menial labor set out as a test of mettle at West Point, we will never escape its yoke.'"

Augusta laughed and gave him a saucy smile. "You haven't had a task like this since your plebe year."

"None too long ago for such an odious assignment," said Nathaniel, cheerfully shouldering the shovel, and heading towards the malodorous undertaking. "Horsey duty...." he mumbled, still laughing.

Nellie felt her waist encircled from behind. *That Lawrence and his bold moves,* she thought.

"'I loved Ophelia,'" was whispered in her ear, but it was Obadiah's voice. Nellie whirled around in his arms.

"Mercy, you startled me," Nellie cried, trying to calm her runaway heartbeat.

Obadiah smiled down on her. "'Forty thousand brothers, if you added all their love together, couldn't match mine,'" he quoted. Pleased with himself, his smiling eyes flickered from her mouth to her eyes. When their eyes met, she saw his brimming with love. "That is the sole declaration of love Hamlet utters about Ophelia in the whole play. I was struck by their tortured relationship when we studied *Hamlet* at Saint John's. I'll wager every man, at some point in his life, cannot fathom the complex nature of his sweetheart. Something about your spectacular performance elicited this gem from deep within the recesses of my memory."

Augusta came toward them, same pointer finger raised, "Do you not have additional boxes to move, Mr. Wright?" she asked, with a look of mock reprimand. "Must I constantly goad you into performing your duties, like a recalcitrant schoolboy on a picture-perfect July afternoon?" She gave a merry laugh and made a shooing motion with her hands. Obadiah pretended to skulk away.

With a whirl of petticoats, Anastasia joined them. "Did I just see *Cadet Baker* talking to one of the technical crew, discussing the limelight? Cornelia, have you taken leave of your senses? You cannot engage one beau's assistance for months on a production and then suddenly also enlist the expertise of his competitor."

"I did not seek Baker—I am equally surprised at his sudden appearance here!" exclaimed Cornelia. "Nay, I am flabbergasted. Utterly distraught!"

She grabbed a hand of each friend. "I beg you to assist me. Can you *please* help me prevent them from encountering each other?" Her two dearest friends exchanged glances.

"I must be on center stage overseeing the dress rehearsal," Cornelia said. "I am powerless to control...."

"We will each take a beau," interrupted Anastasia, quickly catching her drift. "And keep him away from you."

"I am already directing Mr. Wright to 'lift that barge and tote that bale', so I will continue in my efforts to ready the sets whilst keeping Obadiah busy and at a distance," Augusta said with a firm clap of her hands, jumping right on board.

"Right. Then Anastasia, ensure Cadet Baker remains on the cat crawl, fixing the limelight. I'll stay in the footlights, in front of the actors, so neither man has an opportunity to talk with me," said Nellie. The ladies all nodded and scurried away.

Nellie stood in the footlights, anxious at first. But as act after act rehearsed, their plan worked. Nellie saw neither hide nor hair of either beau. Soon, absorbed in the details of scrutinizing the actors and their skits, and writing staging notes, she felt the tension of her behind-the-scenes drama fade to the back of her mind.

Suddenly it was front and center.

Scribbling copious notes about the pantomime and its chosen backdrop, she was startled out of her working calm by Obadiah appearing out of the shadows at her left elbow, whispering, "Golly, you appear both intimidating and endearing standing there absorbed in your work."

Nellie smiled and shooed at him, glaring at Augusta who was three steps behind him. Augusta beckoned for Obadiah and scurried him away.

Less than a minute later, Lawrence, with Anastasia fluttering at his side, slid next to her right elbow and whispered, "I am simply enamored of a strong woman, leading the troops," before Anastasia could pull him back into the shadows.

For the next half hour, while Nellie was correcting and directing the train wreck of a farcical act, every few minutes like clockwork, Obadiah appeared, stage left, whispered a bon mot, and disappeared, and seconds later, Lawrence appeared, stage right, kissed her hand, and vanished into the shadows.

Nellie was completely distracted, but somehow, she kept the skit running, until at last they had a flawless run through.

In the middle of the next act, Mrs. Wheeler's off-key and off tempo aria, just as Nellie was about to stop the orchestra and start again, Obadiah appeared, stage left and picked up her hand. He gave it a sympathetic squeeze as Mrs. Wheeler screeched a high note, completely flat. Seconds later, Lawrence appeared, stage right, simultaneously smiling and wincing at the music.

The love triangle stared at each other, aghast.

Mrs. Wheeler's high-pitched note stuck in her throat. She shaded her eyes with her hand and peered into the footlights, soundless.

The orchestra music petered out, one instrument at a time, like the winding down of a music box. The hum of activity backstage stopped and every person froze in place, *mouths agape,* Nellie thought to herself, before the horror of her situation took root and her brain immobilized too.

"Baker!" said Obadiah.

Baker dropped the screwdriver he was carrying. He bent to retrieve it, pulled himself back up to attention stance and barked, "That would be *Lieutenant* Baker to you, *Mister.*"

"*Wright*. Mr. *Wright*," replied Obadiah. The men glared at each other and then simultaneously each turned on his heel and marched off in the direction from whence they came.

Nellie was so flummoxed all she could think to say was, "*Exeunt, stage right, stage left.*"

A quick, nervous giggle ran through the ensemble, all eyes on Cornelia.

Nellie signaled to the orchestra, who struck up the introduction to the aria. Mrs. Wheeler began to sing, from the beginning. *The incident seems to have jolted Mrs. Wheeler back on key*, Nellie thought, ears burning in shame as she tried to fade back into the footlights and resume the dress rehearsal as if nothing happened.

CHAPTER 32
Did You Ever Have to Make Up Your Mind?

Sing Sing, June 1851

The curtain came down on the last scene.

"Dress rehearsal is successfully concluded!" announced Nellie through a speaking horn. "Stage hands please report three hours before show time tomorrow. Actors, before you change out of costume, come to the front row orchestra seats for notes. I will review your sketches as quickly as possible. I know we all want to retire home for our suppers."

Cornelia, flushed with the success of the evening, swung down from the stage in a happy twirl and almost bumped into her father.

"Cornelia Rose Entwhistle, I am completely disappointed in you," Mr. Entwhistle said.

Nellie burst into tears.

"Now, colleen, I didn't mean 'completely.' I am extremely proud of ye for organizing this fine show. It has all the markings of being a success, both financially and artistically. Tomorrow, 'opening night' is sold out. Sunday's 'closing night' only has a few seats left. Ye have made your parish proud, putting both your literary and dramatic talent and your organizational skills to work for our common goal."

Eyes red, Cornelia snuffled into her handkerchief in confusion.

Her father looked at her with a stern expression on his face. "Ye a' course can surmise, I am not pleased with t' sticky romantic situations you perpetually find for yerself. 'Tis a bit of a farce here," said Mr. Entwhistle, gesturing to the stage.

"Mercy! What a relief! I was afraid no one would think our minstrel show was funny," quipped Cornelia through her tears.

Her father looked at her and suddenly they both burst out laughing.

Cornelia's laugh changed to a loud guffaw, which got stuck in her throat and turned into a sob. She burst into tears anew, laughing and crying at the same time. Finally, her father wiped a tear from his own eye and said, "Ye may be t' belle o' the ball, but ye canna toy with these men's affections. Baker has fine prospects—he will soon receive his commission as an officer. He has all t' markings of a fine husband—a gentleman from the South with a fine practical education in engineering, earned while commanding a salary from our United States Army. Mr. Wright on t' other hand studied who knows what, and aims to become an attorney-at-law. Lord knows we don't need any more o' *those* helping to run this country amuck."

"Papa, you have stacked the deck! Do you mean to say you have chosen for me?" asked Cornelia, lifting her horrified face out of her handkerchief and staring at her father.

"Only wi' yer best interests in mind," said her father. "Interests that you may lack t' knowledge to discern."

Cornelia shook her head. "How can *you* know *me*, better than I know myself? How can *you* know, better than I, what type of man will suit my nature?"

"Would that it were that simple! Many men could suit yer nature, and sure yer fancy too. But it takes wisdom, experience, and an emotional detachment to discern who will be best fer ye in t' long run," said her father, running his hand over his hair and down the back of his head in his 'deep thought' gesture.

"Truly, Papa, you think I am incapable of making the correct choice?" Cornelia demanded.

"Not incapable, no, but perhaps swayed by transient or superficial trappings," her father replied. "Listen to me, it is simple. 'Tis simply a question of faith."

Cornelia looked confused.

"Obadiah is t' wrong faith," said Mr. Entwhistle.

"Whatever do you mean? He was baptized Catholic, just like we Entwhistles were."

Her father shook his head. "Always negotiating and twisting yer words. Yer *Mutter* has discovered that while he may have been *baptized* Catholic, in fact his mother was Episcopalian, and therefore his faith orientation is suspect."

"*Mutter* discovered?" Cornelia almost shouted. "*Mutter discovered? Mutter* discovered his mother was Episcopalian because *I told her.*"

"Well, true enough, Nell, but yer *Mutter* suspects that his father, Silas Wright was Episcopalian as well."

Nellie was flabbergasted. She shook her head. "That would, of course, make Obadiah simply Episcopal."

Her father shook his head. "That's what she thinks."

Nellie threw up her hands. There was no point in arguing this with her father. She tried a different tack. "Obadiah has truer, less tempestuous, intentions than Lawrence, even if Lawrence is completely Catholic."

Her father looked surprised. "'Tis true. I'm a mite surprised at your accurate assessment. T' heart is oft not a reliable judge."

"How do *you* gauge the veracity of that statement?" Cornelia replied.

"By t' fact that Obadiah has already asked my permission to marry you," replied Mr. Entwhistle.

Cornelia drew in her breath. She thought for a moment. "When did this transpire?"

"At our Twelfth Night cotillion," answered Mr. Entwhistle. *So long ago*, thought Cornelia. *Whatever could be cause for his delay in approaching me?*

"Has Lawrence made the same request of you?" she asked.

"No, t' man has not declared his intentions to me, come to think on it," Mr. Entwhistle scratched the back of his neck again.

"Merciful heavens!" Nellie wagged her finger at her father. "Perhaps I might be better able to make sound decisions *for myself*, if I were in command of the same facts as you."

"I'll allow, 'tis a fair point. What say ye to yer *Mutter*, ye and I all sitting down an assessing the information together, after ye finish here tonight?"

"That might be a good start," conceded Cornelia. *However, there is some pertinent information I cannot divulge to you. Furthermore, it is my future, therefore, I will decide,* she promised herself.

By the time Cornelia finished reviewing her director's notes with the actors, it was long past nine in the evening. Nevertheless, Gertrude Entwhistle had a warm supper waiting for her family.

"At last, the hard-working thespian troupe has come home for some nourishment." Mrs. Entwhistle smiled, rosy-cheeked from her hours at the stove. Matthias stretched a grimy hand to the table and stuffed a still-warm piece of cornbread in his mouth. "Stage hands must, at very least, wash the poster paint from their hands before joining us at the supper table," she objected.

Matthias ran off. Loud splashes were heard from the kitchen.

The stew was consumed in minutes, everyone too hungry and tired to eat slowly and make conversation. In less than half an hour, the table was empty of food and all family members, save Cornelia and her parents.

Cornelia was scraping the last bits of creamy butterscotch pudding from her bowl when Mrs. Entwhistle said, "I heard there were one too many stagehands today."

Cornelia looked up in surprise.

"Gossip like this takes only minutes to travel throughout the entire town," said Mrs. Entwhistle. Nellie scrutinized her mother's face, trying to ascertain her level of upset.

"Gertrude, I have already told our daughter 'tis time for her to choose a horse and finish t' race," said Mr. Entwhistle.

"I do not wish her to choose just *any* suitor," said Mrs. Entwhistle. "He must be a Catholic, approved by us."

Nellie's heart plunged to the floor. She snorted, in frustration. *Mutter's face never betrays her position. Her words however leave little doubt as to which camp commands her loyalty. What hope is there I will even have opportunity to voice my opinion, much less persuade these two intractable authoritarians to respect my preferences? It is two against one,* she thought.

Each of her parents spoke in favor of Baker's candidacy, extoling his virtues, but mostly his Catholicism.

"But what of other concerns, for example, each gentleman's integrity and intelligence? Lawrence is almost dimwitted compared to Obadiah. Who is to say his judgment will not be clouded and limited by his lack of mental acumen?" Cornelia asked.

Her parents looked at each other.

"'Tis a fair point, colleen," her father conceded.

"*Mutter*, Papa, I have listened in virtual silence, and with uncharacteristic patience...."

Both her parents burst out laughing.

"Aye," said her father between guffaws. Her mother smiled.

"*Aber*. But, Cornelia, you must confide in us with utter veracity, was Obadiah's father, the Governor, Episcopal?" her mother asked.

Cornelia stamped her foot in impatience. "That would defy common logic—to only divulge that his mother was Episcopalian—if his father were too, making Obadiah entirely Episcopal, and thus the fact that his mother also was, irrelevant."

"A partial truth, which leads to a particular conclusion, rolls off the tongue with far more alacrity than a lie," stated her mother, looking away.

Mutter has just accused me of lying about Obadiah's faith! Nellie grit her teeth. She repressed her anger so she could speak rationally. "Please understand, I value your opinion and give great deference to your view on the merits and considerations of each suitor. I credit your judgment great weight." Cornelia paused as her parents nodded their agreement.

"I have discerned some characteristics and behavior of these suitors unknown, unnoticed, or perhaps even not presented to you, that inclines me in favor of Obadiah."

Her parents started to speak, but Nellie held up her hand. "But be that as it may, my most compelling concern remains — in matters of my own heart, if my reasons are valid and my thought process not flighty or ill-considered, should I not be permitted to exercise my own judgment, a skill, I might add, that you have helped me cultivate?" she asked.

Her parents looked at each other again. Her mother said, "I do trust that judgment we have so carefully nurtured. While at times, some of your actions seem to have sprung from thoughts devoid of any cognitive process — we see that your reasoning here, while swayed by your expansive heart, is sound. Howsoever, you are minimizing the only thing that matters."

"Our investigations have confirmed — t' late Mrs. Wright was Episcopalian. His father is a Jacksonian. I will no' have it," declared her father.

Tears sprang to Cornelia's eyes. "Do you not even care what I have decided?"

"I am t' man. I am t' father. *I* decide," said her father.

Her mother sighed again. "We know this is difficult."

"I'll disinherit ye before I'll allow ye t' marry a man who is *not* Catholic."

"But Papa," Cornelia pleaded, then turned to her mother in a separate appeal, "*Mutter,* I have told you, Obadiah was baptized Catholic."

"To borrow one of his own phrases, I fear t' jury is still out as to whether that gentleman is t' soundest choice.

"We will see what transpires," said her father.

There is hope I can yet persuade them, she thought. *Once, of course, I have persuaded myself.*

Her father gathered her in his arms and hugged her, taking the sting away from his harsh words. His hug held promise of a tiny window remaining open in spite of his door-shutting words.

"We both hope ye will reconsider yer evaluations — but we do acknowledge yer desire to be t' final judge," her father whispered into the top of her head.

CHAPTER 33

At the Least Suggestion, I'll Pop the Question

Sing Sing, July 1851

Cornelia Rose and Obadiah watched the sun's golden orb, radiating light and color, sink over the Highland cliffs on the other side of the river. The last vestiges of its rays suffused the water with Nellie's favorite colors — magenta pink and aquamarine blue.

"Mercy, the mystical beauty of the thinly diffused vapors comprising western sunshine!" she said. "Sunset from the famed Brandreth gazebo. The best viewing spot in the entire world."

"The whole vast world?" teased Obadiah. "I am quite certain there could be finer views say from the California cliffs overlooking the mighty Pacific Ocean, or perhaps from the riverbanks observing the Danube or the Rhine...?" He smiled and tucked her stray strand of hair behind her ear, sending tingles of delight along her neck. She giggled in gladness. Her eyes skittered across his eyes and looked away. She was taken aback by the naked feelings his eyes revealed.

Mercy, we are both wearing our hearts in our eyes, rather than on our sleeves, she thought.

"My opinion does not merely rest on my own experience alone...." Nellie tried to mentally gather herself by resuming their light banter. "All the Knickerbocker poets and writers, well-traveled throughout this wide world, claim these vistas and views are rivaled nowhere." Nellie gave a pretty, merry toss of her head. *It is most fortuitous that I am an avid reader, so I can carry my weight in this scintillating conversation, whilst grappling with my own deep feelings.*

"I concede the point to my lady — a well-read woman with a learned opinion," said Obadiah, and he leaned down and kissed her, teasingly at first. His lips lingered, and Nellie melted into his embrace as his kisses came faster and grew in ardor.

"Mercy!" said Nellie at last, inwardly singing with joy. "Your passion quite takes my breath away."

Obadiah grinned at her. "I ardently desire to hold you breathless your entire life. What say you to a lifetime of kisses and happiness, spent in my arms as we face this world together?"

"Yes, yes, *yes*," said Nellie, blushing with joy.

Just then, George Brandreth charged into the gazebo with Hannah Agate on his arm.

What dreadful timing! This situation is entirely too awkward. Nellie tucked her strand of hair under her hat, as if she were tucking her feelings away. Once again, she would have to contain any outpouring of her heart.

"If this doesn't sour my milk!" exclaimed George. "I see you have taken advantage of your familiarity with *my* Glyndon Estate to sneak off to the best spot in town for a romantic view of the sunset." Brandreth stuck his hands in his waistcoat pockets, the grudge he still held against Nellie apparent. *He seems most unreasonably cross, even for George. But why? He most definitely rejected me before I had the sense to reject him.* Nellie laughed to herself.

"'Tis a great joy to view this sunset unimpeded," George continued, addressing no one in particular.

"Your comportment smacks of ill-breeding," growled Obadiah.

Nellie decided the best course of action was to overlook Brandreth's rudeness and the implied request for them to leave this cozy spot. "Hannah, how very lovely to see you again. Why it has been at least a fortnight since we enjoyed each other's company at Clara Rafferty's quilting bee."

Hannah had the grace to smile. *While she may be self-absorbed and uppity, at least she knows her manners and is always pleasant company,* Nellie thought.

"It *was* such a very special day, helping the bride-to-be prepare her trousseau. She has many patches of good wishes sewn into that quilt," Hannah said, as she gave Nellie a quick but sincere hug.

"Speaking of brides-to-be...." Both George and Obadiah said almost at the same time. Nellie and Hannah exchanged knowing glances.

An awkward tension hung in the air.

"Enough with the fimble-famble. I believe it is time for you to vacate the premises," George said with an imperious waive of his hand.

Obadiah glared and advanced toward him wearing a menacing face. Brandreth change his tack. "I am sure there are still plenty of cakes and tea remaining at the party," he said.

Obadiah kept advancing. George caught him by the elbow and spun him around, walking him back the other way. "Look old boy," he whispered, "I have no desire to affect you injuriously. However, I have an important matter to which I must attend."

The ladies once again exchanged glances.

Nellie said, "Obadiah, 'tis the perfect time of day to stroll along the wharf and watch the sloops moor for the evening. The fading sunset will frame the prettiest of pictures."

Nellie held out her hand.

Obadiah gallantly took it and they waved goodbye.

"They deserve each other," Obadiah muttered as they made their way down the steep trellised steps toward the dock below. "A bully and a hussy: the perfect match!"

Nellie said, "Now, now, let us not judge harshly—lest we be judged. Although I do agree—they deserve each other."

They emerged onto the street from the shelter of the stairway and were hit with a sudden blast of wind from an incoming train that blew half of Nellie's hat straight into the air.

"I thought I had this adequately secured with my hatpins!" Nellie said, but her words were drowned by the nearly deafening toot of the train's whistle.

"...Quite a comic sight!" Obadiah said. Laughing, he reached over and teasingly squished the pretty feathered cap down on Nellie's head while she fished the pins out of her hair and re-secured it. The levity left Obadiah's face as his hand strayed down her hair, along her ear, and lingered on her chin. Nellie forgot about her hat when he cupped her chin and drew her in for a kiss.

"'Tis quite a heady elixir, that magical kiss," said Nellie smiling up at him, eyes brimming with love. He smiled into her eyes, the same love reflected there.

"Come, let us find another cozy spot to nest, now that we have been uprooted from our roost," said Obadiah with a happy lilt to his voice.

They walked north along Water Street toward the Brandreth factory.

"Fiddlesticks, I once knew the perfect destination for such a walk as this, but now the railroads have ruined that favorite summer haunt—

Crawbuckie Beach. The tracks cut off bays and coves from the river causing the water supply to dwindle down to one culvert. The resulting silt and stagnation of the water under the tracks has irreparably damaged the beach terrain."

"I used to fish there during my days at Saint John's. The shad and striped bass were copious," said Obadiah. "It was quite a splendid spot."

"We dug for oysters. I fear the industrialization of the river has reduced the plentitude of both the oysters and the fish. I spent many a happy afternoon, after chores had been completed, of course...." Nellie smiled and winked at Obadiah, who grinned back. "My siblings and I cavorted at the beach or dove in the river, floating in the water. Why, when the tide came in, with its brackish, salty water, we all pretended we were once again at the seaside resort, Coney Island, bobbing in the real ocean, looking for pirates!

"Speaking of which, did you know that Captain Kidd's treasure reputedly lies just a stone's throw from here, just a skip up the river, in Annsville circle?"

"As a matter of fact, I did," said Obadiah. "In point of fact, I have made enquires of a certain Kidd Salvage Company, which runs sloops on Sundays to the site of the shipwreck off Dunderberg Mountain and then back across the river to Annsville Creek. I was thinking that perhaps just such a ride tomorrow would be the perfect way to celebrate the events of tonight." Obadiah winked mysteriously.

Nellie looked confused. "You know I do love a good mystery, which of course is why I am all a twitter at the thought of exploring for Kidd's treasure tomorrow, but what events of today would we be celebrating?"

Obadiah stopped right in the middle of the busy Upper Dock, caught her around the waist and spun her in front of him. She squinted into the brightness of the last vestiges of the colorful sunset.

When her eyes found Obadiah's, her heart leapt into her throat.

"All right then," said Obadiah. Smiling, he got down on one knee. "Now that the interruptions are over, and the whistle has sounded, you must hear the rest of my proposal. Cornelia Rose Entwhistle, will you do this man the greatest honor possible by giving me your hand in marriage?"

The sunset and the color-filled water danced before her. Obadiah squeezed her hand. Nellie smiled as without volition, tears of joy sprang to her eyes. "I too, am quite enthralled at the prospect."

"Then tender your answer!" Obadiah chuckled. "So there can be no mistake."

"Yes, *yes!* Most indubitably, most adamantly, *yes,*" said Nellie. Giggling and giddy, she leaned down to kiss him fully on his most receptive lips.

Obadiah kissed ardently in return, but kept his kneeling position. He drew back, after only a few kisses and cleared his throat, gazing up at her with loving eyes.

"Since I am favored with an affirmative reply—'Love for thy love, and hand for hand I give,'" Obadiah said, slipping a brilliant garnet, reflecting, and flashing the red hues of the sunset's last remnants of sunlight, onto her ring finger.

A ring and *some Shakespeare! I have met my match.* Nellie's beam joined that of the ring and the sunset.

CHAPTER 34
But Can We Still Be Friends?

Sing Sing, September 1851

"I refuse to be married in a warehouse, let alone the pill storehouse of Doctor Benjamin Brandreth! Why his own son, the odious George exchanged marriage vows in the glorious Trinity Church last month, with sunlight streaming through the stained-glass Tiffany windows, like a veritable blessing directly from God!" Nellie came just shy of stamping her foot. She was furious at the thought of a wedding among the pillboxes.

"*Ach du Liebe!*" said her mother. "Doctor Brandreth practically paid for that Trinity Church to be built in time for his son's wedding. A rushed affair, all around—*if* you catch my innuendo.

"Our parish is still short the money required to even begin to build our new church, in spite of all of our best efforts. *Gott im Himmel*, even if they met their financial goals tomorrow, no new church could possibly be completed before January."

Gertrude Entwhistle took a deep breath and continued her tirade. "Trinity is not a Catholic Church. You must exchange your sacred vows in a consecrated place. No daughter of mine will marry outside the Church. If we did not relax our standards to allow Agnes to marry in the multidenominational 'Christian' Chapel at West Point, we will certainly not permit it here at home. Therefore, we must arrange the journey to Saint Patrick's Church in Verplank."

"Good Lord, *Mutter*, even you will concede that the Episcopalian Church is a consecrated place," Nellie said, crimson with annoyance.

"It must be a Catholic consecrated place," said Mrs. Entwhistle, in her 'do-not-have-the-audacity-to-argue-with-me' voice.

"Like the warehouse even *Papa* declared *to Father O'Flaherty* was 'not a proper house of worship at all'?" Nellie did not pause to allow her mother time to interject, nor did she pause for breath. "Like John and Bridget O'Brien's house? Or the stone structure of indeterminate origin on Emwilton Place that many newly forming congregations of different faiths use? Since our Saint Augustine's Parish still does not have a proper Church, and may be years away from having one, save Saint Patrick's in Verplank, just a 'short' *ten miles* from here...." Nellie held up her hands with her ten fingers splayed. "...I propose we make a list of *consecrated places* that would be acceptable to you for the locale of the exchange of my vows of Holy Matrimony." Nellie was practically breathing out steam by the time she finished.

Her father whistled. "Once again, me colleen w' the touch o' the blarney, winning us over! That speech was both eloquent and persuasive. Ye have afresh swayed me thinking. 'T'will all be in front o' the eyes of our Heavenly Father, just as our daily Mass at Bridget O'Brien's, no matter what the venue be, Gertrude dear."

Mrs. Entwhistle, however, was not ready to concede. "I will consult with *meine Mutter* and determine an acceptable Church."

"It must be acceptable to me as well," said Nellie, in a low voice. Her mother flashed her eyes at Nellie, but said nothing further.

"Perhaps we could use the United Methodist Church?" Anastasia ventured. "I am sure they would share. After all, until just a few short years ago that congregation was forced to gather either in Franklin Academy or that stone building to which Nellie just referred, until the Methodists built *their* own church on Spring Street."

"*Ach du Liebe,*" exclaimed Mrs. Entwhistle again and threw up her hands. She turned and bustled out of the room.

"*Et tu, Brute?*" A chuckling Mr. Entwhistle ruffled Anastasia's hair and laughed his way out of the room.

"Thank you, Anastasia," said Nellie. "I so treasure your magnanimous support."

"'Tis not so very selfless," Anastasia said, flashing a sly smile.

"Eureka!" said Nellie. "Do I hear a second set of Wedding Bells?"

Anastasia blushed. "While my Zetus surely is dash-fire, he plumb took his sweet time! It wasn't that he was pigeon-livered. He was busy pursuing employment. First, he was overcome by his responsibilities as apprentice instructor at West Point. Once that was mastered, obtaining a full-time position preoccupied his thoughts...."

"But he has determined and declared his intentions?" Nellie asked.

Anastasia giggled again. "I knew his intentions a long time ago. After all, he gave me his spoony button. But yes, Instructor Searle has finally resolved to ask Papa for my hand."

Nellie said, "If he had declared himself sooner, we might both be wed in January."

"Do not fret," said Anastasia. "If I have my druthers, our wedding vows will be exchanged next spring. I've always had my heart set on a June wedding. Further, with extra time for prodding and persuading, mayhap *Mutter* will agree to the Chapel at West Point this time! It will probably take Zetus until April to gather enough courage to inform his parents, way down south in Dixieland, of our matrimonial plans."

"'T 'will take no courage to announce matrimony," said Nellie. "Informing his family that he has decided to settle up here with us Northerners—that will require fortitude. How will he contrive to make the news palatable to his South Carolinian people?"

Struck suddenly with a terrible thought, all lightness left Nellie's tone. "Unless you will be migrating south after the wedding?" she whispered, trembling.

"No, *no, never!*" promised Anastasia. "I plan to persuade Zetus to purchase the house next door to yours."

Nellie heaved a huge sigh of relief. "May we always be as close geographically as we are in our hearts."

Their father stuck his head back into the sewing room where they still sat. Their mother sailed right by him and sat down, immediately picking up her sewing. Taking the cue, both young ladies picked up their handiwork, and listened.

"I have engaged a cook for the event," said Mr. Entwhistle.

"*Ach du Liebe*, this will make trouble!" Mrs. Entwhistle waved her needle in agitation over her French Knots. "I do not want to hurt the feelings of our Hilda."

Nellie almost giggled, in surprise. *The stalwart cook Hilda with hurt feelings?*

Anastasia leaned into Nellie's ear, whispering, "I do not recall ever seeing any evidence that Hilda *has* feelings, except maybe the one of anger." They both stifled a laugh.

"This chef comes recommended, with the highest of accolades. His many letters of commendation sing his praise," Mr. Entwhistle said. He stepped into the room and handed his wife a neat stack of letters.

Mrs. Entwhistle took the offered bunch, but shook her head in the negative. "Hilda has been with us since Jonas was born. We cannot afford to lose her now—she has finally acquired the skill needed to assist me with baking the Viennese pastries of *meine Mutter*." In spite of her words, Mutter fished her spectacles out of her pocket and perused the notes.

"My competitor in t' shipbuilding business, Thomas Collier, has used this chef for *his* daughter's wedding feast—his letter o' recommendation for this fellow is somewhere in t' bunch. Further, this cook has his own assistant and a crackerjack serving staff," her father said. At his wife's attempt to protest anew, he held up his hand and continued, "Which staff, 'twill be sorely needed if ye intend to invite as many guests as I imagine ye will want...."

Papa's eyes twinkled as he smiled down at his wife of many years, waiting for her to register the import of his words.

She extended her hand and grasped his. "You can be very persuasive. However, I am still not certain this will be a prudent expenditure...."

"I was careful to specify our food must be tasty and delicious. Why, 't would nary do to have it otherwise, since we're surely spoiled by t' likes o' the victuals ye and Hilda always prepare," he said. Another smile beamed upon Gertrude, then spread to his daughters. With his eyes still twinkling, Mr. Entwhistle hustled out of the room.

Nellie dropped her sewing and bounced over to the writing table. "I shall make a list of items we must ready for the wedding day."

"Your father and I will plan the menu and have the food prepared," said Mrs. Entwhistle, embracing the idea of a checklist. Nellie began recording items.

"Invitations," said Nellie. "Let us begin at the beginning and invite the guests."

"Flowers!" exclaimed Anastasia. "Even in January we must have some floral decorations and you simply must have a beautiful bouquet."

"I dream of a bouquet of tulips, in all the colors of the rainbow," said Nellie, hands clasped under her chin, smiling with a dreamy expression. "Do you think we could find a conservatory that grows tulips in the winter? Think of it, pink, purple, red, blue, and combinations of white with blush edges. Oh, it will be spectacular and exotic!"

"Nonsense," said Mrs. Entwhistle. "While we may need to send to the city for an orangery with the right assortment of suitable flowers, your bouquet will consist only of white flowers."

"But I have a penchant for color, In fact, on my wedding day I desire a veritable rainbow of flowers!" protested Nellie.

"Color in the bride's bouquet? Tongues will wag," Mrs. Entwhistle looked shocked.

"*Mutter*! Do not be silly! My dress is white. People will not be scandalized by my fancy for colorful flowers."

"'T would hardly be otherwise, Cornelia," Mrs. Entwhistle said in that famous no-nonsense voice. "The rules of proper society are strict and unrelenting in this matter—a bouquet of flowers in any color but white is simply unsuitable. I will not have my daughter be the subject of raised eyebrows and innuendo. That is the end of the matter." Mrs. Entwhistle folded her hands over her chest and Nellie knew it was senseless to argue further.

She hung her head, but then decided to make the best of it. *Es macht nichts!* she thought with a giggle. "*Mutter*, would you chose a resplendent bouquet for me? You *do* know flowers better than I and, as you have shown daily over the years, have quite the knack for beautiful flower arrangements."

With satisfaction, Nellie observed her mother smile at her gracious demeanor. The conversation moved on to other details.

After luncheon, the postman arrived at the back door and handed Nellie the mail.

Alleluia! A note in Obadiah's hand. But—addressed only to my parents? 'Tis an unsettling surprise, she thought. *An epistle as an emissary of good will is certainly appropriate and desired. But alas! No words for me?*

Nellie had no further time to speculate for her father decided to read the letter aloud to the group at the lunch table.

> *Dear Mr. and Mrs. Entwhistle,*
> *As I finish my last semester at Yale University, I look forward in great anticipation to the next chapter in my life, with great expectations of happiness to come. The joy of completing my studies is eminent (and a relief; 'twas with a heavy heart that I left my dear friends in Sing Sing a fortnight ago). I am entrusting all my bliss and the promise of my future, embodied in Cornelia Rose, to your able care for just a few short months more.*

As I await the arrival of the most holy of seasons, the solemn and blessed Octave of Christmas, I am anticipating the richest gift of heaven – the hand of your daughter in marriage. The thought of at last making Cornelia Rose my wife ignites the light of a thousand hopes of our future joy together. This wedded bliss is the greatest bounty that a man could contemplate. I only wish my dear father, Senator Wright, had not so lately succumbed to the final fate that awaits us all...."

"...He would have to allude to our Jacksonian former Governor!" Mr. Entwhistle broke off his reading to growl. But from the smile that shone on his face, Nellie could see her father was only trying to lighten the seriousness of the mood.

"...Prior to his passing, I obtained his approval of my plans to pursue the hand of your daughter. Therefore, I am certain that my father would be most supportive of my decision to wed your lovely Cornelia Rose. He joined me in my appreciation of her many charms and talents, and I look forward to these same talents enchanting our life together.

If candidates for heaven can feel joy, I discern my beloved deceased mother participates in my happiness on this occasion as well.

I thank you from the deepest recesses of my heart for honoring my request for matrimony. I will strive to confirm and even surpass your faith in my ability to adequately provide for your daughter. Whilst you have given me the greatest gift of all, and its attendant joy, hope, and promise, all I can offer you in return is my undying filial loyalty. I am privileged to join your prodigious Entwhistle Clan and I pledge to add my honor and good name to propagate our new family's greater good.

I count the days until I see you all again, and wish you all the joys of this harvest season, as well as continued blessings from Almighty God above for your entire household.

Your obedient servant,
Obadiah Weber Wright

"Well, sure 'n begora, the lad has a tongue for the words," said Mr. Entwhistle, wiping the corner of his eye.

"Perhaps we did not underestimate his abilities and strengths," said Mrs. Entwhistle.

Is that a compliment? Nellie wondered. *Is Mutter so very critical and so frugal in her accolades that she cannot welcome Obadiah with an open heart?*

Forbearance, Cornelia! She told herself. She looked around at her family, all cozily gathered in the kitchen smiling, listening to Obadiah's missive. *This is not the moment to question Mutter's feelings and motives – I must curb my tongue and await further opportunity.*

She found her moment later in the day. When she ran down the back stairs from her nightly ritual of viewing the sunset from her garret window, her mother was alone on the second floor, completing some necessary mending before the natural light disappeared for the night.

Nellie burst into the room. "*Mutter*," she said loudly.

Mrs. Entwhistle shook her head with disapproval, without looking up. "Charging about like a washerwoman, bursting into a room as if you were about to empty a tub of dirty laundering suds. There is so little time left to ensure your proper ladylike comportment...."

Nellie came to a full stop in front of her mother, chagrined and chastised, and temporarily distracted from her mission. "Is deportment the sole virtue you exalt, *Mutter*? Do you not value other aptitudes besides proper posture, etiquette, and retaining one's gloves?"

Her mother lifted her head and gave Nellie her all-too-well known puckered mouth stare. *It is as if all the criticism she heaps upon the world upsurges from her heart, pulling in her lips before spewing forth,* Nellie thought.

Nellie opened her own mouth to continue, but instead burst out laughing. "I had mentally formulated quite a fine soliloquy, to persuade you with my sincerity and my logic to overcome your negative feelings toward Obadiah and share my euphoria over my impending union to him. But I find that the happiness I derive from contemplating my future life with him obviates any necessity for you to join me in that state in order to maintain it."

Mutter looked back down at her mending, without commenting.

"Well, perhaps I do still desire some expression of felicitation from you, *Mutter*," Cornelia admitted, laying her hand on her mother's shoulder. "Would that be so taxing, so impossible for you to provide?"

Her mother remained silent, still bent over the camisole in need of repair.

"Do you not remember a time when my father's love was so important to you, you were willing to proceed without *your* mother's complete approval?"

Mrs. Entwhistle's head jerked up and she glared at Nellie. "There was never such a time."

"I beg to differ. I remember a time when Grandmama offered many criticisms of 'the Irish boy'." Nellie smiled.

"*Ach, du Liebe,* that was such a long time ago...." Mrs. Entwhistle sighed.

"*Mutter,* I am certain in my heart that Obadiah has the requisite qualities that make a fine husband. My happiness revolves around, nay depends upon, my union with him," said Nellie. She looked into her mother's eyes and smiled.

Her mother sighed again. "I can see that you are smitten, but there is still time to reconsider Lieutenant Lawrence Simmons Baker, or...."

Nellie shook her head with a vehemence that sent her hair combs wobbling.

Mrs. Entwhistle permitted herself a small smile. "...You have resolved your mind. While I am ignorant of the charms you attest, I will concede that I have raised you to have good judgment of character. Therefore, I will trust your decision in that regard." Her mother caught her hands and gave them a squeeze. "I wish you happiness, and more importantly, I hope this matrimony you contemplate will facilitate your journey closer to Our Lord."

Mrs. Entwhistle pulled her hands away and resumed mending.

I guess this is Mutter's manner of blessing? Nellie thought.

She shook her head, as if to clear any lingering doubts and negativity and skipped out of the room, determined not to lose her joie de vivre. She almost collided with their butler. He had a silver tray balanced on the tips of his fingers, which spun precariously. The man's struggle to catch the tray from falling was successful, but the card on the tray fell on the floor.

"Mercy! How clumsy of me, I do apologize for my haste," she said. "What is it?"

"Miss, you have a gentleman caller," the butler announced as he bent to retrieve the card.

"Obadiah?" asked Nellie, her heart skipping a beat.

"No miss," said the man, and turned on his heel leaving her to read the card.

"Lieutenant Lawrence Simmons Baker," she read. "Why in the world...?"

She ran down the grand staircase.

There he was, handsome as ever, standing in the drawing room, officer's cap clutched in his hands. His face lit up when she entered the room.

Lawrence cleared his throat. His hands played with his hat. He seemed to make a decision, and cut right to the chase. "I do fully comprehend your words indicating your lack of reciprocation of my feelings, but I wonder if *you* truly comprehend their precise nature."

Nellie stifled a giggle. *But his feelings are irrelevant now – I have made up my mind.*

Baker did not wait for her reply. "I yearn for you, I truly desire you."

Nellie raised her eyebrows. *Desire, nothing else? That's what I thought.*

"Before you embark upon the gravest error of your life, I feel compelled to declare myself. No man will ever love you as much as I do. You are forsaking a lifetime of happiness and adventure."

Nellie opened her mouth to speak.

Baker held up his hand to silence her. "I am not merely speaking of the ordinary adventures of life. In just a fortnight, just enough time to wed, I might add, I will embark upon an adventure of a lifetime. An adventure I wish to share with you."

"Of what adventure do you speak?" Nellie was reluctant to ask.

"I won't 'draw the longbow', I'll just come right out and state the obvious. I will be taming the wild, Wild West! Going out beyond civilization; in fact, bringing civilization to new territory."

Nellie hesitated, not sure how to reply. *There must be some words that will sweetly, but clearly and firmly, reject this suitor....*

Baker said, "I'll be pushing back Savages, Nellie. My unit will clear the land for people to come."

"Lawrence Simmons Baker that is the most ignorant thing a man could say. Even a West Point class *goat*, graduating *last* in his class should know better than to call people by the word 'savages.'"

Baker blinked, surprised. "People? Those Indians are not people, the same as us."

"Verily, they are not the *same* as us, they have different cultures, ways, and traditions. But they are people, nonetheless. Perhaps my opinion is swayed by my favorite literary genre, *the noble natives*, and the many tales I have read of brave Indian women, but I believe these people to be good, with their own ethical standards and noble ways."

Baker stood there blinking.

"Mercy! I can understand when some sensational flyer, inciting and enticing the masses to view a theatrical performance calls those people 'savages' but I cannot understand *you*, an educated man, espousing that view.

"I am sorry, Lawrence, I hold you in my heart with not a small amount of affection, but I most certainly will not accompany you to the 'wild wild west.'"

"But you *will* marry me?" asked Baker.

Nellie almost stamped her foot with frustration. *How many times do I have to do this?* "No Lawrence, I am sorry. I will not, *cannot* be your wife."

"If you remain intransigent, I might just desist in my efforts to pursue you," Lawrence said.

He is relentless! Nellie thought in exasperation. Nellie stared at him. Her mouth tightened. A hard, determined look appeared in her eyes.

"I see," said Lawrence, looking down at the hat in his hands.

Mercy! His look of abject despair is more than I can bear! Cornelia thought. *Oh, why must I tell him over and over that my heart is elsewhere?* "Lawrence, I will cherish the moments we have shared in my heart, but I fear our association must end."

"But surely, we can still remain friendly acquaintances?" he asked, reaching out his hands to take hers.

"Why, of course," Nellie squeezed his hands.

"Then all hope is not lost. Our paths will cross again, and who knows where it will take us?" Lawrence smiled and leaned in to kiss her.

Nellie wrenched herself free, turned, and ran up the stairs, leaving Baker to see himself out.

CHAPTER 35
Get Me to the Church on Time

Sing Sing, January 1852

Cornelia Rose threw open the shutters—*for the last time from my cozy garret bed?* She expected sunshine to pour into her chamber from the wintery sun aloft in its usual position, sparkling on the frost and ice.

"It's *snowing?*" she shouted.

"Is that a bad omen?" Anastasia appeared at her side, blinking in the brightened light.

"Not necessarily," reasoned Nellie, leaning out to catch a flake on her tongue. "It is just a surprise. I had not considered the possibility that it would snow today. I pictured only bright winter sunshine. I do hope none of the guests' travel will be impeded."

Anastasia dismissed this thought with a laugh and a wave of her hand. "Everyone readied their sleighs long ago. Moreover, the river is not frozen, so the sloops and the steamers are unrestricted in their scheduled travel."

A rush of air made them turn from their window gazing. Agnes stood before them, still in her cloak, cheeks rosy from the outside air.

"Come on lazy bones! Today of all days I thought you would be up before the crack of dawn," Agnes said, positively beaming at them.

Anastasia and Nellie exchanged glances. "I think I see an apparition.' said Anastasia.

"Yes," said Nellie, "it has the guise of Agnes but this specter is far too jovial." They laughed.

"Goodness sisters!" exclaimed Agnes. "How you both still carry on. Come, make haste to get ready and join me for a pre-nuptial breakfast. I have prepared one for you Cornelia, just as you did for me on my wedding day." Agnes gave Nellie and the amazed Anastasia hugs and bustled back down the stairs.

"Marriage certainly agrees with Agnes," said Nellie.

"Agrees with her? It has downright transformed her into a different creature!" Anastasia replied.

The girls scrambled into their flannel robes and rushed to the kitchen.

The morning passed in a quick whirl. The sumptuous *petit dèjeuner*, so lovingly and unexpectedly made by Agnes, was hastily consumed, with Nellie only taking a few bites of her toast in her excitement for the day.

The flurry inside the Entwhistle house was as frantic as the icy one outside. Many fragrant dishes for the feast bubbled and percolated on the stove as the wind howled and snow swirled around the external perimeters of the kitchen. The house teamed with food stacked on tables as high as the snow piles stacked outside its doors. Pies, cakes, and scones, already prepared and waiting, overflowed shelves and nooks in the pantry just as the drifts and mounds of shoveled snow overflowed the lawn edges and nestled against the kitchen's brick foundation.

Cook was giving orders and hyperventilating over some details of a signature dish, but she paused when she saw Nellie to give her an uncharacteristic hug. "Mine grand lady, *zum Feier des Tages*," Hilda whispered, squeezing Nellie tight. "Ach, in English—to the celebration of the day!"

Mr. Entwhistle appeared at the door to mother's dressing room where the bevy of girls buzzed around making their final preparations. "The carriages are ready! To Saint Paul's we go!"

The girls screamed and scurried about even more furiously.

"Saint's preserve us!" he said with his customary cheer, and threw up his hands with a big laugh. He spied Nellie, completely ready, sitting in a cozy armchair watching the antics of her sisters and mother with an amused expression on her face.

"Ye be t' calmest bride the likes o' which I ever did behold," said Mr. Entwhistle and he picked her up and crushed her into one of his big, warm hugs.

"Papa, your hugs are one of my favorite things," she whispered. Nellie hugged him back, and then stepped out of his embrace to right all of the rumpling of her clothing, hair, and veil engendered by his enthusiasm.

"Aye, yer words still warm the cockles o' me heart," he said, and Nellie thought she saw the glisten of a tear in his eyes. *Papa, crying? Why it isn't possible.* Her father spoke again. "There will always be a hug awaitin' ye, no matter how old ye get, nor how far ye travel.... Yer a daughter what does her father proud." He swooped in for another enveloping hug. "If'n ye keep yer heart open continuously yer sure to catch blessings from above,'" he whispered into her ear and squeezed her again. She reached up and gave him a kiss on the cheek.

Mr. Entwhistle smiled again, kissed the top of her head, and then turned brusquely to address the room. "Ladies, to t' carriage entrance, please. We do not want to keep Monsignor Fitzpatrick waitin.' He's come all the way from The City to concelebrate the Mass with Father O'Flaherty and a priest from Saint Patrick's in Verplank. Make haste! It's half eleven now. We should already be at t' Church."

The group of women ignored him, continuing to tie ribbons, button boots, and fuss with their hair.

"Must I remind you—our clergy *are waitin' in enemy territory?* The heretics the rest o' the world call t' Episcopalians will be tryin' to convert them as I speak! Have mercy on these men o' the cloth and 'make foot' into t' carriages!" he shouted.

Mr. Entwhistle let loose another big belly laugh and then ran down the stairs. Mrs. Entwhistle and Nellie followed directly behind him. The rest of the girls finished their final preparations, swapping wraps, and searching for accouterments. They straggled outside long after Nellie boarded the first sled.

Nellie's head was in the clouds, yet something about the handsome footman who helped her into the carriage caught her attention. *What a wonderful smile,* she thought, smiling in return. She turned her head to look at the man as the horse departed. *Those eyes have a familiar twinkle,* she thought. Her mother's squeeze of her hand pulled Nellie, with a rush of joy, back to the present.

"*Mutter*, thank you for permitting our Mass of Holy Matrimony to be celebrated at Saint Paul's Church." Nellie leaned closer to her mother and gave her a hug. The wind turned her cheeks to rose and blew a strand of hair out of her elaborate wedding coiffeur as she said, "I so truly appreciate your blessing on the Church of my choice."

Mrs. Entwhistle returned the hug with her reply, "You were most persuasive in overcoming the objections of the pastor at Saint Patrick's. Even *he* had to concede that as a Mission Church, with such a large congregation, and weekly Mass held in unconsecrated places, a wedding in a church, albeit the wrong one, is better than one in a home—even if it *is* the home of blessed Bridget O'Brien!"

They both laughed in accord.

"I well know you are disposed and equipped for this most important step, Cornelia Rose," her mother said to her. "I believe you have been ready for a long time. I only hope your *groom* is prepared for the responsibilities of a family. I would feel more assured of his sentiments had you chosen a suitor from the ones your father and I preselected." Nellie frowned, *a rain cloud on this fine day?* But Mrs. Entwhistle shook her head, as if to wipe all negative thoughts away. "*Es macht nichts.* Although I did not approve of many of your methods for finding a husband...." Again the shake of the head. "...I believe in the end you have made a suitable choice."

A suitable choice? Nellie felt her temper rise. But she considered the source of the words. She looked hard at her mother, who smiled back in return. *Why, I suppose she thinks 'a suitable choice' is high praise?* Nellie chuckled and squeezed her mother's hand, to compensate for her lack of a suitably worded answer. They slid into the carriage entrance at the St. Paul's, Nellie so breathless in anticipation of her dream wedding she felt she had run the whole way.

She laughed, shaking her head. *Mutter has such a propensity to be negative, even when she is positively disposed toward the events of the day!* she thought. *'Tis immaterial my mind is devoid of a fitting reply; in mere minutes, I will profess my wedding vows!*

As Nellie stepped out of her sleigh, her bridesmaids' bobsled swooshed into the lane behind her. The last of the guests scurried past them into the church and the organ began to play.

"Here we go!" Anastasia cried, squeezing Nellie's hand. Nellie's niece, Theodora Entwhistle, still precocious, but now a demure four-year old, with doll-like with curls clustered around her face and protruding from under her pretty hat, began the march. Carefully, the little girl scattered rose petals, dried and preserved this fall for just this occasion, as she led the bridal party down the aisle.

Agnes handed Nellie her bouquet. She stuck her nose in the hothouse flowers from New York City's finest botanical gardens — freesia, carnation, and snowdrop, all white as dictated by her mother — and inhaled their sweet perfume.

The ceremony was a happy blur of a solemn Mass peppered with beautiful singing. Nellie was glad that the ceremony included a Mass; it gave her time to reflect on this momentous step and cherish the details of the day. She basked in the sunlight, now streaming through the stained-glass windows, just as she had dreamed it should, blessing her wedding. She contemplated her parents, dignified and grand, praying in their pew, her sisters, resplendent in their finery, her brothers, all polished and posh, standing next to her groom. *My groom!* She smiled, her whole face alight. *Tender, amorous, Obadiah... I can no longer imagine living my life without him.*

The entire scene was picture perfect, just as she had always fantasized her wedding Mass should be.

As a special wedding present, Obadiah arranged for the choir from his former Academy, located right behind Saint Paul's Church, to lead the congregation in song. Nellie and her mother chose all their favorite hymns. It was an added blessing to have the double prayer of choir song and organ music.

In an instant, Nellie felt, the ceremony was over and they were sledding back to the house.

"I may not see you alone again until later in the evening. Now that you are officially mine, I am loath to share you," Obadiah said, with mock anger in his voice. Nellie laughed, so happy, so excited, yet so at peace. He continued speaking, "I would like to take this opportunity to thank you for wedding me." Nellie's laugh changed to a giggle. "But it is vital you comprehend the depth of my love. I know that with you at my side, nothing can conquer me." He leaned in, wrapping Nellie tightly in his arms. His lips found hers. The warmth and love Obadiah's kiss communicated fanned the flame of desire smoldering deep inside Nellie. She kissed him back and floated on the wave of passion surging inside her.

Suddenly, she heard laughing.

"Let my sister breathe!" shouted a voice. Nellie pulled out of the embrace to see her brother Patrick, with his daughter Theodora clutching his pant leg, holding on to the reins of their horse, waiting for them to disembark.

"Not on your life!" said Obadiah, and wrapped her back in his arms.

Nellie resurfaced from the bear hug clutching her veil, and looked wildly about. "No, we must ready ourselves to receive our guests."

Patrick said, "The guests will not arrive for several minutes. *Mutter* will warm them with some hot apple cider and mulled wine. You have just sufficient time for a quick spin.

"Driver, take them around the block," Patrick commanded. He slapped the horse on its rump and the animal started forward. "They are in no condition for public display."

Patrick laughed. Theodora giggled and threw a rose petal at them.

The driver gave a nod and a smile, and flicked the reins. The horses broke into a trot.

"Ten precious minutes more, alone with my bride!" Obadiah said, even his voice smiling. "I am beginning to develop an insatiable appetite for time in her presence alone." He kissed Nellie again. With a giggle, Nellie gratefully succumbed to the delight of kissing him back. "I have long awaited the opportunity to surrender to the charms of this alluring neck," Obadiah whispered into her warm, tender flesh.

"Where to, sir?" The driver looked down at them. Nellie looked up and he turned quickly away. "Right, I'll think on it."

Heaven, thought Nellie, *is a glide on the snow in our finest sleigh, 'spooning' with my* husband...*with a wedding feast and celebration complete with dancing as our ultimate destination....* Her heart soared in delight.

All other thoughts flew from Nellie's mind as she yielded to the seduction of Obadiah's lips. When his hand followed his lips, down her cheek, past her jaw, along her neck, diagonally across her shoulder, and landed lightly and teasingly on the Dresden lace at the top of her bodice, she marveled at how suddenly warm the day had become....

"Now compose yourself," teased Obadiah. "We are back on Main Street and this wanton behavior must stop."

Nellie opened her mouth to protest, but Obadiah closed it with a last, most satisfying kiss.

Upon their arrival at the top of the driveway, a cheer rose from the crowd of guests pouring out of the house's entrance, welcoming the happy couple to their reception.

The wedding feast was quite the grand luncheon. The food smelled tantalizingly good and tasted delicious, just as her father requested.

Far too busy dancing and entertaining her guests, Nellie only sampled one tasty crumpet. She and Obadiah exchanged the requisite piece of wedding cake, but after only one bite, a throng of well-wishers interrupted her. Nellie hugged Midwife Rafferty, Dr. Hart, and new relatives from Obadiah's family in turn, leaving the rest of her cake on the table.

All too soon, the weak winter sunlight faded from the dance floor. Nellie breathlessly turned from a Virginia reel to kiss Grandfather Pffernuss goodbye. His departure, she knew, signaled the time for her exit. She ran up the back stairs for one final glimpse of her old garret room (and to make sure her cases were loaded in the sled), made a quick trip to the "necessary" and skipped back to the main stairway in a farewell tour of the upstairs parlors.

Nellie floated down the center hall stairs, like a princess descending from her castle chamber, into the throng of admiring guests. Joined by Obadiah, they began saying their goodbyes. Poised and gracious, Nellie thanked each and every guest for attending, as she embraced them in farewell hugs. She cherished the bountiful congratulations and blessings heaped upon her. With tears in her eyes, but with a light happy heart, Nellie made sure to spend a minute with every one of her sisters, brothers, in-laws, niece, cousins, aunts, uncles, grandparents, and friends as they made their way through all of the festivities to the front door.

She caught her mother in a happy embrace, turning Mrs. Entwhistle away from instructing a footman to pour more champagne. "*Mutter*, I cannot ever thank you enough for this sumptuous feast and magnificent celebration, let alone for the lifetime of love and care you have given me."

Her mother held her in her arms and said, "I know you will do the same for your own children. That will be my appreciation and reward." Nellie pulled back in surprise, but her mother laughed and said, "You know well that is your next responsibility. Yet, I must tell you directly — your accomplishments to date, while unsought and unexpected by me, fill me with happiness and pride."

Nellie blushed and hugged her hard.

She turned and her father caught her into one of his signature hugs. "Oh Papa," she said, "I thank you...."

"Hush now, Nell o' me heart," he said into the top of her head. "'Tis one time when yer words are not required. Yer ready to face the world with a fine young gentleman, but you'll always have a home with me." Her father gave her one more squeeze and then turned her to the door. Behind her, Obadiah shook her father's hand, as Nellie blinked at the guests lining the stairs of the Entwhistle mansion into the street.

Cornelia Rose and Obadiah ran through the barrage of rice into the frosty air, and tumbled into the waiting sleigh.

In less than a minute, they were waving at the tail end of the smiling, cheering crowd, headed down to the Westerly Avenue Dock to take the evening steamboat into The City.

Tonight, the Astor House! In the spring, a honeymoon trip via luxury steamer to Coney Island Resort. Nellie gave Obadiah's hand a squeeze.

So much to anticipate, so much to delight.

Snow crunched under the sleigh's runners. The horse snorted in the cold. Wrapped snugly in a crimson shawl and Obadiah's warm embrace, Nellie looked up at him with quiet joy. "I love you so dearly, Obadiah," she whispered.

"You have made me the happiest of men," he whispered back.

"Our lives will be a grand voyage filled with ecstasy and excitement," she said, her smile growing even bigger.

She nestled back into his arms, eagerly anticipating the trip ahead.

BOOK CLUB GUIDE

1. What excites you about history? What are your favorite types of historical sites?

2. Have you ever been part of an historical event like the true historical event of the ceremonial opening the Croton Aqueduct?

3. Which characters resonated with you? Do you have an "Agnes" in your life?

4. The relationship of Cornelia with all of her family is at once impatient and forgiving. Which of the characters personality traits do you find particularly trying?

5. Midwifes were the exclusive deliverers of babies until doctors figured out how lucrative the business could be (two chickens for delivering a boy!). Discuss the 'home remedies' proffered and their efficacy in modern times.

6. Christian camp meetings such as the one described were common at that time, all over the United States. Discuss how one's faith was a central part of community at that time and dictated more than just where someone worshiped.

7. Compare the home remedies created by the Midwives and Cornelia to the similar salves and home remedies in Tara Westover's *Educated*, which is a contemporary memoir.

8. Benny Havens' is a real tavern that welcomed West Point cadets and the actual old tavern has been relocated to Highland Falls, almost directly across from West Point's main gate. Discuss the antics of the various characters seen there.

9. At West Point, Cornelia meets the famous editor and author, William Cullen Bryant, part of the Knickerbocker school. Whom from the 1850s would you like to meet at a West Point tea?

10. The British ship *Vulture's* launching of a cannonball that went right though a tombstone in Sparta in 1812 is a true historical event. Discuss how Obadiah and Nellie perceive it. Are there any historical markers where you live? Does your community host any events commemorating local history?

11. The social mores at the time were very restricting, yet how many ways can you identify that Cornelia Rose attempts to shape her own destiny?

12. Were you happy with whom Cornelia Rose finally chose to marry?

INTERVIEW WITH THE AUTHOR

Q. What is it about the lore and history of the Hudson River Valley in New York that inspired you to write *Flirtation on the Hudson*?

A. Its pervasiveness! Traces of the history of this area abound, waiting for the observant viewer. Hints sigh from old trees and mountains. Whispers of peoples' stories emanate from old paths, walks and buildings, and clues are found in the cryptic verse on tombstones and monuments.

I live in an area imbued with history and the romantic in me wanted to walk in the shoes of the first occupants of the buildings and woods I enter and see the earlier version of this area, just to feel what life would have been like in that time.

Q. Does writing energize or exhaust you?

A. Energize definitely! When I finally give myself permission to abandon all my other responsibilities and sit down to write — three hours go by in a heartbeat and I find I am late for the next thing on my schedule. Happiness is — -writing all day!

Q. How about the research?

A. I have cherished the time I have spent, retracing the footsteps of my heroine. I have walked the streets of Sing Sing (now Ossining- a different transliteration of the Native American Sinct Sinct) New York gazing in wonder at old buildings, picturing Cornelia Rose there. I have strolled the Old Croton Aqueduct, and the double arches of Sing Sing many times, feeling Cornelia Rose and Obadiah promenading arm in arm next to me.

I have also frequented West Point, both as a giddy teenage girl going to the weekly "Hops," (the current name for the cotillions) and as a friend visiting cadets attending the Academy. I visited the campus often while writing this book. The museum outside the gates was invaluable—I even found a map of the Academy from 1860, only slightly off my time period. I have researched, using all platforms—books, libraries, online, walking tours, anything to make sure my story was historically correct.

Q. Are any characters in *Flirtation on the Hudson* real people?

A. Yes, many: the superintendents at West Point, all of the named cadets, some of the townspeople, shop owners and officials in Sing Sing, and of course William Cullen Bryant and Benny Havens. I have found some great names in the history books of Sing Sing and West Point and snippets of those people's stories. I have taken liberties with the few biographical facts I found, and woven real people into my fictitious characters' drama hence—historical fiction.

An example is that at West Point, the museum of class rings includes Armistead L. Long's actual ring from the class of 1852. I am not sure he actually used it as an engagement ring, but it makes a good story!

Q. How accurately do you depict this time period?

A. Other than the personal events in the novel, all of the historical events actually took place at the stated time. This was often hard to work into the novel—for example, I wanted Cornelia Rose to stay at the Thayer Hotel at West Point, but it was not built yet. I wanted her to attend Superintendent Thayer or even Superintendent Robert E. Lee's tea but the story timeline just could not be altered to have Cornelia visit while either one of these great men were superintendents.

Even some of the fictitious conflicts in the story were constrained by historical facts — for example, I wanted Agnes's to suffer her broken arm from a bicycle ride gone awry, and Jonas to fall off his unicycle — but bikes hadn't yet been invented!

Q. Do you want each book to stand on its own, or are you trying to build a body of work with connections between each book?

A. Can I say both? My goal is the story as a whole, but also that the books can be read out of 'order' or simply as 'stand alones.' I don't want any reader to feel they can't pick up one of the books and begin reading without reading the others. That seems to constraining to me.

Q. From where did you draw your inspiration for the series?

A. I come from a big, close, very loving family who focused on education, hard work, and culture, as my husband and I have done with our four children. As a lifelong student of history, I wanted to create characters set in a romantic period of time with modern day dilemmas so readers of today could feel what it was like to live in the 1850s.

Q. What's next?

A. Cornelia Rose moves out West, but any more than that you will have to get from Book 2!

Acknowledgements

This series would not be possible without the wonderful support team I am fortunate to have!

Thank you to my team of readers: Anne Mulvey Lindstrom, Alicia Zeidan, Joan Smith Grey, Maryse Godet Copans, and Susanna Maher for taking time to read and give me your invaluable insights and your encouraging support.

To my family for all of the love, support, and positive feedback: Jess, Jocelyn, Abigail, Bennett, Alicia, Paul and Lauren.

Thank you, historians and librarians of Briarcliff Manor, Ossining, and West Point. You helped insure I could find and verify the details that tell the story.

And to my editor, Kimberly Goebel, for going above and beyond in her help to edit and tweak the books and bring me to Evolved Publishing.

About the Author

Jane Frances Collen has spent the last umpteen years practicing as a lawyer—but don't hold that against her! She has made a career of protecting Intellectual Property, but at heart always wanted to be writing novels instead of legal briefs. She has written award-winning children's books, "The Enjella® Adventure Series," using fantasy as a vehicle for discussing the real world problems of children. She has tried to use her talent for storytelling for good instead of evil.

But her real love is history. One of her many hobbies is traveling to historical sites around the world and reading the biographies of the people who affected these places. Her books depict modern dilemmas in historical settings, with a touch of humor. Since only one of her parents had a sense of humor, however, Jane feels she is only half as funny as she should be.

Much to her husband's dismay, they still live in New York.

For more, please visit J.F. Collen online at:
Website: www.JFCollen.com
Facebook: Jane.F.Collen

What's Next?

Watch for the second and third books in this "Journey of Cornelia Rose" series to release within a few months of this book, starting with:

PIONEER PASSAGE

Pack up and leave her home? Never see the broad Hudson River, which flows both ways past her sitting room window, again? Eschew the glories of New York City and the wonders of the 1850s modern technology, and head out to unknown territory in the Wild West?

Heeding the call to "Go West Young Man," Cornelia Rose's husband accepts a position as Circuit Judge in the new Utah Territory, and persuades her that it's an exciting opportunity for them all. She thinks leaving the modern comforts of their home in Sing-Sing, New York, and saying goodbye to her family, will be the hardest challenge she'll ever have to face.

Life on the Oregon Trail is full of more deprivations than Cornelia ever imagined, in spite of her research, and preparation of their Conestoga wagon, for the rough road ahead. She summons all her resourcefulness to combat the hardships leading them to the greatest unknown: what would be waiting for them in the Great Salt Lake City?

More from Evolved Publishing

We offer great books across multiple genres, featuring high-quality editing (which we believe is second-to-none) and fantastic covers.

As a hybrid small press, your support as loyal readers is so important to us, and we have strived, with tireless dedication and sheer determination, to deliver on the promise of our motto: **QUALITY IS PRIORITY #1!**

Please check out all of our great books,
which you can find at this link:
www.EvolvedPub.com/Catalog/

Thank you!

CPSIA information can be obtained
at www.ICGtesting.com
Printed in the USA
BVHW030940300920
589958BV00030B/237